THE
LAND
OF LOOK
BEHIND

AARON BLAYLOCK

THE LAND OF LOOK BEHIND

BONNEVILLE
BOOKS
An imprint of Cedar Fort, Inc.
Springville, Utah

ISBN 13: 978-1-4621-1795-6

Published by Bonneville Books, an imprint of Cedar Fort, Inc.
2373 W. 700 S., Springville, UT, 84663
Distributed by Cedar Fort, Inc. www.cedarfort.com

LIBRARY OF CONGRESS CATALOGING-IN-PUBLICATION DATA

Names: Blaylock, Aaron, 1977-
Title: The land of look behind / Aaron Blaylock.
Description: Springville, Utah : Bonneville Books, 2016.
Identifiers: LCCN 2015033433 | ISBN 9781462117956 (pbk. : alk. paper)
Subjects: LCSH: Missionaries--Jamaica--Fiction. | GSAFD: Mystery fiction |
    Adventure fiction
Classification: LCC PS3602.L3995 L36 2016 | DDC 813/.6--dc23
LC record available at http://lccn.loc.gov/2015033433

Cover design by Rebecca J. Greenwood
Cover design © 2016 by Cedar Fort, Inc.
Edited and typeset by Justin Greer

Printed in the United States of America

10 9 8 7 6 5 4 3 2 1

Printed on acid-free paper

This book is dedicated to the people of Jamaica
and specifically to Jermaine "Bigga" Robinson
and all the adventures we had
and to those we never got to.
I miss you, son.

A Soldier's Duty

Three little birds shot down the gully and passed just over his head. In a panic, he nearly fired on them. He exhaled deeply, but that did not slow his racing heartbeat. *I will not die today,* he told himself, in a vain attempt to assert some imagined personal power over death. He leveled his musket at every sound and shadow as he braced for conflict. All the while he crouched low to the earth and kept a wary eye up the gully to the north. When no imminent danger presented itself, he removed his soaking wet wool coat and laid it on the jungle floor as quick as he could. With his knees bent, head up, and back straight, he assumed a military-conditioned defensive posture and waited.

The afternoon showers had faded and the sun pierced through the dispersing blanket of light grey clouds. The heat of the day bore down on him and beads of sweat formed on his sunbaked brow. For the first time since he arrived on the island, Lieutenant Benjamin Jarvis cared nothing for the stifling humidity. At the moment his thoughts were of survival. He hurriedly scanned back and forth between the brush, which sprawled out on all sides, and the jungle canopy above. Unable to take in the whole of his surrounding visually, he listened intently for signs of life.

It had been nearly five years since he made landfall, five years since the battle of Caguaya Bay, five years since being dispatched to parts unknown in the far west reaches of the island to oversee the Spanish exodus. Terms of surrender dictated that its inhabitants leave the island within a fortnight. Jarvis was confident they would meet little resistance from a scattered lot of settlers; after all they were farmers, not soldiers. What they encountered, however, was far more than Spaniards with pitchforks.

The minutes passed like hours now, if they passed at all, and it felt to Jarvis as though time stood still. He tried to collect himself. He needed a plan of action. Captain Willard had given him strict orders and he was a soldier; and a soldier follows orders. But what weight ought he to give the orders of a dead man?

Captain Willard and the rest of his company had only just left his sight when he heard the sound that shook him to his core; the dreaded sound of an abeng. The enemy used the cow horn to signal over great distances or raise an alarm. In Jarvis's experience it had become synonymous with battle and death. The abeng echoed off the gully walls and was followed by the tumultuous noise of battle. There were shouts and shots, then silence. A penetrating silence, an emptiness that Jarvis wished more than anything would be filled with signs of survivors. The void that followed was truly horrifying, more so than the preluding cries and conflict.

Stay here. If we do not return, kill them and make your way back to the outpost. Willard's orders rang in his ears. They were his last words before he led the men through the thick underbrush and disappeared around the bend. *Stay here.* The words sprang to the forefront of his consciousness. *Here* was the problem now. *Here* was out in the open. *Here* was exposed. *Here* was in the middle of this Godforsaken island with no clear path to safety. No clear path to anywhere.

The limestone walls rose up on all sides like a coliseum. He stood in its midst, a lone gladiator waiting to meet his destiny. From the mountains above, the surrounding region looked like a giant basket of green eggs. Bumps of earth were separated by narrow depressions, as far as the eye could see. Their descent into these depressions was like stepping into a labyrinth. The thick overgrowth and crumbling limestone foundation was not only dangerous but made it nearly impossible to navigate. Wicker vines sprawled upward through the rocks and dense vegetation. Waist high ferns thrived in the clearings, the fresh rainfall dripping from their leaves. Being out in the open meant he was free from the suffocating darkness beneath the jungle canopy, however, the occasional breeze was little consolation under the unrelenting sun. At the moment neither shade nor breeze would deliver him from his afflictions.

The order was simple enough. *Stay here. If we do not return, kill them and make your way back to the outpost.* Except, how was he to know if and when they would return? How long would he have to wait? If they did not return how would he make his way back on his own? And how, in the name of all that was holy, could he kill a child much less three?

In all his years of service he had never disobeyed a direct order. He had never, before now, had cause to. Lieutenant Jarvis was a good soldier. He kept his boots spit spot. He was clean shaven and his hair was slicked back away from his face, combat ready. His black trousers were clean and mended if he had anything to say about it. In many ways he was the model soldier. His ambitions were tempered and his devotion absolute. Soldiers have orders, not opinions. They do not need the why, just the when. This, however, felt altogether different. These circumstances were new, nothing he had prepared for, and these feelings were foreign and made him uneasy.

He began to weigh his limited options. He could disobey the first directive, follow after his company to see what had transpired and perhaps save a few of the men in the process. Although he was not a coward this course of action seemed imprudent. He could stay right where he was, obey the first directive and wait for their return, but the thought of staying put grew more unbearable with each silent moment. He could abandon Willard's edict and leave without completing his unthinkable task, make his way south to the Saint James outpost, and hopefully, to safety. If Willard were still alive though, and returned to find Jarvis had not executed his orders, he would be court-martialed for sure. *Willard, you fool, where are you?*

How had his situation become so bleak? Potential court martial or potential death, those were his options? No, if he was going to leave this spot it would be after doing his duty.

Determined to flee from this place as quickly as was possible, Lieutenant Jarvis turned himself about to face the grizzly task at hand. There before him, huddled together on the ground, were three small Arawak children. The arrival of the Spanish spelled doom for the peaceful indigenous inhabitants of the island. They died by the hundreds from enslavement, hard labor, and European diseases. This was the story of the New World, the story of the Conquistadors. Lieutenant Jarvis had never seen an Arawak before these pitiful creatures, nor had anyone he knew of. In all likelihood these three were the last of their kind. How they had survived this long, and what misfortune had placed them in his path, he did not know. It was a question he would not, could not, allow himself to dwell on. Not if they were to meet their end like this.

The child closest to Lieutenant Jarvis looked up at him and met his eyes. The boy's flat face was stoic and accepting, like he knew what was to come. He could not have been more than nine or ten years old, and looked to be on the brink of starvation. His big brown eyes were sunk back behind his broad face and his ribs protruded from his torso. Other than being malnourished, however, he appeared to be well cared for. His dark black hair lay down evenly over the top of his head. His body was clean except for red mud on his bare feet and ankles, unavoidable considering the terrain and the weather. *Where then was his caregiver?* Some kind of animal hide was tied about his waist as a loin cloth. He was crouched back in the impression of the shrubs, made by their three bodies. Jarvis had begun to exam the two little girls when his heinous duty returned to his memory and stung his conscience.

How to do it? Not the musket, of course; the sound would undoubtedly draw Willard's attackers to him. Besides, the other two might run while he reloaded. He laid the musket against a nearby stump and drew the bayonet from his military issued canvas pack. At that moment the other two, still silent, raised their heads and all three looked up at him.

How am I to do it? Jarvis thought. *Run! Run, you fools. Why do you not run?*

He opened his mouth to speak but no words came. He hoped in vain that something would save him from this awful deed. The crack of a branch drew his attention to the trees behind him. He scanned the perimeter intensely. With his back to the children, he thought they might escape. Amongst the thick ferns and undergrowth on the gully floor they could easily slip away. Incompetence, at the moment, was preferable to insubordination. After a thorough perimeter check found no signs of movement, he paused for a moment or two extra to allow for their potential flight. To his great disappointment, however, he turned back to find the three little children right where he left them. There was no use stalling, if he remained any longer he might be discovered and killed. It was time to act. He rolled up the sleeves on his long white shirt and raised his bayonet toward the boy, but immediately lowered it again. *Come on man. Get on with it.*

"Close your eyes," Jarvis commanded the children.

They stared at him as if he had not spoken. Frustrated, he raised his left hand and brushed a long lone strand of ink black hair from his eye. He made a pinching gesture with his fingers and forced his eyelid shut. The children, unfazed, continue to stare up at him.

"Uh, *cierre*, um, *su*," Jarvis said, and pointed to the children. "*Ojos.*" He pointed to his eyes. "*Ojos. Cierre sus ojos.*"

He knew the odds that they understood his rudimentary Spanish were only slightly greater than the odds that they understood English, but thought it worth a try. They just sat there like three pathetic little statues.

"Oh for cripe's sake, close your bleeding eyes!" Jarvis demanded louder, and gestured again with even more exaggerated movements.

It was at this moment of heightened frustration that he observed the most remarkable thing, which brought an unsettling kind of calm over him. With the greatest care, and without breaking eye contact with Jarvis, the girl furthest from him reached forward and gently covered the eyes of the girl next to her. She then took her other hand, pulled the little boy toward her and covered his eyes as well. One could have easily mistaken her resolute stare as an act of defiance, but for the serene look on her face. She had a broad face and flat nose, like the boy, and her long black hair hung neatly down her shoulders and over her chest. Her skin was smooth without a single crease, line, or dimple, which left Jarvis to believe the solemn look she wore was commonplace and not strictly attributed to her current distress. She was clearly the smallest of the trio but not necessarily the youngest.

Not only had she discerned what he wanted, Jarvis suspected she knew what was to come. Her actions were to spare the others the unpleasantness that would soon meet them. This courageous girl gave him pause. If she did know what was to come she was going to meet it with her eyes open. Her penetrating glare chilled Jarvis to the bone. His jaw fell open, his limbs lost their strength, and he swayed backwards as if her eyes repulsed him. Once again he ran his limited options through his mind. After he glanced back one more time in the direction where he had last seen his company, he turned back to the children and made up his mind. He would not reconsider again. If this was the way she wanted it, then so be it. He would be quick and she would go first.

Jarvis raised the bayonet and took a step toward the children. His uncle, back in Yorkshire, was a pig farmer. He had seen him slaughter hundreds of pigs. *Was this so different?* It was. It was different, and he knew it. He stood there frozen, with his arm raised against them, and looked into the tranquil dark brown eyes of the brave little girl. *I can't, I won't.* He did not lower his bayonet but his mind began to race wildly as he looked for a way out. There had to be something he had not thought of. Some way he could execute his duty as a solider but spare the lives of these innocents.

Just when he was about to abandon hope, his salvation was

delivered with a terrible sound that sent a shockwave of fear through his body. A single crunch of a branch gave away the approach of an unseen assailant. The sound was close, just a few yards directly behind him. Jarvis spun around on the spot to see a shadow disappear behind the trunk of a nearby tree. He frantically looked for it to emerge from the other side but saw only bushes and trees. He listened carefully for some sound of movement but heard nothing. His breathing quickened again. This was no friendly, it was not an Arawak and it was not a Spaniard, it was one of them.

In the chaos of the English invasion many Spanish slaves broke free and ran for the hills. The Spaniards who chose to stay and fight enlisted their slaves and former slaves in a ragtag militia. These Africans quickly became of formidable foe. They were skilled hunters who had intimate knowledge of the islands backcountry and were untethered from military training and tactics, which allowed them to wage war as they saw fit. Something the English soldiers were unaccustomed to and ill-equipped to deal with.

Jarvis revered these fierce African warriors above all others. They fought like ghosts, striking from the darkness and retreating without a trace. Rumors had quickly circulated throughout the ranks of entire companies being wiped out by only a handful of these wild Negroes. What chance did he stand by himself with only a musket? *The musket? God save me, the musket.*

Amid his inner turmoil he had forgotten that he set it down. He took his eyes off the tree in front of him and looked to the stump where he had laid his firearm. From his peripheral he saw movement back by the tree. He lunged for the musket and wheeled around back toward the shadows. Everything was still again. No noise, no movement. It was as if the whole world held its breath along with him. Not even the birds or the insects dare to make a sound. He could feel his heart beat rapidly inside his chest.

With his musket leveled at the trees all he could do was wait and watch. With his whole being, he wanted to break and run. But which way would he go? No, he had only one choice. He would have to fight in this very spot, to the death. There was nowhere to hide, there would be no escape.

"Show yourself, you bloody coward!" Jarvis screamed into the air. He hoped to sound brave and terrifying, but feared he sounded desperate.

As if granting his request, a blur emerged from the shadows to his left and struck him in the side, knocking him to the ground. He held tight to his musket, raised it and fired. Smoke plumed all around him as his heart sank. He heard no impact. At point blank, he had missed.

His dark green eyes burned and filled with tears while his vision blurred even further. As the smoke cleared, a dark figure loomed over him, silhouetted by the blinding sun that peaked through the clouds and smoke. The whites of his eyes were fixed on Jarvis like a lion that glared down at its prey. The figure's black chest was bare and around his neck hung a necklace made of bone and teeth; human teeth. He wore a tattered and stained pair of grey pants that came down to his knees. He turned and leaned back slightly, as the afternoon sun illuminated his swarthy muscular frame. A strap hung over his shoulder, which held a musket to his back, and in his hand was a blood covered cutlass. There was a dark marking of some kind on his right forearm, with lines too precise to be a birthmark. He towered over the fallen Jarvis, as if waiting for him to fight or flee.

Eager to oblige him, Jarvis made his move. He dropped his musket and reached for his bayonet. The dark warrior quickly restrained the lieutenant and stepped on his wrist. He reached down, wrested the bayonet from his grips and flung it into the bushes. In the same motion, he retrieved Jarvis's musket from the ground. With methodical grace and precision the assassin raised the musket, with the barrel skyward, and paused for a moment to consider his victim.

Jarvis quickly glanced over at the children and knew without a doubt this was a judgment wrought against him because of his sin. A sin he had yet to commit, yes, but the Good Lord knew he intended to. The sun gleamed from over the shoulder of this angelic assassin, which Jarvis took as a divine sign of his mandate. With that he accepted his fate, closed his eyes, and turned his face heavenward. He would not struggle against his sentence or plead for a reprieve. After all, he earned what was coming by even considering to do harm to those helpless little ones. The glory of the sun pressed upon his eyelids. A dark silhouette encroached upon the light as his assailant stepped forward. An overwhelming peace came over him as he gave in to the sweet release that was about to find him. The painful anticipated strike burst across his forehead and then darkness.

Back to Life

Working the nightshift at the Circle K was not where he envisioned himself at 21. It was the very same convenient store where he purchased gummy worms and made soda fountain suicides as a child. Children know next to nothing about good taste, but they do know the good fun that lies within a 32-ounce paper cup filled with equal amounts of every flavor. In those days thirty-two ounces was a large, the largest cup he could imagine; today it was not even a medium. His imagination, much like the sizes of beverage cups, had greatly expanded over the years. His world was much larger now than the distance from his front door and the store on the corner. However, in this large new world the store on the corner was where he found himself at the moment. And he prayed that it would only be a moment.

Three months earlier he awoke on a beautiful spring morning with nothing to do for the first time in two years. It was unsettling for Elder Goodwin. *You're not an Elder anymore*, he had to remind himself. *It's Gideon now, Gideon again.* For as long as he could remember he had prepared to serve a mission. He saved his money and studied his scriptures. He served when he was asked and in general tried to be a good Christian. Although he was less than fully prepared when he left home, he had some idea of what he was supposed to do. Returning home was a different story, one that he had not prepared for. Why would he? In his heart, he did not want to come home. In his heart, he would have stayed. A part of his heart had stayed.

When the white envelope arrived in the mail from Salt Lake, he read the words *Jamaica Kingston Mission*. He was ashamed to admit it now, but it took him several minutes to even find it on a map. Now, Jamaica and the friends he met there were more familiar to him than the family and friends he had known since birth. But those dear friends on his beloved Caribbean island were thousands of miles away and Elder Goodwin was no more. He reassumed an identity equal parts foreign and familiar. Reimmersed in a forgotten life he had left, with people who had grown and moved on without him, he sought out the one thing he knew, work. His body was behind the dingy counter of the Apache Junction convenient store but his mind had drifted off, as it often did, to join his heart back in the land he loved.

That was the beauty of working the nightshift. He was often left alone with his thoughts and those thoughts, without exception, turned to his cherished memories of his missionary service in Jamaica. Every day there felt like an adventure. Every day there was something new and beautiful, something he had never experienced before. Missionary work was hard and he loved it. Leaving it behind had left a chasm in his life; a void he tried in vain to fill each day with work.

The bell above the door jingled and snapped Gideon back to reality. He looked up to see a large man with long gray hair and a ZZ Top beard walk passed the counter toward the beer cooler. He wore a sleeveless jean jacket and a well-worn orange bandana, which covered his forehead. His belly hung over a pair of dirty, stained Levis adorned with black leather riding chaps. A tattoo of a red heart and the name *Louise* was proudly displayed on his flabby left bicep. Gideon put down the book he had been blankly staring at and stood up from his stool. His left foot slid ever so slightly on the grimy red tile floor, which was mopped repeatedly but never seemed to be clean.

11

"How's it going?" Gideon smiled and greeted the man.

"It's cool," the man replied with a slightly raspy, mellow voice.

The nightshift brought with it a unique clientele. Not that kings and queens graced the doorstep in the day time, but the night crowd was a different breed altogether. Alcohol and tobacco sales peaked in the wee hours of the morning, as did the tattoo and body piercing count of the patrons. The irony of a little Mormon boy ringing up beer and cigarettes in the middle of the night was not lost on Gideon. He justified his part in these transactions by saying he was "in the world, not of the world," a phrase he misappropriated from the seminary lessons of his youth.

He watched the man pick out a six pack and return to the counter. He watched as a matter of duty and not necessarily out of any suspicion that his new bearded biker friend was up to no good.

"And a pack of Camel filters," the man said, and placed his six pack on the counter while coughing in the same breath.

Gideon fought back a smile at this man asking for cigarettes while simultaneously suffering from their effects. "That'll be $11.85," Gideon said. "Do you want a bag?"

"No," the man replied and handed over four wrinkly pieces of paper that bore the image of Abraham Lincoln.

With the familiar cha-ching the sale was registered and the drawer sprung open. Realizing the man had given him one bill too many, he set a five dollar bill to the side and grabbed the proper change from the appropriate slots. He moved right to left from the largest denomination to the smallest, as he always did.

"$8.15 is your change," Gideon said with a practiced smile and handed over the change.

The man dropped the coins into the 'take a penny, leave a penny' tray and turned to leave. Gideon's mind harkened back to the times that very same brown tray had been his salvation when he had come up short on his weekly Circle K run for candy and drinks. He felt part of a larger adult society on the occasions when he could contribute his change to the tray.

He watched as Scooter exited the store. Scooter was the name Gideon had given the large bearded man with the Louise tattoo.

He attributed ironic nicknames to customers to break up the monotony of the day. On the other side of the wall of windows in front of the store, Scooter straddled his Harley and walked it backwards out of the parking spot, and as he revved the engine the countertop and windows rattled. Scooter clicked into first gear, let out the clutch and tore off past the large store sign into the early morning darkness.

Gideon's shift would be over in an hour and the sunrise would shortly follow. He made a mental check list of the tasks he would need to complete before clocking out. The counter was as clean as a well-trafficked and oft-stained convenient store counter could be. The isles were relatively stocked and the items properly faced. He needed to check the restroom but that could wait until his replacement arrived to watch the register.

He took one more look out at the empty parking lot. The single gas pump was lit by the street light above. All else was dark and the neighborhood in the distance lay silent. Satisfied that he would not be interrupted, he sat back down on his stool and reached beside the register to retrieve his book. It was not a book so much as it was a journal; one of the few items he brought home with him from the island. The brown leather cover was worn and scratched. The binding had begun to come loose; however, he thought it was in pretty good shape for its age. The handwritten account, on disparate-sized pages, was stuffed together into one record. It chronicled the adventures of a man who came to Jamaica in the mid-seventeenth century.

History was to be the focus of his studies when school started in the fall. His goal was to teach and coach football. He discovered his love for both in high school. Ms. Jackman made those old textbooks come to life. She spoke of ancient conquerors like Alexander the Great and heroes closer to home like Wyatt Earp as if they were old friends. It was the conquest and struggle for victory that he loved most. It was his great desire to pass on this love and these tales to future generations, to be a faithful steward and become in some way a part of that history.

Football, on the other hand, that was for him. He loved the

game, for the same reason he loved history, the struggle for victory. Although physically blessed with above-average size, he was never the biggest, the strongest, or the fastest, but he gave it all he had no matter the opponent. Coach Gebhardt liked to say he was put on earth for one purpose: "to wear people down." Not a natural-born athlete, he worked himself into a reasonable facsimile; however, he traded two-a-day workouts and weight lifting for morning scripture study and knocking doors. Between a diet of chicken neck and rice, his bike, and the mountainous hills of Jamaica, he had lost some of his formidable size, and with those extra pounds his dreams of college athletics had disappeared. If football was to be a part of his life, it would be from the sidelines.

The sidelines. That is where his life had been stuck all summer long. He worked, he saved, he registered for classes, but ultimately he waited. He waited to get back in the game, anxious to move forward again. Just a few more weeks till the start of term and then this giant dormant ball would finally be off and rolling.

He opened the journal to where he left off and began to read.

Sixteenth of February

When I awoke, night had fallen. I was alive and alone. No sign of my attacker or the Arawak children. He had taken my musket and what rations I had left. He left me with my boots and the clothes on my back. Why he spared my life I do not know.

Unable to navigate in the dark I hid myself near the cavity of a rock, which I discovered at first light, had a strange marking on the wall. At daybreak I made my way southeast. It was little wonder why he left my boots, as they had been torn to shreds in our march through the impenetrable jungle and became virtually useless to me. Near midday I came to a stream that I thought we had crossed before. I followed it further east. I knew I would have no trouble finding water, as this region is rich with springs and fresh water. Luckily, I found some kind of fruit growing down by the stream. It was green with little round bumps covering its skin. The texture of the flesh was not pleasant but it tasted sweet and curbed my hunger pangs. Before day's end the stream disappeared into the ground allowing me to cross and continue southward. I began feeling feverish and weak which slowed my journey considerably. After another day in the bush I finally made it back to the outpost and to safety.

Colonel Tyson looked none too pleased to see me. I cannot decide if this is due to the fact that I returned alone or a personal vendetta he has against me. Nonetheless the fact remains that we failed to meet our objective. I say we, but the reality is that I am all that is left. Twenty-three men did not return from our ill-fated expedition to find the enemy's den.

The jingle of the front door bell jolted Gideon back to the present. A man in a gray hooded sweatshirt sprang through the door, lunged toward the register and slammed his open hand down on the counter. Gideon leapt backwards and struggled to maintain his footing as the stool crashed to the floor. The journal flew from his hands, bounced hard on the counter and knocked over a Reese's Peanut Butter cup display before falling face down next to the stool.

"Your money or your life!" the forced deep voice demanded. He had his right hand in the front pocket of his hoodie, pointed at Gideon.

Gideon froze. His heart pounded hard as his mind ran through one horrific scenario after another. The young man removed his hood to reveal a familiar smiling face that matched the familiar voice. Todd Colbeck stood at the counter and grinned at the distressed look on his victim's face.

Todd was Gideon's roommate, and the pair had been best friends since kindergarten despite that fact they differed in nearly every way.

"You freaking idiot!" Gideon shouted. "You nearly gave me a heart attack."

"Relax," Todd answered his shaken friend. "I was just messing around. Besides you should have been paying attention instead of sleeping on the job."

"I wasn't sleeping, jerk." Gideon turned and bent down to pick up the stool. "What are you doing here? Shouldn't *you* be sleeping?"

"I couldn't sleep, decided to go for a jog." Todd bounced up and down in place.

Gideon drew himself upright to exaggerate his one-inch height advantage over his blond haired friend. He inhaled deeply to enlarge his bulky frame in an attempt to recover from the embarrassment of succumbing to Todd's prank. Todd just grinned innocently with his childlike blue eyes and ignored Gideon's derisive head shake.

"What time do you get off?"

Gideon surveyed the mess caused by his roommate. The individually wrapped peanut butter cups were spread all over the counter and the floor. He reached down and swept the scattered candy into a pile with his hands. Cleaning up after Todd's thoughtlessness was nothing new for Gideon. He stooped down, picked up the journal from the floor, and attempted to straighten the wrinkled and folded pages.

"I get off in about an hour," a semi-flustered Gideon responded without looking at the inconsiderate prankster. "Why?"

"Let's go to the gym."

"I don't want to go to the gym." Gideon wiped some schmutz off the corner of the leather-bound journal and gently tapped it on the counter to nudge the loose pages together.

"Come on now," Todd chided. "We haven't hit the weights together in weeks. Besides, no offense, but you're starting to pack on the pounds, my friend."

Gideon stopped wiping at the worn cover and looked up at Todd with his best 'I am not amused' face. Todd failed to suppress a mischievous smile. Gideon's khaki work pants did feel a bit snug and there was a little pouch that pushed his aqua blue shirt against his belt buckle.

"Listen, I have no desire to go to the gym right now. When I leave here I'm going to go home and get some sleep. That is, of course, after I clean up this completely unnecessary mess you made."

"Take it easy there, tough guy," Todd said. He looked down at the peanut butter cup pile on the counter. "Let me help."

Gideon placed his arms over the candy in a protective motion to block Todd's reach. "No, it's fine. I've got this. Just go." He forced a smile.

"All right, I'm leaving," Todd said as he put his hands straight up and backed away from the counter. "Hey, my dad is coming by tonight for dinner."

Todd looked down to see a small piece of faded paper underneath his shoe. He moved his foot from off the paper and squatted down, slowly, to retrieve it.

"I didn't know Joe was in town," Gideon said, and leaned over the counter to see what his friend was up to.

"Yeah, it was news to me too," Todd said, as he examined the piece of paper. "He got in last night."

Joe Colbeck had always been a favorite of Gideon. He told the best stories, some of them repeatedly, of his wild adventures and the crazy places he visited. No one took Joe too seriously, as treasure hunting was not exactly a conventional profession. But he had a good heart and, like Todd, was fun to have around.

"What are we doing for dinner? Give me that!" Gideon said, and snatched the paper from his hand.

"I was thinking of ordering pizza," Todd said. He stared at his empty hand in front of him, where the paper had been before it was abruptly confiscated.

"Don't do that. I'll grill up some chicken and bake potatoes," Gideon offered. He suspected that was Todd's design all along.

"Sounds awesome, man," Todd said. He continued to back out of the store. "I'll catch you later. Hey, two more days, brother!"

He snatched a bag of sunflower seeds from the display at the end of the gondola as he exited the store and held it up in the air. "Five finger discount," he yelped as he burst out the front door.

Gideon shook his head and watched his friend run through the parking lot like an overstimulated baboon. When he was out of sight, Gideon slipped some cash from his wallet into the register. The cost of his friend's shoplifting was starting to add up. He kept a ledger of all the money this game had cost him. He figured if Todd ever won the lottery he would recoup the one hundred and eight dollars that he now owed him.

Gideon looked down at the small slip of paper he had rescued from Todd. There was a drawing of what appeared to be a decorative looping heart atop a tripod, or a three-legged alien. There were no other markings or explanation as to what it might be, but he was certain it had fallen out of the journal. The faintest memory flickered in his brain but he could not quite grasp onto it. He placed the picture back inside the frayed leather bindings of the journal.

The rest of his shift passed like a dream, with his thoughts consumed by the drawing. His head swirled with questions. What could it mean? *Had* he seen it before? If so, where? When? He wanted to do research, he wanted to know more. *But where to*

start? He concluded the most likely place to find answers were within the bindings of the journal. He set his mind to study it, in earnest, just as soon as he got home and got some sleep.

'As soon as he got home . . .' He was home. He sat behind the wheel of his truck in their driveway. He did not remember the drive home, which unfortunately was a common occurrence. Many early mornings he found himself in front of his house with no memory of the drive between there and work. It was an unsettling feeling. *Did I run any stop signs? Was there anybody else on the road?* Each time he cursed his unintentional recklessness and vowed not to let it happen again.

This morning, however, he simply rubbed his eyes, pulled open the door to his truck and stepped out into the warm morning air. The sun barely peaked over the Superstition Mountains but the heat had already begun to build.

To Gideon the face of the mountain looked like a real-life version of Castle Grayskull, with the head-shaped cliffs at the center and protruding jaws jutting out toward the west. The mystery and legend that surrounded this mountain range was where it got its name. Ancient Apaches believed there was a cave deep in the mountains that led to the world below and was the origin of the terrible storms that swept through the valley.

Settlers had their own legends too. Gideon grew up on stories of the Lost Dutchman, an old German miner who supposedly struck a mother-load of gold and whispered its location on his deathbed. Many people from near and far came in search of the Lost Dutchman's gold but no one ever found it. Cynics claimed it was the ranting of a crazy old man or a myth to cook up tourism.

Gideon soaked up the stories of The Superstitions. He did not care if they were true or not, in a world where nearly everything had an explanation, he was determined to hold on to his sense of wonder and mystery. As far as he was concerned the gold and the Apache cave to the underworld were out there and he hoped that one day somebody would find them.

He reached back into his blue pickup truck to retrieve the

journal from the passenger seat before walking up the driveway. He pushed open the unlocked door and stepped inside of the quiet house. Without turning on a light, he made his way down the hallway back to his bedroom. Too tired to get undressed he kicked off his shoes, removed his belt and placed the journal carefully on the floor before falling into bed. His eyes were closed before his head hit the pillow.

"Craaaaaaap!" he muttered, as he realized he had forgotten to pray.

He slid his lower torso unto the floor and knelt beside his bed. He knew he would not reach that level of comfort again. That was always the case when he had to rip himself from his pillow when he had forgotten to pray, a sacrifice he felt was a test of his resolve. He had a streak of 815 nightly prayers, which dated back to the beginning of his mission, and had no intention of seeing it come to an end this day. Technically, it was early morning, but as it was his bedtime he still counted them as his nightly prayer.

After his usual expressions of gratitude he turned his mind's eye heavenward to consider whom he prayed to. This morning, however, a decorative looping heart sitting on a tripod invaded his thoughts. He shook it from his mind and climbed back into bed. He was in no mental state to tackle this problem now and hoped that clarity would come with rest.

Alliance and Orders and Stares

Although he sat in a proper chair for the first time in weeks, it was little consolation considering his dreary circumstances. Lieutenant Jarvis had not received the welcome he hoped for when he returned to the outpost earlier that evening. He was instructed to get some food, get cleaned up and report to Colonel Tyson without delay.

The young quartermaster's aide scrambled and found him a pair of boots, to replace the shredded pieces of leather that barely clung to his feet. Then he helped bandage his scraped and bleeding souls and ankles. A melancholy settled over him, as this was the first act of kindness shown him in some time. He did not even know the boy's proper name, but everyone called him Smitty. Jarvis reckoned he was fifteen or sixteen years old but his slight frame and boyish face made him appear younger. Smitty was always eager to assist the soldiers and could be seen skulking about by the fire as they swapped stories each night. He was the lone spot of brightness among this gloomy lot and his kindness reminded Jarvis of better times and bygone days he feared he would never know again.

Their base of operations was an abandoned Spanish settlement and the officers had taken up residence in the main farmhouse. It was a crude structure that leaked like a sieve whenever it rained, which was nearly every day. The rest of the troops pitched their tents to the east, in two parallel lines that faced each other. While the atmosphere was bleak for its current reluctant occupants, Jarvis could not help but think that at one time this farm must have been a piece of heaven on earth. The property was positioned near the edge of a mountaintop on the southern end of the Saint James precinct. Wild green grass blanketed the wide-open plateau and an enormous valley sprawled out below. The valley was stuffed with lush green trees and vegetation that stretched right down to the ocean. On a clear day you could just make out the blue rolling sea in the distance, even without the aid of a monocular. The front door of the main house faced to the southwest, overlooking the valley, and was witness to the most spectacular sunsets each day at dusk.

On this day, however, Jarvis had paid no attention to the evening sunset, as his freshly commandeered boots carried his worn feet up the steps and into the farm house to face an unpleasant debriefing. Colonel Tyson sat across from him, absorbing the information he received. The room had grown dark, as the daylight faded and gave way to night. The lone lamp, which hung over the table between them, illuminated the look of displeasure on the Colonel's face. The evening air buzzed with the bugs and insects that infested the island. In the distance, Jarvis heard the muffled tones of soldiers conversing outside their tents. He was never particularly fond of idle blather but would have much preferred that company to this right now. In this dark and lonely room, apart from an unhappy Colonel, his only companion was silence.

His report was complete and accurate. He had stated the facts and the events as they transpired; however, he did not elaborate more than was necessary. He was not anxious to give any reason for a further questioning, and the Colonel was not a man who appreciated embellishment or storytelling. From the length of the pause between the end of his report and this moment, however, he knew that more questions were to follow and he prayed he had the answers.

Colonel Edward Tyson was not a man to be trifled with. He had distinguished himself at the Battle of Ocho Ríos. Despite his forces being reduced by disease and desertion and facing a militia newly reinforced with provisions and men from Cuba, the English prevailed. Governor D'Oyley promoted him and placed him over the troops in the north. His further success at Río Nuevo prompted the governor to dispatch him south where a regiment, which included Lieutenant Benjamin Jarvis, struggled to gain advantage over the Spanish and wild Negroes in their mountain strongholds. The previous colonel had died weeks earlier of influenza and the company had fallen under the command of Captain Willard. Willard immediately put them on the defensive. They broke down camp and moved each day to avoid ambush. This exhausting tactic left little time for a proactive strategy or even proper patrols. Colonel Tyson's first order of business was to establish an outpost, which provided a strong footing and allowed them to strike out more effectively against their opposition.

Most of the men feared Tyson, some hated him, but all respected him. Not solely on the merit of his rank and reputation but because he was a man of results. He demanded results from his men and did not tolerate failure. Failure like the one Jarvis had just recounted to him. The wait was excruciating. *What is he going to say? What is he going to do? Say something. Do something, anything.*

The Colonel had been perched on the edge of his seat while he listened intently to his lieutenant's report. Upon its completion he remained motionless, and appeared to quietly contemplate the situation. Somberly, he leaned back in his chair and inhaled. He pursed his lips, clearly unhappy.

"Why were you not with them?" Tyson finally asked.

"Sir?" Jarvis responded.

"You said that Captain Willard and the rest of the men left to pursue a pair of rebels into the jungle. Explain to me why you were left behind?"

"The children, sir," Jarvis answered, still puzzled by the question. "As I explained, I was left to watch them."

"But why? What value did these children have? What advantage did they offer? What danger were they?"

"I do not know, sir. You would have to ask Captain Willard."

"I can't bloody well question a dead man, can I?!" Tyson bellowed in his deep and penetrating voice. "I'm asking you!"

Jarvis took a moment to collect himself before he spoke. His skin burned from the fever and beads of perspiration pooled on his clammy face. If he were completely honest, he had asked that same question many times on his journey back to the outpost. He still did not have a good answer but as he sat there, in the teeth of Colonel Tyson's interrogation, he knew that now was the time to imagine one.

"Well sir, like I said, we had come upon these children on our march and they were collecting birds, from a trap. We commandeered the birds and planned on eating them. Perhaps Captain Willard thought they might be valuable to us in obtaining food, as our rations were running low." Jarvis tried to appear confident in his attempt to read the mind of his fallen commander.

Tyson continued his questioning as if he had not heard, or did not care for, the answer he received. "Two men appear before a company of twenty and you all give chase? Did nobody see it was a trap?"

"Twenty-four, sir." Jarvis interrupted.

"What?" an irritated Tyson shot back.

"There were twenty-four of us, sir, twenty-four men."

"And yet only you return. Tell me something, Lieutenant, if you care so deeply for each of these twenty-four souls, then why did you not go with them?" Tyson demanded.

"I had my orders, sir."

"And did you execute those orders?"

"Yes sir!"

"So then the children are dead?" Tyson continued to push.

"Yes. Well . . . uh, no. That is, I am not certain, sir, but I suppose they are." Jarvis did not know where this line of questioning was going, but was certain wherever it was headed it would not be good for him.

"You suppose?" Tyson made no attempt to disguise his contempt. "And do you suppose that those twenty-three other soldiers, whom you abandoned, are dead as well?"

"Yes sir." Jarvis said and suddenly realized where this was headed.

"But you don't know?"

"No, sir." Jarvis slumped down in his chair and looked down at the floor, wishing it would swallow him up.

"No, you don't. Because you didn't bother to investigate; you simply ran away to save your own skin!" Tyson said, as he sprung his verbal trap.

Jarvis raised his head to speak but wisely said nothing. He wanted to protest, wanted to proclaim that he had followed orders. They did not return so he made his way back to the outpost, but he knew it was not as simple as that. He could have pursued them. He could have sought after their whereabouts, but he did not. He was afraid. He could admit that to himself, even if he had no intention of confessing to his superior.

As Colonel Tyson rose from the chair his face disappeared above the lamps light into the darkness of the room. He was not a tall man but was considered, by any reasonable person, a large man. He was nearly as wide as he was long with club like forearms. He had a round face beset atop a thick neck, like the trunk of a tree. Most prominent on his round face was his hoof-like chin, which looked as if it could double effectively as a nutcracker. His dark eyes were set close together and gave him the look of a primal predator. He leaned forward and placed both hands on the table in front of him. The light from the lamp once again lit his stony expression.

"I need more than men following orders, Lieutenant. If I cannot trust your judgment," Tyson stated plainly, "then you are a burden, not an officer. Dismissed."

Lieutenant Jarvis stood up and stared straight ahead at the wall behind the colonel. For a moment he swayed on the spot as a bout of lightheadedness nearly overcame him. He steadied himself, saluted his commanding officer and turned to leave. *That's it,* he thought. *My career is over.* He stepped around the chair, where he had endured interrogation, and made his way to the doorway toward the dimly lit room beyond.

"One more thing, Lieutenant," Colonel Tyson added. "How would you evaluate Captain Willard's actions?"

Jarvis quickly weighed his options, as this was clearly another test or trap. Either his answer would satisfy the Colonel and provide a degree of redemption, or it would drive another nail into his coffin. With nothing left to lose, he stopped in the doorway and turned to face Colonel Tyson. He straightened himself up with his shoulders back and mustered all the confidence he had left.

"Captain Willard's actions were rash and shortsighted, as he all too often was," Jarvis spoke boldly, and begged forgiveness in his heart for speaking ill of the dead. "The risk and likelihood of ambush far outweighed the reward of capturing or killing those men and I did not need the benefit of hindsight to see that."

He stood, rooted to the spot, and waited to be dismissed once more. Instead, Colonel Tyson grabbed his hat from the hook on the wood planked wall and walked toward him. Jarvis was not sure if the colonel could see his face in the darkness but kept a blank expression just the same, as not to give away his trepidations. He took Jarvis by the left elbow with his right hand, spun him around and began to lead him through the doorway.

"Walk with me," Tyson instructed.

The two made their way through the empty entry way and out the front door, into the fresh night air. With not a cloud in the sky, the stars filled the heavens. Jarvis allowed himself a moment to enjoy God's splendor before turning his thoughts to his walking companion's possible motives and their potential destination. With only the moonlight for guidance, they made their way due south away from the main house and followed a muddy, well-worn path. As they reached the bottom of the steps Colonel Tyson had released his grip on Jarvis's elbow and placed both arms behind his back. He gazed up at the stars while Jarvis's mind whirled. *Does he mean me harm? What did I say to provoke this?*

Jarvis again began to weigh his options, which seemed to

dwindle by the moment. If it came to that, he was certain he would not prevail in a physical confrontation with the Colonel. Even in top form he figured he had a fifty-fifty chance, at best, against the stout battle tested officer. When he factored in his wounded feet and feverish condition he did not like his odds. Fortunately, given the opportunity, he could talk his way out of almost anything. But what he would need to talk himself out of he did not yet know. The prudent course was to wait and see what was in store for him.

"Willard was a fool," Tyson said as he broke the silence. "His stupidity is what brought me here and it is what got him and his men killed."

Jarvis tried to decide if this statement made him feel better or worse, as it pertained to his current standing with the Colonel. The fact that he had finally said something did put him at ease, although only a little. He considered agreeing with him but thought it wise to hold his tongue, at least for the moment, and wait to see where this was headed.

"By here, of course, I mean this region and this outpost and not this mosquito-infested island. No, we have grander fools than Willard to thank for that," Tyson continued. "We failed to take Hispaniola and captured this booby prize instead, an island the Crown did not want which the Spanish did not think enough of to properly fortify. Now we grapple over it as if it were Christ's cup."

In the distance Jarvis saw the light from a small fire and could make out at least two figures that stood near a lone tent. *What are they doing out here so far away from the rest of the camp?* This was obviously the Colonel's intended destination, but for what purpose Jarvis could only guess. He kept his eyes on the approaching encampment and listened as the colonel continued.

"We have a problem, Lieutenant. We fight a foe with no great ambition," Tyson explained. "Their only desire is to hold on to what they have, however insignificant it might be. How do you reason with someone like that?"

Lieutenant Jarvis rightly assumed that the question was rhetorical and said nothing.

"You don't." Tyson went on. "There is no reasoning with Ysassi or men of his kind. That is why we must drive him out or destroy him."

Don Cristobal Arnaldo de Ysassi was the leader of the Spanish resistance. He was not a soldier but had been given command of the military forces that remained. Being outmanned and outgunned, Ysassi had taken to the mountains. His forces consisted of a rag tag coalition of Spaniards, Indians, and Africans. Their objective was to gain whatever advantage possible and wreak havoc on the English any way they could. His single-minded determination to keep the island of his birth out of Britain's control was a personal thorn in Tyson's side. While Jarvis would never utter a kind word of Ysassi, he had a quiet respect for his resolve.

"The Spaniards would be long gone if not for Ysassi and his dark cohorts. He has convinced these Negroes they have cause to fight against us. They pose a greater threat to our mission than the Governor and his advisors wish to acknowledge. If we are to succeed against Ysassi, they will have to be dealt with first," Tyson concluded.

Upon recognition of their approach the two soldiers turned and stood at attention. It was a standard canvas A-framed tent, nestled back between two large red ebony trees. The soldiers stood with muskets at the ready. From their positions outside the tent, Jarvis surmised that they did not occupy it but guarded its contents. Neither of the soldiers made eye contact with their new visitors. They stood straight and tall and stared into the blackness beyond the fire, as if they expected them. Tyson stepped between the guards to the front of the tent and placed one hand on the flap that covered the entrance. He turned back to Jarvis and beckoned him closer with a nod of his head. Jarvis suppressed an uneasy feeling in the pit of his stomach and drew closer. His better judgment was completely overwhelmed by a burning curiosity for what he was about to be shown.

"There are fewer than five men in this regiment that have any knowledge of what I am about to show you. Each of them knows he will be shot dead, without questioning or trial, if these things come to light," Tyson explained, with a tone attuned to the gravity of his message. "Do you understand?"

Jarvis nodded, feeling that whatever lay beyond that flap was about to change his life. "Yes, sir."

"Very well," Tyson pulled back the flap and gestured for him to enter.

After a moment's hesitation, Lieutenant Jarvis stepped forward and entered the tent. Five African men, seated on the ground, lined the walls inside the canvas room. They ate off of metal field plates and drank from tin cups. They all stopped eating and looked up as Jarvis entered. The man in the center, at the back of the tent, stood slowly while the others simply looked on. Colonel Tyson entered behind Jarvis. He removed his hat and came to a stop to Jarvis's left.

"Lieutenant Jarvis, this is Juan de Bolas," Tyson said.

Whether out of courtesy or sheer force of habit Jarvis stepped forward and extended his hand in greeting. The man stared back with a stony expression that gave no clue as to whether he did not understand or did not care to partake in the gesture. In either case, Jarvis withdrew his hand quickly, as to not prolong the awkwardness. The man was a head shorter than Jarvis with broad shoulders that, through his threadbare shirt, he could see were perfectly rounded. He wore a pair of navy blue trousers and what appeared to be a brand-new pair of boots, identical to the ones Smitty had acquire for Jarvis. The whites of his eyes set prominently amidst his black skin. He briefly surveyed Lieutenant Jarvis before he turned his attention to Colonel Tyson.

"De Bolas here has agreed to assist us with our Spanish infestation," Tyson explained, with one arm opened wide to the room, in a grand gesture to its occupants. "He and his men know these mountains inside and out. They have traveled the back channels and know how to navigate the terrain that confounds our own troops. More importantly though, they know all Ysassi's haunts and hiding places."

"De Bolas?" Jarvis questioned, as he turned about to face the Colonel. "Sir, this is not the one called Juan Lubolo?"

"The one and the same," Tyson responded. He raised his hand immediately to preempt his protest. "He is with us now, Lieutenant, and that is that. Do you understand?"

Lieutenant Jarvis nodded in submission, although he most certainly did not understand. Juan Lubolo had been a fierce opponent of the English occupation and an ally to Ysassi. He led a significant number of Africans in a settlement somewhere in the mountains. This group was infamous for their bold attacks and night raids on English troops and settlers. Their ambushes had reached legendary proportions and were a source of great fear and trepidation for soldiers throughout the island.

It was men of this sort who had lain in wait for poor Captain Willard and his men. The sort that would have no doubt killed him if given the chance. *But one of them did have the chance,* he thought, and wondered again why he had been spared.

"You are to provide de Bolas and his men whatever they require," Tyson ordered. "And you are not to leave his side. Is that understood?"

"Yes sir!" Jarvis responded, purely out of conditioning, before he gave the order proper consideration. He would not trust Lubolo, no matter what Colonel Tyson said. Not due to the stories the men told but for the fact that he would betray Ysassi this way. A man who exhibited such disloyalty could never be fully trusted. If a lack of loyalty was all Jarvis had to concern himself with, he would have considered himself lucky. His greatest fear was that Lubolo *was* loyal and that this façade was a trap designed to lead them into the hands of their enemies.

"Sir, may I have a word with you in private?" Jarvis requested.

Colonel Tyson momentarily ignored Jarvis as he noticed Lubolo admiring his hat. Tyson raised the hat in front of him and enticed him to take it. Lubolo reached out and took the hat. He looked extremely pleased. He placed the hat on his head and, with a smile, turned to face his men.

"General de Bolas!" he declared proudly, with his hands on his hips in a majestic pose. He and his men laughed loudly.

"Whatever you have to say, Lieutenant, you can speak freely;

they do not understand English." Colonel Tyson said, as he watched with pride the reaction to his gift.

At Tyson's declaration Jarvis noticed that Lubolo stopped laughing and glanced briefly in their direction. Cautiously, Jarvis chose to omit his original question and substitute a new curiosity that arose from Tyson's statement. "Sir, if they do not speak English how did you come to an understanding?"

"What?" Tyson said. He took his eyes off of Lubolo and turned his attention to Jarvis.

"That is, sir, how did you communicate this arrangement with these men if they do not understand English?" Jarvis clarified. He attempted a casual tone and did not wish to be seen to question his superior.

"An interpreter, of course. How do you think?" Tyson responded testily. "A Spanish slave, Demingo, I believe, translated for me."

"And you trust this Demingo?"

"Of course not! That's why I've assigned you to them."

"Sir?"

"I want someone to watch them and ensure they keep up their end of the bargain."

"Why me, sir?"

"You speak Spanish, do you not?"

"Just a little, sir. I can understand more than I can speak."

Jarvis was briefly assigned to guard the prisoners at Spanish Town. They used an opulent local residence as a makeshift prison. The inmates consisted of merchants and farmers, most of whom had come to terms with their defeat in short order and were quite submissive.

During the long hours and due to the close quarters, Jarvis had picked up a bit of basic Spanish out of necessity. Although he could speak little more than threats and curse words, as that is what he found most useful.

"A little will do. It's far more than the rest of this lot," Tyson said, with a nod toward the men outside the tent. "Now get some rest, soldier. We depart at daybreak."

"Depart, sir?" Jarvis asked. "Where are we going?"

"We're hunting Spaniards," Tyson proclaimed with zeal, as he pulled back the flap and exited into the night.

The Symbol

With the drawing burned into his consciousness he did not even need to look at slip of paper anymore, but still he held it up in front of his face. Hopelessly he tried to grasp onto a memory just out of reach. It taunted him like a flickering flame blowing in the wind. This symbol *was* familiar to him. He had seen it before, not on this small slip of square paper, but somewhere. *Where?* This was not some random doodle. It meant something; he knew it. In an act of desperation he attempted to relax his eyes, as if he stared at a stereogram with leaping dolphins hidden in the background. Of course it was not visions of dolphins or hidden sailboats that he sought. Still, he hoped in vain this exercise would engage some long-lost memory.

The unrelenting desert sun seeped through the blinds that covered his window and heated the room to the limits of his comfort. Still dressed in his work clothes from the night before, he sat up in bed as beads of sweat began to pool in the small of his back. He laid his head back against the wall and gazed up at the ceiling fan in the center of the room.

All was silent except for the whirring of the fan blades that whished through the air and the rhythmic clinking of the pull chain bouncing off the glass sphere that covered the light. The air conditioning unit cycled on, which created a euphoric blend of white noise and cool air that washed over Gideon like a wave of serenity.

His room was kept plain and simple. Outside of the twin bed in the far corner, there was a desk and a chair against the opposite wall near the door. The Tuscan yellow walls were bare, except for a red, yellow and green striped poster that hung over his bed by the window and had a black silhouette of a lion at the center. The tan shag carpet was in need of vacuuming but otherwise in good shape and uncluttered, aside from the shoes he kicked off before he fell into bed. A single, packed suitcase was placed neatly against the wall between the desk and the closet.

Gideon moved in with Todd shortly after he returned from his mission. For Gideon the house offered two peaceful moments each day, in his otherwise full and somewhat noisy life. In the early morning hours when his roommate, and most of the world, still slept, and late afternoon when he awoke and they were out and about. Today, however, his solitude was invaded by wisp of a memory. Where in the world had he seen this symbol?

Hunger pangs temporarily preempted his obsession. He swung his feet off the bed unto the plush carpet, bent down and scooped up the journal from the floor. He walked across the room, put the journal on his desk, placed the piece of paper on top and took one last look at the symbol. Gideon opened his door and stepped into the darkened hallway, which was at least ten degrees cooler than his room at all times.

He turned the corner and walked passed their shared living space, which included a futon, a 27-inch television and two bean bag chairs plopped haphazardly in the middle of the floor. Todd's No Doubt poster, which featured Gwen Stefani and her classic bare midriff, hung on the wall above the futon. It was a memento of the day they saw them live at the Electric Ballroom in Tempe. Despite a not-so-secret crush on Stefani, Gideon was slightly embarrassed to have her displayed so prominently in the house. The thick red curtains were pulled shut over the large front room window to keep the heat out and cast a red hue over the room.

Gideon turned another corner and flipped the switch just inside their tiny kitchen. The long fluorescent tubes flickered and blinked as white light filled the room. He pulled a box of Golden Grahams from the pantry and placed it on the counter. The night-shift had not affected his eating rituals; afternoon or not, it was breakfast time. He grabbed a bowl from the cupboard and a spoon from the drawer beside the dishwasher. He placed them on the counter, turned to his right, and pulled a carton of milk from the ancient green refrigerator, which matched the dishwasher. Gideon closed the fridge and stopped for a moment to look at a handful of pictures taped to the upper door.

In the center was a picture of Todd and Gideon preparing to tube down the Salt River earlier that month. Todd wore mirrored aviator sunglasses and a red-and-white striped tank top over a pair of red basketball shorts. Gideon wore a sombrero, which he won in an eating challenge at Carolina's Mexican Cantina, and a torn and faded Nevada Wolfpack t-shirt he got at football camp. The pair had their arms around each other and grinned ear to ear.

Above it, to the left, was a photo from graduation. Again it featured Todd and Gideon, in cap and gown, all smiles with their arms again around each another. Only this time there was a young man squeezed between them, mortarboard in hand. He sported a bowl cut and bright red hair and his round freckled face was almost oval when he smiled. Gideon felt a twinge of guilt that settled into a profound sadness. Glenn Bicklesby was a childhood friend and a constant tag along who never quite fit in. Through-out their school years he was teased and bullied mercilessly about everything from his hair, to the gap between his front teeth; his obsession with science fiction and his extensive Lego collection did not help either. Gideon always stood up for Glenn who seemed not to have the capacity or desire to stand up for himself. He gen-uinely liked Glenn, but with each passing year they had less and less in common and grew slowly apart. Glenn's mother had given him this picture when he went to pay his respects, shortly after he returned home. She expressed her gratitude to him for his friend-ship. She told him of the love her son had for him and suggested that if he had been around her son might still be alive. She meant it as a tribute to the positive impact he had on her son, but her words bored into Gideon heart. He felt burdened by a deep and abiding responsibility for his death, a burden he could not shake free of. He purposefully placed the picture where he would see it every day as a reminder of the impact we have, for better or worse, on our brothers and sisters here on earth. He reached out and gently touched the photo with his index finger.

Partially tucked behind it was a picture he had sent to Todd of himself on a hike through the cockpits of Jamaica. He wore a pair of dark blue sweat pants, which he cut into shorts, a *Hard Work All Day* missionary t-shirt with a yellow, green and black Jamaican flag bandana on his head. With a triumphant look he gazed heavenward, with his hands on his hips in his best Superman pose. Behind him, over his left shoulder, a lush green landscape spread out in the distance beneath a gray sky. The entrance to a cave poked out over his right shoulder.

The cave. All at once it struck him. Gideon snatched the picture off the door and stared at the cave in the background. He placed the milk carton on the counter and raced back to his bedroom. He burst through the door and placed the picture on his desk, next to the journal. In his haste he tripped over the suitcase, on his way to the closet, and fell to the floor. He muttered a substitute swear word, flung open the closet door and crawled in on his hands and knees. The third box from the left was labeled 'Mission Stuff' in black Sharpie.

"Yahtzee!"

He slid the box out from the wall and carefully removed one item at a time. On top were his own journals, followed by picture albums and souvenirs that included a twelve-inch machete with a wooden hand-carved sheath and ganja-leaf necklace. A smile broke across his face when, at the bottom of the box, he saw a few Jamaican five-dollar coins and a video cassette labeled 'Video for home May 1998.' Leaving the contents of the box spread out on the floor, he tucked the VHS tape under his arm and moved back toward his desk. A surge of joy nearly burst from him as he made his way to the TV in the front room with the video cassette, journal, photo and slip of paper in a neat stack in his arms.

The television, a black square tube monitor set in a brown faux wood box, rested on milk crate beneath the front window. Beside the crate was an old gray Samsung VCR with a black piece of electrical tape over a blinking 12:00 because no one cared to program the time. Gideon pulled on the silver dial at the top right corner of the television to the sound of the familiar pop and buzz that signaled the picture tube was warming up. It was a relic, nearly as old as the kitchen appliances, but no one complained as it was free and worked reasonably well. He squatted down on the floor and pushed the videocassette past the cheap plastic flap on the front of the VCR. He anxiously leaned back against the futon with the remote in one hand and the journal in the other. His thumb held the small piece of paper firmly against the cover. For a few seconds the white letters PLAY displayed on a blue screen followed by a black and gray fuzz that gave way to an out of focus figure.

"Is it on?" an off-camera voice asked.

As the camera came into focus Gideon saw a younger, tanner version of himself on the screen. "Yeah, man, it's on. Hello family . . ."

He pressed the fast forward button and watched himself step through, at super speed, the rooms of the Mandeville house. When his patience gave out, he pressed stop and fast forward again. He counted to sixty in his head and pressed stop again and then play.

"All right, we just saw a mad man taking a dump on the side of the road back there," his younger self stated, from behind the wheel of a car. He pointed out the window and laughed. From the shaky images he could see the inside of a car, filled beyond capacity, with four missionaries crammed in the backseat and his companion operating the camera from the passenger seat. Gideon wore the same *Hard Work All Day* missionary t-shirt and Jamaican flag bandana as in the picture, along with a pair of silver framed sunglasses he had bought off a street vendor on Red Hills Road.

He pressed fast forward again. Imagines of merriment and general foolishness whipped passed him with five white zigzaggy horizontal lines spanning the screen. After a flash of momentary blackness Gideon saw lush green bush beneath a grayish white sky. He pressed play and watched forgotten memories, as the herky-jerky camera movements gave the impression that the cameraman was either drunk or walked on uneven ground. Another flash of blackness and again he looked at a slightly younger version of himself striking a superman pose and looking triumphantly off camera. There was a click and a flash of light, from a 35mm camera, and young Elder Goodwin broke pose and smiled.

"Thanks, man," the young Elder Goodwin said, as he took the camera from a Polynesian elder with a black backpack and the same white *Hard Work All Day* missionary t-shirt.

"Hey Goodwin, say something," a voice from behind the camera said.

"Something." Elder Goodwin quipped and looked into the camera with a wry smile. "Wha ya wan mi fi say?"

"I don't know," replied the off-camera voice. "Tell them where we are."

"Well," Elder Goodwin began as he spread his arms wide. "We are in the cockpit country somewhere in St. Elizabeth, I believe, or maybe Trelawney. I don't know; we've been walking forever."

"Elder Goodwin, come and see this," another, slightly nasally voice said from behind him.

"Our intrepid guide, Bammy, is somewhere back there trying to find the trail as we are most certainly lost." Elder Goodwin pointed at the thick bush to his left while he walked in the direction of the beckoning voice. The cameraman followed him toward a pale missionary with glasses, who stood in front of the vine covered opening of a cave. This skinny young man wore a pair of black Doc Martens, dark slacks with a short sleeved white collared shirt with the top button undone.

"What is it, Elder Penny?" Elder Goodwin asked as they drew nearer.

"Check this out," Elder Penny replied. "There's something carved in the rock."

Young Elder Goodwin moved to the side to reveal an etching on the western wall of the cave. It had three legs and the looping swirls formed a heart shape. Gideon quickly clicked pause and stared with joy and disbelief at the symbol from the paper. Excitement welled up inside of him and he felt as if his heart had become lodged in his throat. He knew he had seen the symbol before and there it was on the screen, right before his eyes. He held up the paper next to the screen and looked back and forth between the television and the paper. He could not remember clearly what happened next so he pressed play and the video continued.

"Cool," Elder Goodwin said. "It's a hieroglyph."

A voice in the distance could be heard faintly shouting, "Helders, Helders, no!"

"Technically it's a petroglyph," Elder Penny corrected him. Elder Justin Penny, from Pocatello, Idaho, was a bit of a know-it-all and a stickler for the rules. He stood out in Jamaica like a sore thumb, literally. The tropical sun gave his light skin a reddish hue that made him look like a large sweaty thumb had been hit by a hammer.

"No one cares, Penny," said the voice behind the camera.

The camera panned to the approach of a short thin man, who made his way frantically toward the group of missionaries at the entrance to the cave. There were deep grooves in his dark brown face and gray specks in his thick black hair that showed his age. He wore a tattered, cream-colored, short-sleeved shirt left unbuttoned to expose his washboard abs. His pants were brown and appeared to fit in every way, except the pant legs were three inches above his ankles. In his hand was a machete that had been used and sharpened so often that the blade was now only half the width of the handle.

"Helders, come now man," he said breathlessly. "Lef it an come."

"Hey, Bammy," Elder Goodwin greeted him. "Look what we found man. It's a hieroglyph."

"Petroglyph!" Elder Penny again corrected.

"Shut up, Penny!" they all shouted.

39

"Mi know mi know," Bammy said. He pulled on Goodwin's arm and led him away from the cave. "Yu must come."

"Why?" Elder Goodwin asked. "We were going to check it out."

"No man," Bammy said and attempted to guide him away. "Lef it an come. Night soon fall 'pon wi, yu know."

"Bammy, mi na wan fi lef it," Elder Goodwin responded in patois and wrestled his arm free. "Mi wan fi see it."

Patois was a Jamaican creole, which, like the Jamaicans themselves, was shaped by their rich history and contained components of Spanish, Portuguese, Arawak, and African. Gideon took pride in his patois, as it had taken him months of practice to produce a passable imitation.

"Helda Goodwin uno c'yan't," Bammy pleaded. "A duppy cave dat."

The word *duppy*, patois for *ghost*, had always tickled Elder Goodwin. He laughed at how people could say such a funny sounding word so seriously. Many Jamaicans believed strongly in spiritual things, some even believed in the supernatural. As a rule they had a healthy fear of caves and did not mess with duppies. This knowledge, combined with the look of distress on Bammy's face, caused him to relent.

"All right, Bammy," Elder Goodwin said with a nod. "Come now, Elders, wi gone."

The television displayed static as the camera operator stopped the recording. Gideon immediately rewound the tape to see the symbol. He paused the tape and sat and stared again. There was no doubt that the symbol carved in the rock was the same symbol on the piece of paper he held in his hand. The piece of paper that came from the journal, the journal that was over three hundred years old. Excitement bubbled up again. He did not believe in fate or destiny but could not reconcile this connection as mere coincidence. He opened the journal and turned back a couple of pages. He scanned for a reference he remembered. After a few minutes he found it.

I hid myself near the cavity of a rock, which I discovered at first light, had a strange marking on the wall.

Could this have been the marking that Lieutenant Jarvis had seen? Had he drawn it and kept it in his journal? Even if that were the case its origin and meaning were still a mystery. Gideon wondered how unique this symbol was. Were the author of the journal and the artist behind the drawing the same man? Had the artist seen the very same rock carving from his video or were there more of them? Did the drawing come from the carving or the carving from the drawing, or were each of them derived from a separate source? His mind spun and he turned to the journal for answers. With the video tape still paused, he turned back to where he had left off and began to read intently.

I have serious doubts about the wisdom of Colonel Tyson and the faith he has place in the Negro Juan Lubolo. We have been marching through the mountains for nearly ten days and have only discovered two encampments, both of which had been abandoned for some time. The self-appointed "Governor" Lubolo has assured me that he knows where Ysassi will head next but I hold little hope based on our experience thus far.

I have additionally been put upon with the task of teaching Lubolo and his men the English language, so as to increase their value to our forces. Lubolo has picked it up with great ease, due either to his superior intellect or to the fact that he has exaggerated his ignorance of our language. I suspect the latter. In any case I have not left his side since the outpost and, with few exceptions, we communicate entirely in English. To be honest though, the majority of our communications are initiated by myself, as Lubolo seems reluctant to articulate his thoughts. Colonel Tyson is convinced this is due to a language barrier but I believe he has not been forthcoming with us as he has much to hide.

With each word his hopes of finding a clue to the origin and meaning of the drawing faded. If only the symbol had some kind of explanation attached or if it had not been dislodged from its original location. He took a moment to curse Todd's mischievous nature. Almost on cue, Todd stepped through the front door and let in the blinding outside light.

"What's up, fatty?" Todd greeted him in his usual fashion.

Todd closed the door and stepped further into the room. He stopped directly in front of the TV and looked at the symbol on the screen. He furrowed his brow for a moment and looked down at Gideon then back to the screen. Todd opened his mouth to speak. As he did Gideon sat up straight in anticipation of his question. He could almost see the wheels turn inside his head. He thought for certain his friend had connected the dots.

They looked at each other knowingly for several seconds before finally Todd asked, "Have you started on dinner yet?"

"What?" Gideon responded with chagrin. "No, man, I have not started on dinner yet."

"That's cool, he won't be here for a couple of hours," Todd said, as he took off his shirt and started down the hallway. "I'm going to hop in the shower. Two days baby!"

"Dude, I've told you nobody wants to see that," Gideon shouted.

He shook his head as his regrettably oblivious roommate disappeared through the archway and left him alone again with the mystery of the symbol. He got to his feet and took one last look at the symbol on the screen. *Two days.* He thought to himself. In two days he might be in a better place to get some answers. He dreaded, however, the potentially unpleasant reunion he would have to face to get them.

Ysassi's Last Stand

They moved like a black current through an ocean of bushes and trees. Swiftly and silently they sailed forward with remarkable ease. Lieutenant Jarvis, weakened and harrowed by fever, could barely keep up the frenetic pace. His heart pounded so hard he felt it might escape his chest. He fought the impulse to cry out for a halt. He did not dare. To do so might alert the enemy to their approach, his foremost concern, and further weaken his tenuous position with this lot. His pride aside, he was not even sure he had the authority to give such an order.

According to Lubolo, Ysassi's encampment was set back between two high summits, ideal for concealment but a nightmare to defend if discovered. The plan was for Colonel Tyson to march the regiment north, in plain sight, directly between the summits. Lubolo and his men would scale the summit to the east and position themselves for a surprise attack. Jarvis considered Ysassi and tried to place himself in his shoes. With superior numbers and, fighting from a position of strength, Jarvis could not help but take pity on the man about to be overwhelmed by conspiring circumstances.

The men came to a stop a few yards ahead. Each of them crouched down and became still. Jarvis mimicked this action, and after a moment he crept forward slowly to see what lie ahead. He saw Lubolo, who spoke softly to a few of his men, and crawled up next to them to hear what was being said. However, as he approached they ceased speaking. Lubolo turned to him, gestured toward his torso and said, "Off."

"What?" Jarvis answered with confusion.

"Off off, tek it off," Lubolo replied, and tugged at his coat.

Jarvis looked down at his military issued, red wool coat. He wore the uniform with pride and saw no good reason to remove it. He may have been assigned to serve, temporarily, with this ill-conceived militia but he was a British solider. His uniform distinguished him further from this riffraff and he had no intention of capitulating. Furthermore, he did not like being ordered around by the likes of Lubolo.

"No," he whispered sternly, and pushed Lubolo's hand away. "I will not."

"When uno wan fi hide uno na light a fiya." Lubolo replied.

Lubolo looked at him with hostility. Jarvis did not wish to appear weak and returned his stare, determined not to relent no matter the outcome. After several tense moments Lubolo broke away and muttered, "Fool."

Relieved, Jarvis exhaled. Lubolo moved to the front of the men and began to descend down into the gorge. They had separated from Colonel Tyson just after daybreak; about two or three hours earlier, according to Jarvis's best estimation. While their route was significantly more daunting they had no doubt made better time, as Jarvis had never witnessed an English company move so swiftly. He peered down into the gorge and, to his astonishment, saw signs of life. There was a small plume of smoke that rose softly into the air and dispersed in the breeze that swept through the gully. He saw what appeared to be a small structure to the south near the entrance to the camp. His best guess was that the crude shed was most likely where they kept their powder and rations dry. Other than the shed there were no other significant landmarks he could see. No tents or walls, just a few barricades near the sentries, posted to the south of the camp. He looked from the shed back to the smoke plume. What kind of fool would light a fire while trying to hide?

The incline was steep and they had to grab hold of the branches and vines to keep from slipping down the cliff. They descended nearly a hundred feet and came to a halt. This was where they would wait for Tyson to make his move. Jarvis had fallen behind once more and crept his way up to the front, near the advance group. Lubolo looked back, pursed his lips and shook his head.

"*Tonto*," he said to his men as he gestured toward Jarvis.

"This coat represents the greatest empire in the world and is deserving of your respect, as is anyone who wears it," Jarvis proclaimed with as much authority as he could muster.

He was not entirely sure where he would have gone with his speech but would have liked to have finished it. Unfortunately, just as he spoke those words a single shot rang out from the camp below. It struck Lieutenant Jarvis in his left shoulder and knocked him to the ground. Several men returned fire as noise and commotion exploded all around him. Jarvis had been shot at before, but until now he had never actually been hit. A terrible heat ripped through his shoulder, followed instantly by a release of pressure as his flesh burst open. He lay motionless on the ground and stared up at a deep blue sky.

Panic welled up inside of him. With his right hand he felt for the wound in his shoulder. Seconds later, his fingers found a hole in his coat and, to his horror, his middle finger plunged into a warm wet hole in his body. With a twinge of pain he rolled unto his side and struggled to sit up. His ears rang from the volley of shots released by Lubolo's men as they returned fire. The smoke still hung in the air, but most of the men had disappeared down the gully leaving Lieutenant Jarvis alone. He lurched forward, rolled unto his knees and with great effort stood up. He pulled his coat off his right shoulder and allowed it to slip free. One painful wiggle of his left side and the coat fell from his wounded shoulder in a heap on the ground. He quickly got his bearings, retrieved his musket and followed the sounds of gunfire in the distance.

As he crashed through the perimeter of bushes he beheld the

fruits of war. At least eighty men were locked in the grips of battle. At this moment these men did not fight for land, power, or even victory, they battled for their lives.

Unlike previous skirmishes, Jarvis was not entirely sure who his allies were. This was not a civilized conflict with colors and formations; this was a mêlée between Spaniards and Negroes, Indians and farmers, slaves and soldiers. A large man, with skin like coal, charged toward him with a frightful yell; his wild eyes filled with rage and desperation. Jarvis took a step backwards, swung his musket up with his good arm and fired. He hit the man at close range in the neck. At once the man fell violently to the ground in a lifeless ebony heap. As a conditioned reflex Jarvis immediately began to reload, a task made exceedingly more difficult with one good arm. He drove the butt of the musket into the ground and steadied it against his leg. Frantically, he poured powder down the barrel and dropped in a shot before setting it in place with the ramrod. All the while he kept a wary eye against further attacks.

Directly to the north he spotted Lubolo, with a handful of his men. They pursued a group attempting to flee to the summit at the far end of the gorge. Between Jarvis and Lubolo were at least fifty or sixty men, of whom he had almost no indication who was friend or foe. When he finished reloading his musket Jarvis fixed his bayonet and looked briefly to the south, hopeful for the arrival of Colonel Tyson and his troops. Not surprisingly, they had yet to arrive. The plan had been for the Colonel to advance on the camp at midday and prompt Lubolo's attack. Even if Tyson had been in position he would not have been prepared for this divergence from the plan. Jarvis determined to make his way through the carnage and rejoin Lubolo, as he had been ordered to stay by his side. It would be next to impossible to distinguish Ysassi's Negroes from Lubolo's, so Jarvis decided to fire only when advanced upon.

Jarvis gripped his musket tightly with his right hand, plotted a course through the bodies and brush and raced forward with reckless abandon. Two men grappled with each other and fell against him, knocking him off balance. As he reached out to steady himself, a searing pain shot down his left side. He struggled on, in spite of his pain, with a single objective in mind; reach Lubolo. In a few seconds he was beyond the largest clutter of men, and his path forward seemed relatively clear. He turned north, where Lubolo had caught and engaged the group who fled from him. Toward the western summit he saw a man atop a small bulwark who waved his arms wildly. He wore a bright white shirt and tan pants with a red sash and a saber at his side.

"*Cobardes! Permaneced y luchad!*" the man shouted.

Jarvis had never seen him before but was certain this was Don Cristobal Arnaldo de Ysassi. His dark wild hair was matted to his scalp with perspiration. He looked as if he had not had a proper shave in weeks. He reeked of desperation, from the sound of his voice to his manic gestures. A large group of his men fled south, toward the entrance of the camp, and ignored the pleas of their exhausted leader. Their retreat, however, was cut off as Colonel Tyson and his company at last arrived.

Jarvis's heart leapt in his chest, as the sea of red coats poured into the little green valley. They quickly formed a line and fired a volley of shots, which dropped a handful of men. Jarvis looked back to the bulwark, where a crestfallen Ysassi removed his white shirt. He fastened it to his saber and stood still for a moment. He breathed in deeply and surveyed the scene. After the second volley from the redcoats, he raised his saber high above his head and waved it back and forth. It was over. A young steward near Ysassi blew three times on a horn. The sound of gunfire ceased and Ysassi's remaining forces laid down their weapons and put their hands in the air.

There was a commotion behind him and Jarvis turned to see a young man at a full sprint. Whether it was toward him or away from Lubolo he could not tell and, in the moment, did not care. With no time to fire a shot, he used his musket to impede the boy's progress and whipped him to the ground with the butt of his gun. The boy scrambled to get to his feet but Jarvis leveled the barrel at him.

"Don't!" Jarvis threatened.

The boy froze, in a prostrated position, on his hands and knees. Jarvis winced as intense pain shot through his wounded shoulder. Slowly, the boy raised both hands above his head and knelt backwards on his heels. He kept his eyes fixed on the ground and did not make eye contact with Jarvis. His breathing was labored but steady and gave him an air of calmness, despite his current predicament. He was, quite literally, skin and bones with a gaunt face and bloodshot eyes. There was no doubt the boy was of African descent, but with markedly lighter skin than many of the other Negroes Jarvis was accustomed to. On his right forearm there was a marking of some kind, which stood out against his brown skin. A quick check of the boy and the area around him revealed no weapons, and Jarvis relaxed slightly

Back toward the entrance of the camp Ysassi's troops were being lined up and their weapons collected. Colonel Tyson had made his way to the bulwark and Ysassi personally surrendered his saber to him. Jarvis felt a great sense of relief, as it appeared that not only the battle but the war was at an end. Terms of surrender would need to be negotiated, of course, but he prayed that the fighting was done.

Lubolo approached to his right. Jarvis greeted him with a nod, but kept his musket on the boy. When Lubolo came to a stop beside Jarvis, the boy looked up and his once calm face tightened and filled with anger. He scowled up at Lubolo with a look of intense hatred. Jarvis looked over at Lubolo, who returned the boy's look with a glower of his own. Lubolo's shirt was bloodstained and torn. Jarvis could not immediately tell if he had suffered an injury or if it was the blood of another. Lubolo reached out with his left hand, placed it on the barrel of Jarvis's gun and firmly pulled it from his hands. Without a word he cocked the hammer, held the butt of the rifle to his hip and fired. The boy, who never took his eyes off of Lubolo, fell dead to the earth.

"What was that?!" Jarvis demanded.

Lubolo handed him back his musket, wiped the fresh blood spatter from his pants and said, "No medicine c'yan cure hate."

His voice was cold and expressionless but in his eyes there was no malice, just a shocking cool that complemented his matter of fact tone. Jarvis felt Lubolo believed his actions were justified. He pushed past Jarvis and began to walk toward the bulwark. The shot had drawn the attention of everyone in the valley and all eyes were now on them. Jarvis looked down at the boy's body. He had seen death before, more than he cared to, but this was different. He was able to justify, at least in his own mind, the death and killing in war. Friend or foe, dying in battle was just a part of it. Whether you fought for the cause or against it, you died for a reason. This death, however, was so senseless that he could not come to grips with it.

With purpose, he followed after Lubolo. The bulwark was near the base of the summit in an elevated position. Jarvis labored to make his way up the incline and close in on Lubolo, who was still several yards ahead of him. Colonel Tyson left Ysassi in the custody of Captain York and came to greet them near the east side of the barrier.

"Sorry to be late," Tyson said with a rare smile. "Had a run-in with a band of pirates, believe it or not."

Lieutenant Jarvis wasted no time with pleasantries. "Colonel, this man shot an unarmed Negro boy who had surrendered!"

"Have you been shot?" Tyson asked. He examined Jarvis's wound as if he had not heard the accusation.

"Yes sir, in the shoulder. Did you hear what I said?" Jarvis replied.

Colonel Tyson stepped forward and took him by the right arm, just as he had done that night at the outpost. With a firm grip he guided him away from Lubolo, who stood defiantly. With their backs toward him, Tyson lowered his voice and answered, "Yes, Lieutenant, I heard you. You seem to be missing the big picture here. You've played a role in bringing a multi-year conflict to an end and have won this island for King and Country. You want to talk about one Negro boy? Pull yourself together, man."

"Due respect sir, this is not how gentlemen wage war," Jarvis replied.

"And he is not a gentleman!" Tyson responded in a slightly raised voice. He paused and looked back over his shoulder at Lubolo, who watched them with his arms folded. Tyson composed himself and spoke again with a calm demeanor.

"You did well, Lieutenant. You have won your way back into my good graces. Stay there and you are most certainly in line for a promotion. Let this go," Tyson urged. He released his arm and turned to walk back toward Lubolo.

Jarvis looked back where the fallen Negro boy lay. Two of Lubolo's men stood over him. He considered what the Colonel had said. Why had he gotten so upset about the death of this Negro? *Respect*, he thought. Respect for how you live and how one meets his end. Respect matters. His respect for Colonel Tyson had begun to erode and what little respect he had for Lubolo had all but evaporated.

"Congratulations, Governor," Tyson said, as he extended his hand to Lubolo.

Lubolo uncrossed his arms and reached out to clasp hands with the Colonel. As he did so, the rolled up sleeve of his shirt pulled back to reveal a black mark on his forearm. Jarvis squinted hard and tried to examine the mark. It was a tattoo of what looked like a bird that faced backwards toward its hindquarters. A recent memory flickered and a burning curiosity rushed over him. Jarvis quickly turned and trotted down the hill toward the fallen boy. The two men had lifted him off the ground and were about to carry him off to place him with the rest of the dead.

"Stop!" Jarvis shouted. "Wait."

The men dutifully halted and put the boy back down.

"*Gracias*," Jarvis said. "I'll take it from here."

With a slightly befuddled look the men glanced at each other and then back to Jarvis. He could not be sure if their looks were due to a language barrier or because they too had questions as to his authority over them. In any case, Jarvis decided decisive action was needed to accomplish of his designs.

"Dismissed!" he said sharply.

To his relief, the men left without question or protest. He

waited a moment until they were a good distance away and stooped down to examine the boy. He turned him over onto his back and picked up his frail right arm. Directly in the middle of his forearm was the same tattoo he had seen on Lubolo's right arm just moments ago, a bird that stood and looked backwards at its tail. He could not be sure what, if anything, this meant. Was this the marking of his master? It was not uncommon for Spanish slave owners to brand their property but a slave would not willingly hold still for such an intricate marking; a branding iron was much more likely. All he knew for sure was that Lubolo and this dead Negro boy had the same marking in the same place. Perhaps this had something to do with why Lubolo had shot him in such a brutal fashion, without warning and seemingly without cause. His thoughts were cut short by the sound of footsteps behind him. A shadow moved over top of him and he looked up to see Lubolo.

"What's done c'yan't be undone," Lubolo said.

His voice had a gentleness that Jarvis had not expected. In his face he saw a twinge of remorse, a singular crack in his steely demeanor. Clearly there was more to this man than he had originally surmised.

"Come," Lubolo said. He bent down next to Jarvis and lifted the boy's legs. "We ago lay 'im to rest."

Jarvis grabbed the boy by the arms and began to walk toward a group of bodies laid side by side further down the hill. He was conflicted by what he had seen and what he felt at the moment. All he thought he knew unraveled right in front of him. He was unsure what he had been fighting for or whether his, or anybody's, cause was just. They reached the place where the men gathered the dead and with a single heave unceremoniously flung the boy in line with the rest of the bodies. Lubolo made a hand signal to one of the men who stood by, the man repeated it to the group down across the gully and swiftly and silently they all began to move toward the eastern summit.

"What you did was wrong," Jarvis stated boldly.

Lubolo paused. For a moment Jarvis thought he would walk on, as if nothing had been said, but suddenly he rounded on the lieutenant and in one motion the two men stood nose to nose. He was so close that Jarvis could feel the warmth of his breath on his face. Jarvis stood straight and tall and tried not to blink. He looked Lubolo right in the eye and did his best to mask any signs of the panic that surged through his body. If he could cut down that boy in cold blood there was no telling what he might do. Lubolo reached out and grabbed Jarvis's hand; he thrust the handle of his cutlass into it. Then he slowly knelt down on the ground, without breaking eye contact. Lubolo raised his hands over his head, just as the boy had done mere minutes ago. He looked up at Jarvis with the same hate filled look the boy laid upon Lubolo. Jarvis's hand closed tightly on the cutlass and his arm flinched, almost involuntary. Instinctually, his body wanted to react. He could have easily struck down this man who knelt before him and recoiled at the thought. He took a deep breath and remained perfectly still. Then the marking on Lubolo's forearm caught his attention again. There it was; a backward facing bird, identical to the boy they had just laid to rest. Lubolo too looked at his own tattoo and then back to Jarvis. With a deliberate but unhurried motion Lubolo put his arms down and rose to his feet. He took the cutlass from Jarvis and pulled him close until they were cheek to cheek.

"Yu mek yur choice, I mek mine," Lubolo whispered in his ear.

He released Jarvis and moved to join his men, who watched from a safe distance. Jarvis swallowed hard and glanced over his shoulder as Lubolo marched down the gully. A thought crept into his head, that his choice had just changed both of their lives. He only hoped it would be for good.

Dinner and a Decision

Carefully, he closed the journal and examined the well-worn cover. A smile broke across Gideon's face as he observed the man who held the journal from the opposite side of the table. Joe Colbeck's callused hands grated against the journal's leather spine. His thick beard covered his entire face; aside from his eyes, nose and the tops of his sunbaked cheeks. His blue plaid shirt and denim jeans completed the reclusive hermit look. The most remarkable thing about him was that behind his facial hair, set back against his leathery skin and crow's feet wrinkles, were a pair of childlike eyes. For all his personal faults and failings Joe had never lost his sense of wonder and adventure. Gideon admired that most.

"And where did you say you got this again?" Joe asked.

"From a friend of mine." Gideon remained purposefully vague and hoped he would not ask for further explanation.

The three of them, Gideon, Joe, and Todd, sat around the small rectangular dining room table; littered with half empty plates and glasses. The dark room was lit by an orange umbrella shade lamp, suspended by a brass colored chain over the table. The lamp shone down on the center of the table like a spotlight on a stage. The journal hovered over the table, suspended carefully in Joe's rough hands, illuminated like a fine piece of art in a museum. Gideon tried to read Joe's face and discern what he might be thinking. His best guess was that he was either amused or intrigued by this journal and his story. Joe retrieved the slip of paper from the table, held it up to the light to examine the symbol more closely.

"And you say that this paper was in the journal, but you've found no reference to it?"

"That's right," Gideon said. "Not yet, that is."

Joe placed the slip of paper on top of the journal and laid them to rest gently on the table. He leaned back in his chair and ran his fingers through his thick brown hair, until they connected behind his head. He inhaled deeply and his eyes widened, as he stared intently at the symbol.

"Have you ever seen anything like it?" Todd chimed in.

"No, man, I haven't," Joe replied solemnly as he looked up at his son seated next to him.

Gideon's heart sank. Although farfetched, he had maintained some small hope that Joe might have answers. His travels had taken him far and wide and, while not institutionally educated, he was extremely knowledgeable; particularly when it came to the offbeat and obscure.

Todd and Gideon had grown up on his outrageous tales of adventure and legend, which could easily be dismissed as wild embellishments or outright lies. However, Joe had the innate ability to make them just believable enough that one could suspend disbelief and enjoy them as tales of truth. Gideon imagined, in great detail, the wild and wonderful pictures Joe painted in his stories.

"The part I'm really geeking out on is that you saw it carved in the rocks," Joe continued and gestured toward the symbol. "I mean, here stuffed in a book is one thing, but carved in stone? That's got to mean something. People don't just chisel things without reason."

"But what is the reason?" Gideon wondered aloud.

"Well that's the question, isn't it?" Joe replied. "You said the petroglyph was near the entrance to a cave?"

"Hieroglyph," Todd corrected.

"What?" Joe responded.

"It's a hieroglyph, right?" Todd stated uncertainly, and looked over to Gideon for reassurance.

"No, man," Gideon answered. "Drawn on stone is a hieroglyph, carved in stone is a petroglyph."

Joe shook his head at his son with a bemused look of disbelief. After a moment of awkward silence, Todd shrank back into the shadows of the dark dining room.

"We found this symbol just outside a cave," Gideon said.

"Interesting," Joe said. "Y'know, ancient inhabitants of the Americas both feared and revered caves. Some believed that humankind originated from caves and that they led to the underworld. The Spanish explorers and early buccaneers used this superstition to their advantage. They often concealed their valuables in caves where the natives would not venture. Given the Caribbean's rich and colorful history, particularly in the sixteen and seventeen hundreds, I'd say there's a better than average chance this symbol is a marker of some kind."

"Wait a minute," Gideon began, and failed to conceal his disbelief. "You're saying this symbol is a marker? For treasure, pirate treasure?"

"Pirates, buccaneers, conquistadors, whatever. All I'm saying is that it's possible, if not likely, that this marking was left as a guide; for someone or to something. It was important enough that it was carved in stone and it was important enough to stay tucked inside a journal for three hundred years!" Joe said in a slightly raised voice.

Gideon realized he may have offended Joe, who carried with him a lifetime of rejection and derision when it came to his many theories and fruitless expeditions. He could not help but be skeptical, as Joe's theories often revolved around treasures unknown and yet Joe had next to nothing to show from a lifetime of chasing them. Still, Gideon could not deny the idea of a hidden treasure was not out of the realm of possibly. He tried to ignore the excitement that tingled in his stomach.

"You said yourself, you didn't go in the cave," Todd piped up from the corner. "And that it was difficult to get there. You needed a guide, Barney . . ."

"Bammy." Gideon corrected.

"Whatever, man. Bammy. And he wouldn't even go in there," Todd finished.

"So?"

"So it's possible that no one has explored that cave. It's possible that somebody hid something in there and it's possible that it's still there!" Todd shouted with both excitement and aggravation.

"Sure it's possible but . . ."

"No! No buts! This is where you take a fun idea and throw logic and reason at it, like a monkey flinging poo, until you've covered it with your stink of doubt. Not this time!" Todd demanded. "Look, we're going to be there in just two days. We can either play around on the beach sipping frozen daiquiris and eating rice and beans . . ."

"Rice and peas."

"Or!" Todd shouted, tired of being corrected, and pointed a threatening finger at his friend for emphasis. ". . . we can say 'forget that noise' and go on a legit adventure where who knows what we'll find."

Todd leaned forward and the light from the lamp shone on his bright hopeful face. He paused for dramatic effect and finally asked, "What do you say?"

Gideon had to admit the thought had crossed his mind, but he could not bring himself to say it out loud for fear of sounding like his friends sounded right now, crazy. He looked from Todd to Joe and back to Todd. He smiled and shook his head. He looked at them and thought he was clearly in the company of lunatics, but they were lunatics after his own heart. He opened his mouth to respond but could not find the courage to say what filled his heart and swirled through his mind.

"When do you leave?" Joe asked.

"Tomorrow night. We're on the red eye to Miami and we'll arrive in Kingston the following morning," Gideon answered.

Todd and Gideon dreamed up this trip the day he received his call to Jamaica, they hatched their scheme to return after his mission was over. He wanted to show Todd around and introduce him to the land and the people that he loved. Now, on the eve of their departure, his ambitions had shifted, which was unsettling to him.

Gideon took comfort in planning and organization and avoided spontaneity whenever possible. Spontaneity, however, was where his good friend lived, a trait he inherited from his father, who would pick up at a moment's notice and be gone for months at a time.

"Where are you headed next?" Gideon asked Joe. "You wanna come with us?"

"You know I'd love to, but I'm headed back to Albuquerque tonight to meet up with Stewart. He says he's got a lead on an Aztec temple buried beneath an old Spanish mission south of the border."

"How is Stewart?" Gideon asked, not particularly caring about the answer.

"Same," Joe responded.

"Did you say tonight?" Todd interjected, with a tone of disappointment. "But you just got here."

"I was just on my way back from Chula Vista and wanted to see my favorite son," Joe said with a wink.

Todd was his only son, his only child for that matter. He had always dreamed of sharing in the extraordinary life his father had pursued. Todd allowed himself to openly romanticize his father's life as a globe-trotting archeologist in search of fame and fortune. However, he knew that reality, as it often does, fell far short of the dream. He could not contain his disappointment at the brevity of his father's visit and did not try to.

"Why don't you help me with these dishes, champ," Joe said to Todd and reached for the dirty plates in front of him. He only called him champ when he knew he had let him down. Gideon was certain Joe was unaware of this subconscious reaction and how much it hurt Todd.

"You don't have to do that, Joe," Gideon said, and attempted to wrestle his own plate from his grasp.

"Of course I do. After fixing a fine meal like that, you shouldn't have to do the cleaning too."

The "fine meal" had consisted of frozen, boneless, skinless chicken breasts thrown on the propane grill in the backyard next to some potatoes wrapped in aluminum foil, served with a glass of ready-made Donald Duck orange juice. He released his plate with a gracious nod to his guest.

Todd removed the remaining plates and glasses and said, "You just sit here and think about what I said."

Dishes in hand, father and son shuffled carefully between the chairs and the wall and around the counter into the kitchen. Gideon sat alone and listened to the barely audible sound of the conversation in the adjoining room. He stared at the new shadow on the journal cast from the kitchen lights. After a moment he reached out and pulled the journal toward him. He turned it right side up and opened to where he had left off.

Although it has been my fervent hope that I be reassigned to a regular company, my petitions have all been denied and I have accepted my lot with the black regiment. I have been promoted to Major and designated as special envoy to Colonel Juan Lubolo. While my mistrust for Lubolo has abated, and his recent appointment would suggest that he has earned the trust of the Crown, I nonetheless have been ordered to stay on. Governor Lyttleton has respected the last wishes of Colonel Tyson and ordered that my post be made permanent. Out of deference to Colonel Tyson I have withheld my formal opposition to this appointment.

By any measure the alliance with Lubolo has been an overwhelming success. However, in the three years since expelling the Spanish forces from the island we have been less successful in dealing with the remnants of Ysassi's allies.

Our orders are to secure the interior of the island and if possible eradicate the outlaw Juan de Serras, who has rebuffed all attempts to make peace and ignored the rules of civilized engagement. We have twice destroyed his camps and driven out his men but have been unable to bring him to justice or prevent him from regrouping elsewhere. I myself have yet to even lay eyes on the scoundrel, however, we recently captured one of his men and he has offered, on his own accord, to lead us to his encampment at daybreak.

A clatter of dishes in the sink brought him back to the present. Gideon looked over through the space between the countertop and the overhead cabinets. Joe was at the sink, while Todd sat on the counter with his back to Gideon and regaled Joe with some tale of excitement. His hands and arms flailed about and the pitch of his voice was several octaves higher than normal. Gideon shook his head with amusement, as his friend had once again masterfully avoided the dishes. He closed the journal and stood up from the table. With the journal in hand, he made his way into the kitchen and stopped at the end of the counter. He caught sight of the pictures on the refrigerator and paused for a moment to look at Glenn's smiling face. Glenn would have loved this idea and Gideon thought of how excited he would have been to go with them. Todd halted his wild storytelling when he saw Gideon enter the room. Joe turned around, leaned back against the sink and dried his hands on a towel, as both waited in silent anticipation.

"Fine," Gideon said. "Adventure it is . . ."

"Yeah!" Todd exclaimed.

". . . but I'm getting me some rice and peas while we're there."

Todd hopped off the counter and leapt at Gideon. He grabbed onto Gideon and wrapped his arms and legs around him, like a koala bear on a tree. "This is going to be boss!"

"I'm already regretting this," Gideon said to Joe as he tried to peel his friend off him.

"Nah, man, this is going to rock," Todd assured him.

"Listen, we need to be prepared," Gideon spoke with all the seriousness he could muster, as he considered his audience. "We're not taking suitcases any more. You need to throw your stuff in a backpack and you can only take what's necessary. Do you still have that backpack I lent you?"

"Yes sir!" Todd answered. He stepped back with a sarcastic phony military salute.

Gideon, like most Mormon youth, had grown up in the Boy Scouts, where he became proficient in camping, backpacking, canyoneering, orienteering, first aid, and wilderness survival. Whether he slept in a snow cave, dug with his own hands, or under a lean-to he fashioned out of fallen branches, Gideon was confident he could survive in almost any environment. He prided himself on being able to start a fire three different ways without a match and knew a dozen different knots. Todd's idea of camping, however, consisted of a plush foam sleeping pad, a six pack of Mountain Dew, and enough kerosene to burn down Yosemite.

"This is serious, man," Gideon continued. "I'll make a list of things you have to bring."

"You worry too much." Todd placed his hands on Gideon's shoulders and squeezed. "We got this."

The implication of "we" was that Todd fully trusted Gideon to take care of everything and that his friend's preparations to bridge the gap left by any negligence on his part. Gideon accepted this and had already compiled a mental list of extra things he would need to bring to compensate for his traveling companion.

"Well it looks like you two have a lot of getting ready to do and I've got a lot of road ahead of me," Joe said. "I think I'd better take off."

"Hold up a second, Pops," Todd said. "I've got something for you."

He pushed past Gideon and hustled down the hallway toward his bedroom. He stumbled briefly over the step down into the living room and Joe and Gideon traded a chuckle at his misstep. All at once Joe's face turned serious and the sudden change in his demeanor sent a tremor down Gideon's spine.

"I wish you were going with us," Gideon said.

"Me too, son," Joe replied.

"Any advice?"

"Yeah," Joe began. "You two think you know what you are doing and what you are getting into. You don't. Keep your mind and your eyes open. These things are never what you expect and they won't go as planned."

"Got it."

"One last thing," Joe said. He stepped closer to Gideon and lowered his voice. "I know my son is an idiot, and I mean that in the best possible way, but he'll come through in a pinch. You get each other's back and you'll be all right."

"Thanks, Joe," Gideon said as Todd re-entered the room.

In his hand Todd carried a plastic bag with a Target logo. He handed it to his father and sheepishly explained, "I've had that since Father's Day but never got around to mailing it."

"Thanks, son," Joe said. He reached out and embraced him. "I love you."

"I love you too, pops," Todd said, and buried his head into his chest with a big grin.

Gideon looked away as to not intrude on this father–son moment. He glanced down at the journal in his hand and gave it a squeeze. *Two more days.*

Death of an Alliance

Bodies lay about the camp on either side of the singular foot-path along the crude mountain road. Much to his regret, this sleep formation was as close as Major Jarvis had come to a semblance of order in the black regiment. The men generously referred to this as a camp, but in reality it was simply the place they halted the previous days march; not that you could call what they did marching either. They had been instructed properly to march in formation; however, they employed this knowledge only once at Colonel Lubolo's official appointment in Kingston. To have witnessed them on that day, filing in orderly and standing at attention, only made their day to day lack of discipline all the more infuriating to Jarvis.

It was midmorning and most of the men still slept; save the blurry eyed night watchmen and a few whose hunger had roused them from their slumber. Despite being deep in enemy territory the men filled their night with song, stories and loud laughter. They used luggage, gourds and hollow reeds as primitive instruments and made the most remarkable music. The words they sang were known to all except Jarvis, ancient folk songs brought over from Africa. He imagined they must have been passed down from generation to generation, as few of these men were likely to have seen the vast continent. Removed over thousands of miles of ocean and by decades of enslavement, these songs were one of the few ways they clung to their culture and heritage. Although Jarvis could have done without noise that gave away their position, he quite envied their lyrical link to the past.

Two of the men sat close to a small fire, where the remains of a boar roasted on a spit. The aroma of salted pork wafted up to meet Major Jarvis as he stepped over and around the scattered bodies. For several days provisions had been scarce and much effort had been expended to find food. Jarvis begrudged the hours the men wasted painstakingly preparing food that he himself would not eat. Although the smell made him salivate and his stomach growl with hunger, he learned by hard experience that his stomach did not agree with his nose. Every man in the regiment had a pouch of spices and seasonings tied to his waist. These strong spices left an indelible impression on Jarvis's mind. From the first bite he began to sweat, his throat burned and his nostrils cleared. If his afflictions had ended there he would have counted himself lucky. Violent stomach pains visited him that night and caused much distress to his bowels. At first he feared he had been poisoned, except a few of the men happily consumed his leftovers and showed no ill effects. In any case he vowed never again to eat what was offered him without question. At his approach, one of the men cut off a piece of boar and mockingly offered it to him. The men by the fire looked at each other and laughed as Jarvis passed by without acknowledging their taunting gesture.

Five trunks lay open and empty on the ground beyond the fire pit. Jarvis stopped and considered the empty trunks for a moment. These trunks, filled with supplies and provisions at the outset, seemed the perfect metaphor for the current state of their expedition. For nearly three weeks they traversed the hills and valleys in search of the rebel Juan de Serras and had come up empty. That is, until yesterday—until Goliath.

A pair of advanced scouts captured a man, just before dusk, who claimed to be an associate of de Serras. He had not given a name but Jarvis dubbed him Goliath, as it seemed to suit him best.

He had massive tree trunk legs, broad shoulders and biceps like buckets. His closed fists looked like huge coconuts and appeared just as firm and unrelenting. His head was shorn on the sides was a bushel of short, knotty, unkempt curls on top. Jarvis estimated the behemoth was at least a foot taller than him, not quite biblical proportions but an intimidating figure nonetheless. He sat calm and upright near a skinny cedar tree. With his arms and legs tied together he watched coolly as the major approached.

"*¿Quiere agua?*" Jarvis asked Goliath. He raised his hand to his mouth in a drinking motion.

"He speaks English," a voice sounded behind him.

Jarvis turned to see Lubolo, who walked up the hill at a slow deliberate pace until he stood next to Jarvis and faced their prisoner. The thick woolly hair atop his head was wet and Jarvis surmised that he had just woken and washed up. With his eyes set squarely on the hulking figure before him, Lubolo cradled a lump in his hand wrapped in cloth. Jarvis studied Lubolo for a moment before he asked, "How do you know?"

"Know what?" Lubolo asked as he glared down at Goliath.

"How do you know that he speaks English?" Jarvis responded.

Lubolo turned his head, fixed his eyes on Major Jarvis and stated flatly, "Mi jus know."

From the tone of his voice Jarvis had no doubt that he knew. *But how?* Jarvis had been at the initial interrogation when he arrived in camp yesterday evening and he had only spoken Spanish. Lubolo was also present at the questioning and had not been in contact with him since. In nearly three years Lubolo had hardly left Jarvis's sight, at least not for more than a minute or two. Jarvis had not run across Goliath's colossal path before. That he would have remembered. If Lubolo had knowledge of their prisoner's linguistic ability it was acquired prior to his defection.

A provision in the Governor's agreement was that Lubolo and his men learn English, an additional task assigned to Jarvis. It had taken his men some time to come to even a rudimentary understanding of the language. Lubolo, however, picked it up quickly. So quickly, in fact, Jarvis long suspected the colonel knew English all along.

Lubolo held up the lump in his hand, carefully removed the cloth and offered it to Jarvis. Hesitantly, Jarvis looked down at what appeared to be some kind of meat. He raised his hand toward the cloth as a reflex but froze mid-reach, unsure of what he was accepting. Lubolo saw his reluctance and broke off a piece and ate it. He shook what remained of the clothbound meat in Jarvis's direction and said, "Pork belly."

Jarvis reached out, took a small piece. While he chewed he watched Goliath, who had turned his attention to the grass beneath his large bare feet. He considered for a moment whether or not to pursue his query further. He was certain Lubolo knew him or knew of him but was unsure the ramifications of such a pursuit. Lubolo was not forthcoming generally and it was a constant battle to extract even the most benign information from him. For his part, Jarvis maintained a healthy suspicion of Lubolo, however, their relationship and mutual respect had progressed much over the years. Jarvis took another small piece of pork and turned to offer it to Goliath. He looked up from the ground and stretched his mammoth hand cautiously toward Jarvis. Lubolo slapped the meat from Jarvis's hand and knocked it to the ground. When Jarvis reached for it Lubolo stamped on it with his boot and smashed it into the grass and mud.

"Really, was that necessary?" Jarvis irksomely questioned.

Lubolo stared down with a look of fiery contempt at the captive giant. He glanced at Major Jarvis for a moment before he turned and strolled away without a word. Jarvis watched him walk down from the small hill until he was confident Lubolo was out of earshot. He then turned to face Goliath, who once again gazed up at him. There was no malice or fear in his deep brown eyes. Despite being imprisoned he looked poised and confident. For the first time Jarvis examined carefully the ropes that bound his wrists and ankles. He wondered how they held such a man. He imagined what would happen if this imposing figure broke free from his restraints and had to suppress a wave of panic that welled up inside of him. He removed the green pear-shaped gourd that hung around his neck and placed it at Goliath's feet. He backed away deliberately a couple of paces and cleared his throat nervously.

"Take this. Water. I am truly sorry about that," he said, and gestured to the spot where Lubolo had stood. "Uh, *lo siento*."

He then turned and pursued Lubolo's path down the hill.

"Thank you," Goliath said.

Mildly stunned he stopped and turned back to acknowledge Goliath. A small smile broke across his face as he thought of how foolish his pantomiming and broken Spanish must have been to a man who understood English. He wondered what could have motivated Goliath to confirm, on some level, that he did in fact understand and speak the language. What advantage had he given up? Did he intend to cooperate and lead them to de Serras as promised? Why would he readily betray his people? Had he fallen out of favor with de Serras? Had life on the run become too much for him? He appeared to be the picture of physical health and Jarvis could not imagine a scenario in which he would tolerate ill treatment from anyone. Jarvis knew firsthand the hardships endured by the people who inhabited these mountains, having spent the better part of the past three years living as they did and he was more than ready for it to be over. His hope was that this Goliath shared his desires and would be the key to ending their struggles.

Normally well-kept, Major Jarvis had by necessity not maintained his own high standard of dress and grooming. His long dark hair was no longer combed, straightened and pulled back in a ponytail, but hung in a mess of waves and curls down to his chin. Once clean shaven, his face was covered in a shaggy beard, as he was three weeks from his last shave. His dingy yellowish brown shirt had started out white as a tulip, not that anyone could tell. His black trousers were torn and stained with the red clay from the ground they trudged through each day. He had somewhat reluctantly abandoned his red wool coat. Lubolo had warned him that his uniform made him an easy target but Jarvis, a soldier for king and country, would not hear it. That is until a lone shot rang out in the jungle. On the outskirts of Ysassi's last haunt a sniper singled him out and a bullet pierced his left shoulder. As he struggled to his feet his first thought was to remove his coat. He left it on that very spot and never laid eyes on it again. Like all wounds his shoulder healed in time, but the memory and the lesson learned remained. Although he struggled to admit it, a part of his allegiance died that day, as it fell from his shoulders along with the stripes he had worked so hard to earn.

Goliath raised the calabash to his lips, as he did Jarvis's heart leapt into his throat. There, on his right forearm, was a tattoo of a backward facing bird. It was the same marking on Lubolo's forearm, the same marking shared by the fallen Negro boy from so many years ago. Goliath finished his drink and extended the calabash back to Jarvis. "Uh, keep it." Jarvis stammered. He left their captive alone by the cedar tree, turned and hurried away.

With caution he approached Lubolo, who stood at the head of the camp and spoke with two of the men. They nodded at the Colonel and departed at a jog. In no time they reached the end of the path and disappeared into the bush. It was standard procedure to send a pair of scouts ahead to ensure their desired route was safe. Their departure meant the regiment would follow shortly. Jarvis stood at attention next to Lubolo and tried to peek at his right forearm. At least three men shared identical markings, on the same arm no less. This was well beyond coincidence and Jarvis was certain this explained Lubolo's prior knowledge of Goliath.

The sun had risen over the peaks to the east and breached the tall trees at its base. The morning was cool but Jarvis knew that would not last long. Jarvis straightened up and looked dead ahead at the men, spread out on both sides of the trail.

"What, may I ask, is the plan?" Jarvis asked the colonel, unable to select one of the more pressing questions on his mind.

"We move north. Dem gone north, two days past," Lubolo replied. "Get dem up."

"On your feet!" Jarvis bellowed.

The men scrambled to their feet and shuffled together into a quasi-organized group. No one stood at attention but they looked on attentively. Colonel Lubolo demanded strict and exact obedience from his men. He kept them in line with a healthy fear of his renowned wrath. What the men lacked in traditional military discipline they made up for with their unabashed zeal for combat. They fought without fear and without reservation. Jarvis had often wondered what the outcome would have been if Lubolo had not become an ally. He found it hard to imagine a scenario where his former company would have prevailed in prolonged conflict against them. The expulsion of Ysassi and the rest of the Spanish forces had been the tangible fruits of the alliance his superiors had forged. However, Jarvis considered it a far greater blessing that he now fought with Lubolo and instead of against him.

Colonel Lubolo scrutinized his men in silence. Every man looked on in anticipation. After Lubolo was certain he had their attention, he turned without a word and started in the same direction that his scouts had gone moments earlier. All the men dutifully followed in stride. No orders were given and none were required. His men's loyalty was unquestioned and their faith in him absolute. They moved in one fluid body and seemed to flow through the bush like a breeze; they barely disturbed the landscape and left almost no trace they had been there. Although Jarvis had improved considerably over the years he still struggled to keep up with their usual pace and on most days brought up the rear. Today, however, their slower methodical march was much more to his liking. The reason for the halted pace was that at the head of the group a still-bound and somewhat reluctant Goliath led the way. There was a guard posted on either side of him that held his ropes. Another man walked behind him and drove him like a beast of burden with the barrel of his musket. One particularly aggressive needling from the musket brought Goliath to his knees.

"Colonel, please," Jarvis began his petition.

Lubolo raised his hand to quell Jarvis's protest. He then stepped forward and took the musket from the soldier who had struck down their giant captive. With as little mercy as the soldier had shown Goliath, Lubolo hit him in the face with the back of his hand. Although the soldier was taller than Lubolo he did not match him in stature or strength. Even if he had foreseen the blow he would have been a fool to try and avoid it. The soldier raised his left arm to cover his throbbing face and staggered back amongst the throng of men behind him. Lubolo handed the musket to the next soldier in line and gestured for him to step up in place of the disgraced soldier.

"Get to the back," Lubolo commanded Jarvis through grit teeth.

Goliath was compelled to his feet once more and the regiment pushed on behind the Colonel. Jarvis stood his ground until the last of the men passed him and then fell silently in line. He knew trouble would follow the moment the words left his mouth. None of the men ever spoke up, or spoke out, and that is how Lubolo expected it. Jarvis spoke when the situation warranted, but it nearly always ended the same; a furious Lubolo would overcompensate to prove a point and then summarily dismiss him.

They hiked for the rest of the morning without a single break. The terrain was difficult to navigate. They climbed up and down the limestone hills and in and out of deep ravines and narrow crevasses. There was no ordered march, or any real semblance of a unit, when on the move. It was more like forty individuals who had the same general destination. Each man kept several feet apart from the next, except where the passage would not allow it. Per his training, Major Jarvis preferred they march two abreast for the many tactical advantages, or in a single file formation at the very least. Still he could not argue with the practical, though perhaps unintended, benefits. With the men spread so far apart it was more difficult for them to be ambushed.

They came to a slow moving stream. The lack of current and width of the stream meant the waters were deep. One of the men stripped down to his pantaloons and began to walk across. When he reached the middle of the stream the water was up to his neck. He waded upstream twenty or thirty yards until the water was only waste deep. There it was decided the men would cross. They held their limited supplies and weapons over their heads to keep them dry. A tall skinny soldier, just in front of Jarvis, slipped as he stepped into the stream. In a flash, he and his provisions were soaked. He sat atop the slippery rocks and pulled the cow horn that hung around his neck out of the water. The black powder it contained was surely ruined.

"Get up!" Major Jarvis ordered. He waded into the stream and quickly retrieved a small burlap sack that floated away. "Get up!"

Only half the men carried muskets and the loss of their limited powder was devastating. The men without firearms were left to fight with sabers, billhooks, and bayonets; most of which were taken off of the dead. Major Jarvis held the wet burlap sack above his head, along with his own single shot pistol and saber. The saber was bequeathed to him by Colonel Tyson, on his promotion to Major, and he considered it his prized possession. Each taunting drop from the burlap sack above was a reminder of his miserable plight.

When he reached the muddy bank on the other side he flung the sack back at the soldier who had dropped it. The soldier tucked it under his arm and headed up the hill shamefully. A few of the men had stopped to refill their calabash with fresh water, while the rest of the group moved on. Jarvis took one last look back to ensure that all had crossed to safety. Just beyond the south bank, behind a tree, he thought he saw a figure move in the shadows. Jarvis quickly crouched down behind a bush and watched silently. He scanned back and forth and waited for another sighting. The few men that remained finished getting water and hurried on after Lubolo and the lead group. Jarvis listened carefully as the sounds of rustling brush and footsteps behind him grew fainter and the regiment moved further and further away. He was sure he had seen something. He paused for another moment, drew in a deep breath and held it. All was still and silent. The sun shone down through the trees and cast hundreds of shadows amongst soft yellow light. When he was satisfied that no one would present themselves, he slowly turned to follow after the rest of the men. *We are being followed.*

From the stream their path turned steeply upward. Jarvis's heart pounded as he labored to climb and keep pace with the group ahead. Old fallen branches mingled with vines amongst the thick brush made his ascent even more difficult. His right boot became wedged between two large rocks and he fell further behind. In an effort to free himself, he took his eyes off the group ahead of him. The solid heel of his boot was the source of his troubles. His first instinct to pull upward proved fruitless. Upon closer examination it appeared that if he forced his foot forward it would free him from this rocky trap. He engaged the muscles in his leg and pushed his foot forward. His boot slipped slightly and he pushed harder, but as it came free he felt a popping sensation in his knee and a surge of pain down his shin.

Jarvis cradled his knee and fell to the ground on his backside. He pressed his lips together tightly and stifled the natural impulse to cry out in pain. Unable to shake the terrible feeling they were being followed, he glanced back down toward the stream. When he looked back up the hill and, to his disappointment, the regiment had cleared the peak and moved beyond out of sight. *Has anyone noticed I am not with them?* With some difficulty he got to his feet and started up the hill once more. With pain in every step he moved even slower than before. At last he reached the summit, and was met with further disappointment as the way forward immediately descended down on an even steeper decline.

Standing atop the precipice he could see the three other summits that surrounded the depression in the middle. Each was nearly covered with lush green bush and vines that wove through the depression and connected the summits. From above, Jarvis thought it looked like a giant bowl. *This would be ideal for an ambush.* To his horror he saw that Lubolo had led them down into the depression. The regiment made their way north toward a small crevasse between two of the summits. A flash of white light drew his attention to the summit directly opposite him. He was certain it was the reflection of a musket hammer or sight. *It is a trap.*

Quickly, he hurled himself down the hill. He clung to the branches and vines and tried to keep himself upright. The thick overgrowth and branches tore into his skin as he slid by. His knee groaned under the impact of each descending step. He reached the bottom in seconds but lost sight of the regiment through the thick mahogany forest on the jungle floor. Frantically, he oriented himself with the limited view of the summits and hobbled toward where he hoped Lubolo would be. A noise up ahead made him stop dead in his tracks. Someone or something was coming. He drew his pistol and steadied it at the rustling bushes. All at once a man he recognized emerged through the brush; it was the same soldier Lubolo had unceremoniously removed from his post. The soldier dropped his billhook and threw both hands in the air when found himself staring down the business end of Jarvis's pistol.

"Where are you going?" Jarvis demanded.

"Colonel sen mi to find yu," the soldier answered in his broken English.

"I have injured my knee. We have to hurry; they are walking into a trap," Jarvis said.

Major Jarvis lowered his pistol and the soldier hurried to his side to steady him. He put his arm around the soldier and they set off through the bush. With his free hand the soldier cleared the thick bush with his billhook and soon they were in sight of the men. In the distance, Jarvis saw they began to funnel into a small crevasse ahead. The space between the towering rock walls allowed for just one man to pass at a time. Like participants in a desperate three-legged race, Jarvis and the soldier pushed through the bottleneck in an attempt to reach Lubolo near front of the tiny passage.

"Mek way," the soldier pleaded, just above a whisper.

"Look sharp, men," Jarvis ordered as they passed through the company. "To arms."

He caught sight of Lubolo, about to step into the crevasse. Just ahead were two men with muskets and the captive Goliath, who appeared to have fallen to a knee once more. The dreaded sound of the abeng reigned down from the hills above. In an instant Goliath rose to his feet and turned to face the guards behind him. In his hands was a small boulder that he hoisted over his head, as he let out a mighty shout. With murderous rage in his eyes he brought the boulder down on the head of the soldier nearest him, who fired a shot in vain before he met his demise. Shots rang out in seemingly every direction now, as the hills had come alive with shouts and movement. Goliath lunged toward the next soldier, who also raised his musket and fired. His aim proved better as he hit Goliath in his massive shoulder. The impact sent blood splattering into the air. The wounded, hulking warrior ripped the musket from the soldier's hand and broke it in two against the rock wall. He grabbed the soldier by the arms and lifted him off his feet. He thrust his head forward, with a force equal to the boulder, and the soldier crumbled to the ground in a lifeless heap as he fell from his monstrous clutches.

Jarvis felt his support give way as the soldier to his right fell to the floor. Whether out of fear or do to an injury he did not know. He knelt down beside the man and rolled him over. His blood soaked clothes left no doubt as to cause of his collapse. Amid the volley of bullets and the chaotic commotion of battle on every side, Jarvis looked back toward the way he had come. A dozen enemy fighters emerged from behind them and cut off any retreat. With nowhere to run, Jarvis attempted to locate Lubolo again. He looked up toward the narrow pass and found the colonel pinned to the ground by another large Negro man, each struggling for the upper hand as they wrestled over the musket betwixt them. Jarvis raised his pistol and fired. He hit the man in the ear and added to the blood which now stained the rocky jungle floor where so many men had already perished. The man's head jolted back and his arm shot up as a reflex, but he was already dead.

Lubolo tossed the man to the side, took possession of the musket and rolled up onto his feet. He looked back at Major Jarvis, momentarily, before he sprang back into action. Although the sounds of gun shots had subsided the sounds of fighting had not. Men struggled for their lives in hand to hand combat. Jarvis drew his saber and looked defensively in every direction. When he found no immediate danger he again made his way toward Colonel Lubolo; he had already found a use for the musket of the fallen soldier and pummeled another would-be assailant. Behind Lubolo, up above the base of the summit, a tall, shirtless man emerged through the trees. The swarthy warrior stood perched on a rock, like a majestic bird about to take flight. The sight of him took Jarvis's breath away. Around the warrior's neck hung a necklace of teeth and bone. He had no doubt; it was the angelic assassin who spared his life.

"Lubolo!" Jarvis shouted.

Before the words had fully escaped his lips Jarvis felt a massive hand wrap around the back of his neck and force his head down. Another hand clamped down on his right arm and wrestled the saber from his grasp. The towering Goliath clenched his neck and pulled Jarvis toward him. His imposing frame blotted out the sun and Jarvis watched helplessly as the dark assassin bore down on Lubolo. Having no weapons that Jarvis could see, he raised his arms over his head and struck down on Lubolo with such ferocity that it knocked him several steps back. Lubolo recovered and swung the musket at him. He ducked the blow and countered by knocking the musket from Lubolo's hands. Lubolo charged forward and the titans locked arms, like two big horned sheep battling for supremacy.

The shirtless warrior was trim and much taller than Lubolo, but Lubolo used his stocky frame and lower center for leverage. He lifted his attacker off his feet and whipped him backwards and over his head. Like a cat, the swarthy warrior landed on his feet and immediately lashed out toward Lubolo. He leapt into the air and kicked at Lubolo. Lubolo blocked with his forearm and punched his assailant in the face. Nearly unfazed, the man grabbed onto Lubolo's oversized shoulders and thrust his left knee into the colonel's ribs. Lubolo punched him in the stomach and raked his elbow across the left side of his face. At that, the warrior took a step back, hung his head with eyes close and placed his arms at his side. This curious move caused Lubolo to pause. All at once he opened his eyes and with one mighty kick to the chest Lubolo fell to the ground.

"De Serras!" Goliath yelled, as he tossed Jarvis's saber to him.

The shirtless warrior caught the saber and struck with precision and power to cleave Lubolo's head from his shoulders in one motion. With terror filled eyes Jarvis watched Colonel Lubolo's headless body slump back to the earth, to rise no more. Panic swept over him as he tried to process the events that unfolded before him. Still in the clutches of his titanic foe, he struggled to free himself to no avail. Goliath turned Jarvis about and lifted him slightly off the ground. He raised Jarvis to his eye level and closer than he had ever been to the mysterious marking of the backward facing bird on his right forearm.

"Run," Goliath said plainly. He released him and Jarvis felt a momentary weightlessness.

He stumbled backwards as his feet met with the ground. Pain surged through his wounded knee. He looked up at Goliath, unable to fully comprehend what had just happened. Men fought and died all around him, but amid this hurricane of violence he stood in the eye of the storm and faced the man who had been his captive that same morning. Now, when he could have extracted a measure of revenge, he let him go. *Why?*

"Go!" the hulking figure commanded again. "Run!"

Not foolish enough to hesitate for a second time, Jarvis quickly looked around. With haste he chose a path and hobbled away from the tiny crevasse as fast as his good leg would carry him. He passed at least fifty fallen soldiers before the horror of the battle was behind him.

The path of least resistance was to trek along the bottom of the gorge. He knew his knee would prevent him from ascending the hilly terrain with any speed, if he were able to climb at all. His intention was to get as far away from the ambush as possible and find a suitable, safe place to rest.

The sounds and commotion dissipated behind him and he stopped for a moment to catch his breath. He looked around at the sloping jungle walls that rose up to the domed peaks above him. Alone amongst the bushes and trees he felt no safer than when he hung at the mercy of monumental Goliath. His mind began to fill with the unknowns before him. Who else had survived? Was he the only one spared? Why was he spared again? Where exactly was he and where should he go from here?

A snap of a branch and a rustle of bushes behind him broke his panicked and dizzied train of thought. He turned toward the sound and braced himself for whatever might emerge. A man crashed through the overgrowth. Unconcerned with where he was headed, his attention and his gaze were set firmly on where he had come from. He plowed into and over Jarvis and both men crashed to the hard jungle floor. Jarvis looked up to see a sight he had not expected. Before him was a man in purple trousers and knee high boots, with a buckle about ankle high. He had on a dress shirt, in need of a good scrub but otherwise of fine quality, with a vest that nearly matched his trousers. The midday sun illuminated his straw blond hair, which shone like a lit torch. His pink sunbaked cheeks were the only color to contrast with his pale white complexion. His wrists were bound together by strong cords, which made it quite difficult for him to sit up. Nonetheless he rose to a seated position, looked over at Jarvis with a glint in his eye and said in a playful tone that did not match their current predicament, "Got a knife, mate?"

Ring Road

Gideon had never seen the Norman Manley International Airport in the light of day. His comings and goings from the island had been at night and the wee hours of the morning. He stepped out onto the sidewalk and squinted into the noon day sun. Behind him loomed the white and blue terminal with a zigzag rooftop, which spanned the numerous ticketing counters and airport entryways. In beautiful contrast to the hot sun, a cool breeze of ocean air rushed up to meet him. He closed his eyes and allowed himself to bathe in the moment.

"Hey, G," Todd called from behind him. "Come take a picture."

He turned around to see Todd back in the terminal entryway. He stood next to a life-sized wooden carving of the Jamaican seal. Atop the coat of arms sat a menacing crocodile on a log that represented the indigenous wildlife of the island. Beneath the open mouthed crocodile was an ornate helmet and shield; clear patronage to the island's British colonizers. On the shield were five golden pineapples, Gideon thought mangoes would have been far more appropriate as they seemed more plentiful on the island. On the right of the shield there stood an Indian man who wore a red and yellow leaf loin cloth, and held a primitive looking bow.

On the left was an Indian woman, bare-chested, with a matching loin covering. Todd stood next to the woman, with his camera outstretched toward Gideon.

"Come on, man."

Dutifully, Gideon walked back to his friend and took the camera. He looked around to ensure he would not be in the way of fellow travelers. "Ready?"

"Yep," Todd answered. He reached up and put his index finger up the nose of the wooden Indian woman just as Gideon took the picture.

"What is the matter with you?!" Gideon rebuked his friend.

In the twenty minutes since they landed Todd had already embarrassed Gideon twice. Moments after they stepped off the tarmac they made their way through customs to exchange their U.S. currency. The exchange rate on the Jamaica dollar was thirty-seven to one. The clerk paid the sum out in one-hundred and five-hundred Jamaica dollar bills. Todd held up his small stack of colorful bills and exclaimed, "I'm rich!" Gideon angrily questioned his friend's upbringing and heritage and ordered him to lower his voice and his arms. He then told him to secure the money in his front pocket and explained that thieves in Jamaica were adept at picking pockets and that his valuables would be safer up front. Gideon heard the haughty know-it-all tone of his lecture and immediately recoiled. He enjoyed feeling superior or more knowledgeable than his friends and hated himself for it.

"Relax, man," the highly amused Todd said loudly. "Nobody cares."

"I care," Gideon responded in hushed tones. "I care. And that should be enough. Please, just be cool."

Gideon looked over his shoulder to be sure that no one had seen, for fear they might have offended a perfect stranger. The handful of travelers that passed through the wide entryway seemed to pay them no mind. He handed Todd's camera to him and walked back to the exit.

The pick-up drop-off curb outside bustled with activity. Cars and people rushed about and weaved between one another, entirely unconcerned by the other's presence. A man with skin like coal approached. He sported a trucker hat, with a navy blue bill and mesh backing. His round mirror sunglasses reflected daylight as he bobbed up and down. He had on a button down navy blue shirt and pants tucked into black high-top boots.

"Where yu wan fi go?" the man asked. He took Gideon by the arm and led him toward a white Mitsubishi mini-bus. Gideon, accustomed to this aggressive tactic to bamboozle flustered tourists, would have none of it. He wriggled his arm free and held his ground.

"Mi wan fi go up a Mona," Gideon replied in his best patois.

"Rotted! A chat yu a chat," the driver exclaimed with delight, as a huge smile broke across his face. "Backfoot, mi neva tink say yu a yardy."

"Mi a yardy right 'ere so," Gideon replied, and tapped his heart twice with his forefinger.

"Zeen," the driver said. "Come, mi carry yu up a Mona."

"'ow much?" Gideon asked.

"Fi yu?" the driver said. "Fifty dollars, U.S."

"No man," Gideon shot back. "Yu a tief mi."

"Mi na tief yu," the driver replied, and furrowed his brow. "A charter bus dis. Yu hafi charter to Mona."

In the city taxis and buses ran predetermined routes in most cases and charged anywhere from forty to sixty Jamaican dollars. Charter drivers would take you anywhere you wanted for a price that depended largely on time and distance or how much they thought they could take you for.

"Mi know dat, mi brudda, but mi na hafi pay t'ree times da rate. G'way!" Gideon shouted with a strong wave of his arm. Todd stood back, arms folded over his backpack, with a thoroughly perplexed look on his face.

"A'right, a'right, just a cool," the driver said. "Twenty-five U.S."

"No man. Mi dun with uno," Gideon replied. He turned and walked toward a taxi that loaded a pair of passengers just ahead of the bus.

"Which part uno run?" Gideon asked the man behind the wheel.

"Parade," the man replied. "A 'undred dollars."

"Jamaican or U.S.?" Gideon asked.

"Jamaican," the man replied.

"Cool. Wi a come." Gideon turned to Todd and waved him over. Alarmed and confused, Todd still carried his backpack like a protective mother holding her baby. Meanwhile, the original driver stood a ways off beside his bus and yelled and cursed at Gideon while he flailed his arms wildly.

"What the heck was that?" Todd questioned. "One minute I thought you two were going to make out and now he looks like he wants to kill you."

"Don't worry about it. We couldn't reach an agreement. This is our ride." Gideon said and tapped the top of the brown rusty Lada.

"What's a teef?"

"It's a thief," Gideon answered.

"You called him a thief?!" Todd exclaimed. "No wonder he's mad. And you were worried *I* was going to embarrass *you*?!"

"Just get in the car."

Todd walked around to the driver's side, opened the back door and slid into the empty seat next to a young couple already in the taxi. Gideon pulled open the front passenger side door and gave one more aggressive wave at the still cursing driver in the blue mesh trucker hat, before he removed his backpack and squeezed into the front seat.

The Lada, a boxy Russian sedan, was a tiny metal beast with limited leg room, particularly for someone of Gideon's height. There were seats for five full grown adults, including the driver, but he had seen them fit a few more. Only bare bone models made their way to the island; with not much more than seats, pedals and a steering wheel. In classic Jamaican fashion, each driver added their own bit of flair. A small Jamaican flag hung from the rearview mirror to give color to the otherwise drab black and brown interior.

With a tap of the horn he shifted into gear and punched the gas without so much as a glance to either side to check if the way was clear. Gideon looked back at Todd who, with his backpack in his lap, desperately searched for a seatbelt. He smiled, as he knew Todd would find no such safety device. The car was at least thirty years old and held together by bailing wire and chewing gum. The driver sat on the right side of the car and they drove on the left side of the road, another remnant of Jamaica's European colonizers.

Gideon laughed to himself at Todd's wide-eyed look and thought he must have worn a similar expression on his first trip down the Norman Manley Highway. It was really a "highway" in name only. The two lane road sat atop a mound of sand and rock, flanked on both sides by crystal blue Caribbean waters.

"This is called the Palisadoes," Gideon explained to Todd. "It's a natural barrier that stretches from Harbor View back to Port Royal, an old pirate town. It was a hub for shipping and trade in the Caribbean until it was destroyed by an earthquake in 1692. Some say it was an act of God because of the sins of the people who lived there and the pirates who frequented it."

With the windows down, the fresh ocean breeze swept through the car as Gideon played tour guide. The crisp cool air touched his cheeks as if the breeze was sent by the island to welcome him home. Out the driver's side window, to the south-east, was the rippling blue Caribbean ocean. To his left, Gideon looked out his window at the calm waters in the harbor that reflected the sky like a sheet of glass. The buildings and homes beyond the harbor filled the mountainous bowl that cupped the city.

As they headed west, up the coast and deeper into Kingston, the freshness of the ocean air gave way to a warmth and a new aroma that was anything but pleasant. This distinct smell could be found across most of the larger towns and cities of Jamaica. It was the same smell that offended the nostrils when he passed too close to a madman. Whether a madman smelled because of the streets or the streets smelled of madmen, he could not be sure but there was an undeniable similarity between the odors. Oddly, Gideon felt a greater sense of nostalgia from this aroma than from the cool crisp ocean breeze that preceded it.

Parade was the southernmost hub of the capitol's public transit system, a pavilion flanked by statues of significant figures in Jamaica's history and surrounded by churches, theatres, businesses and buses. At its center was a rectangular park, named after St. William Grant. The park was bordered by Parade Street on the north, south, east, and west. Nestled between Downtown Kingston and the ghettos of Tivoli and Trench Town, areas made famous by the 'One Love' musical icon Bob Marley, these areas were notorious for violence and civil unrest. The Lada rambled to a stop in front of a large church on the south side of the park. Their driver unceremoniously let them out and turned his attention to attracting new passengers.

"T'anks, y'ear," Gideon said, as he climbed out of the taxi. He reached back through the window to hand the driver a hundred dollar bill. Todd quickly followed him and piled out of the backseat. He briefly fumbled for his money while the driver impatiently waited for his fare from behind the wheel. In the meantime, the taxi had filled with passengers, one of whom had pushed passed Todd to secure a seat. The driver quickly sped away with his arm still hanging out the window, Todd's fare tuck between his fingers.

The streets were full of cars, buses, bicycles, push carts and people. Gideon headed up the road toward the building with the red 'Jamaica Post' sign. He bounded up a pair of concrete steps and walked inside, with Todd in hot pursuit. He produced a postcard from his backpack with a beach scene surrounded by a green and yellow border and handed it to the woman behind the bar-lined counter that separated the post office staff from the customers.

"Where did you get that?" Todd questioned.

"'ow much fi post to Europe?" Gideon asked the woman, while he ignored his friend.

"Sixty," she replied.

"Did you write that before we left?" Todd continued.

Gideon paid the woman and continued to ignore Todd, "T'anks, y'ere," he thanked her and turned to leave.

"That's for your wife, isn't it?" Todd asked, knowing exactly how to upset Gideon.

"She's not my wife, idiot," Gideon responded, as he walked down the sidewalk away from the post office. He tried to pretend the topic was too trivial to address. The truth was he simply did not wish to discuss her with Todd, who mercilessly teased him about the girl whom he had always loved but never successfully courted. Elizabeth Hunter was the girl of his dreams and had been from the moment he first saw her. They had not seen each other in over two years, as she left on a mission of her own before he returned home. Todd found Gideon's unrequited love to be a source of endless amusement, which was why Gideon had no desire to discuss his premeditated postcard with him.

"What did it say?" Todd pressed.

"None of your business," Gideon responded, and tried not to sound annoyed. "Listen, we have to pass through the park so I need you to pay attention. Keep your eyes up, your mouth shut and do not under any circumstances take anything anybody tries to hand you. Do you understand?"

"Was it a love note?" Todd asked and playfully raised his eyebrows up and down.

"Todd!" Gideon chided.

"Fine! I got it. Eyes up, mouth shut, don't take anything."

Passing through the park meant passing through the market; a gauntlet of shops and merchants peddling their wares. The market was full of makeshift structures of wood, tin, and tarps where you could find anything from fruit and produce to flowers and dustpans. Pushcarts, filled with assortments of snacks and sodas, filled in the gaps between shops. There was no discernible order to things but it was quite orderly in its function. Gideon liked to pretend he was Alan Quartermain as he navigated the crowded marketplace and imagined himself a great adventurer.

As soon as they broke the threshold of the market they were surrounded on all sides by merchants. "Jackfruit," "Banana chips,"

"Ice cream c'yake." Gideon politely declined and pressed forward through the crowd with Todd right on his heels. Dead ahead he spotted a young boy leaned against a little red cooler with a white lid on a pushcart. The boy wore an old stretched out t-shirt, two sizes too big. He was skinny as a rail with a long face and two big buck teeth. Gideon walked up to the boy and asked, "Yu 'ave bag juice?"

"Yeah man," the boy replied.

"Ginger beer?" Gideon asked.

"Yeah man,"

"I'll tek two," he said and reached in his pocket for his wallet.

As the name suggested, a bag juice was a clear plastic bag filled with juice. They were frozen and placed in a cooler for purchase. These sealed bags were designed as a low cost alternative to plastic or glass bottles and were more commonly consumed by children or people of limited means. They came in all kinds of flavors; from fruit punch to kola champagne to, Gideon's favorite, cream soda. The crème soda was clear and smooth; the polar opposite of his least favorite flavor, ginger beer. Ginger beer was a brownish spicy liquid made from locally grown ginger root that gave it a spicy flavor with an afterburn Gideon did not expect from a soft drink. Ginger beer had become a ritual hazing, passed down from missionary to missionary, and Gideon felt it appropriate to initiate Todd in a similar fashion. He paid the boy and collected the bag juice. With two icy bags in one hand, he slipped his wallet into his back pocket and threw one of the bag juices to Todd. "Break the ice up a little, then tear open a corner with your teeth and suck on it."

He had no sooner spoken those words than Gideon felt pressure on his pant pocket. No amount of wishing could change the harsh reality; he had been pickpocketed. A surge of shame rushed over him as he had been careless enough to place his wallet in his back pocket, they very thing he warned Todd against. He spun around to see the bucktoothed boy racing away through the crowd. Quickly, he ran after him shouting, "Stop that boy! Tief!"

The market already bustled with a torrent of noise and

movement that now seemed to conspire against him. The boy squeezed between a group of people, completely unaware of the chase that was afoot. Gideon bulldozed his way through the crowd in a desperate attempt to keep up with the diminutive thief. He closed in on the boy but an abrupt turn, just as he was within arm's reach, sent Gideon crashing into a flower stand. The boy slipped between two fruit stands and hopped up on the concrete fountain in the middle of the park. Gideon quickly surveyed his obstacles and plotted a course, parallel to the boy's path, around the opposite side on the fountain. He rounded the fountain and came into clear view of the boy. The boy immediately changed course when he spotted Gideon. He plunged into a crowd of people that waited to load unto a red and yellow bus. As his hopes of overtaking the boy faded he called out again, "Stop dat boy! Tief!"

His cry drew the attention of the crowded bus park. The throng parted like the Red Sea before Moses when they saw Gideon bearing down on them. He briefly lost sight of the boy until the crowd gave way and he found the boy struggling to free himself from the grasp of a dark rotund man with an enormous smile. To his surprise, Gideon recognized him.

"Bigga?" he asked, as he halted his pursuit and tried to catch his breath.

"H'elda Goodwin? Backfoot! A yu dat?" the man replied and held fast to the struggling boy's wrist.

Out of the hundreds of people at Parade at that moment, the man who captured the young pickpocket was none other than Jermaine "Bigga" Robinson. Gideon first met Bigga in the "cool cool" hills of Manchester. Everyone called him Bigga for obvious reasons. Everything about him was big, from his big round belly to his big round head. Even his tongue was fat, which made it all the more difficult to understand his thick country accent. Ever smiling, his big crooked-tooth smile lit up the world when he was around. Elder Goodwin and Bigga became instant friends from the moment he heard his infectious laugh ring throughout the halls of the humble church building in Mandeville. Bigga had recently returned home from his own mission and was full of stories and brotherly wisdom that the green Elder Goodwin soaked up.

"What are you doing here?" Gideon asked.

"A mi? A drive mi a drive?" Bigga responded. "When did yu get back?"

"Mi just a come," Gideon said. "Yu drive a bus d'en?"

"No man, mi a taxi driva," Bigga answered. "A dis likkle tief tek way your billfold?"

"Yeah man, 'im lift it from mi pocket," he said and tapped his back pocket.

"Yu c'yan't keep it back d'ere," Bigga chided.

"Mi know, mi know," Gideon said, as Bigga wrestled his wallet from the boy and handed it to him. "T'anks."

Then Bigga grabbed the boy by the shoulders and pulled him close. He stooped down until they were eye to eye. "Look 'ere yu likkle tief, if I h'eva catch uno tief'n round 'ere again mi ago give yu one hot lick. Yu 'ear?"

He released the boy, who stumbled backwards and quickly ran off. The boy disappeared once more through the crowd as Todd arrived. He pressed through the crowd and stopped when he saw Gideon. Out of breath, he bent over and placed his hands on his knees. He looked around at the crowd and then back to Gideon. Gideon nodded to his friend and held up the stolen wallet to assure him that the situation was in hand. Bigga walked over to the clearly out of place new comer and threw his arm around him.

"A who dis? Mi brudda?" Bigga said with a hardy chuckle.

"Yeah man," Gideon responded. "Your brother from another mother."

With an arm around Todd's neck, Bigga squeezed him and belted out his infectious belly laugh. Many of the onlookers joined in the laughter, while Todd stared at Gideon and looked utterly confused.

"Bigga, this is Todd. Todd, Bigga," Gideon made introductions. "Where's your taxi?"

"Mi baby blue right round d'ere so," Bigga stated proudly with a grand gesture toward an old dented Lada, painted bright blue except for one door, which was replaced by a dingy brown door, riddled with so much rust and wear that it must have been salvaged from the bottom of the ocean.

"Excellent," Gideon said. "Beg yu a ride?"

"Fi yu man, of course," Bigga said with a big smile. "Which part uno headed?"

"Ring road," Gideon said.

"Up a UWI," Bigga said acknowledging their destination. "Yeah man. Come, wi a go."

The trio headed toward Bigga's blue cab. Bigga plopped into the driver's seat making the small boxy car rock back and forth. Todd reached out and placed his hand on Gideon's shoulder to stop him before he got in the car.

"What's u-ey?" he asked.

"The University of West Indies," Gideon answered.

"And why are we going to the University of West Indies?" an annoyed Todd asked.

"To see a friend," Gideon said. "Professor Sterling Gervaise. He's the man I got the journal from. I'm hoping he has some answers."

"Cool," Todd said. He stepped in front of Gideon, pulled open the door and threw his backpack in the front seat. "Shotgun."

Gideon climbed in back without an argument; he figured he owed him that much. Bigga leaned out the window and, in an effort to collect a fare on the last two empty seats, yelled, "Mona. Mona wi a go," as the car rolled gently forward. With no takers, he maneuvered his way through the taxis and buses. The people scattered as they departed Parade and headed deeper into the capitol city.

The University of West Indies was tucked back in the hills of the suburban community of Mona, far from the hustle and bustle of the city. They traveled up Old Hope Road and left behind the zinc shacks and paint-faded walls of Tivoli and Trench Town for slightly more modern high rises and office buildings of the new downtown area. The streets were wider and less crowded flanked by off-white uniformed structures made of block and cement. There was a semblance of order, in distinct contrast to the hodge-podge and chaos of the inner city.

"Where did you serve?" Bigga asked Todd, doing his best to slow down his speech and enunciate.

"What?" Todd said.

"Where did you serve your mission?" Bigga clarified.

"I'm not Mormon," Todd replied nonchalantly, used to getting that question. Gideon had once gotten a kick out of it when this scenario played out, but as they grew older he became embarrassed as it illustrated the narrow perceptive held by many of his friends and loved ones.

"Goodwin, 'ow c'yan yu run with dis 'ere b'woy an not 'ave shown 'im da light?" Bigga said. He turned back to Gideon and threw his arm over the passenger seat with a playful grin.

"Relax," Gideon responded casually. "I've shown him the light; he prefers the darkness. Now watch the road, you lunatic."

They all laughed and any awkwardness melted away as they turned up Mona Road. To the left was the sleepy neighborhood of Mona Heights, where Gideon proselyted as a young missionary. Beautiful mature mango trees lined the nearly empty streets. On the right was the Mona Reservoir, a main source of Kingston's water supply. The landmark which defined the area was the ancient stone aqueducts that used to service the plantations as far back as the mid-18th century. Footpaths and trails still cut back through the brick lined arches to the property that lay beyond.

The baby blue Lada turned left onto Queensway, which led straight into the university. This was by far the nicest road Gideon had found in Jamaica. As the story goes the Queen of England had visited Jamaica years earlier. In preparation for her arrival they repaved only the predetermined route she would travel, which included the university. Hence the newly paved road was dubbed the Queensway.

"Which part uno a go?" Bigga asked.

"Number 14, the Humanities building," Gideon said.

Bigga bent the steering wheel left and they merged onto Ring

Road. The campus was built in and around this giant one way roundabout. The building that housed the Faculty of Humanities and Education lay in the center on the far east side, just across from the Snack Bar; a dome like structure surrounded by triangular awnings. The Snack Bar served as the local hangout for university students. The rambling old Lada pulled into an empty parking spot in front of 14 Ring Road and chugged to a stop.

"Are you hungry?" Gideon asked Todd.

"I could eat, sure," said Todd.

"Bigga, could you take him over to the Snack Bar and get him a patty. I'm going to run inside real quick," Gideon said as he got out of the car and pointed to the Humanities building.

"Come, mi brudda," Bigga said and put his arm around Todd. "Mi a go getcha a taste of Jamaica."

Gideon shook his head and watched two of the most lovable idiots he had ever known cross the street. He turned toward the Humanities building and paused for a moment before taking a deep breath and walking up a pair of steps that led to the entrance. He stepped through the open doors and into the hallway. His stomach sank as he came to terms with the potentially unpleasant reunion he was about to have. Cautiously, he crossed the hallway to his right and stood in front of classroom 108. He peered through the small rectangular window in the blue metal door. Gideon realized he was not breathing and forced himself to exhale. His chest contracted and expanded as he filled his lungs with fresh air. He had come this far and could not turn back now. He reached up and pulled open the door.

Room 108 was just as he remembered. The wall opposite the door was full of large window panes that framed a picturesque view of the courtyard outside. At the far end of the large rectangular room was a man who wrote on an old green chalkboard. The classroom was full of tables and chairs but, save Gideon and the man at the chalkboard, was unoccupied. Gideon walked along the side aisle toward the man whose back was to him. He had only taken a few steps when the door closed behind him and caused the man to stop writing and turn his head to see who had entered.

"Hey, professor," Gideon said with a sheepish smile.

The man at the front of the classroom put down the chalk and turned around to more fully face Gideon with a pleasant, but not surprised, look. "Elder Goodwin, my boy," he said. He brushed his hands together to dust off the chalk.

"It's just Goodwin, I mean Gideon, now, sir," he said. "Just Gideon."

"Of course it is," replied the professor. He stepped out from behind his desk and walked forward to shake his hand. "What are you doing here?"

Professor Sterling Gervaise was one of the only Jamaican-born Caucasians Gideon had ever met. His family, originally from England, had lived in Jamaica for generations. As a young man he studied abroad at the University of Oxford but returned home to teach at UWI as a Professor of History and Caribbean Studies. He had a statesman like quality with a full head of silvery white hair, neatly combed and gelled, that swept back away from his perfectly sun bronzed face. He wore a brown tweed jacket with leather patches sown in the elbows and a pair of dark slacks with freshly polished brown leather shoes. To hear him speak delighted Gideon, a mix of patois and a hint of a proper English accent from his time at Oxford. He had a brilliant mind and was a man of great wit and charm. Gideon regarded him as a father and had a great desire to please him, which made this encounter all the more painful as he was sure to disappoint him now.

"I came to return this," Gideon said. He pulled the journal from the side pocket of his backpack. "I borrowed it before I left. I meant to return it but it got mixed in with my things and I didn't realize I had it until I got back to the States."

The professor's face turned serious—serious, but not upset. "You took that from my office?" he asked plainly.

"I did."

"You had no right to take that without my permission," he said calmly.

"I know, and I'm sorry," Gideon said. He looked him right in the eye and fought the urge to look away, fully prepared to take his medicine.

"You didn't come all this way to return that, did you?" the professor asked, with a smile that broke the tension.

"Yes and no," Gideon began. "The trip was planned; I brought my buddy with me to see the island. I intended to return the book when I came back, but then I read it. It's not a book, it's a journal."

"I know it's a journal, Elder Goodwin . . ."

"Gideon. You can call me Gideon," he interrupted.

The professor nodded. He stretched out his hand and beckoned for the journal. "This journal, Gideon, as you know, belongs to me, and I'm well aware of its contents. So you've read it, then?"

"A good part of it," he answered. "And then I found this."

Gideon opened the journal to the page where he had tucked the slip of paper away; the slip that contained the swirling heart shaped symbol. He removed the small square piece of parchment and stepped forward to hand it to Professor Gervaise. He took it from him but did not look at it.

"This symbol caught my attention," Gideon explained. "Do you know what it is?"

"Sankofa. It's an ancient African symbol," the professor stated. He still had not looked at the paper. "Have a seat."

The professor pulled up a chair, removed his jacket and hung it on the back. Gideon followed suit and pulled up a chair of his own from the study desk behind him. He removed his backpack and sat down directly across from him. They both looked at the journal in the professor's tanned hands and the paper that lay on top of it. "In the simplest terms it translates as 'return and get it.'"

Gideon began to get excited; *return and get it* fit quite nicely into Joe's theory. "Return and get what?"

"No, no, my boy. *Sankofa* means 'to return, to go, to seek,'" the professor explained. "It is a reminder to learn from the past."

Gideon contemplated that for a moment. Return and get it, learn from the past; it seemed like an old Chinese proverb. "Any idea why this symbol would be in this journal?"

"Why do you ask?" probed the professor.

"It's going to sound silly," Gideon said hesitantly.

"Silly, eh? Tell me, just how far have you read?"

"May I?" Gideon asked and reached out for the journal.

He gently took the leather bound journal from Professor Gervaise and carefully opened to the last page he had read. He turned the open journal back toward the professor with a motion that invited him to read. The professor rolled up his sleeves in a workman like fashion and reached into the pocket of his coat to retrieve his reading glasses. After one more interrogative look he took the journal, adjusted his glasses and began to read aloud.

Colonel Lubolo has been killed and the black regiment wiped out. We were led into a trap by one of de Serras's men. I alone, for reasons passing understanding, have once again been spared. My leg is badly injured and although death did not find me in battle I was unsure in my current state if I would be able to navigate these mountains on my own.

My salvation, though, has come, at least in part, from an unexpected vessel. A pirate named John Davis was, himself, in process of making an escape from the Negroes led by de Serras when in an act of serendipity our paths of flight crossed. I'm unsure what I value more at the moment, his company or his assistance with my wounded knee.

In any case I cannot imagine I would have made it this far without either. Although I am hesitant to trust a man who would engage in piracy it seems that our fates are, at least for now, intertwined.

Professor Gervaise closed the journal and removed his glasses. As he did so Gideon noticed a tattoo on his right forearm. "And that is as far as you've gotten?"

"Yes sir. It's the paper that really interests me though. I've seen that symbol before."

"Before?" asked the professor.

"Yes, sir—before I left, in a cave, in cockpit country."

"You saw it *in* a cave?"

"Well, no. Not in a cave. It was carved into the rock at the entrance of a cave. I didn't go inside."

"I see." Gideon couldn't be sure, but he almost seemed relieved. The professor leaned back in his chair and smiled at him. He folded his arms across his chest and waited for Gideon to continue.

"Professor, what I'm wondering is if the symbol on that paper and the symbol from the cave might be connected somehow."

"Connected? They are very much connected. Sankofa is connection. Sankofa is history. It has connected people to their history for thousands of years. I, myself, have dedicated my life to sankofa."

"Sure, I get that, but that's not exactly what I meant."

"Well, out with it then," the professor demanded. "What is it that you meant?"

"Promise not to laugh?"

"I do not," winked the professor.

"I thought that, being that it was carved in a rock, that it might be a marker of some kind," Gideon said. "You know, like a landmark or a trailhead that might indicate something of significance, or value?"

He tried to sound as if he had not put a great deal of thought into it, but feared his hopeful expectations were painfully transparent. He looked for some sign of understanding on the professor's face. The silver haired professor sat back in his chair and cocked his head sideways. He opened his mouth to speak and Gideon could already feel the derision and condescension before he uttered a word.

"My boy, are you looking for treasure?" the professor asked with a snooty half-giggle.

Gideon wanted to crawl beneath the study desk and die. To hear Professor Gervaise be so dismissive of the theory, Gideon himself had taken some time to warm up to, was painful. His mind told him the best course of action was to drop the subject, but his pride would not allow it. With vigor he began to defend a hypothesis that he knew he ought to distance himself from.

"It's not all that farfetched, professor. People don't just carve things in stone without reason," he began with words that were not his own. "It's got to mean something."

"It means a great deal," the professor stated bluntly.

"You said it means return and get it. Couldn't that be talking about something besides just knowledge, something important?"

"Just knowledge?" the incensed professor responded. "Since the beginning of time, man has drawn on stone and carved into rock things of great importance, things that had nothing to do with trinkets or treasure. Just knowledge? You disappoint me, Gideon."

Like a searing-hot knife, the professor's rebuke cut Gideon to his core. The last thing he wanted was to be seen as a greedy treasure hunter. He had come to return what was not his and find answers. He believed his questions were born from a sincere desire for discovery. Now he had been painted as a rube by a father figure who he wanted nothing more than to impress. He collected himself, sat up straight, and resolved to make his intensions clear.

"You know me, and I hope you don't believe that I do not value knowledge," Gideon said. "Reading this journal has been thrilling for me. To discover a possible connection between something I found there and my own life? Well, I can't even put into words what that has meant.

"I'm not after anything in particular, just trying to satisfy a burning curiosity. I will admit I hope to find something extraordinary. The fact is I've been seduced by the prospect of adventure; even if it's only in my mind. To return, to seek and to learn, that is what motivates me and I don't see the harm in that."

"No, of course not, my apologies," Professor Gervaise said. "An inquisitive mind is a moral imperative, as is a deep and abiding reverence of history, and your quest to connect to that history is admirable. Forgive me for jumping to conclusions."

"No need for forgiveness. I misspoke and misrepresented myself. I value your opinion."

"That's very kind," said the professor. "So then, you intend on seeking out this cave?"

"Yeah, I think so."

"You said it lies in the cockpits? All you're liable to find there is trouble. Mi na sen yu na come."

'Mi na sen yu na come' was an old Maroon expression that meant 'Do not come unless you are invited.' *Maroon* was the name given to runaway slaves centuries earlier. These slaves fled to the mountains and organized themselves to fight against their former masters. Eventually they struck a treaty with the British government that allowed them to remain a semi-autonomous society. Many still lived in the hills where their ancestors fought for and won freedom. These remote communities were located in some of the more inhospitable parts of the island and were still led, at least ceremonially, by an appointed Colonel. While many of the Maroon communities were friendly to tourists, there were still some where outsiders were not welcome.

"I'm aware of the dangers. I have a guide. He's the one who originally led us to the cave," Gideon explained. Although he knew full well how presumptuous his statement was, as he had yet to contact his trusted guide. "I don't plan on wandering around on my own."

"You'd be better off taking your friend to Ochi to lie on the beach and drink some Ting, mi know yu love dat," the professor counseled in full blown patois. "Mi c'yan't convince yu fi leave dis crazy t'ing though, c'yan I?"

"'fraid not," Gideon said.

"Well then, I'll wish you all the best and let you be on your way." Professor Gervaise stood up and extended a hand of friendship. As Gideon reached out and shook his hand, he stole an opportunity to examine the professor's tattoo a little closer. It looked like a goose or a swan, with the head craned back toward its tail. "Sorry I didn't have the answers you hoped for."

"Professor?" Gideon started, with some trepidation. "There is a way you could help me. I need to ask you a favor, one I'm afraid I have no right to."

"Sounds serious."

"I'm hoping you'll let me hang onto your journal for just a few more days," Gideon entreated. "I'd love to finish it. I promise I'll return it before I leave. Scout's honor."

Professor Gervaise looked down at the leather-bound journal and back up at Gideon. He thoughtfully furrowed his brow and considered the request. He drew in a deep breath. Gideon made sure to keep his expression blank, to conceal his level of desire for said request. He did not want to sway the professor one way or another by allowing him to see just how much he wanted the journal.

After what felt like an eternity, the professor extended the journal toward him.

"Very well," he said. "You've proved yourself trustworthy. See that you take good care of it and ensure that it makes it back to me in one piece."

"I will," Gideon promised. "Thank you, professor."

"Gideon, one more thing," he said, and held fast to the journal. "Knowledge often comes with a price. If you do go, the treasure you find may not be the kind you seek."

They both held unto the journal but neither tried to seize control. Gideon was unsure what the professor meant and did not know whether he wanted to. He stood and stared back into the professor's gray eyes. He had come to expect words of warning like this from his parental proxy on the island. When he was certain nothing more would be said, he pulled the journal ever so slightly toward himself. Professor Gervaise released it and took a step back.

"Thank you, professor," Gideon said with a smile and an appreciative nod. "All the best."

"All the best, my friend. Safe travels."

Gideon tucked the journal safely back in his backpack. He bid Professor Gervaise farewell with a half salute and left the classroom the way he had entered. The meeting had not gone as anticipated and did not get the answers he hoped for; still, he felt an extra pep in his step as he made his way down the hallway.

The burden over how he had come to possess the journal was lifted. He could now conduct a guilt free study of its contents, although he was left to wonder whether there was indeed a connection between the paper and the cave. If anything he now knew the meaning behind the symbol. *Return and get it*, he thought.

The Code

Pain shot down his wounded leg with each throbbing step and his misery seemed to have no end. His good leg wearied, as it compensated for his injured knee. Without the assistance of his traveling companion he was certain he would have collapsed by now. He had learned little of his newfound friend other than his name, John Davis. It was not the time for pleasantries, as they spent what little energy they had on survival. Their shared, yet unspoken, goal was to distance themselves from Lubolo's massacre as quickly and quietly as possible.

When night had fallen, they hid amongst the undergrowth of the labyrinth-like crevasse. Somehow Jarvis managed to sleep for a few minutes at a time. When he awoke, near daybreak, he was surprised to find that his golden haired sidekick had not abandoned him. In the light of a new day they were able to see their way forward. This unlikely pair hobbled on, with John Davis shouldering the load. They moved with haste but kept a wary eye to the rear for fear of pursuers.

A thunder clap above warned of the impending storm. The clouds had gathered all morning, yet another ominous sign that their journey was about to become more difficult. The mountainous walls on either side seemed to close in with each step. Jarvis could hear the labored breaths of young Mr. Davis deepen. One thing was clear; they were both in need of a rest. Just then the rain came down. It fell softly at first but as the gentle sound of rolling thunder echoed off the jungle walls, the volume swelled to torrential levels. His under garments were already drenched with sweat from the hot humid morning. The cool drops of rain on his head were at first quite refreshing. However, in minutes his soaking wet clothes began to sag from the weight of the absorbed rainfall.

"There," John Davis said. He pointed over to a massive mahogany tree, dead ahead. "Just there."

With great care they made their way toward the tree like a three legged monster. Under the canopy of limbs and branches they found much welcomed respite from the storm. John Davis helped Jarvis over to the base of the tree and sat him down between two large roots, which protruded from the ground. With a graceful and showman-like twirl, John Davis plopped to the ground and leaned against the root opposite Jarvis. Both men cast their eyes upward at the protective natural ceiling. Though hungry and thirsty, Jarvis was above all grateful for the break. He looked over at the man who had been by his side for nearly a day now and thought of how little he knew of him.

"Mr. Davis?" Jarvis began.

"Call me John Davis, mate," he responded as he casually checked the perimeter.

"John, how did you come to be here?" he asked.

"You mean 'ere on this island or 'ere as your 'uman crutch?"

"Both actually."

"Well John Davis was born right 'ere on this island, so in a way 'e's always been 'ere 'asn't 'e?"

Confused by his answer, Jarvis opened his mouth but did not speak. It was improbable, if not impossible, that he was born on this island. The Spanish occupation had ended only a few years previous, and even the earliest English settlers had been there less than a decade. In Jarvis's estimation his friend was at least twenty-five or twenty-six, with a distinctly English upbringing judging by his speech. The most perplexing part of his answer was that he referred to himself as if he were someone else?

"As to the question of 'ow I came to be in your company?" he continued. "Well that's a bit more complicated."

"I think we've got some time," Jarvis said. He looked around at the sheets of rain that poured just outside their mahogany umbrella.

"Right then," John Davis said. "If we're going to get into all that we'll need some nourishment. You got anything to eat in that bag there?"

Jarvis unconsciously patted the satchel that hung from his shoulders. It was a grim reminder of all he had lost. The satchel and the clothes on his back were all he had escaped with. Lost were his limited provisions, powder, and shot; gone were his pistol and saber. *His saber.* He fought hard to keep his eyes open and shake free the image of his saber flying through the air to behead a helpless Lubolo. All that his satchel contained now was some useless old musket wads, a portable inkwell and his journal.

"No," he said with regret. "There's no food."

"All right then," John Davis said. He jumped to his feet and wiped his muddy hands on the front of his trousers. "Let's see what we can scrape up."

He hopped up on the large tree root to attain a better vantage point. After he looked the area over thoroughly, he pursed his lips and exhaled. His shoulders sagged down in mild disappointment. Jarvis sat back and observed. He wondered what this peculiar man had planned and if his quest for food would prove fruitful. John Davis walked up the root toward the trunk of the gigantic tree that sheltered them. When he reached the base, he leapt to the next nearest root and with one more bound was out of sight, around the tree into the bushes.

Despite his perilous circumstances and the daunting journey that lay ahead, Jarvis was quite at ease. He rested comfortably in the crevasse of the tree and gazed up into the canopy, as the occasional drop fell through the branches and leaves above. His knee no longer throbbed and much of the pain had, at least temporarily, been relieved as he kept it elevated slightly. Although he and his companion were by no means safe, he felt no sense of imminent danger. After all, if they had wanted him dead they could have easily killed him in battle. *Why was I not killed?* That question had floated in and out of his mind during their arduous flight. Almost on cue his train of thought was disrupted again as John Davis emerged from the dense jungle bush, carrying something in his hands.

"Success!" he exclaimed and unloaded his bounty at Jarvis's feet.

There were two large, green melons or gourds the size of his head. Jarvis recognized them at once as the outer husks of young coconuts. Beneath them were a cluster of spiny reddish purple fruits that were completely foreign to him. John Davis produced Jarvis's knife from the back of his trousers, a reminder that Jarvis had yet to reclaim his borrowed possession, and set to work carving a chunk out of one of the gourds. He then used the point of the blade and twisted the knife like a corkscrew. When he had bored a hole in the side he handed it to Jarvis, being careful to keep it upright.

"'ere ya are, mate."

"Thank you," said Jarvis. He bowed his head in gratitude.

Jarvis put the dark green husk up to his lips and tilted it back. He drank deeply from the cool liquid inside and gasped and choked as it poured down his parched throat. It tasted like water from a soapy bucket but it was wet, which at the moment was more than good enough. John Davis cut into the second coconut husk while Jarvis drained all the coconut water he could into his mouth. When he was sure it was empty he laid the husk to rest beside him and watched as John Davis drank from the other coconut.

"Well," Jarvis began. "What is a pirate doing so far inland?"

"'old on right there, mate. Let's not be name call'n," John Davis said.

"You are a pirate, are you not?"

"You say it like it's a bad thing. The way I see it we ain't so different you an' me."

"How so?" Jarvis queried.

"You rank an' file type 'ate them Spaniards as much as we do. An' that's all we're after really. We're looking to drive them blokes from these waters an' make a little profit while we're at it, same as you."

"We?"

"Buccaneers. We ain't so different from soldiers. We just don't sail under 'is Majesty's colors, y'know."

"There is a great deal of difference," Jarvis said sternly. He took umbrage at the suggestion that scoundrels and soldiers could dare be lumped into the same group.

"'ow do ya figure? You take what ain't yours same as we. Only difference is you ain't taking it for yourself."

John Davis reached over and picked up the husk that lay beside Jarvis and began, carefully, to excavate the shell beneath. Jarvis sat in stunned silence. It had never been put to him in such a way and he had never considered what he did in His Majesty's army as stealing. In his mind he served King and country in a noble cause. He defended their interest against the Spanish foe. He was not a thief, he was a soldier. He felt foolish and angry all at once. Angry at the family that encouraged him to enlist; angry at his commanding officers who duped him into believing he was part of some grand effort. Most of all he was angry at the pirate who brought this tragic misconception to his attention. When John Davis had removed the outer husk he bashed the coconut shell on a rock between his legs until it burst open. He used Jarvis's knife to carve out some of the white flesh from inside of the shell and handed it to Jarvis. Almost as an unconscious reflex Jarvis took it and ate it. He chewed and swallowed, unsure if he even cared about hunger anymore. He was unsure about a great many things. John Davis cut out the rest of the white fleshy innards of the coconut and heaped them into one of the half-shells. He gave it to Jarvis and began to work on nourishment of his own.

"You have yet to answer my question," Jarvis said, as he tried to disregard his pointed observation.

"'ow I came to be 'ere?" John Davis asked, with a transparent grin that gave away just how much he wanted to share his story.

Jarvis nodded and waited for him to begin.

"Well let's see," he started. "I caught on with this crew outta Port Royal, mostly blokes from Portugal. We answered to a somewhat decent fellow named Bartolomeu. 'e 'ad us loaded up with a good amount of loot an' we was 'eading for 'ome when this Spanish warship set in on us. They waylaid our ship an' we lost a good portion of our crew before it was over. Anyway we tried mak'n it back with what we 'ad but got caught in a storm that blew us clear up to Hispaniola. We was captured up there and they stole our 'ard earned booty. Ole Bartolomeu was a crafty bloke though an' he lifted a knife off a one the guards an' . . ."

He made a throat slitting gesture with the knife in his hand. Jarvis could tell that he took a great deal of pleasure in telling his tale, as his demeanor had grown progressively lighter from the outset.

"We lashed some wine jugs together an' floated a shore before dawn. Then we trudged through the jungle a bit an' commandeered a ship to carry us back 'ere."

"But why here?" Jarvis interrupted. "Port Royal is on the opposite side of the island."

"Well ole Bartolomeu 'ad a stash up 'ere an' we was coming to recover it as it were."

"And where is Bartolomeu now?"

"'e run off when we was set upon by them blacks what ambushed you and yours. I fell be'ind so I got lef'. That's 'ow it goes."

"No honor amongst thieves, eh?" Jarvis said in a condescending tone.

"You watch yourself, mate," John Davis threatened. He waved Jarvis's own knife back at him. "You know nothing 'bout it."

"I only meant to sympathize with you. That is all."

John Davis stared at Jarvis for several seconds, not with contempt but to gage his level of sincerity. Although he was sincere, Jarvis had no intention of revealing any more than he had to and returned his searching stare in kind. Jarvis put the last bite of coconut flesh into his mouth and let it dissolve on his tongue, being sure to maintain eye contact. In turn John Davis took a bite of his own and chewed it thoughtfully. When he seemed satisfied, John Davis turned his attention to the cluster of spiny fruit. He split it open with the knife and removed a small nut. He placed the nut inside one of the empty coconut half shells and repeated this process for each piece in the cluster.

Jarvis watched intently as John Davis ground the nuts into the shell with a smooth rock until they were a lumpy sludge. Then he stood up and walked out from under the canopy to place the shell in the rain. He came back and retrieved the coconut shells that remained and placed them in the open as well. After he was done he sat down beside Jarvis and discarded the spiny coverings into a nearby bush.

"Them things ain't no good," he said, and stuck out his tongue with a fake gag. "Poison."

Jarvis watched the half shells fill up with water and thought about how much he wanted another drink. He turned his attention back to John Davis and asked, "You said that the men who attacked our regiment captured you?"

"That's right."

"Why did they capture you?" Jarvis questioned further. "I mean, why did they not kill you? Have you given that any thought?"

"Well, I s'pose they thought I was one a you at first. They questioned me real good as to where I'd come from an' who I was with an' such. I told them I 'ad stumbled 'pon them accidental like an' I wanted no trouble. I even offered to take them to Bartolomeu's 'ideout an' split the loot with them but they wanted no part of it. These are men of peculiar motivations. They care nothing for silver an' gold."

"How long did they hold you?"

"Just over night. They was waiting for their boss. Some bloke named Ketlore or Keetloora, something like that."

"You mean de Serras."

"What?" John Davis asked confused.

"Juan de Serras," Jarvis clarified. "The men who held you, the men who ambushed us, are led by a man named Juan de Serras. A tall man with a necklace of teeth and bone."

"Aye, a shirtless bloke with the look a death in 'is eyes," John Davis said. "Far as I could tell 'e's not the man in charge. This Ketalora so and so 'is who 'e answers to."

Jarvis did not know what to make of this revelation. Of all the information he was able to glean from Lubolo, and in all official intelligence reports, he had never heard of this Ketlore or Keet-lora figure. Everything he knew about this group of Negroes told him that they were led by Juan de Serras. The idea that de Serras took orders from someone else was difficult to take in amid all the turmoil and questions he already faced. He was certain Mr. Davis was mistaken and could not have gathered any credible information while being held captive for just one night.

John Davis got to his feet and walked back to the coconut shells, which were now nearly full of water. He retrieved two of them, one of which contained the smashed up nuts, and brought them back near Jarvis. He offered the shell to Jarvis, who quickly downed the cold rainwater.

"Thank you," he said to his savior, who had walked back out under the rain to collect a shell for himself. He returned once again with two shells. He held the shell full of water and ground up nuts in one hand and drank down the other. Then he carefully sat down on the ground and began to slowly match the two half shells together. He aligned the two pieces like a puzzle with the now empty shell on top of the shell full of water and mashed up nuts.

When the two halves were pressed back together, in their almost pre-broken state, he turned it ninety degrees and allowed the water inside to seep slowly out.

Although he was mildly interested in what John Davis was up to, Jarvis grew impatient and decided to record current events while they were still fresh in his mind. He removed the satchel from around his neck and pulled out his journal and a long brass cylinder. He opened the cylinder and pulled out an old, worn, featherless quill. In a compartment beside the quill was a tiny glass jar with a cork in the top. He pulled the cork from the glass jar and opened his journal. Gently, he dipped the quill into the jar and let the excess ink drip back into the thin glass vessel. John Davis sat quietly with the two half-shells held in front of him and observed what Jarvis was up to. He paid no attention to the water that continued to escape through the cracks of the reunited half shells. With fresh ink on his quill Jarvis began to write about Lubolo's death, the ambush and John Davis. The brass cylinder was a gift from his mother, as was the journal. With it she had given him a charge to chronicle his adventures abroad, an undertaking he took seriously.

After Jarvis had written for several minutes he glanced up to find John Davis had returned his focus back to the shells. The drip had slowed to a stop and he turned the shells back to their original orientation and removed the top shell. Inside, the nut sludge had congealed into an oily molten black and brown substance. He offered the shell to Jarvis, who declined and pushed it back toward him.

"It's for the pain in your leg, mate," John Davis explained.

"What is it?"

"Dunno really, but I've seen it work wonders before an' for folks far worse off than you." John Davis thrust the half shell at Jarvis again.

Jarvis hesitated, for a moment, before he finally accepted the shell. He slowly pulled it closer for examination and rocked the shell side to side with his hand. The oily goo sloshed back and forth atop the nutty sludge beneath it. Jarvis craned his neck forward and brought it directly under his nose. It smelled of burnt candle wax. He looked back at John Davis, who sat still as a statue and waited for him to drink.

"It won't kill ya. I'm nearly certain a that."

With that tepid endorsement, Jarvis inhaled deeply and brought the half shell to his lips. He tipped it back and ever so slowly it oozed onto his tongue and down his throat. It felt like molasses with small chunks of dirt in it. He imagined this is what tar must taste like. With one big slurp he had all he could handle. He turned his head to the side and tried not to vomit. He swallowed hard and made a face like a child who sucked on a lemon.

"That is awful," he reported to John Davis.

"I've never tried it me self, but that's the general consensus," John Davis said, and failed to stifle a laugh. "You'll feel better in no time." He jumped to his feet once more and walked over to get the last half shell from out in the rain. "'ere, this'll 'elp."

He handed the half shell to Jarvis, who took it and guzzled it down. John Davis left the shell which contained the remnants of oily sludge and returned the remaining empty shells for refill. He looked carefully to all sides as he returned under the protection of the tree's canopy.

"John?" Jarvis asked. "Why do you help me?"

"Why not?"

"Your compatriots would have surely left me behind, would they not?"

"That's their code, mate, I live by me own code," John Davis answered. "Besides, I seen first'and what that's like an' it ain't all that great."

The two men regarded each other for a moment. With all he knew about pirates, Jarvis had prejudged him to be a man whose motives revolved around self-preservation. Pirates, as everyone knew, sought for their own personal fortune and glory. They cared little for those who might be harmed by their actions. Although he had been in dire need of his assistance, he remained suspicious of his intentions and wary of what this union would ultimately cost him. His words cut deep into Jarvis's heart as he realized there was a goodness and selflessness in this man that he himself could lay no claim to.

"So how did you escape then?"

"Well I reckon they 'ad decided that with or without 'is blessing they was gonna off me before I could cause any trouble. But good fortune smiled on me as your lot came along and they all scrambled off to lie in wait, leaving me behind with just this young lad to guard me. When the skirmish started and shots were fired that little yute could 'ave cared less 'bout me so I buggered off right quick."

"And then you ran into me."

"An' it's a good thing I did too, else those black demons would a run you down in no time."

"Well, without my knife you would still have your hands bound together."

"Nah, I'd 'ave gotten me self outta them things eventually, besides it didn't slow me up none. Only thing that stopped me was running into your gimpy arse."

"Fair enough," Jarvis said. "I have yet to properly thank you for that."

"'Tweren't nothing mate," he said. "If I 'ad thought properly I'd 'ave probably left ya."

"Be that as it may, you have my sincerest gratitude." Jarvis said. He touched his heart with a slight bow.

"Don't get all lovey dovey on me or I'll leave you 'ere in the jungle," he shot back with a great big smile. Both men chuckled and then shared an awkward moment of silence. John Davis looked down at the journal beside Jarvis. "What's that then?"

"It is a journal. I jot down things of importance from time to time."

"Did you jot me down then?" John Davis said as he reached for the journal.

"That is private," Jarvis grabbed the journal and quickly moved it back and up near his head out of reach.

"A'right, a'right, don't 'ave a conniption," John Davis said. He threw both hands in the air and eased back against the large root behind him.

"I am sorry. It is not meant for you, that is all."

"Who's it meant for then? A girl?" John Davis ribbed him.

"No, I mean maybe. Not exactly. Sort of?" He struggled to explain himself. "I keep a journal for my mother. Before I set off, she made me promise that I keep it. I write so that if anything happens to me she'll know where I have been and what I've done."

"Well that's a real downer, mate. That's your death diary," quipped the pirate.

"I never thought of it like that," Jarvis said with a grin. "I suppose it is rather morbid."

"So there ain't noth'n in there 'bout rainbows an' sweeties then?"

"No, I suppose I have omitted certain important details as it pertains to rainbows and sweeties." Jarvis reflected on the often melancholy tone in his writing.

"Pity," John Davis stated. "That's the stuff that ought to be remembered. All the rest ya just 'ave to get through, ya know?"

Jarvis envied him for his outlook on life. All too often he had allowed the day to day drudgery to swallow up all that was beautiful and pleasurable. Even now there was beauty all about him. The deep green bush that surrounded them and the lime stone cliffs on either side of the gorge stood as a magnificent reminder of the island's splendor. He had not been sufficiently grateful for the grand old tree that provided them shelter from the rain. The rain itself was refreshing and brought relief from the harsh tropical sun; not to mention the life giving water they so desperately needed. All of these things had been lost to him. His focus had been on the loss and suffering from the previous day's battle and the injury to his knee. "My knee," he said aloud as he realized the pain was gone. "It is not hurting."

"Yeah?" John Davis said. "That's a relief."

"What do you mean?" Jarvis asked.

"Well either that stuff was gonna 'elp you or you was gonna keel over. I wasn't really sure which." John Davis answered with a shrug of his shoulders and a sheepish grin.

"You are unbelievable!" Jarvis said furiously.

"What? I 'ad 'igh 'opes for ya, mate. Truly I did," John Davis responded sincerely.

The rain had let up and there was a small break in the clouds that let in the first piece of sunshine, in what had otherwise been a grey and gloomy afternoon. Jarvis looked out at the newly arrived ray of sunlight. "So where to now?"

"You're asking me? I ain't never been 'ere in me life," John Davis replied, as he came to his feet.

"I have been following your lead for nearly a day now," Jarvis said, as he attempted to stand for the first time since they stopped to rest.

"Me? I've been following you."

"Stupendous. I thought you knew where we were going," a befuddled Jarvis said. He put weight on his injured leg and bounced lightly to test the depth and breadth of this miraculous remedy.

"These parts 'ere is your purview, mate."

"You said you were born here! And what was all that business about Bartolomeu's stash," Jarvis said indignantly.

"'old up there mate. I weren't born in the jungle. An' I 'adn't been to old Bartolomeu's 'ideout yet. That Portuguese blaggard was pretty tight lipped 'bout that sorta thing. 'e 'ad trust issues 'e did."

"But you offered to take de Serras to it and split the booty?"

"It was a bluff, mate. I was trying to not to get run through or shot."

"So you had nothing?" Jarvis continued his interrogation. "What if they would have called your bluff?"

"I didn't say I ad nothing. I said I 'adn't been there . . . yet," John Davis said. He untied a small leather coin pouch from the waist of his trousers. He opened it, carefully removed a small slip of paper and handed it over to Jarvis. "I nicked this from 'im just after we come ashore."

Jarvis looked down in astonishment at the paper. On it was a looping heart shaped symbol sitting on a three-legged post. "I know this."

"Ya do?" John Davis said, matching Jarvis's astonishment. "'ow so?"

"I took shelter for a night in a cave that bore this marking," Jarvis said. The memory of that night and the day that preceded it flooded back into his mind. His current circumstances were eerily similar. Once more his company had been wiped out in an ambush by de Serras, and once again he had been spared for reasons that passed understanding.

"Can you find your way back to that cave?"

"It has been years since I was there but I believe I could. If I had a map."

His mind raced as he thought about what treasure they might find. He mentally berated himself for being so close to it before and not exploring the cave further. *How long had Bartolomeu used this cave? Had there actually been treasure there?* On that night, long ago, his single-minded determination had been to return to the outpost and report. The outpost, he thought. He could find a map there; a map with the potential to change his fortune. No longer would he be at the mercy of a chain of command or bound to service of King and Country. He could finally be his own king, master of his own fate. He tried to push these thoughts to the back of his mind and focus on the task at hand. Colonel Tyson had never shared the cartography of the area but he had seen him reference it many times. Colonel Lubolo did not use maps but navigated by landmarks. He needed a point of reference. Surely, he would find what he needed from the map at the outpost.

"Well then, let's go find you a map," said John Davis with a wry smile.

Quickstep

At our current pace we should arrive at the outpost by early morning. My knee is much improved and is allowing me to walk on my own. However, it is still causing me some discomfort. Even if we could procure the necessary ingredients, I do not dare try Mr. Davis's toxic remedy again for fear of death.

I have no intention of returning to my post. If all goes to plan we will find a map and procure provisions undetected. If we were to be discovered, I would surely be detained, questioned and court martialed. News of our defeat and Lubolo's death could not have possibly reached the company yet, which may prove some small advantage.

If there is indeed a treasure to be had in Bartolmeu's cave, then, with my share, I intend to start a new life apart from all of this awful mess and death.

Also we saw a rainbow this afternoon just over the ridge, thought it worth noting.

"Yo Goodwin," Bigga shouted. "Quickstep right up y'ere so."

Gideon looked up from the back seat of the baby blue Lada. In the rearview mirror Bigga's dark brown eyes looked at him and waited for a response. For nearly two hours they had traveled on the narrow winding mountain roads of Jamaica's elevated interior. Since they left Kingston, earlier that afternoon, they had not passed through a city or town of any significance: just small country settlements. Todd had once again claimed the front passenger seat and got better acquainted with Bigga while Gideon delved further into the journal. He was in search of a sign or a clue that might offer some idea of what lay in store. Brought back to the present by the beckoning voice of his old friend, he looked out the window to get his bearings.

The thick over growth of the backcountry grew right up to the pavement. The pothole infested roadway was barely wide enough for two cars, and often required that both vehicles ease to the far side of the road to avoid a collision. On a road like this it was not out of the ordinary for side mirrors to knock against each other as cars passed. Scattered throughout the hills and cliffs on either side were old shacks and houses of varied shapes and sizes. A particularly quaint little green house, with a zinc roof and a red concrete porch, caught Gideon's eye. He thought about the countless hours he had spent on doorsteps and verandas just like it on his mission.

"Goodwin, ya 'ear mi?" Bigga asked.

"Yeah man, mi hear yu."

"Which part uno wan' me fi go?" he said, speaking to the rearview mirror.

"Relax man, I'll point it out when we get there," Gideon said. He did not remember exactly how to get where they were going, but was certain he would know it when he saw it.

Quickstep was a small roadside community at the bottom of Trelawney and served as the southern gateway to the cockpit country. It also laid claim to the only drivable road into the inhospitable jungle, although the term "drivable" was debatable. Gideon had only been to Quickstep once but was confident he could find their destination along the only paved road.

"Why do they call it Quickstep?" Todd asked Bigga.

"'cause ya better step quick if ya na wan fi get dead," Bigga answered, with his signature belly laugh. "Da land a look behind dis, st'yar."

"The land of look behind?" asked Todd. Gideon was pleasantly surprised that Todd could understand any of what Bigga had said.

"They call this whole area the land of look behind. Early colonial soldiers who came up into these parts used to ride two to a horse. One rider faced front and the other faced the rear as a look out," Gideon explained.

"Look out for what?" Todd asked.

"Yeah Mr. 'istory, a wha dem a look for?" Bigga said. He never missed an opportunity to tease Gideon.

"Runaway slaves that fled to the mountains." Gideon ignored Bigga's mocking moniker and secretly hoped 'Mr. History' would catch on.

"No man! Dem na runaways, dem a freedom fighters. Dem na slaves, dem a warriors," said a defensive Bigga.

"Yeah G, what the crap?!" Todd chimed in, in classic mob mentality.

"Fair enough," Gideon said. He threw his hands up in a gesture of surrender. "I only meant that their origins were from those fleeing slavery. But he's right; some of them were born up here just as free as you and me. The remarkable thing was that they were able to fend off a superior British force for almost a hundred years and eventually struck a treaty with them that granted lands and liberty. Their descendants still live up here."

"Where did you learn all this stuff?" Todd asked.

"They conceal information like that in books," Gideon retorted, and tried to do his best Oliver Platt impersonation.

"Okay, cool guy," Todd said sarcastically.

An orange building with red trim sailed passed the passenger's side window. Gideon spun around quickly. It was the local Pentecostal church and the first thing he recognized. "Slow up Bigga."

"Ya see it?"

"No, but it's right up y'ere so."

If his memory served him, the shop where they were headed

was up on the right. This particular shop had some of the best chicken, rice and peas that Gideon could remember eating. It was Jamaica's answer to the convenient store; part haberdashery, part grocer, part eatery. Up on the right side of the road, as he anticipated, a small gray building with a white sign on top appeared. In blue letters, the sign read Trevor's. Contrary to what the sign suggested, the shop was not owned by anyone named Trevor. It was owned by the man Gideon hoped to find, the man who would lead them back to the cave.

"Here," Gideon directed. "Pull in right y'ere so."

The blue Lada rambled to a stop just passed the gray building. Bigga pulled onto a small grassy clearing north of the chicken shop. Bigga and Gideon climbed out of their respective doors on the driver's side. They stretched their legs from the long journey, while Todd struggled to open his door that was partially blocked by a banana tree. Gideon bent down and reached back into the back seat where he had laid the journal. Carefully, he placed it under the front seat out of sight and closed the car door.

The concrete walkway in front of the shop was swept clean. A domino table was setup out front, which served as a local gathering point most evenings. For now it was pushed back up against the building and out of the way. The sun rested just above the massive peaks in front of the shop. A young man walked down the road and passed right next to Todd, who had finally freed himself from the banana tree. Todd leaned on the trunk of the old Lada and looked gleefully at this outrageous looking Jamaica youth. His hair was matted and coiled into black dreadlocks and partially stuffed into a brown crocheted cap. His long patchy facial hair was intentionally unkempt like his dreads. He wore an oversized pair of bright red shorts with large pockets on the side and his white tank top gleamed against his deep brown skin. In one hand he carried a long brown pod from a Poinciana tree. The slender hard pod was full of seeds and made a distinct rattle sound when shaken. In his other hand he held a lit, smoldering spliff.

"Jah dem a bring corruption of da wicked an' Babylon to mi

doorstep," he shouted, to no one in particular, as he walked past Todd. "Uno haffi g'way white devil! Fire burn 'pon de white man."

"Oy," Gideon called after him.

The young man continued down the road. He shouted at the sky and shook his cursing stick in the air. "Burn down Babylon an' all dem evil conceptions! Lighting an' tunder 'pon da white man!"

"Oy, my yute," Gideon said again. "Ya know what da Docta say?"

The young man turned and looked back at Gideon. His eyes were glassy and bloodshot. Although the tone of his voice had been angry the expression on his face was blank, almost serene.

"'im say," Gideon continued, as he broke into a rhythmic tune. "Too much fire burn a word without works, fire burn up the Obeah man's shirt. Fire burn uno neva learn, nah everything out d'ere ya fi burn."

"Blood fire!" the young dread exclaimed. "Ya know Beenie Man?"

Beenie Man, also known as "The Doctor," was a dancehall reggae artist from Kingston who managed to achieve mainstream success while still staying relevant to younger Rastafarians. Rastafari was a religion, of sorts, that worshipped Haile Selassie, the former Emperor of Ethiopia, or Jah. Their way of life consisted mostly of smoking ganja, listening to and making music, and quoting obscure passages from the Bible. Reggae music was popularized by the most famous Rasta, Bob Marley. Gideon loved Reggae and often used his shared love for music as a tool to build relationships with young people on his mission. Beenie Man's *Better Learn* was his favorite retort to the common 'fire burn' Rastafarian refrain.

"Yeah man, da girls dem sugar fi true," Gideon said.

"Backfoot," he said. "Ya do know da Docta. Respect."

"Yeah man, peace and blessings," Gideon said. He brought his fist to his heart and bowed his head slightly.

"Every'ting cris. I and I must give t'anks and praise, fi mi jus' a live up in a de mountains dem praising 'is name, Haile Selassie."

"Jah," Gideon stated emphatically.

"Rastafari!" the young man shouted as he turned back down the street and walked away, singing.

Gideon and Bigga smiled at each other and exchanged a light fist bump. Then Gideon looked back at Todd, who stood between them. His eyes were still fixed on the young Rastafarian, now a good ways down the street. His mouth was agape and he looked befuddled, the same look he had worn a handful of times now.

"What just happened?" a wide-eyed Todd asked. "That was complete nonsense."

Bigga put his arm around him and led him to Trevor's front door, "Don't worry mi brudda. Mi a go teach yu fi be a Don like Goodwin y'ere."

"No seriously," Todd called back to Gideon over his shoulder. "That made no sense."

The trio walked into the small sitting area inside Trevor's chicken shop. In front of them was an old cracked counter with an antique beige cash register. On the other side was a warming box with a couple of beef patties, leftover from the morning. A skinny little boy sat on a stool and leaned back against the counter, facing the door. He wore bright green tank top and a pair of yellow shorts. To their left was a shoddy, mismatched booth and table set with a faded poster for a Christmas Reggae concert from 1997 above it. On the poster was a woman, in a clear plastic mini skirt and top, performing on a stage before a throng of arm waving fans. Behind the counter an open door that led to a small back room with three half empty shelves. A tall lighted beverage cooler that contained several glass D&G soda bottles and a Coca-Cola was directly behind the register.

"Likkle yute," Gideon said to the boy on the stool. "Where Bammy di d'ere?"

"'im gone."

"Where 'im gone?"

"'im gone a country," the boy said.

'Gone a country' was an expression that meant a person could have traveled nearly anywhere on the island, except Kingston.

Kingston was widely referred to as 'town' and really anywhere else was 'country.' Gideon was used to this type of vague and less than helpful qualification of a person's whereabouts and found it more charming than irritating. Before he could continue to question the boy, a woman quickly emerged through the doorway.

"A lie ya a tell," she scolded the boy. She reached across the counter and smacked him in the side of his head. "Leave 'ere an' g'way."

The boy hopped off the stool and ran out the door. He squeezed between Bigga and Gideon with a mischievous smile on his face, completely unfazed by the minor beating he had received. The three visitors stood in stunned silence at the appearance of this unexpected beauty. Her short black hair was neatly slicked back and swept away from her youthful face. She had dark brown eyes that were warm and welcoming. The proportions of her face were perfectly symmetric from her broad round nose to her strong, yet soft, chin. Her sleeveless shirt revealed her sculpted biceps and clung naturally to her womanly figure. It was only when she cocked her head slightly to the side and put her hand on her hip that Gideon realized they all stared stupidly at her.

"Uh . . . do you, uh, know where we can find Bammy?" he stammered.

"Who's asking?" she replied, with her hand still on her hip.

"Oh, um, my name is Gideon."

Todd pressed up against Gideon and leaned into her field of view. "And I'm Todd."

"Mi friend dem call me Bigga but you c'yan call me whatever you like," his large friend said as he similarly leaned in and brandished a crooked, cheesy smile.

Gideon elbowed Todd in the ribs and he bumped backwards into Bigga. He shot them both a look that pleaded for decorum, although he knew that ship had sailed. She removed her hand from her hip and shook her head slightly. The look on her face and her crinkled brow clearly showed that further explanation was required.

"Bammy and I are old friends," he lied. He had only met Bammy once and knew little about him other than his name and general whereabouts. "I served here as a missionary and he took me hiking back into the cockpits."

"Are you Helda Penny?" she said, and she brightened up for the first time.

"No, I'm not Elder Penny," he said, unable to believe she had even heard of Elder Penny. He thought that if any of his group had been memorable or noteworthy it would have been him; if not him, then certainly not Penny. "I'm Elder Goodwin, Gideon Goodwin."

"Mi neva heard a yu," she said, unaware of the destructive nature of her words.

"So you know Bammy, then?" Gideon asked.

"He's mi fadda."

"Are you running the shop?" Gideon did not wish to press too hard or too fast.

"Dat's right."

"Great," Gideon continued. "We'd like to get something to eat. You 'ave stew peas?"

"Stew peas nah cook till Sat'day."

"Ox tail?" Gideon purposely asked for meals that were out of the ordinary, with the hope that it conveyed his knowledge of the island. He, once again, was met with disappointment as he failed to impress.

"It's finished," she said. "We 'ave chicken, rice and peas."

"Irie. We'll 'ave t'ree plates dem," Gideon said.

She rolled her eyes and went back through the doorway into the small back room. "Having or going?"

"Having." Gideon raised his voice slightly to project into the back room. "So do you know where Bammy is then?"

"'im up a di yard," she said, and leaned through the doorway to point out the window on the southern wall.

They turned and looked out the window to see a small footpath that led off into the bush. In the distance was a tiny zinc shack, atop a small hill at the base of a large cliff face. As they looked toward the window they noticed, for the first time, a small child who sat quietly in the corner of the room near the entrance. Somehow they completely missed this inconspicuous little boy upon their arrival, with their attention on the front counter. This little boy, who appeared to be around five years old, sat on the ground with a single thick brown crayon and drew on a sheet of paper. He wore a light blue t-shirt with a faded picture of ALF above the words *No problem*.

"Hey likkle yute," Gideon said, warmly. "Wha g'wan?"

The boy did not look up but continued to draw as if he had not heard him.

"'im c'yan't 'ear yu," she said and emerged again from the back room with a plate of rice and peas. "'im deaf."

"Oh," Gideon said, embarrassed. "I'm sorry."

"Why ya sorry? Yu didn't mek 'im dat way," she stated matter-of-factly.

"Yeah, well . . ." Gideon said, unsure how to respond.

"I got this," Todd said confidently. He squatted down in front of the boy and touched the floor softly to draw his attention. The boy looked up and Todd communicated something to him in sign language. The boy smiled and signed back.

"When did you learn sign language?!" Gideon exclaimed.

"I wasn't just partying and goof'n while you were gone," Todd said indignantly. "I am a man of many talents and interests."

Gideon did not respond but looked at him with skepticism.

Todd feigned offense at Gideon's unwillingness to accept his explanation but finally said, "Fine! I dated a deaf chick for a while. Are you happy?"

"What did you say to him?" Gideon went on, with smug satisfaction.

"I said hello," Todd answered and repeated in sign as he spoke. "And asked him how he was doing."

Todd glanced over Gideon's shoulder in the direction of their beautiful host. Gideon looked back to see her standing by the table, with the rice and peas still in hand. She smiled down on the boy with great adoration. Her smile revealed two dimples on either side of her bright white teeth. Todd jumped at the opportunity to engage her in conversation. "Is this your son?"

She looked over at Todd and back to the small boy in the ALF t-shirt. Her eyes welled up with tears as she gazed down at her pride and joy. She pressed her lips together and nodded. Her prominent cheek bones almost glowed; perched atop a pair of graceful smile lines.

"Was that your son too?" Todd asked. He gestured to the spot where the other boy from the stool had exited the shop.

"You t'ink say mi mudda every last pickney in town?" she replied, as her face hardened and changed in an instant from kind to furious. "Cha!"

She threw the plate on the table and stormed back behind the counter. Bigga wasted no time; he sat down in front of the plate of chicken and rice, oblivious to the awkward turn that ensued. Todd looked up at Gideon in search of some kind of support, but Gideon folded his arms and shook his head.

A moment later the woman appeared from the back room with two more plates of chicken, rice, and peas. She unceremoniously plopped them on the table and walked over to the corner where her boy colored. She flipped on a switch by the entrance and a light bulb on the ceiling lit up. The light was attached to the switch with bare wire, tacked to one of the exposed 1-by-2s that held the flimsy shop together. As the daylight faded the room had imperceptibly grown dim. The new light was a welcome change that Gideon hoped might lighten the mood.

"What's 'is name?" Bigga asked, with a mouthful of food.

"Corey."

"I didn't catch your name," Gideon said.

"Mi neva t'row it," was her surprisingly playful reply. "It's Tara. Come, Corey."

She signed to him and took him gently by the hand. The little boy stood up and collected his paper and crayon.

Corey looked up at Todd and handed him the paper. Todd looked at Tara to gauge her reaction. When he failed to read her expression he reached out and accepted the paper. "Thank you,

Corey," he said as he brought his hand to his chin and continued to sign. "It was nice to meet you."

Gleefully, Gideon sat down across from Bigga to enjoy the meal he had longed for all the days he had been away. In front of him was a red plastic plate, with a heaping portion of fluffy pink rice, loaded with red kidney beans. What Jamaicans called peas Gideon had always called beans. Initially this was a point of confusion, but he quickly conceded the name game as rice and peas was his favorite. Next to the rice and peas were two small pieces of juicy, dark brown fricassee chicken.

With the white plastic fork he eagerly scooped up his first bite. He hummed with euphoric zeal as he devoured the soft, moist rice and peas. Todd squeezed in beside Bigga, where the other plate was laid, and placed Corey's paper on the table. Gideon looked at the boy's drawing in disbelief. He reached across the table and turned the drawing right side up.

"Holy crap, this is good!" Todd remarked to Bigga as he began to eat.

"Yeah man, inna Jamdown we know what is good," Bigga bragged.

"What's in this?" Todd asked.

"Seasonings," Bigga replied.

"Yeah, but what seasonings?" asked Todd.

"Good seasonings," Bigga answered, with a wry smile.

"What's up with you?" Todd asked, as he looked across the table at Gideon, who was staring in astonishment at Corey's drawing.

Gideon's eyes left the paper and met with Todd's. He slowly turned the page around until Todd could see the image Corey had made. Drawn in the center of the paper was a looping brown heart that sat atop a three-legged stand, identical to the symbol from the journal.

"Ho-ly crap!" Todd exclaimed.

Todd grabbed the paper and stared at it himself. Gideon jumped up from the table and started toward the counter. Tara returned just as Gideon passed the cash register. Startled to see him behind the counter, she lunged toward him and pushed him back into the sitting area. "You c'yan't come back y'ere."

"Where's Corey?"

"'im gone 'ome,"

"I need to talk with him," Gideon said. He leaned back and looked out the window. The small shadowy figure of a boy jogged down the foot path toward the shack, the black landscape shrouded by dusk.

"What? Why?" she asked, bewildered.

Gideon turned around to the table. Bigga had leaned over toward Todd and they sat almost cheek to cheek and stared at the paper. Gideon snatched the paper from Todd's hands and handed it to Tara. She looked at the drawing and quickly back at Gideon. Her eyes were filled with fear.

"Why did yu come y'ere?" she demanded.

"This symbol is why we are here," Gideon said, and pointed to the drawing. "We want find a cave where I've seen this symbol."

Tara pushed passed Gideon and ran to the entrance of the shop. She leaned out the doorway and looked up and down the street. The sun had dipped below the horizon; all was dark and quiet in both directions. She pulled the thick wooden door closed and turned off the light at the center of the shop. The only light in the room was the beverage cooler behind the counter.

"Sit down," she said to Gideon.

He joined Bigga and Todd, who watched intently as all of the action unfolded. She pushed in the booth next to Gideon. Tara leaned in and whispered, "Uno c'yan't go near dat cave."

"Don't tell me it's a duppy cave 'cause I've already heard that from your father," Gideon interrupted.

"Shut up," Tara chided. "Ya know noth'n 'bout it."

Something or someone ran into the front door of the shop. The four of them jumped at the sound. Tara looked back at the closed door behind her and held up her hand to signal for them to stay silent. There were two more bumps against the door, a clear indication someone wanted in. After a third bump, the door slid open and the figure of a tall, skinny man stepped inside. The light bulb in the ceiling burst to life as the man flipped on the switch and startled the nervous quartet at the table.

Gideon recognized immediately the old man who stood in the doorway, it was Bammy. He still sported an opened button up shirt and high water pants, the same ones he had worn on their first meeting.

"Daddy," Tara said with relief.

"Tara, wha 'pon to ya girl?" Bammy said as he stumbled forward. "Why yu sitt'n inna da dark?"

"Daddy, come in 'ere," Tara said. She got up, pulled Bammy further into the room and closed the door behind him.

"A who dis?" Bammy said as he examined the unusual trio that sat around his table.

"Bammy, it's me, Elder Goodwin," Gideon said. He stood up and extended his hand.

"Helda Goodwin?" Bammy said. He reached out, grabbed Gideon's hand and shook it excitedly. Gideon could smell the rum on his breath. "Backfoot. Mi c'yan't believe it. Where's Helda Penny?"

Gideon bushed off another minor blow to his ego and reached back to the table to retrieve Corey's drawing. He wasted no time with pleasantries. "Elder Penny's not here, it's just me. Do you remember the cave with this marking?"

"No man, don't budda with dat t'ing d'ere," Bammy's countenance changed from excited back to agitated.

"Mi try fi tell dem," Tara chimed in.

"Please, Bammy, we need to go here," Gideon pleaded.

Bammy slowly walked over to the empty bench, opposite Bigga and Todd, and sat down. Gideon followed cautiously and squatted down beside the table. Tara stood behind him with her arms folded. All eyes were fixed on Bammy as he inhaled deeply and began.

"Out d'ere is the baddest lands we 'ave. 'hole 'eap a sink'oles an' cliffs dem. Peoper g'wan out d'ere an' ya neva see dem again. All a de dangers out d'ere got nothi'n on dis 'ere so," he said, and gently tapped the paper placed on the table in front of him. "Dis right 'ere will get uno killed."

"Killed?" Gideon said. He shook his head in disbelief. "Killed by what?"

"Da obeah man."

"Obeah man?" Todd asked.

"Obeah is black magic," Gideon explained briefly. "The obeah man is like the boogieman."

"You're messing with me," Todd said skeptically.

"No man, I'm afraid not," Gideon answered seriously.

Elder Goodwin had one unforgettable encounter with an obeah man, which was more than enough. On a beautiful clear spring day, he walked down the main street in St. Ann's Bay with his companion. A black man in a long black robe approached from the opposite end of the street. People and animals outside the market parted like schools of fish before a shark. Elder Goodwin followed suit and fled to the other side of the street before he crossed paths with this ominous figure.

The man's head was covered with thick black hair, from his waist length dreadlocks to his unkempt beard. He wore a thick gold chain around his neck with a circular medallion on it. Although Elder Goodwin had successfully crossed the street, he failed to look away and avoid eye contact. The obeah man's penetrating black eyes locked on to his, and he stood transfixed. His heart felt as if it were being constricted. He had an intense desire to flee, but was unable to move. His companion came to his rescue when he unknowingly stepped between him and the obeah man and freed him from his trance-like state.

Obeah was much like voodoo. Its origins could be traced back to tribes in ancient Africa. An obeah man was somewhere between a witch doctor and a shaman and was said to have supernatural powers. The final initiation of an obeah man was to steal the spirit of a child and Gideon had been told that they could raise the dead and control their minds and bodies. Although he did not fully believe the stories, his lone encounter had taught him that an obeah man was not to be taken lightly.

"A bad man in bad lands my yute," Bammy muttered. He stared blankly at the tabletop. "Da land of look behind out d'ere so."

"Bammy, what does the obeah man have to do with this?" Gideon asked. He picked up the paper from the table and held it in front of him.

The elderly man sat up straight and looked Gideon square in the eyes. "Only 'im c'yan go d'ere. Only 'im c'yan come back."

"I don't understand," Gideon said. "Only he can go where? The cave?"

Bammy stood up without further explanation and walked past Gideon and Tara to the front door. He pulled it open and let in the cool late evening air. "Night a fall. Uno c'yan stay 'ere fi da night but uno hafi go inna da marn'n."

He looked back at Tara with a nod. Then he walked out into the dark street and disappeared from their view. Gideon looked down at Todd and Bigga, still seated at the table. They both looked terrified. Tara walked to the front door and closed it behind her father.

"Wi 'aven't got any beds but mi a go get uno blankets fi share," Tara said, without looking at them. "In da morning just clear out an' lock up."

She turned and started to exit the room through the back door. Gideon saw his hopes of reaching the cave walking out the door. He pursued her and caught her by the arm, just before she got to the counter. She immediately shook herself free and assumed a defensive posture. Gideon realized he had overstepped his bounds and backed off. He put both hands in the air and took a step away to give her space

"Wait a minute," he pleaded. "Just wait a minute, please."

Tara relaxed her stance and looked curiously back at Gideon. He stood quiet for a minute and attempted to collect his thoughts and digest all that had happen. Questions swirled in his mind. What was the connection between the obeah man and the symbol? Why were Bammy and Tara so afraid? What were they going to do if Bammy refused to guide them?

One thought above all the others sprang to his lips.

"Why did your son draw this symbol?" he finally asked and held up the paper.

"Mi na know but 'im draw it all da time," she said, with all the feeling of a worried parent.

"Do you know what it means?"

Tara shook her head.

"It's called Sankofa," Gideon explained. "It means 'return and get it.' That's why we're here. That's what we're trying to do. This is the third time I've run across this symbol. That's got to mean something."

Gideon paused and drew in a deep breath. He determined to make one final plea for help.

"I don't believe in coincidence and I don't believe in fate," he continued. "We all have our own choices and we have to live with them. We can dismiss what we see, what we feel and chalk our circumstances up to luck. Or, we can follow our hearts and minds and choose our own path. I intend to do the latter, but I'm gonna need some help. What do you say?"

She leaned against the counter and folded her arms. Thoughtfully, she stared toward the front door and after a minute said, "'ow much?"

"What?" Gideon asked.

"Mi na go take yu inna da cockpits for nutt'n. 'ow much?"

Gideon smiled broadly. He was relieved his impassioned pitch had at least softened her stance, "How much will it take?"

"$4,000 Jamaican," she said.

"That's everything I have!" he shouted.

"That's mi price," she replied. "You c'yan chalk it up to luck or follow your 'eart."

"Blood fire," Bigga laughed, "A she t'rew dat back de 'pon ya, brudda."

Gideon turned around to see Bigga and Todd grinning like a couple of fools from over the back of the bench. "I don't know what you're laughing about," Gideon said to Bigga. "I'll be paying her with the money I owe you."

"No worries," Todd interjected. "I'll take care of what we owe for the ride up."

"And mi a go t'row in mi good company fi free," Bigga added.

Gideon was glad to know that he had his friends' support and that they had not been scared off by the threat of death or tales of dark magic. He counted himself lucky to have such traveling companions. Although he was not sure what lay in store for them, he at last felt optimistic about their undertaking. His speech was meant to convince Tara but served as his own conversion. He turned back around to face her. If she was agreeable they had all the pieces they needed.

"$4,000 it is, then." He extended his hand and she reached out to grab it. "You're sure you can get us there?"

"Yeah man," she said and shook his hand in agreement. "Mi sure."

"Well then," he said. "When can we leave?"

"First t'ing in da morning before 'e wakes." She turned around and walked behind the counter. "'im a go try an' stop wi if 'im gets da chance. Daddy na romp with da obeah man."

"Don't worry," Gideon said. "Nobody knows we're here."

She stopped at the threshold, looked back over her shoulder and said with an ominous tone, "Don't be so sure."

Abandoned Post

The first sign of morning light began to show, although the sun had not yet risen over the mountain peaks behind them. The weary duo perched on the edge of the wilderness and crouched among the bushes and trees that surrounded the old Spanish ranch. All was silent and still, as most of the inhabitants were fast asleep. There was a small billow of smoke that came from the old house where the officers slept. The house was just as rundown as Jarvis remembered it. The wooden slat walls leaned slightly to his right, as the foundation had shifted. Shoddy attempts had been made to mend the gaping holes in the roof. Crisscross boards were tacked down over the holes and black tar slathered across planks. Several barrels were strung haphazardly across the back wall; a few had rolled out into the grass and lay on their sides. To the east was a line of nine or ten beige canvas tents, far less than Jarvis remembered. They were tattered and stained and, all but one, snagged to one side or the other. It had been months since Jarvis laid eyes on the outpost and he could not believe how quickly it had fallen into disrepair. Notoriously rigid and meticulous in his day, Colonel Tyson would never have stood for this.

"So what's the plan, mate?" asked John Davis.

"See that large tent there, next to the main house?"

He pointed to the first tent in the row, the only one in the lot that stood straight. The poles were upright and the lines were pulled taught and staked down properly. The outside of the tent was relatively clean as well, aside from the unavoidable red clay stains around the bottom.

"Aye."

"That should be the quartermaster's tent," Jarvis explained. "I will be able to find everything we need there."

"Won't the quartermaster be wonder'n what you be doing in 'is tent?" John Davis asked.

"That plume of smoke means he is stoking the fire for the offices in the main house." He pointed to the chimney. "With any luck I will be in and out before he returns."

Between their position and the outpost were several split log barricades with wooden barbed spears that jutted out in their direction. They were set several yards apart and only covered the back perimeter of the ranch house. Jarvis could not imagine this makeshift line of defense would be effective in stopping, or even slowing, an enemy force.

"And what will I be doing then?" John Davis asked.

"You stay here," Jarvis ordered. "It will be easier for one of us to get in and out. As I know what to look for and can explain my presence, if detected, it should be me."

"Aye," John Davis responded, not one to offer an objection to a plan that required nothing of him. "Off you go then. I'll be right 'ere if ya need me."

Jarvis kept low to the ground and left the cover of the trees. He walked with a slight limp but felt only a dull sensation of pain that did not slow his progress. Cautiously, he advanced toward the encampment with his eyes trained on the tents to the east to watch for any activity. Experience told him that he need not worry about the officers. They would not emerge before morning formation and inspection. Formation and Inspection took place at sunrise which, by his estimation, gave him no more than thirty minutes. What concerned him at the moment was a solider or infantry man who might be roused from his sleep by want of food or the need to relieve himself.

He crept forward carefully and was within a few yards of the quartermaster's tent when one of the night watch came round the corner of the main house on a perimeter patrol. Jarvis fell down and lay flat on the ground, with his face turned away from the guard. The wild grass was barely tall enough to conceal him, as he lay on his stomach in his dingy brown shirt and torn trousers. He listened for sounds that the guard had passed. When he could no longer hear movement he turned his head slowly to face the main house. Jarvis saw through the grass that the guard had stopped to lean against the back wall. The solider rested comfortably on one of the barrels. He was dressed in uniform but had failed to button his shirt and jacket properly. The soldier glanced to each side, pulled a flask from behind his belt and began to drink.

Rum, thought Jarvis.

Rum had been a poison to the troops since their arrival and, external forces aside, was the military's greatest foe. Jarvis had seen strong and virile men fall ill and useless from excess drink. Men who were regularly drunk were worse than useless and often became a danger to themselves and those around them. As an officer, Jarvis would have been angry to find one of the night watch drinking. However, in this case an inebriated guard proved advantageous.

As he lay in the open, semi-exposed, he knew time was against him. The rest of the men would soon awake and the camp would be bustling with activity. An object struck the ground to the west of the main house with a great thud. The startled guard quickly capped his flask, retrieved his musket and ran to investigate. Jarvis raised his head slightly to watch as the guard rounded the corner out of sight. He looked back to the bushes to see John Davis with his thumb in the air and a smile on his face. Jarvis scrambled to his feet and raced toward the quartermaster's tent. He hesitated at the door, took a deep breath, and threw open the flap.

Inside was completely dark, except for the dim light of the

dawning of the sun that seeped in through the gap around the bottom of the tent. Jarvis kept the flap open slightly to allow as much light in as possible. There were two tables on either side of the tent with boxes and crates stacked on top and piled neatly beneath them. Quietly and carefully, he rummaged through wood boxes in search of necessary provisions. He found an empty satchel and began to fill it with bags of beans and flour, rice and dried salt fish. There was a musket in the far corner with a horn half full of powder. He retrieved them both and set the horn on the table. He held the musket in his hands and looked for some musket balls.

All at once the front flap on the tent burst open. Instinctually, Jarvis pointed the unloaded musket toward the opening. A young man entered and walked in stiffly with his chin toward the sky. John Davis entered close behind him, with Jarvis's knife pointed at the back of the young man's neck.

"This bloke was wander'n 'round outside," John Davis whispered. He reached back and closed the flap behind him. He pushed the young man into the middle of the dark tent and pointed the knife at him with a threatening gesture. "You make one sound, mate, an' I'll slit your throat."

The scrawny young man cowered between Jarvis and John Davis with his head down and his shoulders slumped forward. He was little more than a silhouette until John Davis struck a match and held it high in the air. Aided by the light, Jarvis got a better look at the lad. His stringy brown hair hung in front of his gaunt face. He wore a leather vest over a white shirt and a blood stained apron. In the darkness and shadows Jarvis could not be completely sure, but thought he knew him.

"Smitty?" he asked.

"Yes, sir," the surprised young man replied, and looked up at Jarvis.

"You know 'im?" John Davis questioned. The flame reached the end of the match stick and burnt his finger. He flicked the hot stick to the side and swore.

"I do," Jarvis replied. "He is the quartermaster's aid."

"I'm the quartermaster now, sir," Smitty corrected, sheepishly. "Ole Casterson took sick an' died, leav'n me with a promotion of sorts."

"Do you remember me?" Jarvis asked him.

"Yes sir, Major Jarvis."

"Jarvis. Just Jarvis, my boy."

"An' I'm rutty Galileo," John Davis interrupted impatiently. "What are we gonna do with 'im?"

"Calm down," Jarvis pleaded. "This one we can trust. Smitty, we need your help. I need to find the map of the northern wilderness area."

"The land of look behind?" asked Smitty.

"That's right," Jarvis said. "Do you know where it is?"

"Yes sir. It's in the officer's quarters."

"Could you get it for us?" Jarvis asked.

"Yes sir," Smitty replied. He rumbled around in a box on the table in front of him. Finally, he produced a lantern and lit another match. The room filled with light. Young Smitty had grown considerably since the last time Jarvis had seen him. In the three years that he served with Lubolo and the black regiment he had on several occasions passed in and out of the outpost. However, they never stayed more than a night and slept far away from the other troops. Jarvis had not seen or thought of the young quartermaster since the night he met Lubolo. "Begging your pardon sir, but what's going on? Who's this and where are your men?"

"I do not have time to explain Smitty," Jarvis said. "But it is vitally important that no one know we are here. This is a mission requiring the utmost discretion. Are you up for it?"

"Yes sir." Smitty did not move or break eye contact. "Forgive me for saying sir, but I'm not as stupid as you think. You're not back 'ere with this feller for an important mission, are ya?"

Jarvis paused and weighed his options. He looked at Smitty's shadowed face. This was not the eager boy he remembered. The glint in his eye was gone, replaced with a jaded caution beyond his years. There was a confidence in his voice that disarmed Jarvis. He resolved to come clean with the young quartermaster and let the chips fall where they may.

"No, Smitty," Jarvis began. "There is no mission. Lubolo and his men are dead. We were ambushed in the jungle and wiped out; all except me. We need a map so we can navigate our way back into the wilderness."

"To find the lot what ambushed you?"

"No," Jarvis replied.

"You're deserting then?" Smitty asked directly.

Jarvis confirmed his question with a solemn nod. John Davis looked uneasy with the conversation and the situation on a whole. He still pointed the knife at Smitty and looked anxiously back and forth between him and Jarvis.

"Take me with you," Smitty quickly pleaded. It was as if he had already given it a good deal of thought.

"If you can get the map you can come with us," Jarvis said after a brief pause.

"'old on a bloody minute," John Davis whispered angrily. "I don't know 'im from Adam an' now 'e's com'n along?"

"That's right," Jarvis said. "I vouch for him and that is all you need know."

"Well, 'is take is com'n outta your share, that's for sure." John Davis relaxed his stance and tucked the knife back in his purple trousers.

"My take?" Smitty asked.

"We're going after treasure hidden in the land of look behind. Pirate's gold."

"Buccaneers, mate," John Davis pleaded. "Oh, who bloody cares? Go get the map already."

John Davis pulled back the flap and stepped to the side with a grand gesture to usher the young quartermaster out of the tent. Smitty nodded toward Jarvis before he nervously made his way toward the exit.

"Nice to meet you, Mr. Galileo, sir," he whispered, as he passed by John Davis and stepped out into the cool morning air.

Annoyed by the newest addition to their quest, John Davis

rolled his eyes and let the flap fall closed. Jarvis smiled brightly, amused at his level of frustration, but did not dare speak further. Without a word, the two of them set to work. They filled several shoulder bags with additional provisions and helped themselves to the beef and bread, which had been prepared for the troop's morning meal. Smitty returned just as Jarvis secured a small black cast iron pan for cooking.

"Have you got it?" Jarvis asked.

"Yes sir," Smitty said. He held up a large folded piece of paper. "And I got a compass as well."

"Brilliant, Smitty, just brilliant," Jarvis praised the young steward.

"We'd better go now," Smitty warned. "The coast is clear, but the men will wake soon."

Jarvis took the map and compass, placed them carefully in one of the bags, and threw it over his shoulder. He slung the powder horn over the other shoulder and grabbed the musket. With the barrel, he pulled back the flap and peered out toward the main house, on the lookout for the night watchman who would most certainly still be on patrol.

The sun crested over the peaks to the east and ushered in the morning. There were still no sounds of movement or activity but in the light of a new day they were exposed and had to move quickly. Each of them carried a shoulder bag, filled with provisions enough to last several days. Smitty opened the tent flap fully and held it back while Jarvis led the way outside. He immediately turned right and headed back toward the cover of the thick jungle bush to the north. John Davis followed close behind him and Smitty brought up the rear. With purpose, the men trotted away from the camp. Jarvis kept low to the ground and did not bother to look back.

"Hey!" a voice from behind them shouted. "You there, where do you think you're going?"

All three of them stopped and spun around. An officer sat on the step, just outside the back door to the main house. He was not yet fully dressed for the day and was bare foot, with a shiny black boot in one hand. Jarvis, who had been away from the outpost for some time, did not recognize the man. The officer had a thick bushy mustache and sideburns. He wore a pair of white trousers with white suspenders to match. His shirt had yet to be buttoned and his raspy voice indicated he had only recently woken up. His general level of angst aside, Jarvis could see he was in no position to pursue them.

"Run," Jarvis directed his companions.

An anxious Smitty reacted faster than John Davis and lurched forward. He smashed into the blonde buccaneer and nearly knocked him to the ground. Jarvis, meanwhile, had broken into a run, although he still limped ever so slightly. Smitty and John Davis recovered from their collision and headed after Jarvis.

"Stop!" the officer on the back step yelled, as he hurriedly put his on his other boot. "Stop right there!"

His shouts aroused several of the men from their tents and the camp suddenly came to life. The flask toting night watchman staggered around the side of the main house, musket in hand. The stunned soldier looked toward the back door at his commanding officer, who had finished putting on his boots and come to his feet.

"There!" The officer pointed to the fleeing trio. "Over there!"

The soldier looked out toward the jungle and saw Jarvis, John Davis, and Smitty. Surrounded by a sea of green bush, they bounded toward the wall of trees. Unsure what had happened or what to do the soldier looked back at mustached officer, who now stood several paces from the main house.

"Don't just stand there, you idiot," the officer shouted. "Shoot them!"

The soldier briefly fumbled with his musket before he hastily raised it to his shoulder and fired a shot. Jarvis reached the tree line first, just as the shot was fired. He stopped behind the safety of a tree, out of the line of fire, and looked back to see Smitty sprawled out flat on the ground. Instinctively, he dropped his pack and started to go back. John Davis, who had just reached the trees himself, caught him by the arm and said, "What are ya doing, mate? Leave 'im."

Jarvis shook free of his grasp and glared at him. He thrust the musket into his hand and continued toward the fallen quartermaster. As he did, he looked back up toward the camp. Four men, from up near the tents, advanced on their position. The soldier who had fired the shot was busy reloading in the distance. Another man had emerged from the main house and was engaged in an animated conversation with the officer with the bushy mustache. From behind the barricade they shouted inaudible instructions at the soldiers that bore down on them. Smitty stirred and started to stand before Jarvis reached him.

"Are you all right?" he asked. He bent down and quickly helped him to his feet. "Are you hit?"

Smitty patted his torso and shook his head, "No, I'm fine."

"Let's go," said Jarvis. He turned and led Smitty back toward the sanctuary of the jungle bush.

They breached the tree line and looked around for John Davis, who was nowhere to be seen. Jarvis glanced back over his shoulder. The group of soldiers from the camp had slowed at the bottom of the hill and spread out, with the muskets ready. With his hand still closed tight around Smitty's arm, Jarvis hurried deeper into the jungle. They raced through the knee high ferns, all the while being sure to keep trees between themselves and their pursuers. Jarvis moved with purpose. He zigged and zagged through the overgrowth, as if on a predetermined course. He did not look back but could hear the soldiers as they grew closer with each step. Smitty stumbled along behind him, for the most part being dragged by the former Major. They turned uphill and began to climb, sure to keep themselves as low to the ground as possible while still at a near run.

Another shot was fired, Jarvis heard the musket ball impact a nearby rock and felt a piece of debris deflect off his boot. At the top of the hill they passed between two large trees. Jarvis threw Smitty to the ground behind a large tree root that jutted up out of the earth. His look to Smitty conveyed that he expected him to conceal himself. Smitty dutifully tucked himself back behind the large root. Jarvis ran up ahead another hundred paces and dove into a tall patch of ferns. Moments later, the group of soldiers thundered passed their hiding places. The soldiers shouted to one another about which way they should go and where they might have disappeared to. They passed by like a herd of cattle and soon the sound of their footsteps faded into the distance.

When he was certain they were gone, Jarvis got up and headed back toward Smitty. He stopped dead in his tracks when, between the two large tree trunks, he saw the officer with the bushy mustache. The officer's face was clenched and troubled, whether from anger or his trudge up the hill Jarvis could not tell. He drew his pistol and took aim at Jarvis, who stood frozen with nowhere to turn. All of a sudden, the officer's head lunged forward and his body crumbled to the ground. His fall revealed John Davis, who stood behind him with the butt of the musket held at shoulders height. Jarvis breathed a deep sigh of relief. Smitty climbed out from his hiding place and he and Jarvis walked over to meet John Davis, who stood over the fallen officer.

"Ya could 'ave left me with some shot an' powder, ya know," John Davis said testily, as he stooped down and picked up the officer's pistol. He tucked it behind his belt in the front of his trousers.

"There needed to be something to entice you to remain," Jarvis said. He stooped down to examine the body of the mustached officer.

"Is 'e dead?" Smitty asked.

"No," Jarvis replied. He held a finger under his nostrils. "He's unconscious."

"No need to thank me," John Davis added sarcastically.

Jarvis performed a quick check of the officer's unconscious body, in search of anything that might be useful. He had nothing on his person other than the clothes on his back and the pistol, now in John Davis's possession. When he finished his inspection Jarvis stood up and extended his hand toward the pirate.

"I'll take that," Jarvis said. He looked down at the musket his buccaneer friend leaned on. John Davis turned over the musket without protest. Jarvis beckoned further, "And my knife as well."

"A'right," John Davis said. "But I'll be keeping the pistol."

Somehow, the idea of him being armed was both comforting and mildly unsettling. Jarvis wrestled with the esteem he had built for the man and the mistrust of people of his ilk. After a brief hesitation, Jarvis nodded in agreement and the moment of tension passed. John Davis handed over the knife and Jarvis tucked it in his boot.

"We'd better be going," Smitty said. "When Colonel Swanson comes 'round 'e won't be 'appy."

"Comes 'round," John Davis said. He pulled out the pistol and pointed it down at the officer's body. "Who said we was letting 'im come 'round?"

"Are you mad?" Jarvis rebuked. "One shot will bring that search party right down on top of us."

"A'right, give me your knife then."

"I have seen more than enough senseless killing, thank you," Jarvis said and stepped back to move the knife out of his reach.

"Senseless?" he shot back. "You think 'e's gonna wake up an' go 'bout 'is business like we was neva 'ere?"

"He knows nothing of our intentions or our destination," Jarvis said. "Pursuing us where we are headed would be foolhardy."

"Good thing 'is Majesty's officers ain't neva done nothing fool'ardy then," he retorted.

"We are wasting time. We are leaving him as he is and that is final," Jarvis declared.

"Well excuse me, mate, but I don't remember coming under your employ."

"We can't just kill 'im," Smitty spoke up.

"There, two against one. It's settled," Jarvis said.

"'e doesn't get a bloody vote," John Davis argued, and waved the pistol at Smitty.

Jarvis looked over his shoulder back up the hill, in the direction the search party had marched off. He turned back to look at Colonel Swanson, who lay immobilized on the ground between them. It was easy to argue the morality of sparing this man, but he knew doing so with a pirate would prove unprofitable. The practicality of such an act could be skewed in either direction. Killing him would mean one fewer pursuer, but it could also mean rallying all the forces in the region to bring them to justice for murdering an officer. In either case, Jarvis knew that they had little time to make a clean escape. He looked John Davis directly in the eyes, took in a deep breath, and attempted to plead to his sensibility.

"It does not profit us to kill this man," Jarvis said, and pointed to the body on the jungle floor. "It will only cause us additional grief and motivate his men to pursue us further. If we make our way down into that ravine, just there, and head north without delay we will be long gone before he awakes and the soldiers return."

John Davis shook his head in disgust but returned the pistol back behind his belt. "A'right mate, but on your 'ead be it if 'e comes back to 'aunt us."

Each of them glanced back up the hill for any signs of the soldiers return. When they determined the coast was clear they regarded each other, one more time, before Jarvis led the way down into the ravine. Smitty followed after him, as they lumbered down toward the bottom. John Davis stood over the fallen officer for a moment longer. He did one last perimeter check and headed down the hill after them.

Mi Na Sen Yu Na Come

Rhythmically, he strummed his fingers on top of the closed journal in front of him. He stood bent over the countertop and rested his weight on his elbows with one hand covering his mouth. The bright fluorescent lights from the beverage cooler illuminated the small dark storefront.

Gideon was accustomed to being awake in the early morning hours but usually it was the end of his day, not the beginning. He contemplated the events that had taken him from behind a dingy storefront counter in Arizona to this dingy storefront counter in Jamaica. Although he was very tired, from a semi-sleepless night, he could not keep a smile from his face. He felt alive in a way he had not felt since he left his beloved island. He looked over the counter and out into the room. His two friends lay on the floor fast asleep. Gideon had known them in what felt like completely separate lives, but there they were sharing a blanket on a dusty floor in a remote town, in the middle of his island home away from home.

Bigga snored loudly as he had done throughout the night. Somehow, despite the bone rattling reverberations that came from the gentle giant, Todd was tucked up comfortably by his side. Gideon could not blame his lack of sleep entirely on his large and loud friend. He felt a restless energy, a nearly overwhelming desire to get to the end of a journey that had only just begun.

He heard the back door open and turned around to see Tara enter through the doorway. She looked mildly surprised to see Gideon behind the counter. He greeted her with a smile and a nod. She carried with her a small JanSport backpack over her shoulder with a black plastic bag in her hand. Jamaicans called these black plastic bags scandal bags, because it concealed whatever scandalous items that might be in them. However, most times they simply concealed toiletries or groceries of no real interest.

She placed the blue backpack and scandal bag on the counter and walked back through the doorway. She reached out the backdoor and retrieved two machetes that leaned against the wall. With a glance to either side, she pulled the door closed behind her. As she rejoined Gideon behind the counter, Todd rolled over onto his side and threw his arm around Bigga. Tara and Gideon exchanged amused looks at the unlikely cuddle buddies before them. Gideon could not help but be drawn in by her warm smile. It made him question his first impression of her from last night where she had been rather harsh and abrasive.

The sound of Bigga's snoring stopped and he began to stir. As he awoke he looked down to see Todd's arm across his chest. He pushed it away as if it were a poisonous snake and rolled away from his sleeping companion. His sudden movement caused Todd to wake up with a start.

"Wha the rotted a gwan y'ere so?!" Bigga shouted at a still groggy Todd.

"Shhh!" Tara chided and looked out the window to the south. Everything outside was still dark as dawn had not quite begun to break.

"Wha ya do y'ere st'yar," Bigga continued in a whisper. "How ya hug up 'pon me so? Ya love man?"

"What?" a confused Todd asked.

"Mi say, do you love man?" Bigga said slowly and enunciated each word.

"No!" Todd answered emphatically. "I don't love man. I love women."

"Relax, Bigga," Gideon said, coming to his friend's rescue. "Ya just too cuddly, mi friend."

All four of them laughed and Bigga said, with a big smile, "Ya know dat's true, my yute."

The moment passed and the smiles fell from their faces as Tara hefted the machetes onto the counter. Gideon knew the terrain would be rough, nearly impenetrable in certain places, but that realization only just dawned on Todd and Bigga at the sight of the machetes. While much of their discussion had centered around the cave itself, and the mysterious symbol, they had given almost no consideration to how they would reach their remote destination. Gideon worried that his friends were not up to the challenge.

"Ya ready?" Gideon asked Tara.

"Yeah man, come wi a go."

"Wait man," Bigga interjected. "Me 'ungry. What 'bout breakfast?"

Without a word Tara reached into the scandal bag and pulled out a round brown cake, wrapped in cellophane, and tossed it toward Bigga. Todd reached up in front of him and snatched it out of the air. He looked down at it curiously, before Bigga wrestled it away from him and tore open the wrapper. Todd's blond hair stuck straight up, uncharacteristically messy from a poor night's sleep on the floor of the shop.

"What is that?" Todd asked.

"Bun," Bigga replied, as the crumbs shot from his mouth.

Tara tossed another bun to Todd and handed one to Gideon. He looked down at the familiar red and yellow HTB logo on the wrapper. This brown sweet bun was a common snack in Jamaica. Spiced bun was a dense brown cake with cinnamon and nutmeg, most often served with a chunk canned cheese. Gideon loved bun and cheese, although he questioned if the yellow substance sliced from the circular can was indeed cheese.

"Come now," Tara said again.

She handed one of the machetes to Gideon and kept the other

for herself. She discarded the black scandal bag in the waste bin and threw the backpack over her shoulder. Gideon quickly gathered the journal and followed her out the back door of the shop. Outside it was still dark, cool and quiet. They made their way down the back side of the shop toward the baby blue Lada to the north. Bigga and Todd talked excitedly as they exited. Tara turned around and shot them a dirty look. Todd, who was in mid-sentence when he caught sight of Tara, froze and pointed a finger of blame at Bigga. In turn Bigga slapped at Todd's finger and flashed a boyish smile at Tara. She held her finger to her lips, in a silent rebuke.

When they got to the taxi Bigga got behind the wheel and Todd squeeze passed the banana tree to reclaim the front seat. Tara walked to the back of the car and looked cautiously up and down the street. Gideon joined her. He rested his hand on the trunk and glanced down the dark street toward the south.

The dead silence of the morning was disrupted as Bigga turned the ignition. The Lada chugged and churned and attempted to turn over.

"Come on baby," Bigga pleaded.

One more chug and churn and the engine revved to life. Gideon turned and pulled open the back passenger's side door. He looked back at Tara, who had not moved. She stood and stared up the street to the north. Gideon spun around and leaned over the car in an attempt to follow her gaze. Twenty or thirty meters up the road there was dark silhouette, shrouded in blackness, beneath a tree. The sprawling tree grew on the other side of the street and shielded the ominous figure from the glow of the lone street light. Gideon looked nervously back at Tara.

"Get in da c'yar," she said. She did not blink but kept her eyes locked on whoever stood beneath the tree.

From her tone Gideon thought it best to save his questions for later. He jumped in the car, threw the journal on the seat next to him and closed the door. Through the dirty window he could still make out the haunting silhouette beneath the tree. Tara climbed in the back seat next to Gideon.

"Bigga, drive!" Gideon ordered.

"What's wrong?" Todd asked.

Gideon and Tara looked anxiously out the window toward the tree and did not answer. Bigga shifted the Lada into reverse and backed out onto the road. He spun the wheel to the right and the car swung onto the street, parallel with the front of the shop. As the headlights panned across the road they illuminated the man, who had stepped out from underneath the large tree into the middle of the road. The man had long thick dreadlocks and wore a sleeveless maroon shirt and black pants. Around his neck was a white and tan colored necklace, which appeared to be made of bone. The light from the street lamp behind him and the headlights in front shadowed the peaks and valleys in his muscular shoulders and forearms. The four occupants of the baby blue taxi stared out at the human roadblock that stood before them.

"Move dis c'yar now man," Tara told Bigga.

"A who dat?" Bigga asked.

"Move!" she shouted.

The gears grinded as he shifted the car into gear and jammed the gas pedal to the floor. The Lada lurched forward and threw them back in their seats. They sped straight toward the man in the middle of the road. Todd and Bigga's simultaneous shouts cascaded together as the car accelerated forward. Unflinching, the man stood straight and tall in their path. The beam from the headlights rose rapidly from his feet to the top of his head. His shoulder length dreadlocks and beard gave him the appearance of a black lion. He trained his eyes on the car, without fear, like a predator stalking its prey. At the last moment Bigga swerved to the left. The metal beast missed him by inches as they sped by. Todd, Gideon, and Tara all spun around to look out the back window. The man turned around to face the fleeing vehicle. With the glow from the street light directly over him he was once again a dark silhouette, framed by a bulb of light overhead. They watched anxiously for him to make a move as the car moved further and further away. A minute later they had rounded a bend and the man drifted out of sight. Bigga kept the pedal down as they sped down the narrow mountain road.

"What just happened?!" Todd shouted. "Who was that?!"

"'im right name is Marcus, but dem call 'im Mucaro," Tara answered calmly.

"Mucaro?" Gideon repeated.

"What is a Mucaro?" Todd asked.

"Not what, who. Mucaro is 'is name. Da local rude b'woys an' Rastas follow after 'im. Dem t'ink 'im 'ave powers," Tara explained.

"Powers?" Gideon asked. "You don't mean . . ."

"Yeah man," Tara confirmed solemnly. "Obeah."

Inside the car, all fell silent. The only noise was the sound of the bald tires squeaking and squealing around the turns of the road and the clinking and clanking of the old rusty frame. Gideon's attention was drawn out the driver's side window where the sky grew slowly brighter. A shadowy horizon had begun to form in the distance. He tried to make some sense out of the appearance of the mysterious man back in town. It could not be a coincidence that this obeah man was on the street in the early morning hours. Gideon considered a dozen possibilities all at once. It seemed the obeah man knew they were there, but did he know why? And did he know where they were headed? The questions remained, if he did know, why would he care and what were his intentions? He had tried to convince himself that Bammy's fear of the obeah man had been the trepidation of a superstitious old man. Now that he was faced with the reality of such a figure, he was forced to consider potential obstacles greater than those posed by nature.

"So let me get this straight," Todd began, and broke the momentary silence. "Mufasa back there is some kind of witch doctor; her old man is scared to death of him; he just faced down a car like a crazy matador and nobody here is overly concerned about that."

"'im was jus' trying to frighten you," Tara said.

"Well it worked," said Todd.

"Yeah man, mi nearly pooped mi pants," added Bigga.

"Tara," Gideon spoke and attempted to ignore the hysteria from the front seat. "How did he know we were here?"

"Nobody comes round 'ere without 'im know'n 'bout it," she said.

"You didn't tell anyone?"

"No man," she replied.

"Bammy?"

"No man, 'im na 'ave to fi do with 'im," she said. "Mucaro watches over da cockpits. If 'im na wan yu up y'ere den yu c'yan't come."

"Mi na sen yu na come," Bigga said to the rear view mirror.

"Yeah, man," Tara replied.

Bigga, who momentarily took his attention off the road, had to turn sharply to avoid veering into a ditch as the road banked right. The tires squealed and everyone was thrown to the left side of the car. Tara was flung into Gideon's lap. Bigga regained control and steadied the car. Tara pushed herself back into her seat and for a moment Gideon thought he saw a faint smile on her face. He smiled back, but she frowned at him and looked out the front window.

"Slow down man," Gideon barked at Bigga. "He's not going to catch us on foot."

A beautiful sunrise broke over the mountains to the east, bathing the sky in orange and red. Bigga lifted his foot off the pedal and the car slowed slightly as they reached the top of a plateau. On both sides of the road they could see the rolling hills of the cockpits. It looked like a field of giant green eggs as far as the eye could see. There was a misty white fog that filled the crevasses beneath the egg shaped summits. Gideon had seen many beautiful sunrises, growing up in the valley of the sun, but none had moved him the way this particular sunrise did. This sunrise ushered in a new day that brought with it endless possibilities. He usually took great comfort in routine, but suddenly felt exhilarated for a day like today, a day outside the routine. His apprehension over their encounter, with the frightening figure in Quickstep, all at once swept to the back of his mind.

"Why are they called cockpits?" Todd asked, as he stared out at the surrounding scenery.

"I read somewhere that the depressions between the peaks reminded people of cockfighting arenas; the cockpits," answered Gideon.

"And we're going in there?" asked Todd. "Super."

"Yeah man," answered Tara.

Todd shook his head softly with a look of awe on his face. Gideon looked at his friend with an odd sense of envy. The island was brand new to him and Gideon was certain he had never seen anything like it. Although he could not imagine being any happier than he was right now, he remembered how excited he had been to experience this beautiful country for the first time. He could hardly wait to explore the cave, to see something he too had never seen before.

Perhaps only a few people had.

He reached down to the floor of the car where the journal had slid during their flight and picked up the leather bound book. He looked around at the other passengers. Thankfully, Bigga had his attention back on the road. Todd and Tara gazed out their windows at the landscape that whisked by. Gideon looked around at the mist slathered peaks, shone down upon by the newly risen sun. He took a moment to enjoy his majestic mountain surrounding, but felt compelled to read on while he could. He knew once they reached the end of the road their long hike would begin. He opened to the page he had marked.

We have twice evaded the troops sent from the outpost to capture us. I foolishly believed that once clear of their perimeter they would abandon all attempts to pursue us, a fact that Mr. Davis reminds me of constantly.

Young Smitty has proved to be a great asset, a fact even the reluctant Mr. Davis cannot deny. He is eager to pull his weight and has seen that we are well fed, which was a blessing that has become our curse. We lost some of our provisions in our hasty escape. Still, we were confident we had more than sufficient for our trip and failed to ration properly. We ate well for several days but are now running short on food.

It seems I was overconfident in my ability to navigate through the wilderness, another fact that Mr. Davis brings up with regularity. We have come across many caves, but none with the proper marking. Fortune though seems to have finally smiled on us as we happened upon a stream that I recognized from my retreat and I believe the cave is less than a day's journey due north.

"What is that?" Tara asked.

Gideon looked up and saw that Tara watched him read. Her tone and expression were soft and it was clear her interest had been piqued. Gideon closed the journal and placed it on the seat between them.

"It's a journal."

"Yours?"

"No," he replied without elaborating. He attempted to walk the fine line between mysterious and enticing, and aloof and off-putting.

The look on her face told him which side he had fallen on. She pursed her lips, cocked her head sideways and stared intensely at him.

"It's the journal of Benjamin Jarvis, a British soldier from the sixteen hundreds," he explained. "It's why I'm here."

"Why we're here," Todd piped up from the front seat.

"Yeah man, we," Bigga added.

"Fine," Gideon conceded. "It is why we're all here. I believe he was up here in this area and may have gone to the cave that bears the marking from Corey's picture."

"So what?" she said.

"So what?" Gideon replied with surprise. "So what? That doesn't interest you?"

"Na really, what do yu 'ope to find?"

"That's not important. I just want to go up there and have a look. Maybe we find something and maybe we find nothing but I have to know."

"All you're gonna find is trouble."

"And what makes you so sure?"

"From da time mi was likkle mi fadda 'as taken mi up inna da cockpits," she said. "An' wi a go everywhere up d'ere except fi dis cave. 'im say wi mustn't bodder with it. 'im say di obeah man come an' take yu 'way if yu go dung inna dat cave."

"That dude back in town?" Todd asked.

"No man," Tara said. "Mucaro 'as taken after 'im fadda. A 'im 'ad da real power. 'im name was Chaka and nobody mess with 'im."

"Was?" asked Gideon.

"A 'ole heap a y'ears ago 'im disappeared," she said. "'im come up 'ere an' nobody ever saw 'im again."

"So is Bammy afraid of Mufasa or Shaka Zulu?" Todd asked.

"A Chaka 'im a fear," she said. "A 'im could cause man fi disappear."

"So then what do we have to worry about if Chaka is gone?" Gideon asked.

"Bammy say 'im na gone. 'im up 'ere an' 'im watching over da cockpits," she said.

"Do you believe that?" he asked.

"Mi na know," she said.

"If Chaka had the real power, do we need to be worried about Mucaro?" Gideon asked.

"Ya always need fi worry 'bout a man trying to live up to 'is fadda," she said.

The car slowed rapidly and caused Tara and Gideon to sway toward the seat backs in front of them. Gideon looked out the front window as they shuttered to a complete stop. They had reached the end of the road. In front of them was nothing but green trees and bushes. From this point on they would be on foot. Todd was the first one out of the car, followed by Tara and Bigga. Gideon looked around inside the car to make sure nothing important was left behind. He collected the journal and the machete Tara had given him and joined the others in the fresh morning air. Tara, with her machete in hand, put on her backpack and scanned the perimeter to get her bearings. Bigga walked to the back of the car and opened the trunk with his key. In the trunk were two backpacks, a tire iron and a spare tire with an old rusty rim. Gideon removed his backpack from the trunk and attempted to wipe off some of the dust and rust stains from the shoulder straps. Todd unzipped his pack, almost unconsciously, and checked the contents briefly before he quickly zipped it up again and swung it over his shoulder.

"Where's my pack?" Bigga teasingly asked.

"We weren't counting on having you with us, big fella," Gideon said. He tucked the journal safely in one of the outer pockets of his backpack.

"Yeah man, mi know."

"It's gonna be quite a hike. Are you up for it?" asked Gideon.

"Yeah man. Ya 'ave some snacks in d'ere fi me?"

"Sure thing," Todd said, as he patted his pack. "Beef jerky and granola bars from the good ole U.S. of A."

"Jerk beef?" Bigga said excitedly. "Mi c'yan't wait fi try dat."

Jamaica jerk was an all-spice mixture, traditionally used with chicken or pork. It was a spicy blend of pimento, scallion, thyme, garlic, salt, and scotch bonnet peppers. Once applied to the meat, it was slowly smoked all day in custom metal oil drums, cut lengthwise and held together with hinges. In the evenings the drums were wheeled out on pushcarts to roadsides all across the island where mouthwatering chicken and pork were bought and sold. Gideon did not have the heart to tell Bigga that the hard and dry beef jerky was nothing like the succulent, fall-off-the-bone chicken and pork he anticipated. He just walked by him and patted him on the back with a smile.

"Come," Tara said. "If wi move wi c'yan make it d'ere and back before dark."

"How far is it to the cave?" Todd asked.

"Jus' up d'ere so."

Gideon laughed. He knew it was a good distance to the cave and had learned not to put much weight in a Jamaican's proclamation of time or distance. Tara looked at Gideon with a confused expression. She shook her head and walked off in the direction she had pointed, followed by her three outsiders. A few steps away from the car and they found themselves waist deep in the lush grass, bushes and ferns. They stepped through a wall of trees and the car and road disappeared behind them. Crossing this threshold was like stepping back in time. Gideon listened to the wild birds whose chirping and singing filled the air. With every step his heart filled with energy and optimism.

They had hiked only a few hundred meters when Gideon looked back and, to his disappointment, found that Todd and Bigga had already fallen behind. Todd, who was never in a hurry, walked several paces behind Bigga. He had his camera in hand and looked to be enjoying the scenery. He raised his camera toward the hills in front of them and took a picture. Then he turned his camera toward Bigga, who struggled to bushwhack his way through the dense overgrowth in front of him. He giggled and snapped another photo.

"Hold up a second," Gideon said to Tara.

She stopped and waited for them to catch up. Gideon instructed Todd how to use the machete. He pantomimed the necessary motions, and then handed over his machete. Bigga, who breathed and heaved heavily, took out a red handkerchief from his back pocket and wiped his sweaty brow. Gideon had his doubts about his friend's ability to make the journey and already regretted allowing him to come.

Tara stood impatiently with her hand on her hip and Gideon held up an open hand toward her in a plea for patience. He pulled out one of his water bottles and offered Bigga a drink. He took the water bottle with a grateful nod, tilted it back and guzzled it down.

"You sure you want to do this man?" asked Gideon. "No shame in waiting in the car."

"So da obeah man c'yan come an' take mi 'way?" Bigga squealed. "No man."

After they rested for just a couple minutes, Tara again led the way into the jungle. They made their way through the thick brush and down into a ravine. They had no sooner reached the bottom when they started a steep climb directly opposite from where they entered. With the machete that Gideon had given him, Todd was able to keep pace with Tara and Gideon, however, he stayed back and helped Bigga along.

For the first hour there was a quasi-discernable trail; although it was apparent that this trail was seldom traveled, as the overgrowth of bushes and vines all but covered the small footpath. It was just wide enough for a single person to stride along, which meant Gideon had to walk behind Tara. He kept a wary eye on his friends and each time he could no longer see them he would call for a halt. This scenario played out again and again as they made their way through the dense vegetation and mountainous terrain. Finally, in the early afternoon they broke for lunch at the base of a particularly large limestone cliff face. Bigga plopped down on the ground and Todd shared a half-empty water bottle with him. Gideon found some shade beneath a cluster of bamboo stems and Tara walked over to sit down next to him.

"Wi shoulda been d'ere already," she whispered, and shot an accusing look toward Bigga.

"He's doing his best."

"'is best isn't good enough. If wi don't 'urry wi won't make it back before nightfall."

He was less worried about being in the jungle after dark than he was about their limited supplies. Between the four of them they only had six water bottles. Gideon and Todd had each shared their water with Bigga. His best estimate was that, between the three of them they barely had a bottle and a half. He knew there was an abundance of fresh water in the cockpits but had little clue where to find it.

"We can't leave him," he said. "He doesn't know the way back and even if he did we don't have any water to spare for him."

"Fine," she agreed. "D'ere's a spring back up d'ere so. It's outta de way but wi c'yan go up d'ere an' leave 'im fi da way back. 'e'll 'ave water an' wi c'yan leave 'im somet'ing to eat."

Gideon had to admit it was a good plan, and he was just as anxious and impatient as Tara to reach the cave. Todd walked up to where they sat and stood just outside of the shaded area. His face was red and sun-beaten as he looked up at the cliff in front of him. Gideon looked skyward and back behind him to the top of the cliff. He sat in awe of the majesty of this beautiful country and felt small against the towering backdrop.

"You know what I've been thinking about?" Todd asked.

"What's that?" replied Gideon.

"Glenn would have loved this," Todd replied. He still looked up at the massive cliff face. "Everything about it."

When they were kids it was Glenn who always led the games of make-believe. He laid out scenarios of grand adventures in magical lands and painted beautiful mental pictures with great detail. While his vivid imagination generally centered around science fiction and super heroes, it was always a product of his own invention. The game he loved most was called "Lost Boys." They would pretend that the three of them had no parents or anyone to look after them and they traveled the country in a Lamborghini helping people in distress. There was a sense of liberation pretending you were on your own and that nobody knew where you were. This imagined freedom, especially to a child, opened up a whole new world of possibilities.

"While you were gone, he drug me all over The Superstitions looking for some Apache wind cave. That chubby little guy couldn't play ball for five minutes, but he could hike up in the mountains all day." Todd squatted down into the shaded area in front of Tara. "He ever tell you about that cave?"

"Yeah," Gideon said. "He wrote me about it once."

The truth was Glenn had written him several letters that featured his obsession with the mythical Apache storm cave. Matter of fact, it was the topic of the last letter he ever received from Glenn. It was a short letter and, from the barely legible handwriting, Gideon could tell it was written in a hurry. It mentioned a cave and a discovery. He sounded almost paranoid about the fact that nobody believed him. He told Gideon that this would be his last letter to him. Gideon remembered the worry and fear his letter caused him. He wrote to him immediately to ask what he meant and assure him they would talk more about it at Christmas, when he could call home. From the states to Jamaica a letter could take a couple of weeks to arrive and the return took the same. This month long lag was like a bad long distance connection on the telephone, only in writing. The week after he received Glenn's letter, Gideon got a letter from his mother saying that Glenn had gone missing and people were looking for him. The following week, when the mail arrived, he was handed the biggest stack of letters he had ever received. There was another letter from his mother, one from Todd, one from Liz, and one from Mrs. Bicklesby. They all said the same thing: Glenn was gone. It felt unreal. He was so far removed that he could not fully wrap his mind around it. Glenn's funeral had already come and gone, without him even knowing what happened.

"They said he must have fallen down a mine shaft or something," a melancholy Todd said, to no one in particular. "We looked for him for days."

"Yeah," Gideon said, as a conversational reflex, still deep in thought.

"He never shut up about you," Todd said.

Gideon swallowed hard. The notion that he might have changed things plagued his mind.

"I miss him, ya know?" Todd said.

"Me too, man," Gideon replied.

"Sorry 'bout your friend," Tara said.

Both Gideon and Todd looked over at their beautiful guide. They were so engrossed in their conversation they had forgotten she was there. Gideon recalled the conversation Todd had interrupted and the issue at hand. The only problem now was that their plan involved, at least temporarily, abandoning his friend. He thought of Glenn all alone in the desert wilderness of the Superstition Mountains. He imagined his body lying at the bottom of a dark abandoned mine shaft. He looked over at Bigga, who had just come to his feet and bent over to wipe the mud off his pants.

The cockpits were full of sinkholes and sudden drops, without an experienced guide they stood little chance of making it through without serious injury or worse.

"Tara knows a place we can get some water," Gideon told Todd.

"Good, 'cause I'm almost out," Todd said. He gestured toward Bigga. "It takes a lot to keep the big fella hydrated."

"About that," Gideon started.

"Yeah?"

"Any way you can prod him to go a little faster?"

"Not with beef jerky," Todd quipped. "If ya had some fried chicken I could dangle it in front of him. That might help."

"Todd!" Gideon exclaimed. "That's racist."

"What's racist?" Tara asked.

"Well, uh, you know," Gideon replied hesitantly. "They, um, say, uh, black people love fried chicken."

"We do," was her matter-of-fact and slightly amused reply.

"Yeah, uh, I know," Gideon said. "I just, ah, never mind."

"I'll get him moving," Todd said. He smiled and winked at Gideon's awkwardness. He turned, walked back toward Bigga and shouted, "Oy! How do you say 'hurry your round rump up' in Jamaican?"

Gideon turned to face Tara. He leaned in slightly and said, quietly but firmly, "I can't leave him. We'll stay closer together and try and go as fast as we can."

She furrowed her brow, pursed her lips and sucked in air through the gaps in her teeth, making a derisive hissing noise. She offered no objection but set off angrily toward the east, with no regard for the rest of the group. Gideon waited for Todd and Bigga to reach him and the three of them followed quickly after their guide. Although their pace had slowed a bit, they stayed closer together and took fewer breaks. Tara stayed far ahead of them, as both Gideon and Todd hung back to encourage Bigga. They climbed up a particularly daunting incline and the afternoon sun beat down on their backs. Gideon wondered if Tara had chosen this route to intentionally punish him for not going along with her plan. Their descent down the other side caused them to fall even further behind Tara and about half way down they lost sight of her. By the time they reached the bottom she was nowhere to be found.

"Tara!" Gideon shouted.

They waited quietly and listened for a reply. Gideon scanned up and down the ravine. After a few moments they heard the rustling of bushes and the snapping of twigs; someone or something approached their position. They all turned toward the sound and watched the immature bamboo stocks move as the sounds drew nearer. Gideon felt a wave of panic wash over him as the thought occurred to him that Tara might not be the only one out there. His fears were quelled; however, as Tara emerged from the bush with one mighty hack at the bamboo stalks with her machete.

"What's wrong wit' yu?" Tara demanded. "Uno c'yan't come out 'ere yelling up an' down da place."

"Sorry," Gideon said. "You're right. I wasn't thinking."

Just then they heard the sound of snapping branches and rustling bushes from behind them. Gideon, Todd and Bigga spun around to look back toward the new sound. Shoulder high bushes moved in the distance. They could not yet see who or what was the cause of the commotion. Gideon was certain he did not want to find out.

"Come," Tara said firmly.

She turned and headed back in the direction from which she came, opposite the rustling bushes. With ease she circumnavigated the trees, bushes, and branches in her path. Gideon had to run to keep up with her and plowed through leaf laden branches. He glanced off tree after tree with his broad shoulders on his way through the thick jungle foliage. It reminded him of the gauntlet drills in football practice. He heard Todd behind him, as he panted and gasped for air in his friend's wake. At the moment, their shared fear was of the unknown. Gideon did not know where they were or where they were headed. He did not know who or what was behind them and whether it meant them harm. His thoughts turned to the man in the middle of the street earlier that morning. Had he followed them? What did he want? Did he have cause or the authority to stop them? His biggest fear was not the threat he might be to their journey, but that he might be a threat to their lives.

He continued to run after Tara as fast as he could. She was within of few paces of him and hopped to the left around a tree trunk. Gideon did not react quickly enough and slammed into the tree with his right shoulder. The impact spun him around and Todd smashed into him at full speed. They grabbed hold of each other to steady themselves and somehow kept their feet. To Gideon's horror he looked back and did not see Bigga. Immediately, he ran back the way they had come to rescue his friend. He rounded a tree, cut through two tall thick bushes, and caught sight of Bigga's body. He lay face down on the ground, amongst the ferns. Quickly, Gideon ran to where he had fallen.

"You all right?"

"Yeah man," Bigga said. "Mi jus' tripped."

The bushes behind them began to rustle and shake. Gideon reached down and grabbed hold of Bigga's hand to help him up. His heart raced and another wave of panic overcame him. Before Bigga could get to his feet a wiry old man emerged from the bush next to them.

"Bammy?" Gideon said, with relief and confusion.

The old man stood there, tall and strong, with a familiar well-worn nub of a machete in his hand. He wore the same clothes as the night before, the same clothes as he had worn on their first expedition, with high water pants and his shirt still unbuttoned. Unlike Bigga and Gideon, he did not draw heavy breaths after all the pursuit. He did not look tired, but his face wore a worried and anxious expression.

"Where Tara da d'ere?"

Almost on cue Tara and Todd crashed through the bushes and stopped in an attack position. Their arrival now filled the small clearing and its five occupants eyed each other. Tara looked first at Bammy and then to Bigga, who Gideon now helped to his feet. Todd stepped in front of Tara toward Bammy.

"Judas Priest, old man!" Todd exclaimed. "That's twice I've nearly crapped my pants because of you."

"Daddy, mi told ya na fi come," Tara said.

"An' mi told yu na fi take d'ese b'woys out 'ere."

"Mi a grown woman an' mi c'yan make my own choices."

"An' what about your son?" Bammy asked.

"Mi lef' 'im with uno."

"An' what if ya na come back?" he asked. "All 'im will 'ave is a broken-down old man fi care fi 'im. A dat yu want?"

"We'll be back dis eve'ling," she assured him.

"Not like dis ya won't."

She did not immediately answer him but exhaled and hung her head. Gideon was uncomfortable with his role in the tension between father and daughter. In his single-minded determination to reach the cave he had given little consideration to the impact his quest would have on others. He wanted to say something, to try and help, but nothing came to mind so he stood there quietly and watched Tara to see what she would do.

"Uno 'ad an 'our 'ead start an' mi catch yu," Bammy went on. "An' if mi c'yan find uno d'en 'e c'yan find uno."

"Dem jus' wan' fi see da cave an' look 'round," Tara argued. "D'ere's no 'arm in dat."

"Uno t'ink say 'im fi let yu?" Bammy said. He raised his voice and pointed his machete into the bush.

"Who him?" Gideon said, as he finally found his voice. "Mucaro?"

Bammy turned his head and faced Gideon with a look so serious that a chill shot down his spine. "Mucaro will try fi stop uno. Chaka *will* stop uno."

A gust of wind whipped through the group and rushed further down the ravine, entirely unconcerned with their standoff; whether coincidently or not, it added to the drama of the moment. Bammy continued to stare at Gideon, who stood in the thick of the group. Bammy was directly in front of him with Bigga just to his right. Behind him Tara and Todd stood silently by and watched and waited. Gideon began to question if any of this was worth it.

He did not know what, if anything, he hoped to find. In his heart, he believed there was something significant that awaited them but was afraid he might be wrong. He looked over at Bigga and saw the exhaustion in his face. He looked back at Todd and wondered how motivated he was to continue. He thought about how easy it would be to turn back. He remembered Professor Gervaise had urged him to forget the cave and go lay on the beach. He shuddered at the thought that they might encounter the dark shadowy figure from Quickstep in this inhospitable wilderness. Still, there were so many questions that remained. If he stopped now he would never know. That he could not live with.

"How far is the cave from the spring?" he asked.

"Two, maybe t'ree 'ours," Tara said. "But we 'ave to move quickly."

"All right then," Gideon began. "Here's the plan. We're going to go to the spring and get some water. After that, Bammy, if you take Bigga back to the car we'll head up to the cave just to see what we see. I promise we'll be quick and careful, no unnecessary risks. You have my word."

"No amount of quick an' careful c'yan guarantee your safety out 'ere," Bammy said.

"Daddy," Tara started, but Bammy held up his hand to silence her. He gently took Bigga by the arm and led him forward past his daughter, without another word. She watched as her father walked away, toward the spring. There was a soft rolling sound of thunder to the west. Light gray clouds began to show over the summit against the clear blue sky. A cool breeze cut through the heat of the day.

"Come," Tara said and she walked after Bammy and Bigga.

The trek to the spring took less than twenty minutes but the climb was arduous and, despite the storm clouds that threatened in the distance, the heat from the afternoon bore down on them. On either side of the spring were tall trees that grew close together. Their canopies formed a beautiful green ceiling.

Bigga collapsed as soon as he reached the shade. Tara and Bammy stood a few meters from the edge of the water and looked cautiously up and down the fern-laden shoreline. Knee-high wild grass grew amongst the ferns along the bank to conceal where the ground stopped and the water began. Todd and Gideon got out their water bottles and removed the lids. They walked to Tara and Bammy and stood between them. After a brief pause they stepped forward and began to stoop toward the water. In unison Tara and Bammy raised their machetes and formed a broadsided X to block their way forward. When they stopped, Tara removed her machete from Todd's chest and pointed at the water. Gideon squinted toward the spot. Just above the grass he saw the water gently rolling over a small cluster of rocks. As he looked closer though, the cluster moved slightly. He shook his head to clear his eyes and looked again. The outline of a dark scaly body lurked in the bushes at the water's edge, a crocodile lay in wait. Todd let out a groan when he saw it.

"Mind da waters, dem thick with dem t'ings d'ere," she said.

"You saved my life," Todd said to Tara.

She smiled and walked up the bank. Gideon smiled at Bammy and nodded in appreciation.

"Thank you," said Gideon.

"I think I'm in love with her," Todd whispered to Gideon.

Unfortunately, he did not whisper quiet enough that Bammy could not hear. From the look of displeasure on his face it was clear he did not appreciate Todd's level of affection for his daughter. Bammy pushed passed them and joined Tara up the bank. After several minutes a safe spot was found to refill the water bottles. Todd carried water back to Bigga and soon they all had their fill. They refilled the bottles once more and prepared to depart. The clouds crept up behind them and the sky was now a light gray. The noises of birds and insects still filled the jungle all around them, and Gideon felt a familiar euphoric calm well up from inside him until it burst out in a wave of serenity that enveloped him.

Todd walked over to a large green tree full of reddish orange fruit, which they passed on the way to the spring. He picked a piece of fruit and examined it.

"What's this?"

"Ackee," Bigga replied, still seated on the ground.

"Can you eat it?"

"Yeah man, it cooks nice. Yu h'eat it with salt fish," Bigga said. "But uno 'ave to cook it right or it's poisonous."

"Poisonous!" Todd exclaimed, hysterically. "Is there anything in this place that's not trying to kill us?"

"We better get going." Tara looked up at the dark clouds above.

Gideon walked over to Bigga and helped him to his feet. He handed him one of his water bottles. "If you don't want to wait for us, I understand."

"No man," Bigga said. "Mi a go stay. Sorry mi couldn't go all da way with uno."

"Me too man," Gideon said, as he leaned in to hug him.

Bigga recoiled away from him, threw up his arms and pushed him back, "Wha'pun to ya Goodwin? Uno c'yan't come huggle up 'pon me like dat. Ya love man?"

Gideon laughed, having momentarily forgotten his friend's aversion to male affection of any kind. "No man, mi na love man, Bigga, mi love yu!"

"Wha?! Don't bother tell mi say ya love mi, cause mi na tell no man mi love 'im," Bigga shouted.

They both smiled and Gideon grabbed him by the shoulders. He and Bigga shook hands and he walked over to join Tara by the stream bank. Todd threw the ackee fruit into a bush and walked up to Bigga.

"We'll see you in a little while," said Todd.

"Yeah man, likkle more," Bigga said and extended his fist toward him. "Respect."

They bumped fists and Todd joined Tara and Gideon. With a frown on his face, Bammy looked over at his daughter. She stood straight and strong with her arms folded and gave her father a gracious nod. Bammy returned her nod and left without a word. Before he left, Bigga forced a smile onto his round face but could not conceal the disappointment in his eyes. While Bammy and Bigga headed back to the west, into the brewing storm, Gideon,

Tara and Todd followed the stream north. As the group parted the rain began to fall.

Somewhat sheltered from the rain by the trees they made their way along the banks of the stream, but soon left its protection when the stream turned back to the west. They crossed at a spot where the water ran ankle deep and continued north, deeper into the cockpits.

The rain made an already treacherous journey even more difficult. Within minutes their clothes were soaked. It was impossible not to slip as they climbed up and down the mountainous terrain. The vegetation was thick and lush and now dripped with rain water. Gideon felt more exhausted than he had under the heat of the sun. In spite of the weather, they made better time without Bigga. Gideon was hopeful it would not be much longer before they reached the cave. Tara stopped underneath a massive mahogany tree, which allowed the group a brief respite from the rain. Beyond the tree was a clearing, full of bushes and vines that ran along the jungle floor and stretched out several hundred yards to the base of two giant summits. She pointed ahead beyond clearing at a gap between the summits.

"Wi go t'rough d'ere," she said. "It's na long afta dat."

The two summits were at least sixty meters tall, the one on the right was covered in green bush and resembled the hundreds of other egg shaped peaks they had passed or climbed during the day. The summit on the left, although still covered by dark green bush on the back, showed an ashy limestone face and was bare on the top with light green moss between the rocks. It stood in stark contrast to the darker green that span the rest of the landscape. Gideon tried to take in the panorama, framed beautifully by the limbs that hung from the tree overhead. Despite the rain and the difficulty of their journey he felt grateful to be where they were. Todd had taken off his backpack and placed it on the ground; he squatted down and looked for something to eat. Tara rocked back and forth on the spot where she stood and looked at the ground. Gideon studied her for a few moments. He had not seen her behave in such a way. The strong confident woman that led them now seemed diminished, unsure and hesitant. Todd removed the wrapper from a granola bar and held it between his teeth as he stood up and put his backpack on. He too noticed the change in Tara's demeanor. He looked over at Gideon with inquisitive raise of the eyebrow. Gideon shrugged his shoulders and shook his head.

"What's wrong?" Gideon asked her.

"Nutt'n," she replied, but did not look at him.

"You ready then?"

"Yeah man."

She did not move though. They stood silently under the tree for another minute. Tara stared up toward the summits ahead while Gideon and Todd watched and waited for her to lead the way.

"Tara?" Gideon said softly. "Why aren't we going?"

"Mi 'aven't been past dis tree since mi was a likkle girl," she explained pensively. "Daddy say mi mustn't pass dis spot y'ere and so all d'ese years a 'ere mi stay."

Gideon was unnerved to see her vulnerable for the first time. He had not realized how much strength he drew from her confidence and to see it disappear before his eyes brought fresh worries to his mind.

"It will be okay," Gideon spoke, and attempted to assure them both.

She broke from her trance-like state and shot a furious look at Gideon, "Of course it will. Uno t'ink say mi need yu fi say dat? Cha!"

She stormed off toward the summit. While Gideon felt foolish for being rebuked, he was glad to see Tara return to her normal powerful self. He picked up his backpack and started to hike after her, but before he took a step Todd caught him by the shoulder.

"Hold up man," Todd said. "What's that?"

Todd pointed to the bald ashy top of the limestone cliff of the western summit. Gideon looked and saw what appeared to be the silhouette of a man that stood atop the clearing. He could not be sure from this distance but he could swear it was a man in a maroon shirt.

"Tara!" he exclaimed in a whisper.

She stopped and looked back at them. They both pointed urgently up toward the summit. She spun around and saw the same thing they saw atop the peak. She quickly crouched down behind a bush and urged them to do the same. They found cover behind a large fern and she made her way back to them on her hands and knees. Together they huddled behind the ferns and looked up at the man who stood near the edge of the cliff.

"Is that . . . ?" Gideon began.

"Yeah man," she said in answer to the obvious question. "Mucaro."

"He's looking for us."

"Perfect, just perfect," Todd said.

"Is there another way?" asked Gideon.

"No man," she said. "It will take too long."

"What do you mean?" asked Gideon.

"Wi won't mek it before dark," she said. "Mi na sleep'n out 'ere with yu. Uno only paid fi da day."

"I paid you to take us to the cave!" Gideon argued.

"No man," she said and shook her head. "Dis wasn't da plan."

"Please, Tara," he said. "We're so close."

She closed her eyes and scrunched up her face. With her eyes close she sat and thought for a minute.

"A'right," she said. "But yu 'ave fi do somet'ing fi me."

"Name it," Gideon said.

"Sponsor me an' Corey," she said. "Take us to the States. Take 'im 'way from all dis an' 'elp us start fresh."

While Gideon loved everything about Jamaica, he recognized that, for the most part, it was a hard life that Jamaicans lived. Many lived in poverty, with little opportunity to escape it. The American dream was hardly confined to Americans. Immigration was one way for Jamaicans to seek a better life. Except immigrating to the United States was not easy and took connections and money. He had known entire families that lived in one room shacks. Children so hungry they stood outside restaurants and stores to beg for leftovers. He thought of Corey sitting on the dusty floor of the chicken shop drawing with a single crayon. His heart ached as he longed to help all those he found in need. He could not deny her request, especially when he considered it would advance his cause as well.

"Deal," Gideon promised, although he did not know fully if he could deliver. "You take us to the cave and I'll get you and your son to the States."

He extended his hand and they shook once again to bind the agreement. They all turned their attention back toward the man atop the peak. He stood there, nearly motionless, like a sentinel at the gate.

"Wi mus' go further east, round dat peak over d'ere," Tara instructed. "Mi know a place where wi c'yan sleep an' reach da cave in da morning."

They stayed low to the ground and crept along the tree line, sure to keep out of sight and avoid the watchful eye of the guardian atop the summit peaks. Gideon felt like their hike in the jungle had suddenly turned into more of a military operation. In his mind he imagined them, camo-clad, stealthily sneaking behind enemy lines, evading an opposing army to complete their mission. The reality of their situation, aside from Todd's bright white t-shirt, was not far off as they would need stealth to avoid their opposition and achieve their objective. As this military fantasy played out in his mind he thought again of Glenn who, without question, would have tried to engage them in just such a ridiculous game. Gideon had to remind himself that this was no game and that they were opposed by a very real person and not an imaginary army. He would not allow himself to indulge in fantasy any longer. In short order he returned to his senses and continued to plod behind Tara through the bushes and vines of the cockpits, toward a destination unknown. *Now this is a good day*, he thought.

Dark Waters

Smitty stooped over a smoldering metal pot, with his hands cupped together to catch the warmth and disperse the rising steam. Dented and dinged from its many travels the pot rested on four quasi-flat pieces of shale. White smoke seeped through the gaps between the pot and the shale fragments. The coals beneath were barely adequate to heat the black bubbling liquid contained inside. Any fire had to be kept small, so as not to give away their position. With the cuff of his shirt Smitty reached down, grabbed the handle of the pot and lifted it from the coals. He quickly stamped out the remaining embers with his boot and carried the pot over to an empty tin cup. He lifted the bottom of the pot with his cuff covered hand and filled it to the top. He placed the pot back on the shale and picked up the full tin cup.

Jarvis sat a few feet away, with his back to Smitty and his make shift shale stove. With a dead-eyed stare he gazed down on the map that taunted him. The map lay open on top of a round piece of limestone that jutted out of the earth like a foot stool. Jarvis straddled the rock so as to peer directly down at the map. To his great disappointment, the map had proved to be wholly unhelpful. Any landmarks on this rudimentary outlay were along the coasts to the north and south of the island. This map marked only the main rivers that ran to the oceans and none of their inland tributaries. The mountainous region they traversed were simply designated 'Unnamed,' with several hand-drawn hills and trees. His pride would not allow him to admit the uselessness of the map after all the trouble they had gone through to get it. So he spent a healthy portion of each day addressing the map as if guided him to where they ought to go. He worried this exercise fooled no one; however, Smitty and John Davis allowed him to save face and had not directly addressed the matter. Smitty walked quietly up to his side and extended the warm tin cup. Jarvis sat up straight and reached out to accept the offering.

"Thank you," he said. He took the cup and held it under his nose.

The warmth rose up to meet his skin and cut through the coolness of the morning. He took a sip and instinctively recoiled, as the liquid passed his lips and flowed over his tongue. It was not from the heat of the liquid but due to an affront to his sense of taste. It looked and smelled like coffee but tasted like Smitty had soaked burnt tree bark in the pot. Jarvis noticed Smitty stood by and watched for his reaction. He suppressed his repulsion to the tree bark broth and forced a smile.

"It is a bit hot," he said, in an attempt to cover up his initial response. "Good and hot."

Smitty collected the sought approval with a smile and walked back to the shale stove. Jarvis looked over his shoulder to ensure Smitty was not watching but abandoned his plans to dump the brew in the bushes when he saw John Davis emerge through the tree line. Just a few yards beyond the perimeter of trees was the stream they crossed the previous evening, which made it an ideal spot to make camp for the night. John Davis carried two green gourds in each hand. The gourds were suspended from thick twined rope that hung around his neck. He placed the gourds at Smitty's feet as he passed by and sprawled out on his side opposite Jarvis with the map in between them.

Jarvis offered the unwanted cup of coffee to John Davis, which he happily accepted.

"Thanks, mate."

He lifted the cup to his lips and took a drink; immediately, he sat up straight and spat the liquid on the ground. Half of it splattered on the shoulder of his tattered and worn dress shirt.

"Blimey! What is that?" he demanded, and examined the new stain on his once beloved shirt.

"It's coffee," Smitty submitted defensively.

"No mate, that ain't nutt'n like any coffee I've ever 'ad."

"Major Jarvis liked it," Smitty rebutted. He boldly stood up and faced the pirate directly.

"Oh 'e did, did 'e?" John Davis said. He looked over at Jarvis, who did not look up. He turned back to Smitty and continued. "Well 'e liked it so much that 'e gave me 'is cup without so much as a sip outta it. 'ow well d'you think 'e liked it?"

Smitty stood for a moment with mouth agape and looked at the back of Jarvis's head. Jarvis stared even more earnestly at the map, as he had no desire to face the disappointed young quartermaster. When it became clear he would not receive any reassurance, Smitty sat back down, picked up a stick, and brooded while he poked at the ash and dirt in front of him. John Davis tossed the remains of the cup into the bushes and lay back on his side with a satisfied look over at Jarvis.

"Ya got this figured out yet?"

"I believe so," Jarvis replied, as he looked up from the map. He pulled a slim square box from the pocket of his trousers and rested it neatly in the palm of his hand. The box was made of ivory with vine shaped designs etched into its surface. He carefully opened the lid and held it up at eye level. Inside the box was a circular depression with a spinning dial at the center. Four ornate arrows were painted in the circle and pointed in opposite directions, marked with the letters W, N, E, and S.

"If we head north about a half day's journey we should reach Bartolomeu's cave," Jarvis said, and pointed in the direction the compass indicated as north.

"An' what makes you so sure?" John Davis challenged Jarvis.

"I have traveled these mountains for years and have only encountered one such tributary of this size and volume that flowed east to west. I do not know precisely where we are, but I know that the cave that bears your captain's marking . . ."

"Former captain," John Davis interrupted.

"Former captain's marking," Jarvis corrected with an apologetic nod, "is in that direction."

"A'right mate, that's good enough for me," John Davis said. "Shall we be off then?"

Jarvis closed the compass and tucked it back in his pocket. He folded the map and came to his feet. John Davis and Smitty followed his lead and Smitty packed up the few odds and ends from breakfast into his shoulder bag. He emptied the black remains of the pot into the bushes with a derisive look toward John Davis; who was unaware of the evil eye shot his way. The golden haired pirate stood and stretched both arms high above his head. When the bed rolls were rolled up and the assorted cookery had been packed away, Smitty dispersed the pieces of shale that had corralled the cooking coals and buried the ashes from the morning fire.

Most of their energies, beyond their march through the mountains, were spent to conceal themselves and cover their tracks. This was necessitated by the relentless pursuit of Colonel Swanson and his men. They had twice been fired upon by his troops. Luckily, each time they found themselves on a summit opposite Colonel Swanson, with a deep ravine in between them that kept them safely out of reach and provided ample time to make their escape and elude capture. Each encounter, however, precipitated a change in course which was not conducive to reaching their objective in a timely manner. They lost some of their supplies in their initial flight and had gone through the remainder in the days that followed. No one spoke it aloud but each of them understood that if they did not reach the cave soon, their quest and their lives hung in the balance. In addition to their individual satchels they carried water in the gourds that John Davis had fashioned for them.

Although he had no more powder or shot, Jarvis still toted the musket from the quartermaster's tent and his knife. John Davis carried Colonel Swanson's pistol and Smitty was armed only with the cast iron skillet on his back.

They left the stream behind them and headed north, making sure to keep the morning sun on their right. Whenever possible they took the path of least resistance and held to the ravines. Even though the ravines were thick with vines and vegetation it was easier than scaling and descending the summits, which seemed to stand in their way in every direction. They moved in a single file formation as they had done for the past two days. Jarvis led out, followed by John Davis and finally Smitty. Less than an hour into the day's march they encountered a rock wall fifteen feet high. Jarvis stopped and looked for a way around. He removed the satchel from his shoulder and a smile crept across his face.

"I know this," Jarvis said.

"Oh yeah?" John Davis replied. "So we're on that right track then?"

"Yes indeed," Jarvis said thoughtfully, as he looked for a way up. He grabbed onto a group of vines to his right and climbed up the east side of the crevasse. In moments he reached the top and swung his leg over the ledge to pull himself up. From the top, he looked up the ravine and saw, as he expected, that it continued northward. He turned back to John Davis and Smitty and motioned for them to throw up his satchel. John Davis heaved the nearly empty satchel up to him. He caught it and swung the strap over his shoulder. Then John Davis threw up his own satchel to make the climb. He took hold of the same grouping of vines Jarvis had just ascended. It was only after Smitty threw his satchel that Jarvis remembered it contained the metal pot and skillet. He caught the strap and managed to avoid the skillet, but the bag flew up and hit him in the jaw. He closed his eyes and winced in pain. Jarvis put down the bag and rubbed his chin. When he opened his eye, he looked down on Smitty who had a startled look on his face. Jarvis nodded and waved to assure him no harm was done. Smitty looked relieved and started to climb the vines. Jarvis and

John Davis reached down and pulled Smitty up the last stretch onto the top of the rock wall.

They moved onward, up the ravine, until it turned decidedly to the east. Jarvis feigned a study of the map and decided they should climb up and over rather than follow the ravine any further. It was not as steep as some of the other inclines they had climbed, but the summit was high and the climb was long and it was decided they would rest once they reached the top. From the summit's peak, they had an unimpeded view of the wide world. The dark green egg shaped hilltops stretched on as far as they could see in every direction, with little to distinguish one from the next. The sky was a brilliant bright blue with soft white clouds that sailed serenely toward the eastern horizon. A cool breeze caressed their sunbaked skin. Jarvis sat in awe and wondered if heaven itself felt any sweeter.

"No view like this back 'ome, that's for sure," Smitty said.

"An' where is 'ome, Master Smitty?" John Davis asked, as he plopped down in the grass and looked over at his companions.

"I'm from Jamestown," Smitty answered.

"The colonies, eh," said John Davis. "I knew a bloke from up that way. So what brought ya to this glorious island paradise?"

"Bad luck I suppose, me mum an' dad died when I was little an' I didn't really 'ave much family to speak of," Smitty began. "Their parents died before I was born, when the Powhatan attacked back in '22. Me one cousin was in the army an' convinced me it was a good idea. 'e died on the ship on the way down 'ere."

"Well ain't you a sad little tale," John Davis said mockingly.

"An' where are you from then, Mr. Davis?" asked Smitty.

"From the sea, mate, from the sea."

"You told me you were born here," Jarvis interjected accusingly.

"This is a part of the sea, ain't it? An' that makes it a part of where I'm from then, doesn't it?" John Davis argued as he sat up and opened his arms wide in a grand gesture.

"Fair enough," Jarvis said, still skeptical of John Davis and his tales, but uninterested in a battle of wits with a shiftless foe.

"So what brought you to this point, then?" Smitty asked.

"Pursuit of fame and fortune, mate. Same as most."

"An' you, Major? Where are you from?" Smitty asked.

"Yorkshire," Jarvis answered.

"An' what brought you 'ere?" Smitty asked intently.

"Fame and fortune, like he said," Jarvis answered after a long pause.

He only wished he had such a tangible reason for being here. In reality the series of choices that led him to this point hardly seemed his own. The truth was he enlisted in the military because he did not know what else to do with his life. When he spoke of his service he spoke of conviction and duty, he had spoken it so often that he actually believed it, but his motivations were not quite so succinct and noble. His upbringing had been entirely unremarkable. His father worked a small plot of land that was enough to support their small family; which consisted of his father, his mother, an older sister and brother. His father was a quiet and unambitious man who worked from sun up till sun down every day except Sunday. On Sunday his family went to church, his mother made sure of that. She was a pious woman who exemplified the tenants of her faith. When not caring for her own children she could be found helping her friends and neighbors, or really anyone she came across who stood in need. While his older brother took after his father and his older sister took after his mother, Ben Jarvis was set apart. He was well cared for and looked after, but often wondered throughout his childhood if his presence would be missed at all. His parents groomed his siblings as their replacements on this earth and, by and large, Ben was an afterthought in his own family. Not in a cruel way, mind you, it was just simply the way things were.

He thought back to the circumstances that led to his enlistment. As a young man, each fall he served as a beater on the pheasant hunt. One particularly long and dreary day he unintentionally snickered when Sir Arthur Ingram's eldest son Henry missed a pheasant perched just a few yards away. Angrily, Henry challenged him to do better. Ben had never fired a gun before but was not about to back down from a challenge. At the next opportunity, with Henry Ingram's gun, he took aim and shot a pheasant in midflight from a hundred paces. Sir Ingram remarked to his son that Ben must possess some natural ability and should consider a career as a soldier. It was the first genuine compliment young Ben could remember. At his suggestion, and with Sir Ingram's recommendation, he enlisted and shipped out before Christmas. He left home certain he would not see his family again but wanted nothing more than to make them proud. In large part he kept his journal for them, but also to calm the ever present fear that his life might not be remembered when he left this world. It was not fame he sought as much as a life worthy of remembering.

"Major?" Smitty began hesitantly. "Can I ask you a question?"

"Certainly," Jarvis replied, as he was snapped from his sober reflection.

"What exactly happened to the black regiment, sir?"

The scenes of gruesome images raced through his mind, his saber hurtling through the air toward the waiting de Serras, Lubolo lying on the ground defenseless as it cut through the flesh and bones in his neck, and the face of the hulking Goliath, who had held his life in his hands. The question returned: *Why was I spared?* A question he had no answer for.

"It was a trap," he began. "We captured one of the rebel Negroes and coerced him into telling us where de Serras was. He agreed to show us but led us into an ambush."

"How did ya escape?" Smitty asked eagerly, his tone made evident his expectation of some grand tale of heroism.

"He let me go."

"'e?" asked Smitty.

"The prisoner who led us into the ambush," Jarvis explained. "The biggest man I have ever seen. I just dangled there in his massive hands and he put me down and told me to run, so I ran."

Smitty was clearly disappointed to learn how Jarvis had survived the ambush. Jarvis could not blame him, as he too would have preferred a different tale to tell. He would have much rather fought his way free or died in battle than owe his life to another; particularly when he considered that person to be an enemy.

"Speak'n of your new found friends," John Davis interjected. "'ave ya given any thought to what ya might do if an' when we cross paths with them again?"

"What do you mean?" asked Jarvis.

"I'm asking 'ave ya thought about what might 'appen if we run into them out 'ere?"

"No," Jarvis lied. "If they wanted to do me harm they have had ample opportunity."

The truth though was that Jarvis had thought a great deal about the possibility they might encounter them again. Whether his angelic assassin or the giant Goliath, Jarvis wondered if they would be so merciful if confronted again. Only they had the answers to the questions that gnawed at him, but the thought of coming face to face with them again brought about a fear that robbed him of all desire to seek out those answers.

"An' what 'bout ole Smitty an' me?" John Davis said. "Will they show us that type of 'ospitality? I doubt it."

"There are no guarantees, my friend. We do not even know if we will survive to the bottom of this cliff," Jarvis said, and pointed to the edge of the peak. "You knew that going in."

"That ain't the point."

"Then what are you getting at?" Jarvis replied testily.

"What I'm asking, mate is, are ya planning on staying clear a these blokes or do you 'ave any thoughts in your 'ead of a rutty reunion?" John Davis said pointedly.

"The plan is to find the cave and lay claim on Bartolomeu's treasure. It is in our best interest to remain undetected," Jarvis said.

"That's true, but you still ain't answered my question," John Davis responded.

"Why would I seek out these men?" Jarvis asked.

"To find out why 'e didn't tear your bloody 'ead off!" John Davis shouted.

Jarvis could not decide if his friend was far more perceptive than he had given him credit or if his internal desires were more transparent than he liked to believe. In any case, he was shaken by the fact that John Davis had surmised an ambition within him, which he himself had not fully come to grips with. A defensive instinct kicked in and he began to shake his head.

"That is ridiculous," Jarvis said. "I would have to be a fool to purposely seek them out."

"That's right ya would be," John Davis said. "We don't want noth'n to do with their type."

"And what do you know of their type?" Jarvis shot back incredulously.

"Plenty, mate. I sailed with a Negro named Duarte. 'e was some kind of priest or something back in Africa an' a warrior to boot. 'e 'ad scars all over 'is body to prove it. 'e was the scariest bloke I ever laid eyes on. 'e only spoke to Bartolomeu an' when 'e laid 'is eyes on you, 'e would get inside your 'ead."

"Bollocks," Jarvis interrupted. "I have heard these bedtime stories before. It is utter superstition and nonsense."

"It ain't superstition, mate," John Davis argued defensively. "I seen it with me own eyes. We was off the coast a this little nutt'n island when we was set upon by 'alf the Spanish fleet. Duarte jumped up on the bow an' started mumbling some sort of curse or something an' next thing we knew we was in the fit of a storm an' it blew them bleeding Spaniards to the other side of the sea."

"Blimey," Smitty said, with amazement.

"That ain't the 'alf of it," he continued. "I 'eard tell these African priests can't be killed by any one man. They 'ave all sorts of powers, on account of black magic. They can raise the dead an' control their minds. Bartolomeu told of when Duarte put a hex on a crew mate what stole 'is boots an' 'e turned 'is guts inside out."

"Good 'eavens," Smitty exclaimed.

"'eaven ain't got noth'n to do with it, mate," John Davis said.

"Enough of this foolishness," Jarvis demanded. He stood up and collected his satchel. "We've rested long enough. Let's get on with it, shall we?"

"But, sir, what if we run into one of them priests with the dark powers?" Smitty worried.

Jarvis was not as concerned with John Davis's exaggerated stories of the supernatural as he was with the actual real live men they might soon encounter. He thought of his angelic assassin, who moved with speed, agility and ferocious power and shuddered at how helpless he had been in the grips of the monstrous Goliath. These men were a force to be reckoned with all on their own. Still, he took small comfort in the fact that they were indeed men and not the unholy specters that Smitty feared.

"They are mortals like you and I," Jarvis said calmly. "If any of them possessed the powers that he suggests then they would have never found themselves in bondage in the first place, would they?"

"'e's got a point there," Smitty said to John Davis.

"Believe what ya want, mate," John Davis said. "I saw what I saw an' I know what I know."

Eager to change the subject, Jarvis produced the compass from his pocket and held it up. He looked out to the north in search of something that might indicate they were headed in the right direction. A scan of the horizon proved fruitless, as each summit looked like the next and Jarvis began to lose hope. Just then, he spotted a peak that showed a grey limestone face amongst the sea of green. Jarvis had a vivid memory of such a peak. It was not far from that peak that he saw Captain Willard and his company for the last time.

"There, just there," he said and pointed excitedly over the top of his compass. "Our destination is dead ahead."

"Where?" John Davis asked.

"That summit there with the grey stone showing," Jarvis replied.

"Is that where the cave is?" Smitty asked.

"It is not far from there," Jarvis answered. Although he was not exactly sure how far, he knew he could find the cave if they could reach that peak. Jarvis took advantage of their elevated viewpoint. He plotted a course through the labyrinth below so they would not have to scale any of the dozen or so summits between them and their destination. He folded up the map and put the compass back in his pocket. He removed his satchel and retrieved his journal and writing quill from the brass cylinder, squatted down and positioned the opened journal on his lap. With great care, he plotted a way through the ravines to the grey limestone face. In the top right corner he wrote 'To Bartolomeu's Cave.' When finished he blew the paper dry, placed the cork back on the ink and gently tucked the quill and glass container back in the brass cylinder and returned it to his satchel. He kept the journal out to reference his directions.

He, John Davis, and Smitty began their descent down the north side of the summit. The decline quickly became too steep for them to keep their footing without the assistance of the vines and bushes beneath them. They hung on tightly and slowly made their way down to the ravine. The pain in Jarvis's knee briefly returned during the treacherous drop down the side of the summit. Once they reached the bottom, they followed the crevasses between the summits and avoided any more steep climbs. Jarvis meticulously crossed off each turn he had mapped out along the way. This meant frequent stops, necessitated by Jarvis's ritual removal of his ink and quill, to be certain they were on track to reach the grey limestone cliff wall.

John Davis folded his arms and tapped his foot impatiently each time they halted. A trek through the jungle floor presented its own obstacles, however, no one complained as they were glad not to have to climb the steep peaks of the surrounding summits. Still they had to expend great effort to push through and climb over the innumerable bushes and vines of the much thicker overgrowth in the ravines and crevasses. They reached a convergence of ravines which seemed to present two options to the right with a third ravine that ran back behind them to the southwest. Jarvis stopped and consulted his journal. The notes he made indicated that their next turn should be to the right. However, he was not certain which right to take. He got out his compass in an effort to determine the correct path. John Davis walked up behind him and examined the journal from over his shoulder. The ravine that lay just ahead bent right to the northeast and was broad and far more welcoming, while the ravine next to it turned decidedly east with a narrow entrance that seemed almost impassable.

"So which right is it, then?" asked John Davis.

"I say we go east," Jarvis said.

"Through that?" John Davis questioned and shook his head. "It looks a might easier up that way, an' it seems to be going the way we ought to be 'eading."

"The Good Lord said wide is the gate and broad is the way that leadeth to destruction," Smitty interjected.

"Well Jesus ain't never 'ad to crawl back up in something like that," John Davis retorted with a gesture to the small crevasse to their right.

Jarvis had to concede he would much prefer an easier route. He looked down at his instructions again and wished he had made a detailed drawing instead of his list of rights and lefts. Even though Jarvis believed the eastward crevasse to be the right way he could not be sure and therefore could not mount a strong argument.

"Very well, we'll try your way," Jarvis decided.

He started to get out the brass cylinder that contained his inkwell before John Davis grabbed his hand to stop him. "Blow ya down! There's a 'andful left. I think we can remember without the 'elp of your flogging list."

He appeared to have reached the end of his patience with Jarvis and his need for order. Jarvis looked into his serious face and chose to capitulate rather than press the issue further. Gently, he pulled his hand free of John Davis's grasp and gave one last look to his list before he closed the journal and placed it back in his leather satchel. Without another word he led the way up into the wide ravine in front of them. There was a gradual incline as the summit walls on either side of them closed in slightly toward each other. As it plateaued, they could see that, as they had hoped, the ravine did indeed turn to the northeast.

"I told you mate," John Davis said proudly. "This is the way."

No sooner had the words escaped his lips than they heard the sound of an abeng blow from somewhere overhead. Frantically, they looked up at the trees and peaks above them and tried to determine the origin of the sound. Soon, another horn blew and then another. The jungle quickly filled with noise from the horns as their hearts filled with fear. Jarvis collected himself and made sure he had the attention of his friends. Without another word he turned and forged ahead quickly. He moved up the ravine as fast as he could. He did not dare look back but kept his eyes dead ahead. They had been discovered and this was the alarm that would alert others of their presence. The sounds echoed off the canyon walls and seemed to come from every direction. For all he knew they were headed directly into the arms of the enemy. *But who was the enemy?*

He abandoned the ravine and pushed upward, following a gradual incline of footholds in the limestone. He raced along the surface of the rocks, as they rose like giant steps up and out of the crevasse and ascended up from the ravine floor. To his left the summit wall raised some twenty feet above him, to his right the jungle opened into an expanse of trees and bush. The sounds of the abeng horns abated and only then could he hear the footsteps and labored breaths of his companions behind him. Quickly, Jarvis looked back to see who was still with him. He saw John Davis, who trudged up the incline right on his heels.

Jarvis had only looked away for a moment when his right foot found nothing but air where he expected it to meet the ground. He tumbled forward and fell down the side of the cliff. Between his momentum and the steep drop, he hurled downward at an alarming rate. He made efforts to cover his head as he bounced off roots and branches in his way. At last his descent was slowed as the terrain leveled out and he came to rest, on his back, in the mud at the bottom of a large sinkhole. He stared up in shock at the bright blue sky. His head rested in a shallow, muddy puddle of water. He took a quick inventory and appeared to be no worse for wear. He lay there for a moment and listened to the sound of running water somewhere over his head. As he tilted his head back, he saw a small waterfall that emptied into a deep blue pool of water. Grass and reeds surrounded the pool, except where he had crashed through them on his downfall.

"Major Jarvis," Smitty called out from up the hill.

"I am all right," Jarvis called back.

He began to sit up when the water behind him exploded in a torrent of white and blue. A sharp pain ripped through his shoulder as, what felt like, hundreds of blades tore through his flesh. He cried out in agony as he was pulled backwards into the pond; his legs dragged through the mud and grass. Blood poured into the pool as his head was pulled under water. Panicked, he strained to crane his neck and look up and back. As waves of water washed over his face he could make out a dark monstrous shadow that had seized upon him. Jarvis struggled against the force that pulled him deeper into the water to no avail. Briefly, his head sprang above water and he gasped for air before being plunged back below into the murky mess. The brown silt swirled with the deep blue water and his dark red blood. The shadowy creature that gripped his shoulder thrashed him back and forth like a child toying with a ragdoll. Once more his head breached the surface of the water and allowed him to draw in desperate breath.

A sense of doom settled upon him. He was not ready to die, but that had little bearing on what was happening. He looked to the shoreline and blinked rapidly, in an attempt to clear his blurred vision. For a moment he thought he saw three or four figures who bounded down the hillside toward him. The foremost amongst them came down into the sinkhole and leapt into the water. All too quickly he was drug back under. This time the beast flipped him over to face the muddy floor beneath him. Confronted with the darkness he was rolled over and over again, unable to draw breath. Clouds crept in from the corners of his mind and filled his consciousness as the blackness swallowed him whole.

In the Mist

A bout how much longer till we reach the cave?" Todd asked. "Not too long," Tara replied and pointed off into the darkness. "It's right 'round d'ere so."

Once night had fallen their progress slowed. They hiked through the bush, aided by flashlight, until they found a suitable spot to rest; in a clearing near a patch of wild banana trees. Their clothes, and the tall grass where they sat, were still wet from the afternoon showers. Todd offered the last of his beef jerky to Tara, who declined. Gideon and Todd rationed out what would get them through the next day's activities and, hopefully, back to the car. The bananas on the tree were still green but they each ate one anyway.

Thanks to the full moon, the night never completely gave into darkness. Although all were cast in shadow, they could still make out most of the mountains, trees and bushes that surrounded them. There had been a brief and awkward discussion about the night's sleeping arrangements before Tara made clear her intentions to sleep on the other side of a small bamboo thicket a few yards away. The three of them sat mostly in silence. Gideon happily gazed up at the star filled heavens while Todd occasionally tried to engage Tara in small talk.

"So why don't we just go up there tonight?" asked Todd.

"Mi c'yan't see inna da dark an' mi na wan fi step inna sink-hole an' die," Tara replied.

"Good reason," Todd said, embarrassed by her obvious answer.

He looked over at Gideon, who just shook his head and smiled at his friend's failed attempts to connect with their guide. Gideon dug down in his pack and pulled out the journal and a flash-light. He lay down on his side with his back to Todd and opened the journal to where he left off. He used the slip of paper with the symbol as a bookmark. Having no intention of giving away their location, Gideon held the flashlight close to the journal and flipped it on. The sole reason they found themselves in the jungle at night was Mucaro, the maroon-clad obeah man, who had pur-sued them from Quickstep. Todd sat thoughtfully with his legs crisscrossed and his arms resting on top of his knees. Tara was nestled in the thick grass and leaned back against a rock near the edge of the clearing.

"It's a beautiful night," Todd stated. He waited for several sec-onds with no reply.

"I love camping," he lied. "Tara, do you like to camp?"

"Camp?" she asked.

"Yeah, you know, sleeping out under the stars in the great outdoors. Camping," he clarified.

"Na really," she said. "Mi prefer mi bed."

"Me too," Todd said excitedly. "I mean, not your bed, my bed. I'm sure your bed is nice though. Nice for sleeping, I mean. Not that I think about your bed, because I don't . . . I just meant, I prefer my bed."

Gideon looked up from the journal to see Todd's horri-fied and dejected face. Tara raised an eyebrow and gave him a sideways look. Todd hung his head in defeat. She smiled until she saw Gideon watching and her stony expression returned. Gideon turned his attention back to the journal. He grimaced as he tried to discern what he found on the page. It appeared to be a series of directions, with about half of them crossed out. In the top right corner of the faded and well-worn page something was written that was no longer legible. He decided to give his friend a break from his self-inflicted travails and offered a change of subject.

"Hey Todd," he said, and turned around toward him. "What do you make of this?"

Todd lifted his head and looked over to see what Gideon referred to. Gideon handed him the journal and the flashlight and Todd examined the page.

"I dunno," he said. "Looks like it could be directions?"

"That's what I thought too," Gideon responded.

With her interest piqued, Tara stood up and walked over to Todd. She drew near, sat down next to him and looked over his shoulder at the journal. The flashlight illuminated the page and the list of words inscribed on it.

~~Right~~
~~Right~~
~~Left~~
~~Right~~
~~Left~~
~~Right~~
Right
Left
Right
Left
Left
Right

"Directions to where?" Tara asked.

"The most pressing question would be *from* where?" Gideon said, with a smug tone that he immediately regretted. "Without knowing where to begin, we'll never reach their intended end."

"That was poetic, man," said Todd.

"Thanks, brother," said Gideon, impressed with himself.

Thoroughly unimpressed, Tara rolled her eyes. Gideon scooted over next to Todd and Tara. The three of them stared at the nearly barren page in the journal. Gideon closed his eyes and tried hard to engage all his mental faculties and possibly decipher what the list might mean. To his disappointment, he drew a complete blank.

"I got it!" Todd blurted out.

"What?" Tara and Gideon replied in unison.

"I know what this is."

"What?" Again Tara and Gideon chimed together.

"It's directions to the treasure."

"Todd," Gideon began dismissively.

"No man," Todd stopped him. "Just hear me out. He wrote this in his journal, right? So it's got to be something that was important, like you said. What could be more important than directions to a treasure?"

"Even if that's the case we still don't know where to begin," Gideon said.

"At the entrance to the cave," Todd stated confidently. "Look right there, doesn't that say cave?"

Chills shot down his spine and goose bumps formed on his arms. Gideon sat dumbfounded and had no rebuttal. As soon as he heard Todd say it aloud it seemed so logical and so apparent that he was ashamed he had not thought of it first. Although he could not read the words at the top of the page his imagination allowed him to see the word cave. Had Jarvis recorded the twist and turns of the cave in his journal? Did they possibly have the key to find a treasure, hidden for over three hundred years? The prospect of such a discovery was thrilling and the ramifications life altering. Gideon had to remind himself to temper his expectations in order to avoid disappointment. In all likelihood it was nothing more than a cave with an old marking on the entrance. He told himself that it was history he chased, not gold. Still he felt that this seed of thought had already been planted firmly in his mind and had begun to sprout into a full grown obsession. He shook it off and sought to insert reason into the discussion.

"That's a huge assumption, Todd," Gideon said. He tried to quell both he and his friend's growing enthusiasm for this theory.

"We don't know anything about this cave. Following these directions could lead us nowhere, or worse, they could lead us to a bottomless shaft of death."

"Really?!" Todd interrupted. "A bottomless shaft of death? I shouldn't speculate about a series of directions, but you have us falling down a bottomless shaft of death?"

"Fair enough. I'm just saying, let's not get too far ahead of ourselves here."

"Bro, we've flown over two thousand miles and driven and hiked at least a hundred; we're in the middle of a jungle trying to avoid some terrifying witch doctor and the ghost of his dead father, all because you found an old piece of paper with a picture you once saw carved in a rock. I think we've gone clean past 'ahead of ourselves.'"

"Speaking of Mucaro," Gideon said. He had no retort and wanted to change the subject. "Tara, how could he possibly know why we're here?"

"Quickstep is a likkle town. When white men come 'round word travels quickly."

"I get that. He could have found out that we were there but not *why* we were there. The only people we told about the cave were you and Bammy."

"What's your point?" she said, with a slightly defensive tone.

"I've been thinking and it doesn't make sense that he would be protecting this cave or its imagined contents. For argument's sake, let's say Todd is right. If there were pirate's treasure in there and he knew about it, he wouldn't just chase people off; he'd claim it and be rich. And if there isn't something valuable in there, then he's going through a lot of effort to keep people from exploring a cave. It's got to be something else."

"What then?" she asked.

"Ganja," he said.

"That's racist," Todd said mockingly.

"Shut up, Todd," Gideon continued. "My companion and I once ran across a field of marijuana, just outside Porus. It was concealed within a yam field. The Rasta who owned it freaked out when he saw two white guys in shirts and ties. He thought we were federal agents or something. He chased us off with a machete."

"So?" she asked.

"What if Mucaro doesn't care *jack* about the cave? What if he's trying to keep us from something else that just happens to be near the cave? What if generations of 'obeah men' have spun these bedtime stories of duppy caves to keep the general population out of the area and away from their stash?"

"You're fulla what ifs, aren't ya?" she said.

"All right," Gideon conceded. "I'm just saying, we might not have as hard a time as we think reaching the cave, provided our path doesn't cut through a giant field of weed."

She shook her head dismissively. Todd stared at the ground and smiled. He appeared to be amused by Gideon's theory or Tara's reaction to it. In either case, Gideon was annoyed. He reached over and took the flashlight and journal from Todd. He turned off the flashlight and said, "Let's try and save the batteries for tomorrow."

Tara stood up and wiped at the mud on the back of her shorts. She walked over, picked up her backpack and machete and turned back toward Gideon and Todd. She nodded and made her way around the small bamboo thicket. Gideon returned the journal and the flashlight to his pack and slid it over, behind where he sat. He lay back on the ground and used his pack as a pillow. With a deep breath he looked back up into the moonlit sky. Todd did the same, and used his backpack as a pillow.

Todd closed his eyes and lay still. Gideon raised his arms up and placed his hands behind his head, atop the backpack. With his gaze heavenward he could not help but marvel at the seemingly infinite amount of stars in the sky. The full moon shone down on him like a flashlight. His anxious excitement melted away as he lay there in the quiet of the night and a powerful peace settled over him. He let his eye lids fall shut and hoped for sleep to come quickly. To his left, Todd had begun breathing deeply, as sleep had already found him.

Gideon wrestled with his own consciousness. His mind

churned with possibilities. Whether it had been minutes or hours he could not be sure. The only thing he knew was that the restful sleep he desired eluded him. Gideon finally opened his eyes and looked over at his slumbering friend. He raised his head and looked down toward the small bamboo patch where Tara had made her bed. All he could see of her was her shoes, which stuck out from behind the thicket. Just beyond the thicket, a fog swept into view. The wispy grayish-white fog moved silently and rapidly; unlike anything Gideon had seen. It billowed into the clearing like smoke from a raging fire, only there was no flame to be seen. He sat up as the fog enveloped Tara's feet and legs and advanced toward him. It was as if they sat in the eye of a hurricane with the unnatural fog closing in on all sides.

"Todd," he called out.

Todd stirred just as the wall of fog overtook him; a cold and damp mist swallowed the two of them and everything in their field of vision. Although he was only a couple of yards from him, all Gideon could see was Todd's shadowy silhouette.

"What's going on?" Todd asked.

"I don't know," Gideon answered.

He got up and stood on his tiptoes in a futile attempt to see over the fog. He peered into the grayish white mist. His racing heart beat wildly in his chest. This was no ordinary mist. For the first time on their journey Gideon felt alone. This momentary isolation sent a surge of adrenaline through his body. He clenched his fists and fought the impulse to run. Somewhere to his left he heard what he assumed was Todd's movements.

"Follow the sound of my voice."

In seconds, Todd was at his side. He could just make out the frightened expression on his face through the thick fog. Gideon tried to quiet his mind and concentrate. Something was not right, he could feel it. He needed a plan, a course of action. Nothing came to mind. He tried to think back to his scouting days but there was nothing like this in the handbook. The visibility was down to only a meter or so. He heard new movement directly in front of them.

"Tara?" he called out toward the sound.

Gideon and Todd stood close together. They looked dead ahead and waited for a response. Not one, but two silhouettes emerged through the mist. One was slender, bone thin, and in the thick fog had the look of a corpse's skeleton. The other was short and round, together they resembled a giant teapot and a spoon. The shadows closed in on them. When they were nearly close enough to touch Gideon could at last identify them. He shook his head, as he could not believe his eyes. The short round figure on the left was Bigga and the gangly figure to his right was Bammy. The relief at seeing his friends was short lived, however, when he looked into their eyes. Their eyes were glossed over with a white haze that enveloped their entire eyeball. At first glance it appeared their eyes had rolled back into their skulls; except there was a slightly darker shade where their pupils should be. Without a word, Bammy raised his machete and swung it at Gideon's torso. Instinctually, he leapt backwards as the blade just missed his stomach.

"Ah!" Todd cried out in pain. The blade meant for Gideon had cut across his friend's bicep. Todd grabbed his arm and staggered backward.

"Bammy, what are you doing?" Gideon asked frantically. Again, Bammy raised his blade and swung. Gideon crept backwards cautiously, unable to see properly through the dense mist. Step by step, Bammy and Bigga slowly advanced on him. Their movements were forced and unnatural. They moved like puppets, puppets with machetes. With mouths agape and blank expressions they showed no recognition of what they were doing. Like a morbid waltz, Gideon and Todd reversed their field and mirrored each forward motion of their attackers. Gideon glanced to his left to check on Todd. He was still upright and moved with him, for the moment that was enough. Bammy swung his machete again, which caused Gideon to stumble backwards and fall to the ground. He looked up at Bammy, who raised his machete above his head and stepped forward. Todd threw himself in front of Gideon and thrust his left forearm in the air to block Bammy's downward blow. Bigga, who had been a bystander to this point, latched onto Todd. The two of them fell on top of Gideon's legs, as they grappled with each other. Without acknowledging this momentary interference, Bammy stepped over their entangled bodies and advanced on Gideon once more. Gideon struggled and finally pulled his legs free from the pile of bodies.

"Bammy, don't!" he shouted.

Gideon lay flat on his back and raised both feet in the air. He kicked Bammy square in the chest. Bammy stumbled backwards into the mist until he was just a silhouette again. Gideon scrambled to his feet and turned his attention to the struggle on the ground beside him. Bigga was on top of Todd and appeared to have the upper hand. Gideon wrapped his arms around Bigga's wide body and pulled hard but was unable to budge him. Out of the corner of his eye, he caught a glimpse of Bammy's shadow to his left. He swung around to meet him head on, but just as Bammy was within striking distance another figure emerged from behind him. Tara had finally found them through the mist. She grabbed Bammy's machete wielding arm, and wrapped her other arm around his neck. With a smooth ninja-like motion she flung her body backwards. Bammy sailed over her with his legs flying into the air. Gideon froze for a moment, not sure who to help. Chivalry mandated he help the girl, but she seemed to have things well in hand. He could hear Todd gasping for air as Bigga's two chubby hands attempted to choke the life out of him.

Quickly, Gideon leapt onto the back of his oversized friend and heaved upwards again. When this second effort proved futile he stepped back and looked around for something he could use. Just a few feet away he found Bammy's machete where it had dropped in the tussle. He reached over and scooped it up. He stood next to Bigga, who paid him no attention, and raised the machete in the air.

"Sorry big guy," he said and sent the handle of the machete crashing down on the back of his head.

After a sickening thud, as the butt of the machete impacted his skull, his body went limp and collapsed on top of Todd. Gideon dropped the machete, pushed on Bigga's unconscious body. With one heave he managed to roll him onto his back and free Todd from beneath him. Todd drew in several deep breathes and rubbed at his neck with his hand.

"Are you okay?" Gideon asked.

Todd nodded, not yet able to speak. Gideon leaned over Bigga and checked his breathing. With his fingers he pried open his eyelids. He was relieved to see his big brown eyes, where there had been solid white moments earlier. Traffic through his mind came to a screeching halt as he failed to process what just happened. They were attacked by their friends. Clearly their friends were not themselves, but what had come over them? What possessed them . . . or who? A chill shot down his spine. One solitary answer, most obvious, sprang to his mind. Obeah. Todd sat up and still caressed his throat, however, his breathing had calmed. Gideon noticed the shadow of a tree behind Todd, which had not been visible a moment ago. The mist had begun to dissipate. Then he remembered Tara and Bammy.

"Tara?" he called out.

No answer came. No sound at all. No indication of a struggle, no stirrings of a victor, only silence. Gideon stood up and tried to peer through the receding fog. He looked down near Bigga's feet and found the machete where he had dropped it. He stooped down and retrieved it while he kept his eyes up on the lookout for more trouble. Cautiously, he walked forward in the direction he had last seen father and daughter. He held the machete upside down with the blade tucked back against his forearm. Although he wanted to be ready for anything he did not want to accidentally harm either of them, should they come upon him suddenly. The moonlight at last penetrated the thinning fog, but it was still difficult to discern details in the gray and black tapestry. With each step, however, the visibility improved. In an instant his heart both leapt and sank as he could make out a lone body, lying face down on the ground. He raced to it and fell to his knees. It was the body of a skinny old man. He reached out and rolled him over. Bammy flopped over like a lifeless ragdoll. Gideon was relieved to find him still breathing. He peeled his eyelids open to see his brown eyes and black pupils. He crouched next to Bammy and turned to all sides in search of Tara. When he found her nowhere, he began to fear the worst.

"Tara," he spoke in a whispered shout.

Each second that passed in silence brought with it a fresh fearful thought. If she had fallen, there would be a body. And if she was conscious, surely she would answer. A new light shone down from above. Gideon looked up to see that the mist had parted and he could once again see the night sky. He stood up and looked behind him. Todd slowly walked toward him. They both looked down at Bammy, who still lay motionless on the ground.

"Is he alive?" asked Todd.

"Yeah," answered Gideon. "How's your arm?"

"It's just a scratch," said Todd. "What the heck just happened?"

"I don't know."

"Where's Tara?"

"I don't know."

"She's not here?" asked Todd. "Where did she go?"

"I don't know!" barked Gideon, frustrated he did not have the answers to his questions.

The mist had all but retreated, with only a remnant that settled just beneath the tree line in the distance. Gideon walked over to the bamboo thicket where Tara had made her bed for the night. Her blanket and blue backpack lay where she left them. He rolled up the thin wool blanket and stuffed it in her pack. He walked back over to where Todd stood and began to look around for some clue as to what might have happened.

Even with the full moon it was still too dark to see properly. Gideon found his backpack and dug into the side pocket for his flashlight. With a better source of light he returned to where Bammy's unconscious body lay and began to scan the area. A patch of grass caught his eye and he got down on his hands and knees for a closer look. There was a deep depression in the ground from the heel of a shoe. The grass around the depression was smashed into the mud. A trail of flattened grass led off into the bushes, littered with small depressions in the ground every foot or so.

"What is it?" asked Todd.

"The ground and grass is torn up around here," Gideon said.

"So," Todd said.

"So, these are footprints, two pair," Gideon went on. "There are signs of a struggle. They lead off this way."

Gideon stood up and shined the flashlight back and forth along the trail of smashed grass.

"How come everyone who runs across a pair of footprints in the mud thinks they're a tracker?" Todd asked. "And what makes you think there was a struggle? I didn't hear a struggle."

"To be fair, you were being strangled at the time," Gideon said dismissively.

He walked around to Bammy's head and slid his arms underneath his shoulders. He lifted his upper body off the ground and dragged him over next to Bigga. Gently, he placed him parallel to his concussed companion. Todd watched silently while Gideon removed Tara's blanket and placed her pack in between their bodies. With all the care of a new parent, he spread the blanket long ways over his slumbering friends; only able to partially cover Bigga's plus-sized frame. Gideon then picked up his own backpack and slung it over his shoulder.

"Ya ready?" he asked Todd.

"Ready for what?"

"We gotta go find Tara," said Gideon.

"Just so we're clear," Todd began, "we were just attacked by our zombie buddies over here amid a crazy magic fog. I probably have tetanus, by the way. And now you want to go running off after whoever or whatever drug our guide off into the jungle in the middle of the night? Is that about right?"

"Technically they can't be zombies; zombies are undead, and they are very much alive," Gideon said, in an attempt to break the tension.

"Oh, you got jokes, huh?"

"Look, I don't like this anymore than you do," Gideon said, in a more serious manner. "But what's the alternative?"

Todd put his hands on his hips with a chagrinned look on his face. He inhaled deeply and looked off into the jungle in the direction Gideon indicated. Gideon would not admit it aloud, but he was frightened at that thought of heading into the dark jungle after an unknown assailant. He would have much preferred to stay right where they were until morning and hope Tara returned on her own. Although a rescue mission was not what he wanted, he knew it was the right thing to do. He screwed up his courage and attempted to steady his voice and project confidence.

"She is out here because of me," Gideon continued. "If anything happens to her it's my fault. The longer we sit here the harder it's going to be to find her. I have to go."

"We," Todd said. "We have to go."

Gideon nodded gratefully to his friend. In the moonlight, Todd's hair almost glowed as he stood distinctly apart from the darkness all around them. He remembered what Joe had said before they departed: *You two stay close to each other, get each other's back, and you'll be all right.* Gideon had no idea what awaited them but felt a calm reassurance to have his idiot best friend with him on their fool's errand. With one last glance over his shoulder at the blanketed pair of unconscious bodies, they set off in search of Tara and her captor.

His hopes of using the light from the moon to guide their way were quickly dashed as they stepped into a grouping of trees and beneath a canopy of complete darkness. Gideon turned on his flashlight and shined it on the ground in front of them. A few meters into the darkness the trail of smashed grass disappeared. He knelt down to examine the area more closely; there were two deep footprints in the mud.

"He picked her up," Gideon whispered to himself.

"He? You mean Mufasa?"

"Mucaro," he corrected. "But yeah, that's my guess."

"Ya still think he's protecting his weed?" asked Todd sarcastically.

The idea that Mucaro was uninterested in the cave or their journey had been a stretch and he knew it. Still, Todd's condescension was hard to take. Gideon hung his head and wished he could go back in time and take his words back. If he could go back in time though, he would not stop there. He would go back to Professor Gervaise's classroom, leave the journal behind, and go to Ochi as he suggested and drink Ting on the beach. Instead, Tara was missing and Bammy and Bigga lay unconscious in the middle of the cockpits and he had to face the seriousness of the situation. Humbled by the gravity of his naiveté, as he had embarked on this quest so unprepared and by the consequences of those actions, he could not muster the strength to answer Todd's query. Mercifully, he did not press further and brought the conversation back to the matter at hand.

"How do you know he picked her up?" Todd asked curiously.

"The grass was mashed into the ground because something was being drug through it," Gideon explained. "There were two sets of footprints before the dragging started. The dragging ends here and there is now one set of footprints. Plus, look how deep they are. Whoever this is, they are carrying something."

"Okay, Columbo," Todd teased.

"I'll take that as a compliment," Gideon responded proudly and rejected his mocking tone. A feigned cavalier attitude was a mechanism Gideon had used since childhood to regain his confidence whenever it waned.

They made their way methodically through the jungle. Gideon kept the light low, pointed down directly at the ground. The purpose was twofold; first, he followed an erratic trail which required concentrated light and second, he did not wish to give away their position. The slow pace caused Gideon to grow even more anxious. Traveling through the bush was twice as difficult and ten times as dangerous at night. In addition, they were without an experienced guide and unsure who or what they were following. They walked for almost an hour without exchanging a word. Both of them kept a keen eye up and listened carefully for any signs of life. Aside from the sounds of birds and bugs that filled the trees, they heard no noises that were out of place. Gideon lost and found the trail several times but kept it to himself; always sure to point to a fresh footprint or broken branch when he happened upon one to show Todd they were still on the right track.

"So what's the plan?" Todd finally asked after an hour's long silence.

"What do you mean?" asked Gideon, as they continued to move slowly forward through a patch of wet, waist-high grass.

"If and when we catch up to them, what are we going to do?"

Gideon had given a great deal of thought to that very question. Whoever had taken Tara was unlikely to be a friend. Catching up to them would surely mean a conflict. Gideon had never fared well in physical confrontations outside of the gridiron. He had only been in two real fights in his life and neither of them ended well for him. The first was actually with Todd. The two of them were at scout camp when Todd, as a prank, ran a pair of his underpants up a flag pole. Incensed by this betrayal, Gideon attacked in a fit of rage. He flailed his arms wildly in an attempt to inflict a measure of pain on his best friend. Todd had the high ground and retreated until he found proper footing. With one punch he belted Gideon on the chin, which left him with more than just a bruise to his ego. If by some miracle they were able to find Tara and her captor, Gideon was not confident he would prevail in a fight. He clung to the hope that his wit and powers of persuasion would be sufficient to get the job done.

"Between the two of us, we'll come up with something."

Even as the words escaped his mouth, doubt set in. They had no idea who or what awaited them, plan making was irrelevant, right now circumstances demanded action. They continued to make their way, in the black of night, through the treacherous cockpits. Their only real break was that they followed after someone and thus their path way was cleared somewhat for them. Gideon had thought they would have overtaken them by now. From what he could tell they were in pursuit of a single individual who carried another person. He could not imagine that even at their current careful pace they would not have gained on them.

"Oh my GAH!" Todd shrieked suddenly.

A black and gold snake had slithered out in between them into the light of Todd's flashlight. Gideon looked back to find Todd, recoiled in fear, about ten or twelve steps from him. He shined his light from Todd to the snake. It was a Jamaican boa at least two meters long. This was their natural habitat, and Gideon was surprised it had taken this long for them to see one. The snake slowly continued on its path, seemingly unaware of the angst it caused.

"Relax," Gideon whispered. "It's not going to bite you. It's a boa."

"Relax?!" he exclaimed in his loudest whispery voice. "That snake's as big as I am!"

"Just step over it," he said. "It's not going to hurt you."

"Are you crazy?" Todd responded angrily.

"Look, just jump quick and it can't get a hold of you," he stated in a calm confident voice.

"Okay, Tarzan. Since when are you a snake wrangler?"

"We did service at the zoo, and we fed the snakes. Move fast and you'll be fine."

Every Monday, Wednesday, and Friday, in the six months he served in Kingston, he and his companion rode their bikes to Hope Zoo and helped feed the animals. It was a small zoo with mostly snakes, birds, and reptiles, plus a few mongooses, peccaries, two lions, and a crocodile. Gideon did not particularly like snakes; but the zoo and a childhood in the Arizona desert provided him enough exposure where he could handle running across one.

"What is that?" Todd said, and pointed over Gideon's shoulder.

"I'm not falling for the 'look over there' trick, Todd."

"No, I'm serious, look," he said, and pointed more aggressively over Gideon's shoulder.

As he turned and looked over his right shoulder, he saw an orange light on the side of the summit, just around a bend from where they stood. The glow cast long dark shadows on the hillside. It was the light from a fire that looked to be set amidst a large grouping of trees.

"That's gotta be them," said Todd.

"Well come on then," said Gideon.

Todd took in a deep breath and exhaled. He ran and jumped over the snake. As his feet hit the ground he shivered and bolted passed Gideon. The two of them hurried off toward the orange glow. Neither spoke of Todd's momentary cowardice.

Gideon gained a new appreciation for the expression, like a moth to a flame. Being immersed in darkness all night, he truly felt drawn to the light. The allure of the light was not only for the physical illumination, but the potential light it would shed on who was out here with them.

Within minutes they had come to the edge of the trees, just a stone's throw from the fire. They crouched down low and crept forward, being sure to keep out of sight. Through the bushes and trees they could see the flames from the fire. They held up at a safe distance, behind a perimeter of bushes. Gideon could make out two figures on opposite sides of the fire pit; the closest to them was Tara. She sat on the ground with her hands and feet bound with rope. His heart sank down into his stomach as he saw that it was the maroon-clad Mucaro, who sat across from her on a stump and stared intently. Gideon looked over to Todd, who already knelt on the ground and looked back at him.

"We need a plan," Gideon said, stating the obvious.

"We could try the 'hey look over there' trick."

That sentence summed up everything Gideon loved about his friend—and at the same time found so vexing. Todd had the innate ability to remain lighthearted at the most inappropriate times. Gideon enjoyed and needed the levity he offered, as the gravity of the moment was about to swallow him whole. Still with his nonchalant nature, Gideon could not tell if he had the proper mindset to address the situation properly.

"No, we need to draw him away. You flank them over in that direction and draw him off into the bush. I'll go get Tara."

"That's a terrible idea," Todd raised his voice to a loud whisper. "How 'bout the homicidal obeah man chases you and I rescue the girl."

"Rock, paper, scissors?" suggested Gideon.

They had settled every standoff, as long as he could remember, with a game of rock, paper, scissors.

"Fine, but no two out of three," warned Todd. "This is it."

Gideon nodded and they both held their fists in the air. They pumped their fists up and down twice in unison. On the third time they showed their hands. Gideon extended two fingers set apart, like a pair of scissors. He looked over at Todd's opened hand, faced palm up.

"Crap," Todd whispered.

The bushes that kept them out of sight also blocked the light of the fire. They crouched in the shadows in silent contemplation. Gideon felt relieved and yet guilty for his victory. He thought hard how he might help Todd in his task. He felt around in the darkness until his hand ran across a hard, fist sized, stone. He picked it up and offered it to Todd.

"Jump out from over there and chuck this at him," Gideon said. "Maybe you'll hit him and knock him out. If not? Run."

"What if I hit him and it just pisses him off?"

"Well, I wouldn't let him catch you."

"Great, thanks. Super helpful," Todd responded sarcastically, and took the stone.

"Once I get Tara free I'll make some noise and try to draw him back toward us," Gideon explained. "We'll haul butt out of there and meet you back by the trees where we stopped."

"With the snake?!" Todd exclaimed, still in a whisper.

"You got a better idea?" Gideon responded.

"No," Todd glumly admitted.

Gideon peaked back over the top of the pinguin shrubs and saw Mucaro stoking the flames with a stick, while Tara did not move at all. He pushed from his mind the thoughts of all that could go wrong. Instead he chose to focus his energies in a more positive vein. He read a book once on the power of visualization. In his mind he imagined the scenario play out. *Todd and Tara would escape and they would regroup safely.* He said a prayer that all would go well and that God would keep them safe. His choices had brought them here, and he only hoped now that God might help get them out of it.

Todd rose, still slumped over beneath the cover of the bushes. "Wish me luck."

"Good luck, brother."

"Hey, give me a Jamaican swear word."

"What? Why?" asked Gideon.

"I want to yell it at him before I huck this rock."

Gideon shook his head and smiled. "Try *bumba ras clot*."

"Got it," Todd said. With that, he hurried off around the perimeter of bushes and trees until he rounded a large bush and was out of sight.

Gideon turned his attention back to the fire pit and began to focus on his piece of the plan. He figured he was about thirty yards from Tara. From his limited field of vision it did not appear there were any major hurdles in his way. He factored in the uneven ground and guessed he could reach her easily in less than twenty seconds. Then he would need to untie her and break for the trees. From his peripheral vision he saw Todd emerge from the other side of a large cedar tree and step into the clearing, in plain view of Mucaro.

"Hey bumble ross!" Todd shouted. He heaved the stone at Mucaro, turned around and ran back into the bush. Mucaro jumped up from the stump and leaned to the side as the stone flew past his head. His body lurched toward Todd, and launched into instinctual pursuit, but he halted suddenly and did not give chase. Instead he tilted his head and stared in the direction Todd had fled. Then he looked back at Tara, walked slowly around the fire, stooped down and untied her arms and legs with a series of rough tugs. He flung the ropes to the side as she rubbed at her wrists and glared up at him. Then he walked back to his stump, picked up another stick and sat down to poke at the embers of the fire.

There was a rustling in the bushes behind Gideon. Quickly, he spun around and braced himself for what was coming. Todd stumbled through the leaves and branches; his once white shirt was stained brown and dingy from trumping through the cockpits all day and night. At the sight of his friend, Gideon relaxed his defensive stance. Todd shrugged his shoulders and held his hands in the air.

"What now?" Todd asked.

He honestly had no idea how to answer. His ill-conceived plan had been an utter failure. They had played their hand and given away the element of surprise. Mucaro appeared entirely unconcerned at their presence. In a perplexing move he had even untied Tara. Gideon felt this might be a show of strength to intimidate or confuse them, and it had worked, because Gideon felt both confused and intimidated. The only thing left to do now was talk or fight. He preferred the former but felt he would soon have to face the latter.

"Gideon Goodwin," Mucaro called out loudly, without looking up from the flames in front of him. "Yu don't give up, do yu?"

To hear his name come from this man's mouth was unnerving. Not only did he know Gideon was there but he knew who he was. His mind whirled as he wondered what else he knew. He had completely underestimated Mucaro. What was the extent of his knowledge? More importantly, what was the extent of his powers and what were his intentions with them? He felt paralyzed. He wanted to flee but was unable to. Even if he could have fled he did not know where he would have gone. Besides, he knew he could not leave Tara. Whatever happened next, he no longer held to the illusion he had any control over it. The next play was entirely up to Mucaro.

"Come," the young obeah man said. "Let's chat."

A Discovery and a Confrontation

His head felt as if it was filled with sand and he lay on his back unable to lift it. Gently, he shook his head side to side in an attempt to clear the cobwebs from his mind. His vision was blurred and hazy, but he swore that he looked up at a rocky surface. A soft orange glow kissed the gray stone ceiling. The orange light mixed with a white light that came from somewhere back above and behind him. He felt a cool breeze sweep across his bare chest. His head was drenched in sweat and he felt a single droplet slide down his cheek into his beard. He felt as if the life had been drained from him. Just keeping his eyelids apart proved daunting. He let his eyes close and lay very still to listen for some clue as to where he was. He heard the crackle of a fire and felt its warmth down by his feet. With great effort he tried to lean forward and sit up. Immediately a dull pain filled his left shoulder and he cried out.

With his right arm he reached across his body and felt a damp cloth on his shoulder. Just then he felt light pressure on his wound, as if a bird had perched upon it. Instinctively, he reached out and grabbed at the source. It felt like a tiny branch. He forced his eyes open and tilted his head downward to see what it was he held.

The yellow and orange light that emanated from the fire cast a shadow over the figure that hovered over him. When his vision came into focus, he saw long black hair draped off the figure's head. He followed the dark locks up to a round face with caramel brown skin. All at once, like the flash from a powder keg, he recognized the face. He had gazed into her serene brown eyes before, in what seemed like another life. Unable to believe what he saw, he lay there in stunned silence. He still held fast to her wrist and she, ever so gently, pulled her arm free and placed it back atop his bandaged shoulder.

The thought occurred to him that he might be dead. *If I am dead then surely this is purgatory*, Jarvis thought. He could not imagine a more fitting punishment than for him to lie in agony for eternity at the mercy of the child he nearly murdered. Only, she was not a child any more. She had grown into a young woman. Her hair was longer and her face much fuller. She was not the scrawny little girl he remembered from the visions that haunted his memory. In her eyes, however, was the unmistakable evidence that this was the girl whose life had once rested in his hands.

She did not speak but peeled back the bandage from his shoulder. He peered down at the wound. His flesh had been gashed open and appeared to have been stuffed with some kind of mud or clay. She removed several pieces of hardened clay from the depressions in his shoulder. She reached down to retrieve a coconut half shell, which rested on the loin cloth that covered her lap. With her fingers, she scooped out a gelatinous oily sludge from inside the shell and massaged it into the wound. This nutty sludge looked identical to the substance John Davis had created from the red spiny fruit in the jungle. He winced at her touch.

"Ah," Jarvis cried. "Is that medicine?"

She repeated the process, dipping and rubbing the sludge on his wound, but did not answer his question or even look up at him.

"Where am I?"

Still she did not answer. After she emptied the contents of the half shell she placed it back in her lap and reached down to the ground. She carefully lifted a large banana leaf with both hands. On top of the leaf was a mixture of clay, green leafs and tiny black seeds. She rested the clay laded leaf on Jarvis's stomach, scooped out generous handfuls of the mixture and slathered it on his wound. As the cool clay touched his skin he realized that he no longer felt any pain.

"Do you speak English?" he asked. "Uh, *habla English*, uh, *inglés?*

Without an answer or even a glance in his direction, she finished her work and covered his wound with the same damp cloth. She returned the empty banana leaf to the ground and picked up the coconut half shell in her lap. Quietly, she stood up and turned to leave. Jarvis struggled to sit up but she quickly turned back, raised both hands in front of her, and beckoned him to lie down.

"*Tie-toca,*" she said. She looked at him for the first time and waved downward with her hands. "*Tie-toca.*"

"I do not speak your language," he said. He had no sooner spoken the words when the irony of him trying to explain that to her in English struck him.

When he ceased his attempt to sit up, she again turned to leave. She disappeared through a man sized opening in the rock wall. Jarvis looked around the small room. The smoke from the fire, near his feet, rose up to a stone ceiling and drifted gently out through the man sized opening. The soft daylight of early morning shone through the breach in the wall. All at once he noticed a dusty old trunk in the center of the room. The brown walnut chest had brass handles on both sides and three leather straps over the top. The room, aside from himself, the trunk, and the fire, appeared to be empty. All that separated his body from the ground was a patch of dark green banana leaves. A narrow passage on the far side of the room led off into the darkness. If not for the passage he would have supposed this small room to be his tomb.

"Hello," Jarvis called out toward the opening. "I need water. Please."

Nearly unable to swallow, due to the dryness of his throat, he sought relief from yet another physical discomfort. He called out, unsure whether he would be understood, and hoped someone might respond to the sound of his voice. He listened and waited. A few minutes passed and he heard movement outside the dagger shaped opening. A shadow crept up the rock wall across from him until it almost completely blocked out the daylight.

"Water, please," he repeated his petition.

"*¿Quiere agua?*" a deep voice answered.

He craned his neck to look upward. A large hulking man filled the entrance to the cave. He held a calabash in his over-sized hands. He took several steps toward Jarvis and the light from the fire revealed his face. Jarvis's stomach lurched and his jaw tightened at the sight of him. The appearance of such a massive specimen, when he had expected a little girl, would have been a shock all its own. However, what sparked such a visceral reaction was not his size, Jarvis knew him. It was the man whom he called Goliath. It was the man who had led Lubolo and his men to their deaths. It was the man to whom he owed his life. Goliath approached Jarvis and bent down to offer him the calabash. Hesitantly, Jarvis accepted the gourde and nodded in gratitude. Goliath sat down on the trunk at the center of the room and studied Jarvis.

"Drink," he said.

With some trepidation Jarvis sat up and pulled the cork from the top of the calabash. He lifted it to his lips and tilted it upward. The cool water washed down the back of his throat. Energy surged through his body as the life giving liquid swept down through his insides. After he drank to his satisfaction, he lowered the calabash and looked back toward the monstrous man that sat on the trunk next to him. His massive forearms were just as big as he remembered. His head was still shorn on the sides, the top adorned by a bushel of knotty curls. He wore no shoes or shirt, only a dark blue vest and black pantaloons that barely went down to his knees. The two men regarded each other silently until a new shadow crept up the rock wall next to the entrance.

A tall shirtless African warrior, with a necklace of teeth and bone draped across his chest, emerged through the opening. At his side was Jarvis's saber, a gift from Colonel Tyson. The memories of the battle flooded back to his mind. He looked into his cold black eyes and thought that those eyes must have been the last thing Lubolo ever saw. Before him were the two men who had held his life in their hands and, for some reason, had spared him. Jarvis wondered again if he might be dead, for this was indeed Hell. The tall shirtless man leaned against the far wall, folded his arms and stared down at him smugly.

"My name is Keitloa," said the hulky figure who sat on the trunk.

"Jarvis," he said after a momentary lapse in decorum. "We know who you are, Major Jarvis," said Keitloa.

To hear the words 'Major Jarvis' come from his mouth was jarring. The fact that he knew something about him, other than his name, was unsettling. *How much did he know? And how?* The unknown, as always, was a breeding ground for fear and there were so very many unknowns that he was unsure what to fear first. He did not wish to appear eager with a barrage of questions and thus tip his hand. Instead, he chose to focus on a question more immediate to the situation.

"The girl, where is she?"

Keitloa laughed loudly and turned back toward the man against the wall, who also smiled broadly. When his laughter faded, Keitloa turned back to Jarvis. "Such concern for a girl who is only alive because she was rescued from you."

Jarvis could not answer, as he had no defense against the accusation. He had indeed been confronted with the gruesome task of dispatching the girl, along with two other Arawak children. The man who lay broken in a cave on a bed of leaves would never have dreamed of harming those children. He was far less certain about the moral convictions of a young frightened Lieutenant left alone in the middle of the jungle so many years ago. Truth be told, Jarvis still did not know what would have happened that day had the angelic assassin not intervened. Jarvis's eyes met with the tall shirtless warrior and turned away from the shame.

Rather than dwell on this unsavory recollection Jarvis sought to change the topic. "Your English is excellent."

"So is yours."

"Where did you learn it?"

"In Accra, from a slave trader named Ellis."

"Where are the men I was traveling with?"

"They are safe. I will ask the questions now," Keitloa said. "Why did you return?"

Jarvis was not about to trust him with the truth. Instead he chose to employ a bold, and possibly reckless, tactic in the hopes that Keitloa might reveal something he could use.

"I returned to bring the war criminal Juan de Serras to justice," he lied.

His statement seemed to amuse the swarthy giant. With a big smile he gestured over his shoulder to the warrior against the wall, "See him there. Go and take him."

The two of them smiled down at Jarvis as if daring him to act. Jarvis shifted his shoulders slightly to determine his level of pain. To his surprise, he felt nothing in his wounded shoulder. Carefully, he rolled onto his side and sat up. His strength had not yet returned so he leaned backwards and rested against the rock wall. Jarvis smiled back at Keitloa and de Serras.

"Will he go quietly then?"

"No," Keitloa replied, with a great big smile. "I do not believe he will."

Another slender shadow crept up the wall next to de Serras from outside the triangular opening. The girl returned and in her arms she carried several pieces of violate green fruit. She offered one to de Serras, who declined. She then reached out and gave one to Keitloa.

He took the piece of fruit and with his left hand removed a small knife from his back pocket. Jarvis thought that it was probably a knife of standard size and length, but it looked small in his massive hands. Keitloa waved toward Jarvis with his knife, to permit her to offer him a piece of fruit. As he waved, Jarvis saw the marking of the backwards facing bird on his forearm. The girl dutifully stepped forward and extended a round piece of fruit to Jarvis.

"Thank you."

Jarvis waited and watched his host. With his knife, Keitloa sliced a piece from the side and ate it whole, skin and all. Jarvis followed his lead and took a big bite. As he sunk his teeth into the fruit's juicy flesh, he marveled how this tiny morsel of nourishment provided an almost immediate renewal to his ailing body. The inside of the fruit was a deep purple, speckled with black seeds, with white veins that ran through it. Jarvis could not remember ever tasting anything so delicious, although he conceded that may be due to his malnourished and dehydrated condition. The fruit bearer returned to Keitloa's side. He gently reached up and caressed her cheek with the backs of his rough fingers.

"You know who suffers most from man's thirst for power?" he asked rhetorically and gazed solemnly upon the girl to his left. "The innocent. They understand nothing of greed or ambition, yet they are doomed to fall victim to both."

Jarvis sat in stunned silence. He was taken aback by this well-spoken man. In the time he spent with Lubolo, he had grown to respect his tenacity and intellect, as it related to waging war, but he did not consider him an articulate man. Lubolo had a decent command of the English language, but it was obvious English was not his native tongue. Keitloa, however, spoke as if he had learned it from birth.

"And who will stand up for them, Mr. Jarvis?" he asked, as he turned back to face him.

"Is that what you are doing here?" Jarvis inquired abruptly. "Standing up for the innocent?"

"No. Neither you nor I associate ourselves with the innocent," Keitloa said. "But what is to be done when they stand before us? I will not suffer their blood to cry out from the ground against me."

"So you *are* here to protect the innocent?" Jarvis asked.

"I am here because of the same greed and ambition that has plagued these people to extinction. The same arrogance and ignorance that caused man to lay claim on a people and a land where he had not the right," he said with fire in his eyes. "I am here to tear down power and lay waste to those who seek it."

"That sounds terrifying" Jarvis said, nonchalantly, although deep down he was terrified. "But I am still not exactly sure what you are after."

"I would no sooner share that with you than you would with me."

"But I have told you."

"No!" Keitloa stood straight up and pointed at de Serras. "You have not returned for him!"

He reached down and threw open the lid of the dark walnut trunk. Inside it was filled with gold coins, silver jewelry, and trinkets. Of all the times Jarvis had imagined Bartomoleu's treasure it had never been in the shadow of the massive man who stood before him. He tried to remain composed; although it was clear that in this game he played his opponent held all the cards.

"This is what you are after," Keitloa continued. "Your yellow-haired friend came for this before and now he has returned with you."

"I would very much like to see my yellow-haired friend and the boy," Jarvis said. He refused to confirm the accusation. He looked Keitloa directly in the eyes, careful to keep his gaze from the object of his desire.

"When you can walk I will take you to them."

Unsure whether he could stand or not, Jarvis rolled up unto his knees. He reached out with his right arm and used the wall to steady himself. Slowly, he raised his left leg in front of him. When he gained a proper footing, he pressed upwards and came to his feet. His head swirled for a moment and he wobbled back and forth. When he had collected himself, he bent his knees to test the sturdiness of his legs. Keitloa, de Serras and the girl all watched him with great curiosity. He let go of the wall and turned to proudly face them.

"Very well," said Keitloa.

He closed the lid to the trunk and stepped aside, with a gesture toward the entrance. The girl and de Serras exited the room

209

through the opening in the wall. Jarvis put one foot in front of the other and made his way, gingerly, across the room. His legs had not felt this unsteady since he stepped off the ship onto the shores of Caguaya Bay, nearly a decade ago. As he reached the triangle opening, he put his hand up to shield his eyes from the blinding daylight. There was not a cloud to be seen.

He paused in the entrance and looked to his right. There was a large clearing of green grass and short bushes that sprawled out toward a group of trees. Several green egg shaped summits rose up in the distance behind them. When he glanced back at the wall to his left, as he suspected, he saw the looping heart shaped symbol carved into the rock just over his head. This had indeed been the cave he had spent a dark and sleepless night in, after his first brush with de Serras.

A dozen men congregated, beyond the entrance to the cave, around the smoldering remains of a small fire. As Jarvis exited the cave they all turned to watch him. Their dark expressionless faces showed no reaction whatsoever to his appearance. He could not discern if they wished him harm or if they even cared of his presence in the least. Jarvis followed after de Serras and the girl, with Keitloa close behind him. Just beyond the men and the smoke filled pit there were thirty or forty Negro rebels strewn about on the ground. They lay amongst the grass and bushes, much like Lubolo's men had done so often. Oddly, this scene made Jarvis feel at home.

Many memories returned of the years spent with the black regiment. A narrow footpath led to several tall trees just ahead of them. As they drew nearer Jarvis made out two men, who sat on the ground at the base of a tree. John Davis and Smitty appeared to be tied to the trunk the tree with several long vines. Jarvis lost his footing on the uneven ground, stumbled and fell flat on his face. He lay motionless, face down in the dirt, and lacked the strength to draw himself up again. The injuries he sustained had clearly taken more out of him than he thought. Within moments he was scooped up by the powerful arms of Keitloa and placed on his feet again.

"Come," Keitloa said. He led him under the shade of the tree. "Sit."

He sat him down gently on the ground, a few feet from where John Davis and Smitty were tied up. They were bound and blindfolded but appeared to be otherwise unharmed. Keitloa squatted down and watched while de Serras unceremoniously removed their blindfolds. Smitty squinted rapidly and looked around nervously until he spotted Jarvis.

"You're alive," he said with a sigh of relief. "We thought you was a goner."

"And how are you?" Jarvis asked.

"A'right, I suppose," Smitty answered and looked over at John Davis.

"I've 'ad it far worse than this, mate," John Davis said. "They gave us fruit an' water. That's a sight better than the bloody Spaniards ever did. Aside from the minor infringement on me liberties I'm quite well. You?"

"I am fine, all things considered," Jarvis said and looked down at his bandaged shoulder.

"I should say so," John Davis said. "You nearly 'ad your bloody arm bit off."

"It were one of them that saved you," Smitty interjected. He pointed to the Arawak girl, who stood a ways back just beneath the shadow of the tree. "This boy come swing'n in outta nowhere. 'e jumped in the water an' rammed a spear clean through that croc's 'ead. Then these 'ere Negroes showed up and we was tied up like a couple a Billy goats."

It was a lot to take in. First, the dark monster that grabbed him and nearly dragged him to his death was a crocodile. Second, an Arawak boy had saved his life, perhaps the same boy who Captain Willard had ordered him to kill. He looked over at the young girl who stood meekly and look back at him. *This cannot be a coincidence*, he thought.

Had his hand been stayed so that these children might later be his salvation? And if so, for what purpose? He looked from the girl to de Serras to his friends and finally to Keitloa. The massive

African warrior stood up and brandished the small knife from his back pocket.

"Are you going to kill us then?" asked Jarvis.

Keitloa grinned and let out a small chuckle as he walked passed Jarvis over to the tree where John Davis and Smitty were bound. With his knife, he sawed through vine after vine until they were free. He put the knife back in his pocket and turned back to Jarvis.

"If I wanted you dead I would have killed you with Lubolo," Keitloa responded.

"Why did you not kill me?"

"Why did you not kill this child?" said Keitloa, and pointed to the girl.

"I was going to," he replied, and tried to sound convincing.

"No, I do not believe you were," he said. "I was there when Ysassi fell. We arrived too late to help, but I saw you. You could have killed that boy, but you did not."

"He was just a boy," Jarvis said. "Besides, it did not matter, Lubolo killed him anyway."

"Lubolo was a traitor and a selfish, wicked man," Keitloa barked angrily. Then all at once his demeanor changed and soften. "And it did matter. It mattered a great deal to me."

Smitty and John Davis untangled themselves from the remaining vines. They sat, rooted to the spot, and watched the back and forth between Jarvis and Keitloa. Jarvis thought about the events in his life and the circumstances that led him to this moment. He imagined how different his life would have been had he made different choices.

In all likelihood he would be dead now, cut down by one of the men who stood before him. If he had killed those Arawak children, Juan de Serras would have surely killed him. If he had shot the surrendering Negro boy he would have most certainly been strangled by the massive hands of Keitloa, or been beheaded in the same manner as Lubolo. Even if these men had spared him, if he had killed those children it would have meant dying in the clutches of a crocodile at the bottom of a deep blue pond. It was humbling for him to come to grips with the fragile nature of his mortality.

"So what is it that you want from me?" asked Jarvis.

"The gold," Keitloa explained. "It is of no use to us. We cannot spend it. No one with means will trade with us."

"True."

"We will spare your lives and give you the gold. In exchange, you will use a portion of it to obtain muskets, powder and provisions for us," Keitloa proposed. "The rest you may keep for yourselves."

Jarvis considered the offer. Self-preservation dictated that he accept and live. From the looks on their faces, John Davis and Smitty seemed keen to the idea as well. On the surface it appeared to be a straightforward and fair agreement. In exchange for their lives they were to provide these rebels with weapons and provisions and, in return, they would retain what treasure remained as payment for their service. The downside was that the weapons would most certainly be used to kill his countrymen. In addition, there was no guarantee they would not double cross them once they had what they were after.

"What assurances do we have you will keep your side of the agreement?" Jarvis asked.

"I can assure you that if you do not agree, we will kill you here and now," he answered with a devilish smile. "You give me your word and you shall have mine. That is the only assurance I can give you."

Although still weakened and sapped of energy, Jarvis felt the situation demanded that he stand on his feet to seal the deal. He shifted his weight to his right side and rolled up onto his knees. Smitty jumped to assist him and caught him under his left arm. Jarvis winced from the pain that shot down his side. Smitty quickly recognized his mistake and hopped over to Jarvis's right help him to his feet. Jarvis leaned on Smitty for support and extended his hand toward Keitloa, "You have my word."

As the two men shook hands an abeng sounded in the distance. Immediately the camp behind them burst into a beehive of activity. Keitloa signaled to de Serras with a nod of his head toward the sound. De Serras leapt forward to meet the men that headed down the hill toward him.

"*¡Dense prisa! ¡Váyanse!*" de Serras shouted, with an aggressive arm motion toward the sound.

The Negro soldiers, led by de Serras, flowed off into the jungle like ghosts and swept silently through the trees. Jarvis stood in awe at their movements and formation. At first glance, they appeared to move at random but, as he watched closely, he noticed that each man stepped within the footprint of the man that preceded him. An act of brilliance, as it all but concealed their numbers were anyone to follow them. They did so with clocklike precision, beat by beat, as they charged off toward the sound of the abeng. In all his time with Lubolo and the black regiment he had not seen such order and rhythm. Few of their men carried muskets. Most were armed with bladed implements of death; such as sabers, cutlass and billhooks. They disappeared into the jungle almost without a sound. Jarvis pitied whoever it was they were after.

"Well, you blokes look like you've got your 'ands full 'ere," John Davis said casually. "We'll just collect the gold an' be on our way."

Keitloa shot a disdainful look toward John Davis. Wisely, he looked away and playfully kicked at a rock on the ground near his feet. Jarvis was eager to head off any trouble and keep their newly formed agreement intact.

"What he means is, do let us know if we can be of assistance in any way."

Jarvis leaned in and tilted his head into Keitloa's field of view in the hopes of distracting him from the death stare he had locked on John Davis. Keitloa looked over at Jarvis but his expression did not soften. Whatever mistrust they harbored toward him, Jarvis imagined, was returned in kind. He thought it best to tread lightly at the moment, a task made more difficult by his companion's overzealousness to obtain the treasure in question.

"Come," said Keitloa.

He led them back toward the cave. As they stepped out from beneath the shade of the tree the full magnitude of the sun bore down on them. A volley of musket fire rang out between the summit walls, toward the southeast. Jarvis stumbled and fell when he turned to look. He rolled over on his back and looked up into the bright blue sky. A muscle bound forearm came into view, with the mark of a backward facing bird at the center. Jarvis reached up and grasped Keitloa's firm hand and was pulled to his feet. The group continued toward the cave and paid no mind to the battle sounds behind them. Keitloa entered the cave first. Jarvis stopped at the entrance and pointed over at the swirling heart shaped symbol carved into the rock. John Davis and Smitty exchanged a gleeful look. The three of them then entered the cave followed by the Arawak girl.

Inside, Keitloa threw open the trunk and stood beside it. John Davis pushed his way passed Jarvis and slid down beside the trunk on his knees. He lifted out handfuls of gold coins and let them fall back through his fingers. Smitty quickly joined him, removed a single coin and held it up to his face to admired it.

"I knew I'd get the best a you one day, Bartolomeu, you ol' cod," John Davis said, as he lifted his gaze and spoke to the ceiling. "Maybe you'll think twice before deserting the next poor bugga."

While his partners worshipped their treasure, Jarvis stood back toward the entrance with the young girl. She looked up at him but still said nothing. He wondered if she could communicate and simply chose not to do so with him. Not that he would have blamed her, as her only memory of him was not a pleasant one. Still, he felt compelled to try and speak with her.

"What is your name?" he asked.

She did not answer and her expression gave no indication whether she understood him at all. She just stared back at him like a stone monument. Undeterred by her lack of response he tried a slightly different approach.

"I am Benjamin Jarvis," he said slowly, and placed his hand on his chest. "You can call me Ben."

In the distance, somewhere beyond the triangular shaped opening in the wall, they heard an occasional musket being fired. The shots were scattered between minutes of silence but they definitely drew nearer. For the first time Keitloa showed some concern. He walked over to the cave's entrance and peered outside.

"Ben," Jarvis repeated, and patted his chest. "And you?"

"We call her Eve," Keitloa said. He did not look over at them but stared out through the opening. "After the mother of us all."

Once again Jarvis was astounded, as his preconceived notions of this hulking warrior were shattered. Not only did he have a healthy command of the English language, but he had clearly been schooled in the stories of the Bible. What most impressed Jarvis, though, was the reverence with which he spoke of Eve.

"Pleased to meet you, Eve," Jarvis said. He extended his hand. "Ben, Ben Jarvis."

She looked at his hand with a puzzled expression. Cautiously, she reached out and gently pressed down on the top of his thumb before she quickly withdrew her hand. *Close enough*, he thought.

"Take what you can carry," Keitloa ordered. He did not move from where he stood. Something outside had him completely captivated. "Leave the rest until you return."

At that he produced a small black polished stone from his pocket. Again, Jarvis could not tell if the stone was small or just looked small in his gigantic hands. The dark stone had a shine to it and almost appeared transparent. Keitloa held it up to his face, between his mighty hands, and began to chant something that Jarvis could not understand. His best guess was that it was some Africa dialect, but his chants were barely audible to those inside the cave. The light that came through the opening faded and turned to grey. There was a clap of thunder and a flash of lightning. Rain began to fall and the ground at the entrance of the cave showed the splatter of mud and clay as the large drops pounded the earth.

"Stay here," Keitloa warned, before he leapt out through the opening to completely disappear into the torrential downpour.

"Did 'e just make it rain?" a partially panicked Smitty asked.

Jarvis and John Davis exchanged a look of disbelief but did not answer. Jarvis had the same thought but did not dare utter it. He had seen many things in his travels, some of which were difficult to explain, but he had never seen a man with the power to command the weather. It seemed impossible and he wished to chalk it up to coincidence but struggled to reason away what he had just witnessed. Had this enigmatic man just conjured up a storm before their very eyes? None of them spoke. Eve walked over to the dying fire in the corner and laid a few branches across it. As the flame grew larger the room grew lighter. Without delay they began to collect the coins from the trunk. Smitty found some cloth, by the bedding where Jarvis had recuperated, and fashioned a pouch to hold some of the larger bullion. John Davis took off his shirt and stuffed it full of gold and silver. Jarvis filled the pockets of his trousers with coins.

"Is that all your tak'n?" John Davis demanded.

"We can get the rest when we return," Jarvis stated.

"When we return?" he questioned. "Are you mad? I ain't never coming back 'ere, mate."

"You can do as you like, but I have given him my word and I intend to honor it."

"An' you expect 'im to 'onor 'is, eh? 'e'll spill your bleeding guts the moment you turn up with what 'e wants. That's if you don't get yourself killed between 'ere and there."

"You are free to forfeit your share by not returning. Take what you can carry and sell your birthright for a mess of pottage."

"A mess of what?" a befuddled John Davis said. "What the bleed'n . . . what are you talk'n 'bout?"

"It's from the Bible," Smitty interjected.

"I know where it's from, you git," John Davis shot back. "But this ain't no pottage, mate. You two do what ya like. I'm tak'n this 'ere loot an' 'ead'n off to the lap of luxury, I am."

He scooped up his shirt, heavy laden with coins, and tied the sleeves together. He flung it over his shoulder and several coins fell out and scattered along the floor. There was an unintentional standoff as Jarvis stood between John Davis and the opening to the outside. However, as he had no intention of trying to stop him, Jarvis stood aside and the yellow haired buccaneer headed for the exit. John Davis paused at the threshold and looked back in the cave.

"It's been a pleasure, mates," he said with a smile and a salute. "I'll see ya when I see ya."

The powder blast sound of a musket ripped through the cave. John Davis's body slammed backwards against the rock wall as coins spilled out in every direction. He slumped against the wall and slid down to an unnatural seated position. Blood stained the wall behind him from the fresh gunshot wound. Jarvis rushed to his side and knelt down next to him. He looked into the terror-filled eyes of the young pirate. John Davis reached out and grabbed his arm. He struggled for breath. The shot hit him just below his left pectoral muscle and blood flowed down from his ribcage.

"I . . . you," Jarvis struggled to find words of encouragement. "Stay with me."

Jarvis had no sooner spoken those words than the light left his companion's electric blue eyes. John Davis exhaled softly one last time and then he was gone. His body still sat on the ground, only a shell now, devoid of the lively and optimistic soul that had possessed it. Paralyzed by the reality of what had happened, Jarvis stared blankly into the vacant face of one of the few men he had ever called friend. Droplets of rain ricocheted off the walls and smacked against his skin. Coldness swept through his body as if the blood in his veins had frozen.

A commotion to his right snapped him from his trance. He looked out through the entrance and saw three soldiers in redcoats advancing on him. A small plume of white smoke hovered behind them, amidst the grey and gloom of the storm, the discharge from the musket shot that had killed John Davis.

The first soldier came through the dagger-shaped opening. With his bayonet fixed to the end of his musket, he took a swing at Jarvis and just missed, as he rolled backwards out of its way. The soldier stepped over John Davis' body and thrust his bayonet again toward him. Jarvis scrambled, on his back, away from the advancing soldier. Smitty leapt in between them and grabbed the soldier's musket. The two of them grappled with each other as the other soldiers pushed into the cave. The first soldier got the best of Smitty, threw him to the ground and stood over him. Quickly, Jarvis raised his leg and kicked the soldier in the knee with all the strength he could muster. There was a sickening pop as his knee buckled and he crumbled to the ground and cried out in agony. The second soldier through, nearest the entrance, reloaded his musket. Meanwhile his cohort had Eve pinned in the corner of the cave. Jarvis came to his feet just as the soldier finished reloading and leveled his musket at him.

In that perilous moment, a giant black blur exploded into the cave from outside. Keitloa, dripping wet from the storm, wrapped both his massive arms around the head and neck of the soldier and with one violent motion the soldier's lifeless body dropped to the floor. Keitloa caught the musket of the fallen soldier out of the air and fired on the soldier who threatened Eve. The shot hit the soldier square in the back and his arms flailed wildly in the air before he too met an abrupt end. The first soldier, who Jarvis had dropped with a kick to the knee, struggled with Smitty for control of his musket. Keitloa picked him up off the ground with one hand and smashed his body into the rock wall, between Jarvis and the body of John Davis. In one tumultuous minute, Keitloa had slain three soldiers and, in an unsettling way, had restored peace to the cave. This beastly figure that had attacked viciously, and without mercy, now gently knelt down over John Davis's body to examine him.

"He is dead," Keitloa proclaimed.

"I know," Jarvis responded.

His heart sank in his chest. Somehow to hear the words made it more real. There was not time to mourn, however, as the momentary lull was disrupted when another gunshot rang out from outside the cave. The ball impacted the rock wall just above Keitloa's head. He ducked and peered out through the opening.

"You must go," Keitloa said. "More soldiers are coming."

"Go where?" asked Jarvis.

"Take them," Keitloa said, as he looked over at Eve.

Without a word, she ran to the corner and grabbed one of the pieces of wood by the fire. She picked up the pouch that Smitty had fashioned and emptied the bullion on the ground. Quickly, she wrapped the cloth around the piece of wood and stuck it in the fire. Instantly the cloth burst into flames, she pulled it out of the fire and headed down the dark passageway opposite the entrance.

"Go," Keitloa ordered them.

Smitty and Jarvis dutifully followed after Eve and headed deeper into the cave. Another gunshot echoed off the walls just before Jarvis turned the corner. He looked back to see Keitloa engaged with a mustached officer in a redcoat who tried to force his way into the cave. For an instant Jarvis locked eyes with Colonel Swanson. He thought briefly about turning back, as he passed behind a stone wall that blocked his view. But what help could he be to the mighty Keitloa?

In front of him, from the light of her torch, he could see Eve and Smitty advancing into the blackness down a stone hallway. They pressed forward down the narrow passageway, which was just wide enough that his shoulders touched on either side. Eve moved without hesitation through the twists and turns of the cave. Smitty was right on her heels and looked back frequently at Jarvis. Without warning, Eve stopped and ducked under a knee high ledge through a hole in the wall on their right. The rock ledge that covered the opening jutted out slightly and almost completely concealed the hole. Jarvis and Smitty stood in darkness, except for the light from her torch that lit their feet from beneath the ledge. They squatted down and looked into the tunnel. Eve scooted down a gradual decline with the torch held back behind her to light their way.

Jarvis weighed the merits of two unappealing options. He had little desire to crawl further down into the unknown, however, he did not wish to be trapped in the darkness alone; which became a real possibly as Smitty slipped beneath the ledge and blocked out most of the remaining light. Reluctantly, Jarvis sat on the ground and slid down into the oblong shaped portal. They descended on their backs down a smooth rock surface. The ceiling above was just inches from Jarvis's face. His heart beat rapidly in his chest. He could not focus his thoughts on any one thing, as he pushed frenzied and panicked ideas from his head. At the moment he resigned himself to spending his immediate future in this stone sarcophagus, the light beneath him dimmed. He looked down and saw Smitty's shadowy outline in the diminished light, but he could not see Eve or her torch. A minute later, he reached the bottom of the decline and saw the cave had opened into a large cavern. Eve stood at the center with torch aloft and waited for them to join her. Relieved at entering a larger area, Jarvis stood and brushed the dirt from his trousers while he looked around. The flickering light reflected off the walls and ceiling to illuminate the size and dimensions of the space. The room was at least three times the size of the small room back at the cave's entrance. The ceiling was fifty feet above their heads. At the far side of the room there was another dark passageway that Eve already headed for.

"How far back 'ere do ya think this goes?" asked Smitty.

"I do not know, but unless you wish to find that out in the dark we had better keep up," responded Jarvis.

They followed her down another long passageway, this one much broader than the first. Jarvis was grateful they were able to stand and walk. They passed a couple of forks and offshoots that branched off into blackness, but Eve confidently navigated through them with purpose. Jarvis considered, for a moment, that this young girl quite literally held their lives in her hand. She held the lone light in the darkness and they had no choice but to trust she knew where she was headed. It was a humbling experience to cede control of your destiny to another and a strangely liberating one. For that instant, he no longer felt the burden of his own struggle for life. His task was simple, follow the light and live, all other pursuits and ambitions were meaningless by comparison.

The vein they followed grew gradually wider as they progressed onward. The walls on either side rose up into the darkness above. Jarvis stayed close to the wall to his right. Still weak, he occasionally needed steady himself. He began to wonder how much longer he could continue at this pace. His face was cold and clammy.

Soon he was unable to keep up and stopped to lean against the rock wall. The wall was covered with a thin layer of water that flowed down along the rock. He withdrew his arm quickly and made a futile attempt to see through the darkness. The light faded as Eve and Smitty moved further and further away. Jarvis collected himself and hastened his steps to catch up. It was not long before the passageway opened to another large room. At the far end of the room daylight shone through an opening to the outside. There was a crude stone stairway that led up and out through the opening. Eve turned back and handed the fading torch to Smitty.

"*Tei*," she said, and put both hands up in front of her.

Smitty obediently stood still and held the torch. When Jarvis stepped passed him and began to follow her, she stopped and pressed her hands against his chest.

"*Ua'. Tei*," she repeated.

He stood and watched as she ascended the stone steps and disappeared through the archway. Several minutes passed and the lone flame from the torch waned against the breeze that swept in through the cavern from the opening.

"Where do you suppose she's gone?" asked Smitty.

"I do not know," answered Jarvis.

"Why is the light so bright?" asked Smitty. "I mean it was just raining like the dickens out there. 'ow 'as it cleared up so quickly? We 'aven't come that far, 'ave we?"

It was an astute observation. Jarvis thought it could not have been more than fifteen or twenty minutes since he last saw Keitloa, tangled with Colonel Swanson, in the rain at the cave's entrance. He did not believe they had come far enough to have trekked beyond the storm or that there had been sufficient time for a storm of that tenacity to have blown through. Although, he conceded he had no experience with storms of supernatural origin and could not begin to guess where it had come from, how big it was or how long it had stayed. He did not attempt to answer Smitty's query but instead decided to investigate for himself. He walked straight toward the stone steps in front of him.

"Oy, I think she wants us to stay 'ere," Smitty called after him.

Jarvis ignored him and began to climb the stairs that led through the opening. Out in the daylight the steps continued up a small hill. The backdrop on the horizon, beyond the top of the hill, was a brilliant blue sky just as bright and clear as it had been before Keitloa's storm. The rock walls on all sides rose several hundred feet into the air and converged into an over-hanging ceiling. The sunlight shone down through the massive hole in the center. Jarvis climbed the steps to the top of the hill and took in the majestic surrounding. It was like standing inside an enormous stone teapot. The rock walls sloped out and away from the large circular hole in the middle. There was a glisten-ing deep blue pool of water at the far end, fed by a waterfall that emerged through the rock. There were plants and vegetation of all sorts that cover nearly every corner. Birds flew overhead and chirped and sang to each other. There was a rustling sound to his left and the bushes began to shake and move. Eve emerged from the bushes followed by another Arawak girl, a little boy, and an old woman. Each of them had Eve's caramel brown skin and round face. They filed out of the bushes and stood in a line in front of him. Jarvis recognized the other girl and boy as the youth he had captured, along with Eve, all those years ago. They too had grown; especially the boy, who was now taller than both of the girls. The old woman had long grey hair, parted down the middle and pulled to either side of her wrinkled and saggy face. She wore a tanned animal hide that covered her from her shoul-ders to her knees. The other children wore loin coverings made from feathers.

"*Manicato*," Eve spoke to the others and gestured toward Jarvis.

"Ben," Jarvis offered, and placed his hand on his chest with a bow.

These were a people who had, from all reports, been driven to extinction. And yet here they were. Where had they come from? How was it that these four survived? Were there more? He looked into their tranquil brown eyes, and tried to imagine what they had witnessed. He felt a strong desire to share his remarkable discovery and only then remembered young Smitty, who obediently waited back in the dark cave.

"Smitty," he called out. "You must come and see this."

Jarvis turned to look back down the hill. His stomach turned at the sight of a bright red coat. Where he had expected to see Smitty he instead found the mustached officer, Colonel Swanson. Jarvis froze as a dozen questions at once ran through his mind. His primary concern, having already lost one friend, was what had become of Smitty. Colonel Swanson held a rock in one hand and a smoldering extinguished torch in the other. Blood dripped down his face from a fresh head wound. Jarvis could not imagine how this man had gotten by Keitloa. The colonel snarled as he started up the stone steps that led to the top of the hill where Jarvis stood. *The children*, Jarvis thought as his mind turned to the four Arawak behind him. He was certain Colonel Swanson could not see them from his current vantage point. Jarvis hurriedly turned around and made eye contact with Eve.

"Go," he ordered softly and pointed the direction they had come from. "Take them and go. Now!"

She summoned them with her hand and beckoned with opened arms.

"*Guarico*," she said.

The three of them moved to Eve and one by one she gently pushed them back toward the shelter of the bushes. She waited until they were all safely concealed and looked back at Jarvis. He nodded to her and forced an assuring smile. There was complete understanding in her eyes although her face remained emotionless. She followed after her people and disappeared into the undergrowth of the cavern. Jarvis turned around to face Colonel Swanson, who was now only a few yards from him. He intended to make his stand on this spot and would fight or die here. He steeled himself and mustered all the strength he had left for this one man war that had come to him.

A Confrontation and a Discovery

Gideon remained quiet and still. He crouched behind the prickly pinguin shrubs and weighed his limited options. Mucaro had Tara, and did not appear worried at all about their feeble rescue attempt. He had untied her and returned to his seat on the opposite side of a fire. *Why doesn't she run?* thought Gideon. There was really no sense in hiding any more, but before he made a move he wanted some semblance of a plan. As he had zero experience with anything remotely close to this type of situation, he tried to recall movie ploys that might be helpful. When he realized how ridiculous that was, he abandoned that piece of foolishness and looked over at Todd, who had a perplexed look on his face.

"Why didn't he say my name?" asked Todd.

"What?" Gideon whispered.

"I mean, I threw the flipp'n rock. But he said *Gideon*, not *Todd*. What's up with that?"

"Are you serious? You can ask him yourself in just a second."

"Wait," Todd said. "You're not going out there?"

"What's the alternative?"

Todd pursed his lips, bowed his head and exhaled deeply. They had no choice but to go and face Tara's captor. Gideon stood up in plain view of Mucaro; Todd hesitated, for a moment, before he too came to his feet. Together they stepped through the bushes into the open and made their way toward the fire. Mucaro watched patiently, still seated on the stump, and poked at the flames. Gideon looked enviously into his cool, calm and collected face. All at once a plan came to him.

"Follow my lead," he whispered to Todd, as they drew near the fire.

When they reached the clearing where Tara sat, Gideon lifted Bammy's machete over his head and stopped. Slowly, he lowered the machete to the ground and left it there. Todd imitated Gideon and lifted his machete over his head before he too placed it on the ground.

"'ave a seat," Mucaro said. He pointed in Tara's direction with the smoking end of his stick. His eyes locked on them like a predator on its prey.

Gideon walked over next to Tara, removed his backpack and sat down on the ground. He was careful to keep his eyes fixed on Mucaro's. Todd also set a mean gaze on the witch doctor in the sleeveless maroon shirt. He walked around the other side of Tara, removed his backpack and sat down with crisscrossed legs.

"You all right?" he asked Tara.

"Yeah, man. Mi a'right."

The three of them sat shoulder to shoulder and stared through the flames at their adversary. Gideon did not intend to speak first. His play was to let his opponent lead and, hopefully show his hand. Several minutes passed and neither side said a thing. A smile broke across Mucaro's face and he let out a chuckle. "What are yu do'n 'ere?"

"I'm on vacation," Gideon answered plainly.

"Try Sandals, man, it's all inclusive."

"The show here is better," Gideon said. "That fog trick was pretty impressive."

"It's no trick, man," Mucaro stated. "It's power."

"So you have power?"

"Yeah, man," he said, and tilted his head back proudly.

His black mane swung backwards slightly and his long dreads rocked gently forward. Gideon looked closer at his necklace. It was made of bone and teeth, and from the look of it Gideon guessed it was very old. The necklace lay in contrast to his shiny maroon shirt. There was no chance Mucaro was the necklace's original owner. Gideon hoped perhaps this hand-me-down was something he could use to his advantage.

"That's not what I heard," Gideon said. "I heard Chaka was the real deal. You're just a likkle boy wearing his daddy's necklace."

"Do not you speak 'is name!" Mucaro threatened. He pulled the stick from the fire and pointed it at Gideon.

"Easy fella," Gideon said with faux confidence. He put his hands in the air. "Don't kill the messenger. That's just the word on the street."

"She knows nothing" he said, with a contemptible look at Tara.

"I didn't say anything about her," Gideon responded. "Look, you are clearly upset. How 'bout we just take off and leave you in peace?"

"Uno c'yan't go in d'ere" Mucaro said, as he pointed at the summit to his right.

Gideon looked over and saw, in the orange glow of the camp fire, the entrance to a cave. Surprised he had not seen it sooner, he sat in stunned silence. It was right there. In an instant he recalled the distance they had traveled and everything they had endured to reach this point. Now they sat just a few yards away. His primary objective to somehow escape safely with Todd and Tara slipped to the back of his mind. With the cave so close, his thoughts began to circle around the idea of getting inside to have a look.

"Why would I want to go in there?" he said, feigning igno-rance. "We just want to take Tara back to check on her father."

"You're lying. Mi know why you're 'ere."

He reached behind the stump and pulled out a rough leather bound book with mismatched pages. As soon as Gideon caught sight of the journal, in a panic, he reached over and unzipped the side pocket where he kept it. When he found it empty, he searched the other external pockets to verify what he already knew to be true. Somehow Mucaro had gotten the journal. He looked back across the flames into his smug face. Mucaro opened the journal and held up the slip of paper with the heart-shaped symbol.

"Dis is why you're 'ere."

Gideon opened his mouth to refute the accusation but before he could speak Mucaro tossed the slip of paper into the fire. Without thinking Gideon leapt to his feet and took a step toward the fire. Mucaro jumped up from his stump and held the journal in the air, in a motion that threatened it too being cast into the fire. Tara and Todd both stood up and flanked Gideon.

"Please," Gideon pleaded. "That doesn't belong to me."

Mucaro flashed a devilish smile and tossed the journal into the flames. Gideon jumped forward and kicked the journal out of the fire. The journal flew into the bushes along with sparks and pieces of flaming wood. Gideon was still off balance when the muscle bound Mucaro grabbed him by the shoulders and threw him to the ground.

With a huge right cross, Tara stepped forward and punched Mucaro in the face. His dreadlocks whipped through the air as his head snapped back. She swung again but he caught her by the wrist and subdued her attack. Todd had circled behind him and hit him in the upper back with a flaming branch from the fire. Wood splinters flew in every direction as it exploded against his deltoids. Mucaro picked up Tara with both hands and threw her into Todd. He caught her, but the impact flung them both backwards into the fire. Todd quickly rolled out of the flames, with Tara in his arms. They rolled around on the ground to extinguish the embers before they ignited.

Amid the mêlée, Gideon had come to his feet. He burst forward toward Mucaro and dropped his shoulder, opening his arms wide to tackle the witchdoctor. Just before he could wrap his arms around him, Mucaro grabbed him under the shoulders and fell on his back. He used his legs, and Gideon's momentum, to flip him into the air and send him slamming upside down into a tree. Gideon's back smashed against the trunk. He lay on the ground in a crumpled heap, his back throbbed and his head spun. He heard a commotion from above and behind him. When he looked up, he saw Todd and Tara had pounced on the fallen Mucaro and attempted to hold him down.

Gideon staggered to his feet and shook his head to clear his blurred vision. On uneasy legs he cut between the two-on-one wrestling match and the scattered fire ring. He made his way over to where he laid Bammy's machete. With some discomfort from his bruised back, he bent over and picked up the machete. He turned back to see that Mucaro had gotten one arm free and had his hand wrapped around Todd's throat. Gideon stood over Mucaro and pressed the edge of the rusty machete to his jugular. Mucaro immediately ceased to struggle and released his grasp on Todd and Tara. He lay perfectly still and peered deep into Gideon's eyes.

"Tie him up," Gideon instructed Todd and Tara.

Todd stood up, rubbed his neck, and moved to retrieve the rope. Tara sat up in the dirt and stared hatefully at Mucaro. The obeah man rose slowly, with the blade of Bammy's machete still pressed against his throat. He smiled tauntingly at Tara. Todd returned with the rope and handed it to Gideon. Gideon gave the machete to Todd and walked around behind Mucaro to tie his hands behind his back.

"Yu could 'ave kill 'im, yu know," she said to Mucaro.

"Who? Your fadda?" he replied. "'e's too strong fi dat."

She reached up and slapped Mucaro in the face. Gideon finished tying his hands together, and stopped to examine a bird shaped tattoo on his right forearm. When he heard the slap, he looked into Tara's anger contorted face and saw malice born from a place far beyond the words Mucaro had spoken. He walked around and knelt down in front of Todd to tie Mucaro's feet. As he wrapped the rope around his feet, he thought of his old scoutmaster, who mentioned that this very rescue knot could also be used to restrain someone. At the time he could not imagine a scenario where he would have cause to restrain somebody. Now, as he bound the feet of a man who had tried to kill him, he said a little prayer of thanksgiving for the boy scouts. He cinched up the knot tightly and craned his head to try and catch another peak at Mucaro's tattoo. However, from his current vantage point it was impossible to see it. When he was certain the ropes were secure, he stood up and took the machete back from Todd. Tara also stood and the three of them looked down on the bound obeah man.

"What now?" Todd asked.

"I say let's see what he's hiding in that cave," said Gideon.

"No," Tara said. "Mi a go check 'pon mi fadda."

"He's fine," Gideon argued. "We left him resting peacefully back where we made camp."

"Uno asked mi fi take yu to the cave," she said, and pointed over at the petroglyph. "See it d'ere? Mi done."

"Dude, Gideon," Todd pleaded. "What are you doing?"

Gideon realized how selfish he had been and felt ashamed. He thought of Bammy and Bigga lying helpless, with head wounds, in the middle of this treacherous wilderness full of pitfalls and deadly reptiles. When he had come to his senses his instinct was to go back as well and check on his friend, but he felt a powerful pull toward the cave that he could not explain.

"I'm sorry, of course you should go," he said, and handed Tara the machete. "Here, take this."

"You're not coming?" asked Todd.

"No, man," responded Gideon, and looked over toward the cave. "I need to know what's in there. Are you going with her or are you with me?"

"I'm with you, man," said Todd. "Always."

For all his faults and failings, for all the times he had frustrated or disappointed, Gideon knew that when it mattered he could count on Todd. He smiled and gave a grateful nod. Then he looked over to Tara.

"Are you sure you don't want to have just a quick look?"

"No man," she said. "Mi a go. If 'im a'right, mi a come back fi yu a daybreak."

"Okay," he said, and handed her his flashlight. "Can you find your way back?"

She cocked her head sideways and gave him a 'do you know who you are talking to' look. Todd covered his mouth with his hand to stifle a laugh at Gideon's expense. Tara and Gideon both looked down at Mucaro, who sat quietly on the ground and did not struggle against his restraints.

"We'll deal with him when you get back," Gideon suggested.

"A'right," she agreed. At that, she turned away from the fire and started off into the bush.

"Watch out for snakes," Todd called after her.

They stood and watched as she walked through the trees until all that could be seen was a lone beam of light that shone off in front of her. Todd shifted his weight anxiously side to side. Gideon looked back toward the symbol near the cave's entrance and then back down at Mucaro. He walked a few steps away from the dwindling fire and stooped down into the bushes. He felt around in the shadows for a minute until his hand brushed against a course flat surface. His fingertips found the edges and he picked up the charred journal. With great care, he brushed off the mud and ashes and beat it twice against the side of his leg. He walked back, journal in hand, and stood over Mucaro.

"Anything you'd like to share before we head in there?"

"If yu go in d'ere, uno c'yan't come back," he said, and looked up at Gideon with his cold dark eyes. A chill shot up Gideon's spine. For a second he considered the prudence of entering the cave at night, or at all. *Is whatever we might find in there worth our lives?* Maybe the wise thing was to follow after Tara and possibly come back when it was light. He would not let fear determine his decisions. He pushed the doubt from his mind and drew a deep breath.

"Okay, tough guy," he mocked. "We'll see you in a few minutes. Don't go anywhere."

Gideon kicked at the remaining embers from the fire. When he had spread them around, Todd helped stamp them into the mud and extinguish each and every tiny flame. With the light of the fire gone the three men stood shadowed in darkness. Todd removed the flashlight from his backpack and switched it on. He

231

shined the light on Mucaro, one last time, and then up in the direction of the cave. Gideon found himself in the untenable position of following from behind as Todd and his flashlight led the way up the incline toward the entrance. Todd shone the light on the looping heart shaped symbol carved into the rock. Gideon reached out and gently traced it with his index finger. The slip of paper that bore this symbol was gone forever. He felt a sense of great loss and responsibility, although he had not tossed it into the flames himself. His stubbornness had destroyed that small piece of history. Todd moved the light off the symbol and shined it into the cave.

Cautiously, he stepped through the threshold. With a twinge of envy, Gideon followed closely behind. The white circle of light scanned from one side of the small room to the next. It was about the size of his bedroom back home. To his great disappointment the room was empty. He was not sure what he expected, but he was hopeful that once inside they would find something of interest, or perhaps a clue they were on the right path. At the far corner of the room was a narrow passageway that led deeper into the cave. With nothing of interest in the entryway Todd set off down the narrow passage.

"Wait a minute," Gideon called after him.

Todd stopped, turned around and shined the light in Gideon's face. Gideon put up a hand to shield his eyes and Todd lowered the light.

"Sorry."

"Bring the light over here," Gideon said, as he opened the journal.

Todd walked over to him and shone the light on the opened pages. The edges of the paper were brown from their brief brush with fire. Gideon flipped through to the last page he had studied. They looked at the directions.

Right
Right
Left

~~Right~~
~~Left~~
~~Right~~
Right
Left
Right
Left
Left
Right

Many questions shuffled through Gideon's head. Was this a set of twelve or two sets of six? Had the first six been crossed off because they were inaccurate? Were they directions at all and if so where did they start and where might they lead? He decided that Todd's theory was a good one and it was possible they were directions through the cave from this entrance.

"Would you say that is to the right?" Todd asked, as he shone his light down the passageway.

From where they stood the passage was straight across but did sit on the right side of the room.

"Looks like it to me," Gideon answered. He reached over, grabbed the flashlight from Todd and pushed past him toward the narrow passage.

Gideon's broad shoulders filled the hall from end to end. He had to walk at a slight angle to pass through. Todd followed close behind him and just fit between the narrow rock walls. They walked a good distance down into the darkness when the flashlight flickered briefly and dimmed. Gideon banged it against his palm and the light ceased to waver, but was still diminished. He worried about the instability of their only source of light. They had already used the flashlight more than he anticipated due to their unplanned overnight stay and the subsequent search for Tara. Her flashlight was yet another reason Gideon wished she was with them. He was about to ask Todd if he thought they should turn back when something caught his eye.

A ledge protruded out from the wall to his right. Just above

233

the lip was a tiny black drawing etched against the stone. It was clearly old and faded, but the backwards facing bird was still distinguishable. Gideon stopped and shone the dimmed circle of light directly on it. It was an exact replica of the tattoo he had just seen on Mucaro's forearm, he was certain of it. Once more it was the same one on the arm of his old friend Professor Gervaise. He did not believe in coincidence. Even the harshest skeptic would be hard pressed to dismiss the connection.

"It's a hieroglyph," Todd said triumphantly.

Gideon smiled as his friend had, for once, gotten it right. It appeared to have been drawn with some kind of coal. He stuck his foot out under the ledge in search of the bottom of the wall. When he felt nothing but air, he stooped down and shined the light under the ledge. To his astonishment, a small oval-like hole led downward deeper into the cave. Todd bent down next to him and peered down into the tunnel. Gideon held the light down in the hole for a minute before he lifted it back up and shone it further down the narrow hallway. He considered their options with the light resting on the bird drawing atop the ledge.

"It's this way," Gideon stated, as he pointed down the hole.

"How can you be sure?"

"Mucaro has this bird tattooed into his forearm." Gideon pointed at the drawing.

He opened the journal and pointed to the second line of directions, which supported the idea of crawling down into this tunnel to the right. Todd nodded vigorously. Gideon led the way as they slid beneath the ledge and crawled down into the tunnel. There was just enough room that Gideon could scoot, feet first, on his butt. He leaned back on his elbows and crab walked to keep his head from scraping on the hard rock surface above him. They scooted down for only a couple dozen meters before they found an outlet into a larger room. The air was stagnant and warm, much less comfortable than the narrow passage above. The ceiling was higher than before with several jagged stalactites that hung down. However, Gideon was again met with disappointment as this room was also empty. On the far side of the room there was another passageway. He honed the light in his intended direction.

"That way," he said, and started for the passage.

"Wait, man." Todd reached up to grab hold of his arm. "Let me see the journal."

Gideon handed over the journal and shone the light down on it. Todd opened up to the page of directions and pointed to the third line down.

"That way is right, this says here we are supposed to go left."

Gideon shined the light over to the left side of the cave and scanned from end to end. It was a solid rock wall with no gaps or openings. To be absolutely certain, he walked over for a closer look. He pressed and prodded along the unforgiving rocky surface. Further inspection confirmed what he knew at first glance; the left side of the room was a dead end.

"Maybe these directions are wrong or maybe we misread them," offered Gideon.

"Either way, we have no idea where we're going then."

"But the bird," Gideon said. "The bird means something, I know it."

"Look around. There's nothing down here."

"That's why we have to keep going. For it to remain hidden all these years, it's got to be hard to find. I believe we have the key."

"The journal?"

"The bird."

"I thought we were following the journal."

"We were," Gideon said. "The journal brought us here and the bird will take us the rest of the way."

"What are you basing this on?" a frustrated Todd asked.

"Faith. Sometimes you have to walk through the darkness to get to the light."

Todd put his hands on his hips and looked off thoughtfully down the passage. He pursed his lips and took in a deep breath. Gideon watched patiently and hoped that Todd would offer no further resistance. It was a rare occasion to see Todd uncertain and afraid. Gideon could feel it in his core; the secrets of the cave were just ahead. He felt as if it called to him now. *Just keep coming*, it said, *you're nearly there*. After what seemed like an eternity, Todd turned back to face him. From the look on his face Gideon knew, reluctant as he might be, he was on board.

"Fine," Todd consented. "We'll keep going but let's not be stupid. If something doesn't look right or safe, we turn back. Agreed?"

"Agreed."

He threw his arm around his neck and led him down the passageway at the far side of the room. They entered the hall side by side and although it was wide enough to continue that way, they chose a more practical single file formation with Gideon in his preferential lead position. An unpleasant aroma filled the hallway just a few meters in. It was unlike anything Gideon had experienced. It smelled like a mixture of sulfur and tar.

"What is that?" gagged Todd.

"Dunno, but it's getting stronger," said Gideon.

"Oh good," he replied with an air of sarcasm. "Then we should definitely keep going."

The light shone further down the passage. All he could see was that it stretched out of sight into blackness. On the left was an alcove that opened up back and behind them. They paused and Gideon shined the flashlight from end to end. They saw nothing but rock and dust from corner to corner. When they were satisfied the tiny nook held nothing for them, they pressed on. With each step the smell permeated the air around them. It came in waves and nearly overwhelmed the senses, at one point Gideon contemplated turning back. They had pursued a diminutive pickpocket, braved the treacherous cockpits, fought off possessed pals, combatted a crazed obeah man, and after all that a single pungent aroma was about to be their undoing. While he mused on this piece of irony, he spotted a mark on the rock ahead in the halo of his light. He focused the beam on the mark and his heart began to race as they drew closer. They gazed upon another drawing of a bird with its head craned back toward its tail feathers. The smell was just as strong but all thoughts of turning back left his mind.

There was another breach in the wall just beyond the backward-facing bird, which led downward.

Gideon smiled at Todd. "You still want to quit?"

"Settle down, fella," said Todd. "What if these markings are just leading us to the source of the smell? That bird could just be smelling its own butt."

When he could think of nothing witty to say, Gideon stepped through the wide breach to his left and descended down into the passage with Todd behind him. The temperature grew warmer and the air felt heavier. Beads of sweat dotted Gideon's head and pooled in the contours of his back. Up ahead he saw several large horizontal slots, uniformly carved out of the rock wall on both sides. They were set three rows high and spanned the walls as far as the light would show. They approached and stood next to the first set of slots. Gideon shined the light in the waste high center slot. The slot above was at head height, with the one beneath it near the floor. Each slot was several feet deep and not quite as long as his wingspan. The banks of slots in front of them were empty. It reminded Gideon of a set of bunk beds. He reached out and placed his hand on the cold rock bottom of the middle slot. There was no doubt that these were man made and must have taken much time and effort to carve out, even in the soft limestone.

"Someone slept down here?" Gideon wondered aloud.

The light flickered again, and temporarily left them in the dark. Gideon shook the flashlight hard and to his relief the light returned. He shined it further down the passage and could see a lighter piece of material hanging out of one of the slots, several banks down. With urgency he jogged toward it; the light flickered his every step. Todd followed after him and when he reached the slot he froze. Horror welled up inside him as he looked down at a bundle of cloth shaped like a body. The light waned once more; frantically he shook it until it came back. He shined it up the passage and back and forth from wall to wall. The banks of slots from that point on down appeared to be filled with corpses wrapped in cloth.

"It's a tomb," Gideon gasped.

"He's a serial killer," said Todd.

"What?!"

"Mucaro. People don't just disappear out here. He kills them and brings their bodies down here."

"Calm down, man. We don't know that."

Todd grabbed the flashlight out of his hands and shined it further down the passage to illuminate the banks of slots as far as the light would show. They were at least thirty to forty slots in view; with potentially countless others beyond the dim beam that emanated from the flashlight.

"Where did all these people come from then?" Todd shouted.

The flashlight flickered again and the light was gone. Gideon heard Todd mutter a swear word and shake the flashlight but this time no light returned. They stood in complete blackness.

"Give it to me," he ordered Todd.

"I can't see you."

Gideon reached out toward the sound of his voice. His arms flailed around in the darkness before they struck Todd's arm. He grabbed hold of it and stepped closer to him. He felt down his arm toward his wrist until he touched the cold metal flashlight. Abruptly, he pulled the flashlight from his grip and shook it. When nothing happened, he twisted off the top of the light and let the heavy D batteries fall into his hand. He rotated them, careful not to drop them, and placed the last one in first and the first one in last. He said a prayer in his heart as he screwed the top back on. He flicked the switch and the light came on. He could see the look of jubilation on Todd's face but then, as quickly as the light had returned, it was gone. Gideon shook the light to no avail. He swapped the batteries again but nothing worked.

"We're dead."

"We're not dead," Gideon said, as he not only tried to calm Todd but himself as well. "Relax and follow me."

With no point of reference, in the darkness, it was impossible for him to gain his bearings. He reached out for the wall, which he thought was to his right. When his hand met only air he leaned in further. He did not want to move his feet until he felt something tangible. His fingers brushed across a piece of cloth and a cold chill shot through his body. He recoiled away from the cloth and the body that lay beneath it. With his eyes filled with darkness and his mind filled with fear, he imagined the corpses rising up to surround them. His overwhelming desire was to flee far away from this catacomb of death. He spun around in the direction he hoped would lead them back up to the main hall, and eventually out of the cave. *Sankofa*: the word seemed to Gideon to roll through the cave.

"Did you hear that?" asked Todd.

"Hear what?"

"It sounded like a whisper."

Gideon had thought it was all in his mind; however, with Todd's additional witness his concern began to grow. *We are not alone.*

"It's your imagination," he assured Todd with a crack in his voice. "Grab onto my shirt."

Gideon felt a hand smack his side and then fingers grasp his shirt.

"Got it?"

The question was not so much to confirm Todd's grip, as it was to quell the irrational fear that it might be the hand of a reanimated cadaver that had grabbed him. Gideon had always maintained that he was not afraid of the dark. What was in the dark, on the other hand, terrified him.

"Got it," Todd answered.

Gideon made his way slowly forward. The ground sloped upward which indicated they were headed in the right direction, as they followed a downward slope into the tombs. He bumped his knee on the rock wall in front of him and put his hand out to feel for something that he could lean against. Once again he put his hand into one of the slots only this time he touched the cold of the empty bay. He ran his hand along the stone from bay to bay as a guide. In his mind he played out their journey, in reverse. He was certain they had made a left into the catacombs, which meant they would need to turn right when they reached the upper hall.

Then they could find their way through the large room and back up the tunnel. From there, if his memory served, it was a left and then straight back to the entrance.

His fear was that he could not be sure there were no other branches in the cave he had not seen or accounted for. He cursed his foolishness for being so unprepared. Had any one of a dozen decisions been different, they would not have found themselves in their current predicament. They made their way cautiously up the incline with the bony claws of the undead clipping at their heels, at least in Gideon's harried imagination.

"Gideon?"

"Yeah?"

"I hate you."

"I know."

This passive aggressive ritual served to break the tension and assured the other that they still cared when things looked bleak. A quote came to his mind.

"Darkness cannot drive out darkness," he spoke it aloud, almost to himself.

"What's that?" asked Todd.

"Martin Luther King Jr.," he explained. "Darkness cannot drive out darkness; only light can do that. Hate cannot drive out hate; only love can do that."

"Are you gonna love us out of this?" asked Todd.

Gideon did not answer. He continued to use the wall to his left as a guide on their way back up toward the upper hall. In pitch black, with no sure way to gauge distance, Gideon felt they had walked much further than he anticipated. He began to question whether or not they were already hopelessly lost in the darkness, but he did not dare express his worries for fear of causing further distress. The wall to his left bent away suddenly and he stopped. He reached over to his right and, with outstretched fingertips, could just touch the wall on the other side. He took one step forward and spread both arms as wide as he could. He leaned right and then left and could no longer touch on either side. He stepped forward again and reached out in front of him. His hand scraped against the rock wall of the upper hall. He felt around and was about to turn right andfollow the passage back to the large room, but amid the warm and stale air Gideon felt a faint cool breeze against his damp skin. It came from his left.

"Do you feel that?" he asked Todd.

"Feel what?"

"A breeze."

"Yeah, barely."

If there's fresh air, then there's an inlet, Gideon thought. He turned left and started to feel his way down the hall. He took just one step in that direction when Todd tugged hard on his shirt.

"Where are you going?"

"This way," Gideon replied. "There's airflow. It may be a way out."

"No way, man," Todd argued, and tugged again on his shirt. "The way out is back this way. You have no idea what's down there."

"Trust me."

"I am, at this very moment, regretting the last time I trusted you," Todd shot back.

"There's a way out if we head toward the breeze," said Gideon. "I'm certain."

Todd sighed deeply. In the darkness, Gideon could not see his face and did not need to. He knew Todd well enough to know that, in the pause that followed the sigh, his friend quietly eliminated reasons not to follow him. Patiently, he waited for Todd to finish his exercise and capitulate.

"Fine, let's follow the breeze," Todd said. "It couldn't get any worse."

"All right," said Gideon. "We'll take it nice and slow."

At that, they continued further down the passage. The breeze had been a faint one but Gideon was sure he felt it. However, doubt crept into his mind with each step. At the moment, he felt nothing but the stale air that filled the hall. He did take comfort in the fact that the smell faded behind them. Also the passageway felt slightly cooler than back where they had come from. Todd held tight to Gideon's shirt and Gideon kept his right hand on the wall as a guide. He thought of how he had taken light for granted. He felt his way along blindly and prayed they might once again find light. Another faint breeze wafted through the cavern.

"I felt that!" Todd said, excitedly.

They hastened their steps, all the while they kept to the rock wall to their right. They had only walked a few feet when Gideon felt a thin sheet of water flowing over his hand. He removed his wet hand from the wall and wiped it on his shirt. This new development caused him to stop abruptly and Todd smashed into him.

"Why'd we stop?"

"I felt water on the rocks," Gideon explained.

He reached out again and his fingertips breached a thin layer of water that trickled down the surface of the rock. He ran his hand back and forth across the gently flowing liquid. Todd released his shirt and a second later he felt Todd's fleshy hand on the rock wall.

"Weird," Todd said.

Gideon ran his hand down the rock wall till it met the floor. There was a small pooling of water at the bottom but the ground beneath his feet was dry. The water found a pathway sufficient that it did not flood the passageway, but swept downward and carried on.

"It must be runoff from a stream or something," Gideon speculated.

"That's a good thing, right?"

Truth be told, he was not sure if it was good, bad, or indifferent. His cracked lips were as dry as his throat. He had not had a drink for hours now and began to feel desperate for relief. Not desperate enough, however, to put his mouth on rocks he could not see and drink liquid of unknown origins. Though tempting, he thought better of it.

"Let's keep moving."

Todd grabbed hold of his shirt again and they moved forward. Gideon streamed his hand along the wet rock wall. He started to worry they might encounter an area where they needed to swim. The swim on its own would not be a problem, the trouble was the darkness. They would not be able to see where to swim and would have even less of a frame of reference in a pool with no wall to guide them. His fear evaporated as his hand once again touched dry stone. At that moment a breeze, stronger than the others, swept through the corridor.

"That has to be good," said Todd.

Gideon silently agreed. The strong wind meant they were close to the outside world. They moved as fast as they had since they lost the light back in the catacombs. In his race toward potential liberation from the stone labyrinth, Gideon caught his toe on the ground and fell down hard on his hands and knees. Todd, who followed close behind, tripped over Gideon and crashed down on top of him. Sharp pains shot down his back and into his bruised and scraped knees. His head throbbed from the impact, and possibly from a mild case of dehydration. He looked over and saw Todd's black silhouette move to his right.

"Holy crap!" he exclaimed.

"I know," said Todd. "You gotta be more careful man."

"No, not that," said Gideon. "I can see you a little. Move again."

"I can't see a thing."

Against the blackness all around him, Gideon saw the edges of a slightly-less-black blackness in front of him.

"There," he said. "You just moved."

"Seriously dude, I can't see a thing," replied Todd.

"Get up," said Gideon. "We're close."

Gideon ignored the pain in his legs, back and shoulders, and stood up. He reached down until he felt Todd's shoulder and helped him to his feet. Together, step by step, they moved forward. They progressed up a slight incline and Gideon began to make out dark shapes in the blackness. Another gust of wind blew passed them. Ahead, Gideon was certain he saw a hazy dark gray rock wall through a black arch.

"Do you see that?!"

"I see it!" Todd said.

Todd let go of Gideon's shirt and they moved closer to the archway. As they stepped through they saw the five walls of another cavernous room. It was illuminated by soft purple light that bled through an opening at the far end. Ancient stone steps led up through the large crack in the wall, out into the dawning daylight. On the wall just outside the opening was a heart-shaped symbol with three legs carved into the rock. Without hesitation they walked to the steps, as they yearned to step into the light.

Gideon was the first to exit the cave. His eyes were drawn upward toward the giant overhanging walls that rose hundreds of feet above them. The stone steps continued up a steep but small hill and disappeared at the top. Beyond the top of the hill he saw a giant hole, high above, at the center of the overhang. It looked to him like a massive upside down stone bowl with a hole at the top. There were pockets of shrubs and bushes that grew up in between the rocks. Through the hole in the high ceiling, the sky was a dull bluish gray, as a new morning dawned.

"Whoa," Todd said as he exited the cave.

"I know, right?" Gideon added. "This is pretty incredible."

"So this is where he grows his weed," Todd said, never able to resist an opportunity to rib his friend.

"Haha," Gideon replied, unamused. "Let's go check it out."

With great excitement, Gideon led the way up the stone steps that ran along the towering wall to their left. Stalagmites the size of barrel cacti rose up through the earth to their right. Gideon's heart raced in anticipation of what they were sure to discover just over the hill. Visions of treasure chests and old ruins filled his head. He wanted to run to the top but tried to temper his expectations. *No matter what, you've had an adventure for sure*, he told himself.

A few steps from the top, a most unexpected sight appeared just over the horizon. It was a young, skinny, shirtless boy. He looked Indian, with light brown skin and short, black, hair. Shocked to see such a sight, Gideon froze on the spot. The boy too appeared startled and dropped the long stick he held. He wore no shoes and was covered by a single cloth around his waist. He stared at them, and looked back and forth between Gideon and Todd. The look on his face was somewhere in between curiosity and terror. All at once he turned and ran back the way he had come.

"Wait!" Gideon called out.

"*Arijua!*" the boy shouted. "*Arijua!*"

"What's he saying?" asked Todd.

"I don't know," said Gideon, as they started to chase after him.

"It means foreigner," a familiar voice, with a slight English accent, answered from behind them.

The unexpected answer, from where they had just come, stopped them in their tracks. They turned around to see an old man, who stood at the entrance to the cave. His silver hair swept back neatly from his bronze face. He wore a long, dark red robe with a thick orange trim. In his hand he held a lit torch. Gideon shook his head in disbelief.

"Professor Gervaise?" he asked.

A Soldier's Honor

Methodically, stone step by stone step, he climbed toward the top of the hill where Jarvis stood still like a statue. His head tilted sideways as his wild eyes peered suspiciously into the backdrop of the enormous cavern. He clutched a rock in one hand and what remained of Eve's torch in the other. Fresh blood covered the left side of his face and flowed into his dark brown mustache. At the top of the hill was a narrow path that cut through a berm, comprised of pieces of limestone shale, just wide enough for one man to pass. A resolute Jarvis blocked his path and Colonel Swanson halted his progress and stared at the man he had pursued for several miserable days.

Jarvis stared back and tried to discern what could possibly have possessed this man to go to such lengths to reach him. To his recollection they had never before met and he could not imagine having wronged him in anyway. To the best of his knowledge the only imposition he had levied against him was that he absconded with his quartermaster and some minor supplies and provisions. Yet this man had hunted him with such vigor that Jarvis thought he must have some personal vendetta against him. As to what that was, however, he remained clueless.

The tension swelled to nearly unbearable proportions.

Although Jarvis had the high ground, he lacked the strength to mount a proper offensive. Colonel Swanson stood like a coiled spring, ready to explode. The only tactic currently at Jarvis's disposal was to stall.

"Good day, Colonel," Jarvis said in a faux-pleasant tone. "Some weather we are having."

"You no-good piece of pikey garbage," Swanson growled back at him.

"Jarvis," he responded sarcastically. "Benjamin Jarvis. Have we met?"

He hoped to disarm him with wit and force a misstep, or at the very least put off a physical confrontation as long as possible. Jarvis kept his eyes fixed on the Colonel's. Despite the cool air beneath the shade of the stone overhang, beads of feverish sweat formed and trickled down Jarvis's pale face. He fought the impulse to clench his jaw and inhaled through his nose to try to calm himself. His heart pounded rapidly in anticipation of the inevitable, and he gently pressed his trembling hands against the sides of his trousers to conceal the obvious signs of his fragile state.

"We have not, but I know you," Swanson answered sternly. "It's because of cowards and deserters like you that this conflict has drawn on so long."

"I am no deserter," said Jarvis.

"Oh yeah?" said Swanson. "Where is your company then? Where is your uniform, Major?"

Jarvis did not answer. Any explanation, under nearly any form of critical examination, would not portray him in a positive light. For all intents and purposes he was a deserter. His company had been annihilated and he now acted to serve his own ends. He had not been relieved of duty or decommissioned. Through circumstances largely out of his control, he considered himself liberated from the bonds of military service. However, as he stood face to face with a military authority it was clear that this understanding was not mutual.

"You are the worst kind of soldier, the sort who doesn't even know what a disgrace he is. Had we purged ourselves of cowardice and insubordination like yours, the Spanish would have been dispatched years ago and these Negroes would have been subjugated," Swanson said.

"We did dispatch the Spanish years ago, I was there, and it was largely because of *these* Negroes," Jarvis shot back defiantly.

"You have forgotten who the enemy is."

"No, I can see my enemy quite clearly."

"Good, then," Swanson said. He swung his arm across his body and tossed the torch nub in the rocks to his right. He let the large stone in his other hand fall to the ground with a dull thud. The bones in his neck popped as he turned his head side to side and rolled his shoulders backwards. He removed his red wool coat, with the precision expected of one who spent his life in His Majesty's service, and placed it atop the large stone at his feet.

"Listen," Jarvis began. "You saw the trunk back by the entrance? There is gold inside, more than you or I could ever spend; take it and we forget this whole thing."

The corners of Colonel Swanson's mouth turned up in a devilish smile beneath his bushy mustache. With a lightning quick step he lunged forward and belted Jarvis in the jaw with a short jab from his left hand. Jarvis staggered backwards and steadied himself just in time to catch a ferocious right hook to the left side of his face. The blow sent him crumbling to the floor. He managed to get his elbow underneath him and began to sit up when Swanson kicked him hard in the stomach. The pain in his face, which still throbbed from the initial assault, felt somehow muted by the violent pain that shot through his torso. Unable to think of anything but escape, he rolled backwards off the berm into the bushes behind him. Colonel Swanson stepped down off the hilltop and stood over him. Without mercy, he pounced on Jarvis and drove his knee into his ribs. He continued his pummeling by grabbing onto his shirt and pulling him toward him while he smashed his granite like fist into his face over and over again. Jarvis desperately flailed his arms upward and tried to deflect the onslaught. He caught hold of Swanson's ear and pulled down hard. The Colonel cried out in pain and stood up to pull himself free of

Jarvis's grasp. Jarvis took advantage of the momentary opening. He pulled his knees to his chest and thrust both feet at Colonel Swanson's midsection, which knocked the bloody Colonel backwards. With great effort Jarvis rolled unto his side and struggled to get his legs underneath him. He had no sooner stood upright when Colonel Swanson charged back at him. The two men locked arms and Jarvis drove his forehead across the bridge of Swanson's nose. A torrent of blood exploded over his brown mustache and he bellowed in agony and anger. Jarvis felt he had given all he had and lacked the strength to continue. Bloodied and broken he slumped backwards and sat on the ground among the shoulder high bushes, a lone red drop in a sea of green. His face was a mess of blood and bruised flesh. The wound he suffered from the crocodile bite had torn open and the blood from his shoulder soaked through his shirt and bandages. He stared up at the furious Colonel, who held his broken nose and breathed heavily. Jarvis knew it was over for him.

"So that's it, then?" Colonel Swanson seethed as blood splattered into the air with each syllable. "What a disappointment. I wanted to feel you struggle to the last as I choked the life out of you."

With his eyes fixed on the Colonel, Jarvis drug his fingers through the dirt and picked up a handful of tiny pebbles. He feebly flung the pebbles at him and they harmlessly bounced off Swanson's knee. "Does that suit you?"

Colonel Swanson looked down at the small stones for a moment and let loose with an enormous belly laugh. The blood from his nose flipped from the tips of his mustache in every direction as his body gyrated with laughter.

"That's the spirit, soldier," Swanson encouraged. "You're not the cowardly impish dog I took you for. But you are a traitor to the crown and to your country. I promised my men I would make an example out of the next bloody fool who tried to shirk his duty. It is an unfortunate circumstance that the next bloody fool turned out to be you."

He took an aggressive step toward Jarvis but stopped abruptly and arched his back. He threw his head and arms skyward and screamed in pain. As he turned around Jarvis saw a long arrow sticking out of his back. A short distance away, behind Colonel Swanson, Jarvis saw Eve. She stood back in the bushes, with her bow still held aloft. The arrow, however, had missed the mark and only served to enrage the mustached soldier. He turned and charged toward her. She attempted to nock another arrow but Colonel Swanson was on her too quickly. With a ferocious backhand he swept the bow to the side and grabbed Eve by the hair. He dragged her from the bushes as she struggled against him. With a violent tug he pulled her up to his eye level, her arrow still protruding from his back. He looked out past her and scanned from one end of the cavern to the other.

"Where did you come from?" he shouted at her.

Eve stared defiantly back at him. She pulled away, but he had a firm grip on her. Jarvis found new strength and got to his feet to face the colonel once more. Colonel Swanson watched callously as Jarvis steadied himself. The colonel pulled Eve close to him and wrapped his arm around her neck. She ceased to struggle as her eyes met with Jarvis. He looked into that same solemn face he encountered so many years ago and saw the same fearlessness.

"Let her go," Jarvis ordered.

"No," Swanson replied. "I think we'll keep her. And we'll take the gold and the trunk and anything else we like. You see, we are the victors here, and to the victors go the spoils."

From the corner of his eye, Jarvis saw a black blur explode into view out of the periphery. He and Colonel Swanson turned in unison to see a bounding Keitloa charge up the hill like a mighty silverback. In one motion he sprung forward on his hands and leapt into the air, feet high over his head. He twisted like a tornado and grabbed Colonel Swanson by the head with his massive hands. In one violent whirlwind motion the flying Keitloa snapped the Colonel's neck, which catapulted Eve out of his arms. Jarvis leapt forward to brace her fall as they both careened into the bushes. Colonel Swanson's lifeless body fell to the earth like a tree rent from its roots, while Keitloa landed on all fours like a graceful but powerful cat. Jarvis lie flat on his back and looked down at the skinny creature cradled under his arm.

"Are you all right?" he asked, with no expectation of an answer. She looked up at him and, for the first time, the corners of her mouth turned upward into something that resembled a smile.

Keitloa stood stoically over the lifeless body of Colonel Swanson. From the way Keitloa looked down on the fallen soldier a feeling of deep reverence swept over Jarvis. He knew all too well what it meant to take a life, although he rarely allowed himself to dwell on the subject. As he watched this hulking beast stand in quiet reflection over the destruction of his own hands, he was struck with awe. Jarvis contemplated the magnitude of the loss of one man's life. He was grateful to be alive and relieved to be free from physical danger. He did not mourn for the loss of the man who wished him harm, but at the same time he could not help but feel a knot in the pit of his stomach. This man had lost all that he was, with no chance to regain it. For Colonel Swanson it was finished, no matter what the next life held for him he would never know this existence again. That was taken from him. As a soldier Jarvis had, himself, taken six lives. Six men whose names he would never know. But those nameless men never left him. Even now he saw their faces. He imagined all of the sunrises and tomorrows he had robbed them of. This was the agony he avoided at all cost. In the heat and tumult of battle and faced with his own demise, the decision to kill seemed almost natural. However, in the quiet and lonely moments that followed there was nothing he would not give to take it all back.

The wriggling of Eve's tiny body shook him from his stupor. As she struggled to get free of him, he realized how tightly he held her while he agonized over his many sins. He released her and she pushed away from him slowly.

"Forgive me," Jarvis said aloud. The forgiveness he sought was not exclusively hers.

In four thunderous steps Keitloa moved from standing over Colonel Swanson's body to standing over Jarvis. He unceremoniously snatched him up off the ground and lifted him to his feet.

Like a puppet master manipulating his marionette, he shifted the beaten and battered Jarvis back and forth and examined his swollen face.

"It seems that we are the only ones on this island, man or beast, not trying to kill you," said Keitloa.

Déjà vu, thought Jarvis, as once again he had found himself hanging helplessly in the clutches of this massive killing machine. He stole a glimpse of the tattoo on his right forearm, the black bird with its head craned back toward its tail feathers. Keitloa pulled him in and draped him partially over one of his barrel-like shoulders. He helped Jarvis over to the cavern wall and gently lowered him to sit on the ground. Jarvis leaned against the cool rock wall and looked up at the man who seemed to have taken up saving his life as a hobby.

"Smitty?" he began. "Is he . . . ?"

"He is alive," assured Keitloa. "Although I do not envy the headache he will have when he awakes."

He turned and walked down the hill toward the entrance that led back into the cave. Jarvis sat up straight and looked around. Only then did he notice that Eve was no longer with him. He was about to call out to Keitloa when the bushes to his left rustled. A moment later, Eve emerged with the young boy trailing behind her. He carried a satchel that Jarvis recognized immediately as his own. The boy walked contritely up to Jarvis and extended it to him. Jarvis took the satchel and nodded graciously.

"Thank you," he said to the boy.

Jarvis opened the satchel and was happy to see his journal and brass inkwell still inside. He carefully pulled them out and turned the journal over in his hands. The satchel had for the most part protected the delicate pulp when he was dragged into the dark waters by the monstrous crocodile. Almost on cue, the throbbing sensation returned to his left shoulder. He reached up to touch the bandage, which now hung from his shoulder and barely covered his wound. Eve quickly knelt down next to him and gently peeled back the cloth. She turned to the boy and said, "*Cuey che, guaiba'*."

The boy turned and ran back into the bushes out of sight. Just then Keitloa returned. He carried the unconscious body of young Smitty, slumped over his massive shoulder. He lowered Smitty to the ground and rested him on his back, near Jarvis. Keitloa took two exaggerated steps away from Jarvis and Eve, spun around on his heels, and sat on the ground with his legs crisscrossed. Jarvis looked down at his friend. From the looks of him he appeared to be sleeping. His chest rose and fell ever so slightly. Eve tended to Jarvis's shoulder as the boy returned with a dark green leaf full of a light brown, claylike material. Jarvis turned his attention back to the large dark figure who sat directly across from him. Keitloa rocked back and forth, ever so slightly, with his arms resting on his knees. Jarvis could see just the top of the tattoo on his right forearm. A sharp needle like pain pricked his shoulder and he jolted back.

"Ow," he complained.

Eve did not look up but continued in a workmanlike fashion to pack the clay into his open wounds. He looked over Eve's tiny shoulder back to Keitloa, who looked in their direction but seemed to look right through them.

"What does that marking mean?" Jarvis asked and gestured toward his forearm.

Keitloa snapped out of his trance and looked into Jarvis's face. Slowly, he lifted his arm up off his knee and looked down at the backwards facing bird branded on his skin.

"*Se wo were fi na wosankofa a yenkyi.*"

"What?" a befuddled Jarvis replied.

Keitloa flashed a knowing smile and chuckled. He knew full well that Jarvis did not speak the language and Jarvis did not appreciate being toyed with. However, he had to accept, in more ways than one, he was completely at his mercy. Jarvis waited patiently while Keitloa had a good laugh at his expense. The swarthy giant leaned back, quite pleased with himself, and drew in a deep breath. Jarvis could not decide what was more unbearable, the pain in his shoulder or the anticipation of the answer to a long held curiosity.

"Long ago there was a bird called Sankofa. She left her village and traveled far and wide. While she slept, she was collected and bound. Greed and ignorance stripped away her beautiful feathers for profit. She was kept and fed while her pride was plucked from her. After being robbed of all she had, she was left bare and alone. She fell in a nest of snakes. They told her she was a serpent and she believed them. She crawled on her belly and ate mice and vermin until, one day, her beautiful feathers grew back. The snakes would no longer have her and she was once again on her own. Unsure what she was, she wandered into the jungle hopping around through the grass and bush. One day another bird found her and took her home to her people. She remembered that she was a bird and took to the sky in flight. She had seen too much to stay in her village and so she left. But ever since, no matter where she flew, she kept her head fixed behind her."

"To remember where she had come from," Jarvis interjected.

"Sometimes to move forward you have to look back," Keitloa explained.

The meaning behind the backward facing bird became clear but there were still many questions yet to be asked. Eve had finished packing and dressing his wound, for the second time. She and the boy sat on the ground and watched and waited. He wondered how much, if anything, they understood. He looked back to Keitloa.

"You, Lubolo, de Serras, and the boy from the battlefield all bear that mark," said Jarvis.

"His name was Kwasi," Keitloa said, with deep sadness in his voice. His tone all but confirmed what Jarvis had suspected for some time: that these men all knew one another and were somehow connected through this marking. Jarvis waited patiently for Keitloa to continue.

"Men lay claim on all they see. They seek to possess and to keep where they have no right. They give and take what is not theirs," he paused and looked over at Eve and the boy, who still sat quietly and observed them. "We are here to remind man of what he has forgotten."

"We?" asked Jarvis.

"We are Sankofa. We are set throughout the world to put down the abominations of man," said Keitloa. "Greed knows no bounds and, left unchecked, will ravage the whole earth. Our breath is eternal, our strength is limitless. Our light cannot be extinguished. We stand to turn back the haughty ambitions of an ever consuming beast."

"You are here to free slaves?" Jarvis asked.

"We are here to free man," Keitloa responded.

"And Lubolo?" asked Jarvis.

"Those who have forgotten can be reminded, those who know and act contrary do so to their own destruction," he lamented.

Keitloa leaned forward and stood up. Dark red blood stained the left leg of his pants and covered his thick muscular thigh. There was a deep gash in his abdomen just above his waist from which the blood still flowed.

"You are hurt," said Jarvis.

Eve leapt to her feet and rushed to his side. Without a word the boy followed her, with the remains of the cloth they used to bandage Jarvis. After a brief examination of the wound she quickly wrapped the cloth around his waist and pressed upon the spot where he was bleeding. Delicately, Keitloa removed her hand. He reached down and cradled her chin with his oversized palm. She looked up at him and Jarvis thought he saw a tear stream down her face. Keitloa smiled broadly at her. He then reached out and ruffled the hair of the boy who stood beside her.

"Nothing was ever asked of her," he said to Jarvis. "The care she gave you, she gave of herself. The boy leapt into peril on his own accord. In all these years we have let them be just as they are. They have great heart; that is their nature. But this new world, our world, I fear will destroy them."

He reached into the pocket of his trousers and pulled out the black stone. It was smooth and polished and almost seemed transparent. He extended it down toward Jarvis. Jarvis sat mesmerized as the weather stone hovered in front of his face, nestled between Keitloa's muzzle sized fingers. Keitloa shook the stone at him and beckoned him to take it. Jarvis reached out, eagerly but slowly, and accepted the stone. It was much lighter than he anticipated and had barely any weight for its size. At first he was not even sure he had gotten ahold of it properly. As he looked at the shiny black orb in the palm of his hand, Keitloa turned and walked away. He stepped over the berm and headed back down the hill toward the entrance to the dark cave. With his shoulder newly numbed again, Jarvis got to his feet and began to follow after Keitloa. He stepped over Smitty's unconscious body and stopped at the top of the hill.

"What am I to do?" he called down to Keitloa.

The weary warrior stopped, placed his hand on the rock face near the threshold of the cave and turned his head back. Jarvis wobbled slightly at the top of the hill and reached out to steady himself on the wall beside him.

"Look back and remember," said Keitloa.

"Look back? Where?" Jarvis asked. "Remember what? Where are you going?"

The dark giant had already turned and disappeared into the cave. Frustrated by his vague response and mysterious exit, Jarvis kicked at the rocks in front of him. *Look back*, he thought.

Jarvis craned his neck and looked behind him. Eve knelt over Smitty now and the boy stood behind her with the leaf full of clay. The old woman stepped out from behind the hedges followed by the other young girl. She paused and looked up at him. Behind her weathered and wrinkled skin was a pair of soft grey eyes that matched her long straight hair.

Jarvis stared at her and turned the black stone over in his hand several times. Strangely, his thoughts turned to his mother and sister back home. He wondered what they were doing at that very moment. He remembered the day he left them and the bittersweet feelings of pride and sorrow. As a young boy he dreamt of traveling the seas and of adventure in far off lands. His childhood fantasies were filled with fame, fortune and glory. Ever present in the back of his mind was a proud mother back at home.

Sometimes he longed for those innocent naïve daydreams; as

his real life adventures had been nightmarish by comparison. He had now traveled the seas to distant lands but found more death and depravity than fame and fortune. If his mother had witnessed all he had seen and done the last thing he imagined her being was proud. And what of his younger self, and all his hopes and dreams of the future, what would he tell him? His life had become a series of orders and compromises until all he knew was seeking someone else's glory. The shame of just how small his ambitions had become was nearly too much to bare. He no longer cared for fame or fortune or glory. What he sought now was a life of meaning; a life of purpose. What stood before him was redemption, a cause worthy of his life. All at once purpose filled his whole soul and he understood what needed to be done.

To his left Smitty began to stir. Jarvis walked over to him and knelt beside him. His eyes opened and closed, as he tried to adjust to the daylight. He coughed and squinted terribly from the pain.

"Welcome back," Jarvis said, as he helped him to sit up.

Without hesitation Eve produced a calabash full of water. Smitty stared at her and then tilted his head slightly for a better look at the three people behind her. He looked back to Jarvis with a dazed and confused look. Then he leaned backwards to determine where he was. He slowly looked up, from the base to the cavernous cliffs above. Eve handed him the calabash. Smitty took it and tilted it up to drink. He lowered the gourd and wiped a few drops of water from his mouth. He squinted again in pain and felt the back of his head with his free hand.

"What happened?" he asked, and shook his head back and forth. "You look like the devil. Who are they? Where are we?"

"Well the long and short of it is, the late Colonel Swanson, over there," Jarvis began, and gestured to Swanson's body lying in the bushes. "He cracked you over the head and then walked up here and gave me a good beating before young Eve here shot him with an arrow and our Negro savior, Keitloa, nearly twisted his head off. These people behind me, I believe, are the last living Arawak. And as to where we are, the best I can tell this is a secret

God-sent paradise refuge complete with protective walls and a pond."

"Right," Smitty acknowledged, as he tried to process the information presented him.

Jarvis stood up straight and looked out the large opening in the stone ceiling at the sky above. He placed both hands on his hips and inhaled through his bruised and swollen nose. He looked around at the walls in the distance and all the vegetation that covered the cavern floor. He listened to the gentle sounds of water flowing into the deep blue pond at the far side of the cavern. Eve came and stood by his side. They regarded each other and then looked over at what was left of her people. He thought again of his mother and the little boy who dreamed of adventure.

"I remember," he whispered to himself.

Legacy

M y boy, you are persistent," said the silver haired man.
"Professor, what are you doing here?" asked Gideon.

"Come, quickly, and I will explain," Professor Gervaise said, as he stepped to the side and gestured back inside the cave with his torch.

"Who was that? What is this place?"

"I promise all will be answered, but you must come now," he said, with an increased level of urgency in his voice.

Gideon took a quick peek back toward the top of the hill where the boy had run off. He was not eager to return to the darkness of the cave but wanted answers and it appeared Professor Gervaise had them. Obediently, he hurried back down the steps toward the professor. Without hesitation and without question, Todd followed right behind him. Professor Gervaise held the torch just inside the cave to light the entryway. Gideon and Todd stepped back into the darkness, from which they had only just escaped. Once inside Professor Gervaise followed and the three of them stood in the blackness just outside the light from the entryway.

"Professor, what's going on?" asked Gideon.

"In a moment," Professor Gervaise said. "Take off your clothes."

"What?!" exclaimed Todd.

The professor held the torch closer to the ground and shone the light down on a red and orange bundle that lay on the floor. The cloth bundle was tied up neatly with pieces of twine. Gideon removed his shirt and started to take off his shoes. Todd looked at him with disgust and did not move a muscle.

"It's okay," Gideon said. "I think I know what he has in mind."

"So do I," replied Todd. "And it's NOT okay."

Professor Gervaise bent down and pulled a small half-moon shaped knife, with a bone handle, from his robe. He cut the twine from the bundle and put the knife back under his robe. He leaned back toward the cave's entrance and peered outside. Gideon finished removing his shoes and picked up a piece of cloth from the top of the bundle. He held it up and examined it, before lifting it over his head. After some maneuvering he managed to poke his head through a hole in the top. The cloth draped over his shoulders and hung down just past his knees. He looked over at Todd and raised his arms.

"See?"

"Fine," Todd relented and took off his shirt. "But I'm keeping my drawers on."

Now that Gideon wore the cloth covering he saw it was more of a serape than a robe. It was a single piece of red wool cloth with a hole cut in the middle. There was a strip of orange material woven into the edges of the garment. He removed his pants from underneath the covering of the serape. Todd had only just begun to take off his shoes and socks. Professor Gervaise, who looked out anxiously through the doorway to the outside world, glanced back inside to monitor their progress.

"Quickly," he urged when he saw Todd was not yet covered with the robe.

"All right!" Todd shot back.

"Professor?" Gideon began. "Please, what is all of this?"

"There are sandals at the bottom," Professor Gervaise said, and pointed the torch at last piece of cloth that lay on the floor.

Todd bent down and picked up the remaining cloth. Gideon

saw two pairs of sandals along with some more orange material. He reached down and retrieved a sandal. Just then a breeze swept through the entrance from outside and blew past them. The wind cut through the opened sides of his robe and he became acutely aware of his nakedness beneath the single piece of cloth. He had to admit that it felt nice to be out of his dirty, sweat soiled clothes.

"What's this?" Todd said. He held up what looked like a dingy gray sheet. He grimaced as it was not as fine a material as Gideon and the professor wore.

"Just put it on," barked the professor.

Todd grudgingly covered himself with the leftover cloth and undressed beneath it. They fastened the sandals to their feet with the thin leather like straps. Professor Gervaise walked over and kicked their clothes and shoes back into a dark corner. He then picked up the remaining piece of orange material on the ground and handed it to Gideon.

"This goes on your head," he explained and pantomimed placing it across his forehead like a bandana.

The headband was made of intertwined pieces of orange cotton cloth. Gideon dutifully tied it across his forehead and looked over at Todd. Gideon smiled at his friend, who did not look amused. Professor Gervaise had picked up their backpacks and looked through the outer pockets. He pulled out Todd's camera and without warning lifted it over his head and hurled it into the ground smashing it into pieces.

"Hey!" Todd shouted. "What the crap!"

He ignored Todd and headed over to the dark corner where their clothes were. Gideon reached out and grabbed his arm.

"Professor?" he said firmly. "Please."

Professor Gervaise stopped and looked back at Gideon. He placed the backpacks on the ground and turned to face both of them.

"How much do you know?"

"What?" asked Gideon.

"Do you have the journal?" Professor Gervaise said. "What have you learned?"

Gideon reached down and picked up his pack from the ground. He retrieved the journal from the side pocket and placed the pack back on the floor. He extended the journal to the professor.

"I'm sorry about its condition," he said. "This psychopath tried to burn it."

"Never mind about him," Professor Gervaise said. "Did you finish it?"

"No," Gideon said, curious how quickly the professor accepted the news that his journal had been partially burned and of how unconcerned he seemed about the identity of the one who did it. "The last I read Jarvis, Smitty, and John Davis were a day away from the cave. Then we found directions through the cave that weren't at all helpful. Did you pass by a man tied up outside?"

"Yes, yes," said Professor Gervaise dismissively. "He was tied up. You didn't finish it then?"

There was a commotion outside the cave. Professor Gervaise walked over and stood in the daylight which bled through from the outside. The rumblings grew closer and louder. Gideon heard many voices garbled together that he could not understand.

Professor Gervaise held the torch out in front of him and raised his other hand high above his head. He looked back toward them and said, "Stay here and do exactly as I say, exactly when I say it. Do you understand?"

Gideon and Todd nodded and he stepped out through the stone archway. They turned to each other and exchanged a puzzled look. Professor Gervaise called out to whoever had gathered outside in a language that Gideon did not understand. His words were immediately followed by an even greater rumbling from the crowd and Gideon got a sense of just how big the group was. He thought about the boy in the loin cloth and tried to imagine what waited for them. He wondered why Professor Gervaise had not been more concerned with the condition of his journal or the fact that a man was tied up outside the cave.

"Gideon, Todd, you can come out," Professor Gervaise called back into the cave.

"Come on," said Gideon, as he started toward the steps.

"Wait," Todd said, and caught him by the arm. "How does he know my name?"

"What?" said Gideon. "We told him."

"No we didn't."

Gideon thought for a moment and said, "Well, then, I must have told him before."

"Did you?"

"What is your deal?" Gideon said, as he shook his arm free of Todd's grasp.

"Something is off with this guy," he said. "He shows up here in the middle of nowhere all prepared with this crap for us and now he's out there talking with who knows who and you don't have any questions?"

"I have plenty of questions. Let's go get some answers."

He turned and headed up the stone steps and through the opening. Todd lagged behind and stared toward the daylight. When Gideon reached the first step he looked out to see Professor Gervaise who stood just beyond the threshold with one arm raised high in the air and the other outstretched toward him beckoning him to come out. Beyond the professor was a group of at least forty people that he could see. They were bunched together and the group stretched all the way up the hill and cascaded out of sight over the top. Gideon's jaw dropped as he took in the spectacle.

They all had caramel skin and jet-black hair. They wore minimal clothing, the makings of which were primitive at best. Some of the men wore cloth coverings around their waists, while others were made of feathers. Their fine straight hair was cut just below their ears. Several of the men carried long spears or bows. Of the few women he could see, they also had loin coverings made of cloth or feathers, with only their long black hair covering their chest. A few carried baskets that appeared to be woven out of thatch or branches. All eyes were on him and they appeared to be just as interested in him as he was in them.

"Todd," he said. "Get your butt out here."

Todd walked out to the opening and looked over Gideon's shoulder. His eyes widened when they met with the sight before him. Like Gideon, his mouth fell open as he stared up at the large crowd of curious people.

"*Guaitiao*," Professor Gervaise proclaimed.

The dark faces in the crowd looked around at each other and a low murmur rolled throughout their numbers. Professor Gervaise walked back to Gideon and leaned in closely. He whispered in his ear, "Put your hand over your heart and say *datiao*."

Gideon stepped forward and the crowd quieted. He put his right hand over his heart and with a loud voice said, "*Datiao*!"

A prominent looking man near the front of the crowd walked down and stood in front of Gideon. He had many bright colored orange and red feathers covering his loins, and a necklace made of claws and talons wrapped tightly around his neck. In one hand he held a bow, which he promptly slung back over his shoulder. There was so much happening all at once that Gideon struggled to focus on just one thing. He forced himself to hone in on the man's face. He was not an old man but definitely Gideon's senior. His eyes were brown with flecks of gray that almost seemed to sparkle. His cheeks protruded out on the sides of his flat nose. Two prominent lines bookended the thin lips of his mouth. With both hands the man reached out and grabbed Gideon by the shoulders.

"Oh, dear," Gideon said, and tensed up.

"*Datiao*," the man said.

"*Datiao*," Gideon repeated. He looked over the man's shoulder at Professor Gervaise, who smiled proudly at them. Momentarily relieved, he relaxed and unclenched his muscles.

The man gently moved Gideon to the side and reached back toward Todd. With his left arm he lay hold on Todd and pulled him out of the cave and up next to Gideon. The man stood between them and turned back to face the crowd. He took Todd by his right hand and Gideon by his left and raised both hands in the air.

"*Gua' kia yu' guaitiao*!" he declared.

They all began to stomp their spears and feet on the ground and hoot in unison. They were all smiles as the man led them up the hill and through the crowd. They passed by Professor Gervaise, who stood to the side and simply nodded. Those in their path made way before them. Some reached out to touch them as they walked by. In seconds they were near the top of the hill, completely surrounded by the people. Gideon was nearly overwhelmed by the reception, with a feeling of pure elation. He looked back at Todd directly behind him, also being mobbed by the crowd. Todd had a huge smile on his face but wore a worried expression.

"What's wrong?" Gideon asked.

"I've seen this movie before," Todd replied. "They're going to eat us."

"Then why are you smiling?" asked Gideon.

"I don't want them to know that I know," said Todd.

Gideon just shook his head and continued to greet all those he came in contact with on their way up the hill. At the top, he could finally see what he had waited for and it was more magnificent than he could have possibly imagined. Mounds dotted the landscape, not mounds of gold but of mud, leaves and branches. There were countless round huts that filled the bottom of the cavern. In the far corner was a beautiful deep blue pool of water that reflected the sky above and a small waterfall that poured out of the rock wall emptied into it. The crowd stretched on, six men wide, for another fifty yards to where the first set of huts began. More men, women and children made their way toward them from the village. They followed a footpath that led out from the huts and disappeared into the horde of bodies lined up to meet them.

Sporadic drops of water fell several hundred feet from the lip of the stone ceiling above; it sprinkled on them as they passed out under the giant circular sunroof above. Pushed along by the throngs of people, Gideon and Todd followed close behind the man with the bright feathered loin cloth. He led them down into the village and through the many round huts. Each hut was uniformly constructed with a circular roof covered with brown leaves and branches. The sides were made of sticks and branches and covered with a thatch-like material. Each of them had a single doorway, faced out toward the pond. Just outside the door, several of them had small smoldering fire pits with plumes of white smoke that rose up into the air. All of the huts were empty and the fire pits unattended, as everyone in the village had come out to look at the newcomers.

Gideon tried desperately to take it all in. He wanted to see every inch and remember every second. He looked into the faces of the people; he looked from one end of the wondrous cavern to the other. Another gentle breeze passed by them and under his robe and reminded him how little material stood between the world and his nakedness. With a glance over his shoulder he found Professor Gervaise, who followed behind the crowd and carried a small child in his arms.

"Look at that," he said to Todd.

Todd, who looked completely overloaded by the whole ordeal, unsuccessfully attempted to minimize contact with a mob of children who sought to feel the hair on his arms. He turned around and looked back at Professor Gervaise, who had placed the child on his shoulder and was being warmly greeted by several of the villagers.

"Still think they're gonna eat us?" Gideon mocked.

"That just means they probably won't eat him," said Todd. "For all we know, he's the chef."

As he said that, a little girl walked up next to him, stumbled and fell. Todd quickly snatched her up to keep her from being trampled by the crowd. He held her in his arms and she flashed a huge bright smile. Still being pushed onward by the crowd, he kept hold of her and could not help but smile back. Gideon took an inordinate amount of pleasure at this scene. He wanted to point out Todd's inconsistencies but chose not to ruin the moment.

They continued to weave through the huts and people until they turned and headed toward the pond. As they left the cluster of huts, they passed through several hundred waist high mounds of dirt about five feet in diameter. They had little green sprouts coming out of all sides. Gideon thought they looked like a giant Chia Pet farm. He looked out over the pond and saw two canoes, carrying four men each, gliding across the water toward the bank. The men pushed the canoes along with long poles that stuck deep into the water. Beyond the mounds of dirt, there was a large clearing along the muddy shore that sloped into the pond.

The man with the bright feather loin cloth led Gideon and Todd to a large flat rock and the crowd filed into the clearing and formed a huge circle. The man stood up on the flat rock and beckoned for Gideon and Todd to join him. Gideon took his hand and he pulled him up on the stage. After hesitating for a moment, Todd looked around for a safe spot to lower the little girl and finally joined them on the rock at the center of the crowd. Gideon looked around at the gathering and estimated there were at least three hundred people that surrounded them. From their elevated position he could see a thick grove of trees and vegetation to the far side of the cavern, next to the pond. Professor Gervaise made his way through the crowd to the flat rock where Gideon, Todd and the man with the bright feather loin cloth stood. He handed the child to one of the women in the crowd and stepped up on the stone platform.

"*Osama, osama! Ocama-quay-ari' daneke'*!" he shouted, with his hands high over his head. The murmuring crowd fell silent. "*Li, gua'kia yu' guaitiao, guarico cu'. Taicaraya gua'kia ara'guaca. Guaiba' taiguaitiao.*"

The people spoke to one another excitedly and smiled before they happily began to disperse; with the majority of the people heading back into the village. Some stopped among the mounds of dirt and began to pull out some of the green sprouts. Others made their way down to the shore of the pond. A small flock of children milled around the edge of the flat rock and stared up at Gideon and Todd.

"*Guaiba', guaiba',*" Professor Gervaise admonished them, and waved playfully with his hands.

The children giggled and ran away. The last to leave was the little girl Todd had rescued from the crowd. She smiled and Todd waved at her before she turned and ran off after the other little ones. With the children gone, the entire crowd had left except for Gideon, Todd, Professor Gervaise and the man in the bright feathered loin cloth.

"What did you say to them?" Todd asked.

"I told them to go and prepare for a party tonight in your honor," the professor answered.

"Professor, this is incredible," Gideon said. "Who are these people? Where are we?"

"They call it *Roco Bana*," he explained. "It means place of remembrance."

Professor Gervaise stepped down from the large flat rock and Gideon dutifully followed after him. Todd remained atop the stone and looked cautiously at the claw and talon necklace of the man that stood next to him, who pensively studied him in return. The professor held up the journal and opened it to the last page. He turned it over and extended it to Gideon.

"As to who they are," he continued, "I will let Benjamin Jarvis answer that."

Gideon took the journal from him and sat down on the end of the flat stone. He cleared his throat and began to read aloud.

I owe my life to a brave Arawak boy who rescued me from the clutches of a monster and to his selfless sister, Eve, who has nursed me back to health even though she had no cause to. We all owe our lives to Keitloa, a titan of a man whose deeds are worthy of being passed down through the annals of time. He has left me with a noble charge and an enormous undertaking. I intend to devote the life which they saved to them. I lament that I will not see you again but rejoice in the fact that I have found a cause worthy of dedicating my life to. I pray that this journal finds you well. Consider the man you find on these pages dead but take comfort that through these people I am redeemed. Give Millie my love.

Your son,
Ben Jarvis

Gideon closed the journal and looked up at Todd, who stood over him atop the rock. Then he looked at Professor Gervaise who beamed with pride.

"These people," he said and gestured all around them, "are descendants of the girl he called Eve. She and Ben Jarvis established this sanctuary as a means of protecting her people from extinction."

Gideon glanced down toward the pond and saw several men and women who mended fishing nets and stared back at him. He turned around and looked back up toward the village and again was met with the eyes of many onlookers who stood near the mounds of dirt between the flat rock and the huts. He struggled to wrap his mind around what he saw. It was as if he had been transported back in time to a primitive world entirely untouched by modern man.

"How is this possible?" he asked. "How was this secret kept of hundreds of years?"

"Through the great sacrifice of a few," Professor Gervaise answered. "Shortly after he wrote those words, Ben Jarvis, dispatched a young man named Thaddeus Smith to England."

"Thaddeus Smith?" Gideon interrupted. "Smitty?"

"Correct," the professor continued. "They financed the trip with some of the gold from Bartolomeu's trunk."

"So there *is* gold," said Todd eagerly.

"Was," Professor Gervaise corrected before he continued. "Smith found Jarvis's mother and gave her the journal and enough gold for her to live comfortably the rest of her life. His sister, Millie, rejected his farewell and booked passage for herself and her young son Robert on the next boat to Jamaica. Together, with the help of Smitty, they found this cave and her brother. She purchased an estate in Seville where they could farm and procure supplies for this burgeoning colony. To conceal any connection to her brother, she changed her surname to Gervaise."

Gideon stared in astonishment. "Oh wow. So she's like your . . . your great-great-great-great-grandmother."

"Seven greats actually," Professor Gervaise said. "I am a direct descendant of Robert Gervaise. For over three hundred years my family has kept this people secret and safe."

"Wait a minute," said Todd, as he stepped down off of the rock platform. "You're telling me that in three hundred years nobody has stumbled onto this place."

"It was not by accident, I assure you. We have been aided greatly by the terrain and difficult nature of traveling through this area," the professor explained. "And additional measures were put into place to discourage outsiders."

"What kind of measures?" Gideon asked.

"Keitloa and his sons were instrumental at first. He organized the Maroons, who settled in this harsh wilderness. They served as a deterrent and a distraction for nearly a hundred years while they scourged the English settlers," Professor Gervaise said. "Eventually a treaty was struck between the two sides and the undesirable cockpit country was awarded the Maroons. They promptly hung an unwelcome sign on the whole region, *Mi Na Sen Yu Na Come*. Stories and rumors of hidden dangers and ghost inhabited caves were spread as further discouragement."

"What about all these people? Why do they stay? How do you keep them from going out there?" Gideon asked.

"*Cacibajagua*," the professor said, and pointed back toward the far wall from where they entered the cavern. "The Black Cave. Arawak tradition says that life began for man in a cave. The sun and the moon came out of a cave. Cacibajagua leads to the underworld, and no man, while he still draws breath, can enter except their god Zemi permits it. Only those adorned in these colors are allowed to pass through Cacibajagua and help ferry the dead to the afterlife."

He spread his arms wide to show the red and orange covering he wore. Gideon looked down at his own robe. It all seemed so simple, and he struggled to accept this cataclysmic shift in his perception of the world. Clearly, he could not deny what he saw. These people were real and appeared to be well established here in this enormous secret cavern. What he could not quite get his mind around was how.

A caravan of women made their way down from the village. Each of them carried a basket under their arm. They approached the quartet at the round rock without a word and laid the baskets on the ground in front of Gideon and Todd. One by one they removed small clay dishes from the baskets. The first woman offered Gideon what looked like some kind of boiled spinach mixed with nuts. He nodded politely and picked up a bite with his fingers. It gushed in his mouth but as he chewed there was an odd contrast between the mushy green leaves and the crunch of the nuts. Gideon smiled and nodded as if he enjoyed it. He did not wish to appear rude. The first woman moved down to Todd and the next woman in line presented Gideon with a thin piece of bread made of cornmeal. Again he sampled the bread and nodded before the woman shifted over in front of Todd. This procedure was repeated for a gourd of water, a piece of dried fish, and finally a ripe mango.

"Thank you," Gideon said as the women collected their baskets to leave.

"Yes, thank you," added Todd, while he chewed a mouth full of fish and bread.

Gideon held the mango in his hand and examined it. The color was a beautiful mixture of red, yellow, and green. He had eaten many such mangos in the years he lived on the island. Two years he had lived, served, and labored, all the while ignorant of the miraculous community that he circled about on his various travels.

"Professor, the logistics of a deception like this is mindboggling," he said. "How is there enough room and food for them all? In three hundred years shouldn't there be more than just a few hundred Arawak?"

"Right you are, my boy," Professor Gervaise said. "Things have not always been as good as they are now. There was a devastating plague around the turn of the century that wiped out over half the population. But they are a resilient people and have overcome much to survive. As for the food, this is a nearly self-sustained community. They grow all the vegetables they consume in those mounds of dirt you see there."

He stopped and pointed over to the sprout-covered mounds by the huts in the village. Gideon was impressed by the ingenious nature of farming in such a way with limited acreage. Professor Gervaise then directed their attention over toward the pond.

"The underground spring not only brings fresh water but will, on occasion, carry with it fish, frogs, and turtles to be caught. The runoff seeps back underground through fissions in the limestone over there," the professor said. He pointed to the far side of the cavern with the dense vegetation and trees. "That both keeps the water clean and clear and provides rich soil for fruit trees and farming. Beyond that, they are proficient at trapping the birds and bats to round out their diet."

Professor Gervaise directed their attention to a group of men behind them. They sat on the ground and fashioned boxes out of thick branches. The sides and bottom of the boxes were lined with small twines of rope. Three little birds rested peacefully in a larger cage that lay at their feet. All the men looked up from their work with interest at their visitors.

"Aren't they curious about where you come from?" Gideon asked.

"We intentionally limit our contact with them to mostly ceremonial events," Professor Gervaise explained. "Bohiti, here, manages the affairs on the village."

The man in the bright feathered loin cloth stepped down from the flat rock and stood next to Professor Gervaise. Gideon realized for the first time, as they stood next to each other, that the feathers and robes were the same colors. The sun rose high enough into the sky that the bright light of day peeked over the ledge high above them. The daylight splashed onto the rock wall just above the pond. The beams sparkled and danced across the deep blue pool. Somehow the miraculous cavern seemed even more magical than before. With the appearance of the sun, Gideon was finally able to get his bearings. The morning sun shone from the east side, opposite the pond on the west side of the cavern. The village was to the far east side, with the lone entrance on the wall to the north and the dense vegetation to the south. The clearing, with the flat round rock in the middle, was just to the north of the pond nearly at the center of the cavern.

"We?" Todd questioned.

"Beg your pardon," the professor responded.

"You said 'we limit our contact', who is we?" Todd asked.

"There is another," he explained. "We work in tandem. Sankofa is greater than any one man."

"Sankofa?" Gideon asked. "The symbol from the journal?"

He lifted his right arm and pulled the cloth back to expose the tattoo of the backward facing bird and said, "*Se wo were fi na wosankofa a yenkyi.*"

Bohiti knelt down on the ground and bowed his head. Gideon felt a swelling in his chest and a chill shot up his spine. He did not know what was said or what it meant but felt a sense of reverence nonetheless.

"What does that mean?" asked Gideon.

"It is an African proverb that says it is not wrong to go back for that which you have forgotten," the professor began. "We are part of an order and tradition that has operated for over a thousand years. Our purpose here is to protect and honor the past to ensure their future."

"So then you are not the only one, the only protector?" asked Todd.

"No. A pact was formed from the beginning to guard this great secret. That pact was passed down from generation to generation."

"Your partner is Mucaro," Gideon realized aloud.

Professor Gervaise nodded. "They call him the night eagle."

"What?!" Todd exclaimed. "That psycho who tried to kill us?"

As Todd shouted, Bohiti looked back and forth anxiously between him and Professor Gervaise and Gideon.

"We were not trying to kill you," the professor said.

"The mist, the kidnapping, the machete marionette twins, that was you?" asked Gideon.

"It was no accident that the journal came into your possession, my boy," Professor Gervaise explained. "But we had to see to what lengths you were willing to go."

"This was a test?" Gideon said. "Someone could have gotten hurt."

AARON BLAYLOCK

The professor did not answer but simply met Gideon's indignation with a solemn resolute stare. Due to Todd's shouting there was a renewed curiosity from the people in the village. A crowd began to gather just beyond the mounds of dirt. Gideon took a deep breath to calm himself. He studied Professor Gervaise and waited for further explanation. Todd paced back and forth next to him, while Bohiti fixated on his rhythmic movements.

"I am an old man, Gideon," he finally said. "This is the legacy I was given. However, my branch of the family tree will end with me. They will need a new guardian."

It dawned on Gideon, all at once, what he was after. The gravity of the situation set in and he looked around at the villagers who stood in the wings. He stood up and looked directly at Bohiti and then over at Todd. Finally, he looked back at Professor Gervaise, who waited expectantly.

"Are you asking me to take your place when you die?" Gideon asked.

"Actually, I was hoping you would start sooner than that."

"How soon?"

"Tonight."

Gideon liked to envision his life as a book in which each minute was being written. What the professor asked of him was something that, in his wildest daydreams, he had never imagined. This was not simply turning the page or starting a new chapter. No, this was closing the book and starting an entirely new one; a book that no one would ever read. He considered the current state of his life, as a convenience store clerk and junior college enrollee. A straight choice between that life and this would have been an easy one. After all, it was just a job, and the life of a struggling college student paled in comparison with this enchanted cavern and its marvelous inhabitants. However, he struggled to let go of his aspirations for the future and all he would give up. He thought of Liz and the dream of building a life and a family with her. He thought of his family and friends back home and how he would miss them. He looked over at Todd who stood beside him with his hands on his hips.

274

"What would be required of me?"

"First, say yes. Then the work begins," Professor Gervaise said. "You will come back with me to Kingston and take charge of my family's estate. You will need to learn the language and the history of this people and this place. In time you will become their primary contact to the outside world and assume responsibility for their protection from it."

"I'm honored professor, truly honored. How long do I have to consider this?"

"I leave here before the sun sets," the professor said. "I will need your answer before then."

"Are you kidding me?" interrupted Todd. "You can't be serious. Gideon, this guy and his partner tried to kill us and now he wants our help?"

"I want nothing from you," the professor said to Todd. "You were not part of the plan."

"That explains the Oliver Twist bed shirt you gave me," replied Todd, as he tugged at the gray sheet draped from his shoulders.

"That is a burial gown," said the professor.

"Perfect, absolutely perfect," Todd said. "Gideon, let's get out of here." Todd took a few steps back in the direction of the entrance to the cave.

"*Akani!*" shouted Professor Gervaise.

Several of the men from within the crowd jump out and advanced on Todd. They all carried spears and bows. Bohiti leapt between Professor Gervaise and Gideon. The children who played nearby scrambled back to where the people had gathered and were collected by various women. Todd was cut off from his exit by the men with spears and put his hands in the air and walked slowly backwards until he met with Gideon. The two friends stood back to back as the armed men from the village surrounded them. Todd looked in all directions while Gideon kept his eyes locked on Professor Gervaise.

"If we're gonna have to fight these guys I really wish I was wearing pants," Todd said.

The men advanced on Gideon and Todd until they were close

enough to reach out and poke them with their spears. A few men had drawn their bows and stood just behind the circle of spear holders. Todd had his fists clenched and assumed a defensive posture. Gideon raised both hands over his head, with the journal in his right hand and his left hand opened.

"We're not going to fight," he said loudly. "*Datiao! Datiao!*"

"What does that mean?" asked Todd.

"I don't know, but they liked it before," said Gideon.

"*Datiao*," they both shouted in unison.

There was a murmur that swept through the crowd of onlookers. The men in the spear circle appeared unsure and looked at Professor Gervaise for direction. He stepped out from behind Bohiti and cocked his head backwards slightly, to look down his nose at them.

"I do not want this, Gideon," said the professor.

"That makes two of us. So how 'bout you tell them to put down their pointy sticks and we can talk this out."

"I am afraid we are beyond words now."

"What does that mean?" Todd whispered to Gideon.

"It means we're in trouble."

Confidently, Professor Gervaise stepped between two of the centuries, who still pointed their spears at Gideon and Todd. He casually walked around the perimeter and studied the helpless duo in the center. They both had their hands in the air and their eyes locked on the business end of the sticks leveled at them. The professor circled around past Todd and shot him a disdainful look. He strode in front of Gideon and came to a halt with his heels together as he stood at attention. Gideon looked upon this silver-haired gentleman who had been so generous to him so many times. Their love for history had bonded them almost instantly. Elder Goodwin and his companions spent countless hours meeting with the professor in his home and in his classroom. They discussed religion, history, philosophy, and life in general. They had a standing appointment on Saturdays for stew peas and stories. Gideon never would have imagined the secret he held or the plans he must have been concocting.

He looked into the cool gray eyes of the man he had always respected and admired.

"What now?" Gideon asked.

"That entirely depends on you, my boy," Professor Gervaise said. "I will do whatever is necessary to protect these people and keep this place secret."

"We can keep a secret," said Gideon.

"Trust is not something spoken into existence, it is earned," said the professor.

"I haven't earned your trust?" Gideon asked.

"*You* have," Professor Gervaise said, with a nod over Gideon's shoulder toward Todd.

"I trust Todd with my life."

"There is much at stake," said Professor Gervaise. "You are asking me to risk my family's legacy and my life's work on a stranger."

"Am I no less of a stranger?"

"My boy, if I were not certain the caliber of man you were, you would not be standing here."

"Then trust me when I tell you that you can trust him."

"No," Professor Gervaise said in a melancholy tone. "He cannot be allowed to leave here."

"What?!" exclaimed Todd.

"Todd, let me handle this," barked Gideon.

He glanced over his shoulder at his friend, who stared daggers into Professor Gervaise. Gideon leaned into his field of vision and got his attention. He raised his eyebrows and slowly gave him an assuring nod. Behind pursed lips, Todd exhaled through his nose and nodded back. Gideon turned his attention back to the professor, who still stood at attention in front of him.

"You can't just keep him here," Gideon argued.

"No, that would pose an even greater risk to our way."

"I don't understand. If he can't go and he can't stay . . ." Gideon's words trailed off as a dreadful thought entered his mind. He looked down and in Professor Gervaise's hand was a half-moon shaped blade. "You're going to kill him."

"That would be the easy answer," the professor said. "But no. If I killed him, then there is still the question of your allegiance. As I said, what happens next is entirely up to you."

He raised the half-moon blade in front of Gideon and dropped it on the ground at his feet. The white bone handle and polished blade shone brilliantly against the red clay floor. Gideon looked down on the knife for a moment and then looked back up at Professor Gervaise.

"If you think I would kill my best friend, then you don't know me as well as you think you do."

"Who's killing their best friend?" Todd asked with a worried gaze over his shoulder.

"His fate is sealed, it was from the moment you brought him here," Professor Gervaise began. "You, however, have a choice. You can join me in this remarkable undertaking, one that has spanned centuries and will ring through the eternities, or you can choose to be forgotten; another soul who ventured off and was lost in the Land of Look Behind."

The words from his mouth did not match with the tone of his voice. He spoke with a calm and calculated demeanor. His expression bore no contempt or remorse. What he suggested was abhorrent and completely out of character for the man Gideon knew. For some reason, the story of Abraham and Isaac floated through Gideon's consciousness. Abraham was asked to sacrifice his beloved son only to be stopped by an angel before he murdered him. God tested his devotion. Gideon wondered if this too might be a test, but feared there would be no angelic rescue for him or for Todd.

Professor Gervaise reached out and took the journal from his hand. He tucked it neatly in the interior pocket of his robe. Gideon kept a wary eye on the silver haired professor and slowly knelt down and picked up the knife from the ground. He took a step away from Todd and turned around to look at him. This caused Todd to temporarily ignore the threatening instruments of impalement aimed at them and turn to face Gideon.

"What are you doing?" asked a worried Todd.

"Don't speak," instructed Gideon, as he held the knife in front of him.

"What?" Todd asked, with a confused expression.

"You and me, we used to be together," said Gideon. "Every day, together."

Todd tilted his head sideways and looked across at his friend. All at once his face relaxed and his shoulders sank slightly. "Always," he said.

Bohiti entered the circle and stood beside Professor Gervaise. The professor left Bohiti's side and walked quietly around to stand behind Todd. He had his eyes trained on Gideon and looked on with great interest at the exchange between them.

"It's all ending, I gotta stop pretending who we are," said Gideon.

"You and me, I can see us dying, are we?" asked Todd.

Gideon nodded and extended his left arm toward him. Todd reached out and they grasped forearms. Gideon gave Todd's forearm a gentle squeeze and raised the knife up above his shoulders. He tensed up his arm and with one mighty pull they slingshot one another in opposite directions. Gideon twirled around and grabbed Professor Gervaise around the neck. He pulled him close and put the knife to his throat.

The men who formed the circle froze for a moment and then began to shout and thrust their spears at them. Gideon looked over and saw Todd had also grabbed onto Bohiti and had him in a headlock. Quickly, they spun around and backed toward one other until they were once again back to back with Professor Gervaise and Bohiti as human shields from the circle of spears that closed in around them.

"Tell them to put down their weapons," Gideon ordered as he pressed the blade against the professor's skin.

"*Wu'a!*" the professor shouted. "*Wu'a Caribe!*"

The men with the spears backed away but kept their spears pointed at them. Behind them the men with the bows stood with arrows nocked and aimed in their direction. Ever so slowly, the circle widened as Gideon and Todd shuffled their feet, and moved counterclockwise. They remained back to back and held their captives close.

"What's the plan?" asked Todd.

"You think I have a plan?" replied Gideon.

They continued to shuffle around and the circle widened with each rotation. In the distance Gideon saw the berm in the corner and the path that led back down into the cave. The gaps between the men had grown enough for them to fit through. Gideon began to shuffle toward the breach in the circle and Todd followed, with captive in tow. The circle of men shifted with them like a protective bubble. Gideon jerked the professor toward him.

"Tell them not to follow us," he ordered.

"*Tie-toca,*" the professor instructed. "*Tie-toca, han-ha'n catu'.*"

They stopped and allowed the four men to pass by them, although their spears and bows were still at the ready. No longer surrounded, Gideon and Todd moved to stand side by side with their human shields between them and the villagers. They backed carefully up the path toward the wall where the entrance was. The entire population of the small village stood before them once more only this time they appeared far less welcoming.

"No Doubt lyrics?" Todd said.

"Gwen is my lady," Gideon smiled at the break in tension.

"You know that's right," Todd said.

Before too long they reached the berm at the top of the hill. The crowd milled around and looked on from a distance. Gideon looked out one last time at the majestic cavern. When his gaze fell on the people who inhabited it, he was filled with an odd sense of awe and pity. They lived a simple life, which a part of him envied, but at the same time he thought of the world outside and the marvelous advancements they were deprived of.

"If you mean to leave, please, do not take Bohiti beyond these walls," Professor Gervaise pleaded. "Please, I beg you."

His voice was just as soft and calm as it had been minutes ago when he had proposed murder. However, there was a hint of humility that replaced the air of haughtiness from before. Gideon looked over at the man Todd held in a headlock. Although he was a captive, the man in the bright feathered loin cloth stood tall and still. He had a noble quality about him and a quiet confidence that Gideon found admirable.

"Todd, let him go and stand behind me," Gideon said as he removed his orange twined headband and chucked it across the berm.

"Are you sure?"

"It'll be fine."

Todd released Bohiti and stepped back with his fists clenched. The man in the bright feathered loin cloth turned to face them but did not move from the spot. He looked from Todd to Gideon and finally to Professor Gervaise. His face did not show anger or fear, confusion or resentment. He stood before them as gracious and opened as when they first arrived.

"*Guaiba*'," Professor Gervaise said to him. "*Guaiba*', *han-ha'n catu*'."

Bohiti gave a slight bow to the professor. He turned toward his people and walked purposefully back down the path toward them. Todd immediately hopped behind Gideon to take cover, as the bowmen still had their weapons trained on them from a distance. They all watched Bohiti until he reached the edge of the crowd. Gideon took a deep breath and began a backwards descent down the stone steps toward the opening in the wall. Todd was directly behind him, so close he could feel his breathe on the back of his neck. Professor Gervaise came along without struggle.

"Gideon, whatever you think of me, know that everything I have done was in the interest of protecting this place and these people," he said.

"Professor, I have no doubt you feel justified," said Gideon. "I have no intention of harming these people or violating this place. But you crossed a line and this is where we part ways."

Carefully, step by step, they drew closer to the dark entrance behind them. They backed down the ancient stone staircase and watched the crowd disappear beneath the hills horizon. Just a few steps from the bottom Gideon ran into Todd, who had come to a dead stop. He turned around to chide Todd for stopping without warning. His heart sank as he saw a machete held to the throat of his best friend. At the other end of the blade was Mucaro, with a bedeviled smile, dressed in a red robe with an orange trim. Gideon swung the professor around to face them. Mucaro pressed the machete harder into Todd's carotid and gestured toward the knife Gideon held. Todd squirmed but did not cry out; he looked more angry than scared. Reluctantly, Gideon yielded. He released Professor Gervaise and held the knife in the air over his head. Professor Gervaise reached up and took hold of the knife. He stepped back and stood near Mucaro and the captured Todd.

"It appears as though we will not be parted just yet," the professor said.

Duppy Cave

Mucaro removed the blade from Todd's neck and pushed him toward Gideon. Todd caught his toe on a rock and tumbled to the ground. Gideon quickly stooped down to help him up, as Todd struggled to his feet.

Shoulder to shoulder now, they looked back at the men who stood between them and escape. Despite their matching red robes they were quite the odd couple. One was a young, strong, virile black man with an unshaven face and long dreadlocks; while the other was a much older, clean shaven, distinguished white man with silver hair.

Nevertheless, they stood unified against them and blocked their way to the cave beyond and to freedom. The menacing Mucaro held the machete down toward the ground and stared at them. Professor Gervaise placed his hands beneath his robe, presumably to return his knife to its proper place.

"It was not meant to be this way," the professor said. "I had hoped to change your life, to change both our lives."

"And now?" Gideon asked.

"Unfortunately, only one of our lives will change today," Professor Gervaise said.

Suddenly, a dark blur exploded through the opening behind

them. Mucaro was knocked to the ground when a coconut-sized stone made thunderous impact to the back of his skull. The machete in his hand flung forward and Gideon reached out and caught it as the blade bounced off the step in front of him. He looked up again and saw Tara standing over the fallen Mucaro. She breathed heavily and held a large stone with both hands. Before any of them could move she dropped the stone, unsheathed the filed down machete that hung around her waist and held it to Professor Gervaise's neck.

"Holy crap!" Todd exclaimed.

"Tara," Gideon said in disbelief.

Bigga and Bammy stepped nervously out through the threshold behind her. Bammy looked very uneasy and Bigga's mouth was agape, as he looked up in awe at the monolithic stone cathedral they had just entered.

"Rotted," Bigga said.

With Mucaro hunched on the ground, Professor Gervaise removed his hands from beneath his robe and stared callously at Tara. In his hand he held a black polished stone. Gideon stared at Tara in amazement.

"How did you find us?"

"Mi followed dis fool fool b'woy y'ere," she said, as she nudged Mucaro with her foot.

"I'm just gonna say it," Todd said. "I'm in love with you."

She smiled at him, a real genuine smile, before she turned her attention back to Professor Gervaise and his fallen companion. Mucaro still held the back of his head where he had been struck but had uncurled from the fetal position. He slowly came to his feet and rubbed a burgeoning bump on his skull. Backed up against the towering rock wall, with the rusty blade of Tara's machete held to his throat, Professor Gervaise lifted his hands in the air. A slightly disoriented Mucaro stood next to him. Professor Gervaise glowered at him.

"You let them follow you?" he asked with contempt.

"Mi told yu not fi bring dem y'ere," Mucaro shot back.

"Stop uno noise, now man," Tara ordered.

The two men in the red robes stopped their bickering and submitted to the blade-wielding woman. Gideon watched Professor Gervaise and looked closer at the black stone in his hand. It appeared to be almost translucent and reminded him of an Apache tear, a volcanic black stone found in the Arizona desert.

"What is all dis?" Tara asked Gideon, as she stole a brief glance at the hole in the rock ceiling above.

"It's not my place to tell," Gideon said, with a nod at Professor Gervaise.

The professor turned the black polished stone over and over in his hand and muttered something under his breath. As he did the light in the cavern dimmed and a clap of thunder echoed and rolled throughout the cavern. Gideon, Todd and Tara looked up at the sky beyond the ceiling to see dark gray clouds rolling in to block out the sun. Bigga stumbled forward and ran into Gideon. He turned around and grabbed Bigga by the shoulders to prevent his fall. His eyes were closed and he shook his head back and forth violently.

"Bigga, you a'right?" Gideon asked.

His eyelids sprung open and he looked right through Gideon, with a white haze over his pupils. Bigga thrust both hands in the air, pushed Gideon away and knocked him backwards. He turned to his left, seized Tara and pulled her arms behind her back. Mucaro reached for her machete, which was now pinned to her side. She lifted her feet off the ground, raised her knees to her chest and kicked Mucaro back against the wall. Then she rocked her weight forward and rammed the back of her head into Bigga's face. Her forward momentum carried him into a devastating reverse head-butt and caused Bigga to release her. He staggered backwards and grasped onto his nose as blood poured out. Gideon regained his balance just in time to step forward and stop Mucaro, who bounced off the rock wall and advanced on Tara again. Gideon put the tip of his machete into his chest.

"No," he threatened Mucaro.

A white eyed Bammy leapt at Tara. Without hesitation she drove the palm of her right hand into his forehead. The blow knocked him back and he crumbled to his knees. She quickly swung her machete back over top of Gideon's blade to its original position against the professor's jugular. They stood in a criss-cross standoff. Gideon held Mucaro at bay and Tara kept one eye on Professor Gervaise and the other on her father; who knelt on the ground. Todd jumped forward and ripped the black polished stone from the professor's hand. Rain poured down from the dark sky, through the hole in the ceiling. The wall of water cascaded through the circular opening like a giant showerhead. The overhang shielded them from the storm.

"Awoo," Bigga groaned. "Uno broke mi nose, Tara, whaapun to ya?"

The white haze was gone from his big brown eyes. He looked down at his blood covered hands. Todd rushed around behind Gideon to check on Bigga. No one else moved. Gideon had his gaze trained on Mucaro and his machete fixed to his chest. Tara still had the edge of her rusty machete to the side of Professor Gervaise's neck.

"Daddy, ya a'right?" she asked, and ignored Bigga's complaint.

"Yeah man, mi a'right."

He slowly stood up and rubbed his sore forehead. The color too had returned to his eyes.

"A yu di obeah man, a na 'im," Tara said to Professor Gervaise with a flick of her head toward Mucaro.

"In this life you observe or act, give or take, learn or teach," Professor Gervaise said with a cool calm demeanor. "His time soon come."

Gideon was amazed at how unflappable he was. All that had transpired, through all the tumult, the professor had remained steady with a staggering level of confidence. Unsure what to do next, Gideon looked from Professor Gervaise to Tara and from Tara to Mucaro. Although Gideon had his machete pressed to his chest, Mucaro had not taken his eyes off of Tara. The rain fell in the distance like a steady drum roll.

"Okay, I think we've all had enough of this," Gideon said. He removed his machete from Mucaro's chest and lowered it to his side. He turned to face Professor Gervaise directly. "Professor, we're leaving now."

"I cannot allow that," he said with his hands still raised in surrender.

"And wha ya a go do fi stop wi?" Tara asked defiantly.

A rush of wind shot passed Gideon's ear, followed by a dull thud as an arrow caught Tara just below her collarbone. She cried out in pain and fell backwards into her father's arms. Bammy crumpled under her weight and they both fell to the ground. Mucaro leapt forward and knelt by her side. He reached out his arm but stopped just short of touching the arrow. Gideon spun around to locate source of the arrow. Bohiti stood on the berm at the top of the hill with seven other men, who all had their bows drawn and pointed down at them. A wall of rain water flowed down behind them. Bohiti drew another arrow from his quiver and nocked it. Gideon dropped his machete and raised his arms in the air. Todd and Bigga likewise made the customary gesture of surrender. Professor Gervaise stepped forward and kicked Gideon's machete to the side. It rattled and clanged off the rocks and came to a rest near Tara. With his arm still overhead Gideon turned to look behind him. Tara lay in Bammy's arms with the arrow sticking straight up in the air. Mucaro hovered over her on bended knee as she winced in pain.

"Stay still," Mucaro's voice quivered slightly.

She looked out past Gideon to the warriors lined up at the top of the hill where the stone steps disappeared. After a few pensive moments she turned her gaze back to the suddenly gentle Mucaro.

"Dis place," she said. "Dis is where you'd come. When ya lef', it was to come 'ere."

Mucaro exhaled a sigh of relief and nodded to affirm her assertion.

"Not another woman?" she asked, with a hint of embarrassment.

"Fi mi, d'ere could neva be another," Mucaro said, as he tenderly reached out and caressed her cheek.

Todd looked over at Gideon, unable to keep his jaw from dropping, "What's happening?"

Gideon did not answer, as he himself had the same question. The man, who had hunted them for two days and kidnapped Tara, now showed compassion like they had never seen. Mucaro rolled Tara carefully onto her side. There was no protrusion or blood so he rolled her over to rest on her back again. With his left hand, he pressed down on her wounded shoulder with the arrow between his thumb and index finger. With his other hand he took hold of the shaft and snapped it at the point of entry.

Tara screamed in agony. Mucaro discarded the broken arrow and lifted her to him. He turned and looked to the men at the top of the hill.

"*Cuey che, guaiba'*!" he bellowed to the warriors.

"*Wu'a!*" Professor Gervaise shouted, and held his hands high in the air, with arms outstretched toward Bohiti and his men.

A few of the men, who had begun to leave, froze and looked over at Bohiti. He made a gesture and spoke to them but Gideon could not hear what was said over the rain. The men filed back in line and raised their bows again.

"She needs c'yare or she could die," Mucaro said to the back of the professor's head.

Professor Gervaise turned around slowly and stepped toward Mucaro, "Her death was a foregone conclusion from the moment she stepped foot in here."

"She's da boy's mother," Mucaro argued.

"You think I will let this place, and all it stands for, be destroyed to save your baby mother," Professor Gervaise said coldly.

"If yu let 'er die, an' if yu kill d'ese boys 'ere," he said, and gestured toward Gideon, Todd, and Bigga. "Yu'll 'ave destroyed dat yourself."

The two men traded deathly stares for what felt like an eternity, before Mucaro broke away. With one arm supporting Tara, he reached down to brace himself with his free hand. Bammy stood up and helped Mucaro raise Tara to her feet. The muscle bond Mucaro glared at the silver haired professor. Then he looked over at Gideon, who still had his neck craned backwards to watch the drama behind him. His hands were raised in the air, toward the men on the hill, as he had no desire to get shot with an arrow.

"Take her and go," Mucaro said.

Mucaro beckoned for Gideon to come to Tara. He dutifully responded and quickly hopped down next to Mucaro. Bammy stepped forward and he and Gideon took hold of Tara and braced her on both sides. They began to walk toward the entrance to the cave with Todd and Bigga behind them. Mucaro stepped between them and Professor Gervaise.

"Do not test me," the professor warned.

Professor Gervaise glowered down at Mucaro with disdain. Bammy and Tara made their way beyond the threshold into the dark cave. Gideon nodded gratefully to Mucaro before he turned to leave.

"Stop!" Professor Gervaise ordered.

"*Han-ha'n catu*," Mucaro whispered to the professor.

With a mournful look on his face, Professor Gervaise bowed his head and closed his eyes. Gideon, Todd and Bigga all stood silently and looked back at the standoff. Professor Gervaise looked up, shook his head and shouted, "*Ari'! Bara!*"

Mucaro leapt forward and slammed Professor Gervaise back into the rock wall. He drove his forearm into his chin and pinned him against the cold limestone. "Run!" he yelled to Gideon.

Gideon quickly led the way through the opening in the wall, as several arrows rained down and ricocheted off the rocks beside them. The large room was dark and still, in contrast to the commotion and chaos that took place outside. Bigga pulled a flashlight from his pocket and switched it on. The light shone directly on Tara and Bammy, who were still coupled together with their arms around each other. Beyond them was the main passage they followed on their way in. Todd hustled over to the corner where their clothes and backpacks were. He picked up the backpacks and reached back down for their clothes.

"No time," Gideon hollered, as he ran up to the narrow passage way where Bammy and Tara waited.

They heard the voices of Professor Gervaise and Mucaro as

they shouted and argued with each other. Gideon imagined that Bohiti and his bowmen made their way down the hill and could come bursting through the archway at any moment. He started down the passage way even though he could not see in the dark, after all he had done it once before. Bigga pushed past him and led the way, with his flashlight pointed directly ahead. Gideon filed in the second slot with Tara and Bammy right on his heels. Todd threw a backpack over each shoulder and scooped up their shoes and clothes in his arms. They moved swiftly down the corridor.

Gradually, the voices and commotion faded behind them. The light from the flashlight bounced vigorously around the walls of the narrow passage as Bigga jogged along. Gideon could not be sure, and was not about to stop and check, but he thought he saw red blood stains and handprints drug across the walls. Periodically, he looked back to be sure Tara, Bammy and Todd were all still behind him and that they were not being pursued. In no time, they reached the place where the water flowed down the side wall of the passage. The beams of light reflected off the liquidy surface of the wall. They hurried down the passageway and after twenty or thirty feet the wall on their left was dry again. Immediately the passage grew warm and humid.

Bigga began to pant and gasp for air. He was in no physical condition to move at such a frenetic pace and, once the initial surge of adrenaline wore off, he quickly slowed down. A little ways up the corridor his light shone on a marking of a backwards facing bird drawn on the side wall, Bigga used it as a convenient excuse to stop and rest. He bent over and shined the light down the off shoot.

"Not that way," Gideon said. "It's a dead end, literally."

Gideon took the flashlight from Bigga's hand and shined the light briefly down to the catacombs before he turned it back on his friends. Bigga leaned against the wall and tried to catch his breath. He tilted his head backwards and pinched his nose closed to stop the blood. Beads of sweat pooled and dripped down his face. Behind him Tara and Bammy, still arm and arm, glanced back over their shoulders with worried looks. Todd arrived and he and Gideon quickly traded their robes and sandals for shorts and shoes. They all recognized Bigga needed a moment to recover, so no one spoke the worry on their minds. Gideon temporarily pushed aside his natural flight impulse. However, so as not to waste a minute, he purposefully placed Todd's gray linens at the fork that led to the catacombs and threw his red and orange robe further down into the darkness. Hopeful this ruse would mislead any pursuer and buy them some time. With that, his anxiety for their current rest stop abated. His best guess was they were less than a hundred yards from the large room and the tunnel that would lead them up and out.

Beyond Bigga's breathing, Gideon heard no other sounds. The silence was more frightening than anything else. He did not know what had happened back at the entrance to the cavern. Had Mucaro prevailed or Professor Gervaise? Would the bowmen pursue them? What would happen if they were captured? Would they be captured at all or simply killed? He did not intend to wait around to find out.

"Ready?" he asked Bigga.

He nodded and pushed off from the wall to stand upright. Gideon rushed onward down the passage. They reached the large room and made a beeline to the tunnel at the far end. Gideon stepped to the side and shined the light up the tunnel. He ushered Bigga toward the oval hole near the floor. Once Bigga was through, he helped Tara stoop down and begin her ascent. She was followed closely by Bammy and finally Todd. Gideon held the light under the lip to shine their way up the oval tunnel. He looked back into the pitch black cavern behind him. There was no sign of trouble, no sign of anything, only darkness. A lump formed in his throat and pressure grew in his chest.

He slipped under the lip and scooted his way up the tunnel, anxious to be near his friends. He reached the top to find his way blocked by a cluster of feet and legs. Bigga, Tara, Bammy, and Todd had exited the tunnel but stood in a tight knit group at the top in the narrow passageway. Gideon forced his way out of the tunnel. He wedged his body into the group and pulled himself up until he stood shoulder to shoulder with them. He faced the exit but noticed they all stared the wrong way down the narrow hallway behind him. From the looks on their faces he could not tell if they looked at something strange or wonderful. Whatever it was they were all mesmerized.

His heart began to beat rapidly and his arms trembled uncontrollably. Although he did not yet know what, he knew that something was behind him. Gideon shifted his feet and forced himself to turn around. His flashlight was pointed down at the ground and even though the light was buried amongst their bodies he perceived a soft glow on the walls in his peripheral vision. When he had turned fully around toward the glow, he leaned to his left to see around Bigga's head. In the narrow hallway there was a tall thin man. He wore an old tattered white shirt and a pair of dark trousers. The glow appeared to emanate from his person and his body was translucent like the polished black stone. His skin was white with a gray ashy hue; and his wavy, silver, unkempt hair matched the long stubble on his face. He had a distinguished chin and well defined crow's feet wrinkles around his dark green eyes.

Very calmly he lifted his arm and motioned for them to follow him. Without a word he turned and headed deeper into the cave, away from the exit. The soft glow that surrounded the man lit the dark passage as he moved away from them. His movements were fluid and smooth but unnaturally slow. A smoke like vapor of light lingered in the spaces he vacated, for just a second, before they disappeared after him. Gideon stood in stunned silence with his friends as they watched this specter of a man walk away from them. His shirt sleeves were rolled up and Gideon noticed a black marking on his right forearm. Gideon felt a stirring in his gut. The same stirring he felt when he found the slip of paper with the heart shaped symbol on it. He felt drawn to this man and compelled to follow him. After a moment of hesitation, he gently nudged Bigga to the side and started off in the direction of the man with the soft grayish glow.

"Gideon, what are you doing?" Todd asked.

"I think he's here to help," Gideon said.

"But that's a . . . he's a, uh," Todd stammered.

"Yeah, yeah he is," Gideon replied.

He took a step back toward his friends, huddled close together like frightened puppies in the narrow corridor. Todd had a worried anxious look on his face. A stunned Bigga had his mouth wide open and stared over Gideon's shoulder at the ghostly figure, who moved deeper into the darkness. Tara winced slightly as she shifted her weight and braced herself against her father. Gideon flipped the flashlight in the air and caught the front end with it facing back toward himself. He extended the handle to Todd, who reached out and took it from him.

"The exit is that way," he said and pointed over their heads. "Get out and get help. I've got to see what he wants."

"Gideon, this is crazy," Todd argued. "What if they catch you?"

"You're the ones in danger," he said. "They won't hurt me."

"There's about a dozen spears and arrows back there that beg to differ."

"Yeah man, an' uno c'yan't follow da duppy down d'ere," Bigga added.

"That too," Todd said.

"Look, we're wasting time." Gideon glanced over his shoulder at the mysterious man. "I'm going."

"D'en we're coming with yu," Tara declared.

Shocked, Todd and Bigga turned around to look at her. She steadied herself and stood on her own. Bammy hovered near her with his hands in front to catch her if she fell. Boldly, she stepped forward and stood in front of Gideon. He smiled at her and she smiled back.

"You're mad fi true," she said. "An' uno mek one fool decision afta da next, but mi t'ink dis is our destiny. So let's go and get it."

Gideon nodded in gratitude and turned down the dark passageway. He started off once more after the soft gray glow, followed by Tara. Bigga filed off reluctantly behind them. When Bammy stepped around him to join the others, Todd stood by himself and held the lone flashlight.

"Oh good, so we're all crazy now," Todd said, to no one in particular. He hung his head in defeat and sighed before he hustled to catch up with the group.

The ethereal being led the way up the narrow corridor. They climbed a moderately steep incline as the serpentine passage banked and turned through the interior of the mountain. Gideon hung back several paces behind their otherworldly guide. The glow that emanated from him lit the way and provided a broader perceptive of their surroundings. The rock walls rose twenty feet about them and came together in a point at the center, like a long gothic archway. The ground beneath their feet also sloped together from the water runoff responsible for the cave's existence. The uneven ground meant they had to walk bowlegged to maintain a good footing. They moved onward and upward and passed several offshoots. Gideon could not explain why he trusted this mysterious figure so easily and so completely. It was a feeling born in his core that grew and expanded until it filled him. He knew that wherever they were headed he was meant to go. Behind him he heard the panting breaths of his companions. Although he had no doubts about the path he had chosen, he could not help but worry for their wellbeing.

The passage widened into a small funnel-shaped room, no bigger than an elevator shaft. A flat rock wall, ten feet high, stood in their way. They shuffled into the small room and looked around for a way forward. Their ghostly guide turned to face them.

"It's a dead end," Todd said, as he glanced over at the man who glowed gray. "No offense."

Gideon looked back at Todd, grimaced and shook his head. The man with the wavy silver hair looked up and back behind him. Slowly, he pointed up to the top of the rock wall. Todd held the flashlight up in the direction he pointed. The ceiling of the tiny room was set high above the flat rock wall and the light shone up and beyond it.

"It's a ledge," Tara said.

She and Gideon stepped up to the wall. He turned to face her and put his hands together. He interlocked his fingers and held them just below his waist. Tara raised her leg and stepped into the manmade stirrup and stood up. She reached for the top of the ledge with her good arm. Gideon leaned back against the wall and hoisted her up higher until she grasped the top of the ledge. Tara moaned with pain but did not waver. She gripped the wall with her shoe and climbed atop the ledge.

"T'row mi da light, d'ere's room up 'ere," she said.

Todd tossed the flashlight up to her and stepped forward to stand next to Gideon. With the flashlight up top with Tara, the only light in the small room was the soft gray glow that came from the apparition with the wavy silver hair. Todd and Gideon motioned to Bammy to come to them. They bent their knees and stood close together so he could use their bodies as footholds. Without much trouble, he climbed up on their knee steps and hand stirrups until he lifted himself over the ledge. Next, Bigga came forward with much trepidation. The trio stood and faced each other. Gideon smiled and gave them a reassuring nod. Bigga began his ascent the same way Bammy had done. He stepped up onto Gideon's knee and then Todd's; they both groaned beneath his weight. Then he braced himself on their shoulders and stepped into their hand stirrups. The higher he rose the more unsteady their formation became. He managed to get his knees up onto their shoulders and they stood closer together so he could brace himself against the wall. With great effort he finally stood up. Gideon and Todd reached up to steady him and push his legs upward toward the ledge overhead. One final heave sent him up over the ledge and out of sight.

"You first," Gideon said to Todd.

Todd stepped into the stirrups and thrust upwards as Gideon lifted his body into the air. He grabbed the ledge, pulled himself up and turned around to sit down, with his legs dangling over the side. Gideon looked to his right where two of the walls met and found a foothold about four feet up that he thought he could reach. He turned back around to the silver haired man, who was stood silently by. He looked into his dark green eyes and his stubbly stoic face.

"You're Jarvis," he said. "Ben Jarvis?"

The glow around him seemed to brighten slightly. The corners of his mouth turned upwards to reveal dimples just above his distinguished chin. Jarvis nodded. Gideon wondered if he might be dreaming. Was it possible that he stood beside a three-hundred-year-old spirit? If not for the pain in his shoulders and the soreness of his muscles he would have sworn he was asleep. But he was very much awake: awake and sweaty. Before he could ask any of the myriad of questions on his mind he heard movement back down the passage. He looked to see an orange light that grew rapidly against the wall of the corridor. Quickly, he spun around and leapt toward the foothold on the far wall. He pushed off the wall and turned to reach for the ledge. He caught Todd's outstretched arm and grabbed hold. Todd leaned back and pulled him up onto the ledge. Gideon looked back down to see an empty funnel shaped room. The ghost of Jarvis had disappeared without a trace. The orange light advanced toward the room and had nearly reached it. Gideon and Todd looked behind them to see Tara, Bammy and Bigga, several yards ahead. Without hesitation, they got up and ran to them.

"We gotta go," Gideon said.

Tara held up the flashlight, to cut through the darkness, and led the way forward. The space above the shelf was much wider than the passage below, but the ceiling was lower. They had not gone far when the cave turned sharply to the right. Gideon could not tell if the rock ceiling overhead descended or if the floor ascended, but the two converged slightly and forced them to crouch down so as not to hit their heads. A soft gray light bled through the wall up ahead on their left. Gideon's heart began to race again. He hoped Jarvis had returned to lead them further. However, when they reached the crack in the wall, the light which came through was not an apparition but an exit to the world outside. They squeezed through the thin crack one by one. Once through, they were able to stand fully upright again. A curtain of rain hung over the arch shaped exit. Behind it, the green hump landscape of the cockpits sprawled out in the distance beneath the gray stormy sky. In just a few paces they made their way through the room and to the threshold of the cave. They stopped and looked out into the pouring rain. There was a small rock balcony that sloped down dramatically on either side. Straight ahead was a precipice that dropped down some fifty feet into a pool of deep blue water.

Gideon stepped out into the rain, onto the somewhat slippery rock ledge. The fresh air and the cool drops of rain were a boon to his soul. For a moment he felt free and at peace; two feelings which had been scarce in the time amongst the darkness. He looked down into the pool of deep blue water and saw three black rocks that floated near the bank at the bottom of the precipice. Millions of tiny ripples exploded across its surface, as rain drops pelted the deep blue pool. The black rock on the right moved and a black tail appeared. A chill shot up his spine as he realized those were not rocks but crocodiles lurking in the water below. Todd, Tara, Bigga and Bammy stepped out onto the ledge and stood beside him. It was just big enough for the four of them to stand shoulder to shoulder. They all peered down at the pool below.

"Left or right?" Gideon asked loudly over the wind and rain.

There was a narrow lip to the left that sloped down gradually, but the bare rocks looked slippery and one false step would send you hurtling to your death. To the right was a much wider slope, but it was steep and covered in green moss. Both choices were perilous in their own way but considering the physical limitations of the group Gideon felt that the slope to the right was the way to go. When no one readily spoke up, Gideon made the call. *Choose the right*, he thought.

"This way," he gestured down the steep slope.

Todd was the closest to the slope on the right so he went first. He turned to face the mountain and went down feet first. He moved carefully, but quickly, and descended a couple dozen feet until it plateaued into a larger landing. Next, Bigga made his way down. He sat on his rear end and attempted to scoot to the bottom. A few yards from the landing he slipped and careened into Todd. Gideon, Tara and Bammy all tensed up and froze, helpless to stop his slide and the inevitable collision. Bigga and Todd collapsed onto the rock landing.

"Royal flat!" Bammy exclaimed.

"Are you all right?" Gideon shouted down at them.

Bigga rolled off of Todd and lay on his back. Todd, already on his back, gave a thumbs-up to let them know they were okay. Gideon breathed a sigh of relief. The slightly shaken Bammy began his descent down the moss covered slope. Gideon and Tara watched anxiously from the top. Before he reached the landing, Gideon sensed movement to his right and spun around in time to miss a blade as it sliced passed his cheek. Behind the blade was a wild eyed and desperate Professor Gervaise.

Gideon stepped backwards into a defensive position, dangerously close to the edge of the precipice. Tara turned around and grabbed the arm of the knife wielding professor. He savagely threw her backwards and she fell over the side and down the mossy slope. Gideon recovered in time to catch the arms of the bull rushing professor and stop the knife, just inches from his face. The two men grappled with each other atop the ledge. The rain poured down harder than before and the rock surface provided little traction for either of them. Gideon was as much concerned with the knife as he was with falling off the cliff to the man-eating monsters below. He dropped to a knee and pulled down hard, using Professor Gervaise's momentum against him and the silver haired professor fell forward. The journal flew out from the pocket beneath his robe and landed near the mouth of the cave. Professor Gervaise fell on top of Gideon, who grabbed hold of him and rolled them both away from the edge. He smashed the professor's hands against the rocks in an attempt to knock the knife loose from his grasp. When that failed he changed tactics.

"Professor, please."

"You had your chance."

They continued to wrestle over the knife until Gideon drove his knee into the professor's groin. Only then was he able to pry the dagger from his hands, as the professor recoiled in agony. Gideon took hold of the bone handled half-moon blade and rolled away from Professor Gervaise. He leapt to his feet and stood over his former friend. The professor lay on the ground, defeated. Gideon looked down the mossy slope and saw Todd as he struggled to climb back up to him. Bammy and Bigga tended to Tara, who sat on the landing and held her head.

"Is she all right?" Gideon shouted down.

Todd stopped his ascent up the slippery wet rocks and looked up at Gideon.

"She's fine," he said. "You all right?"

"I'm good."

He looked back down at Professor Gervaise, who rolled over onto his back. The professor breathed heavily and looked up into the gloomy sky as the rain fell upon him.

"I bet everything on you," said the professor. "Now I have destroyed it all."

Gideon tossed the knife over the edge and it dropped swiftly out of sight.

"What are you doing, man?" Todd called from down below.

"Darkness cannot drive out darkness," Gideon replied.

He stepped forward and extended his arm down to the professor. Professor Gervaise reached up and took hold of his hand. Gideon pulled him to his feet and the two men stood eye to eye.

"Nothing is destroyed," said Gideon. "We can fix this."

The professor tightened his grasp and pulled Gideon closer.

"No," Professor Gervaise said calmly. "I can fix this."

With a firm grasp on Gideon's right hand the professor pushed him toward the ledge. Gideon fell backwards helplessly, unable to find solid footing on the wet rocks beneath his feet. His left leg slipped over the ledge. He leaned forward and grabbed onto the professor's robe. The force of his pull flung the professor forward. Gideon fell down, with his right buttock landing on the ledge, as Professor Gervaise stumbled over top of him and went over the cliff. His knee hit Gideon in the ear, which sent him falling head first down the precipice after him. Something caught hold of Gideon's ankles and held him to the ledge. He watched helplessly as Professor Gervaise fell, amongst a torrent of rain drops, toward the pool below. His red robe flowed like a cape trailing after him. Gideon closed his eyes when the professor's body impacted the water and the black rocks sprang to life and engulfed him. On cue the heavy rain fall ceased as the last drops fell from the sky.

A cut on his chin, from being slammed against the cliff face, began to drip blood up into his mouth. He hung upside down from the ledge, completely at the mercy of his rescuer. The grips on his ankles tightened as he was pulled back up toward the ledge. He reached up with his hands and tried to get a hand hold and help with his ascent to safety. When his waist cleared the landing, he lifted his torso and rolled up onto the ledge on his back. His legs were released and his feet dropped to the rock surface. The dark clouds parted and the sun sprayed through directly over him. He looked up at the dark silhouette of his savior as the sunlight poured in around him. It looked like a black lion hovered above him. He strained his eyes to adjust and the figure came into focus. His black dreadlocks hung down over a red robe. Mucaro reached down and extended a hand to Gideon. He took hold of it and was lifted to his feet.

Todd scurried over the slope to the side of the cave. He panted with his hands on his knees and looked back and forth between Gideon and Mucaro. Even though he had been too late to be of any help, Gideon could not help but be grateful for his efforts. He smiled over at him and Todd straightened up and collected himself.

"You all right?"

"I'm fine," answered Gideon. "You?"

"Yeah, man," said Todd. "I'm good. Your chin's bleeding."

Mucaro stepped up to the edge of the cliff and looked down at the tranquil blue pond below. The black rocks had disappeared and there were no signs of life. Gideon wiped at the blood on his chin and quietly moved to stand beside Mucaro. He felt a strange sense of loss and relief. The man who tried to kill him and his friends was gone and they were safe. Still, the memories of that man, before today, filled his mind. He remembered a kind and generous mentor who had imparted so much to him so freely. Those memories were now forever tainted by the actions of this great and terrible day. How had he so misjudged the professor? He looked over at Mucaro, another man who he had misjudged; the man who saved his life.

"Thank you," he held out a closed fist toward him.

"Yeah man," Mucaro responded as he reached out and bumped their fists together.

"So . . ." Todd called out from behind them. They both turned to look at him. He shifted his weight side to side apprehensively. "You're Corey's father, huh?"

"Yeah man," answered Mucaro. He turned his attention down the slope where Bigga and Bammy helped Tara to her feet.

"He's a good kid," said Todd.

"Yeah man," Mucaro replied, without taking his eyes off of Tara. She steadied herself and looked up at them. When she saw Mucaro she nodded to him. He nodded back and looked over at Gideon.

"Well this has been seven kinds of awful, so . . . ," Gideon said, and pointed to his right. "We're gonna go now."

"Yu c'yan't leave," Mucaro said.

"Not this again," Gideon said in exasperation.

"Give me the stone," Mucaro said, with his hand outstretched toward Todd.

All at once, Todd realized what he was talking about. He hurriedly rooted in the pockets of his pants. He pulled out the small polished black stone. He turned it over in his hand and the shine reflected on his face. He willingly handed it over, relieved to be rid of it. Mucaro held it in his closed fist.

"Listen, we need to get her some medical attention," Gideon pleaded.

"She will get da 'elp she needs," Mucaro said. "I will see to dat."

"Okay, you have your stone," he said. "You're going to see to Tara. What do you need us for?"

"Uno came 'ere for a reason," said Mucaro.

"I came here because I'm an idiot," said Gideon. "I came here because I listen to idiots. I came here because, foolishly, I thought I might find fame and fortune."

"No," argued Mucaro. He walked over near the entrance to the cave, picked up the journal and held it up. "Yu came because a dis. Yu came because a 'im."

He raised his thick muscular arm and pointed back into the cave. The sleeve of his robe dangled like a flag that waved on the breeze. Gideon craned his head to look past it and inside the cave. He saw a soft gray-ish glow from behind the crack in the wall at the back of the room. Mucaro lowered his arm and crossed between Gideon and the cave. With one hop he slid down the mossy rock slope like a skateboarder down a half pipe. When he reached the bottom he drew near to Tara and examined her wounded shoulder. She smiled at him and he tenderly took her by the hand. Bigga and Bammy stood by and watched anxiously. Mucaro looked back up at Gideon and Todd and, with a nod of his head, gestured for them to re-enter the cave.

"Gideon," Tara called out.

She tossed the flashlight up to him. Gideon caught the hefty mini-mag with two hands. He saluted with the flashlight and turned to enter the cave. Todd was right by his side as they stepped into the small entry room. Gideon negotiated his way back through the crack in the wall and into the hallway beyond. Like a man sized night light the silver haired ghost of Benjamin Jarvis stood in the distance. Todd slipped in behind Gideon and stared at Jarvis. It occurred to Gideon that he did not fear this apparition, nor had he at any time since his appearance. There was an odd sense of calm when he was around that was entirely against the nature of things.

Jarvis turned and headed back up the passage, again trailed by the smoky white vapor in his wake. Gideon and Todd allowed him to get a good distance down before they followed after him. They headed toward the shelf above the funnel shaped room. They stooped down as the floor and ceiling converged. When they reached the spot where they could stand upright again, Jarvis took a hard right and appeared to step through a solid rock wall and vanish. Gideon turned and looked back at Todd. The befuddled look on his face told Gideon he had seen the exact same thing.

"Where'd he go," Todd asked.

"Dunno," Gideon said.

The soft gray glow that filled the corridor had all but extinguished as the light from the mini mag became the most prominent source of light. However, Gideon thought he saw traces of the gray light from the spot where Jarvis had vanished. He lowered the flashlight to his side and turned it off. There was indeed a remnant of the soft grayish light that came from the wall where Jarvis had disappeared. Gideon turned the flashlight back on and drew closer. When he reached the wall he put out his hand toward the glow and felt nothing but air. It appeared to be a rock wall but there was another chamber that went on, much deeper than his eyes perceived.

Cautiously, he made his way forward a step at a time. The gap was so narrow he had to turn sideways and slide along between the rock walls, which hugged him snuggly on either side. The gray glow grew brighter and he found himself standing in a circular room where Jarvis waited at the far end. Next to him was a dusty old trunk with brass handles on both sides and three leather straps over the top. Jarvis gestured toward the trunk with his left arm. Gideon's heart leapt. *This is it*, he thought. He was in a hidden room, of a protected cave, with an old pirate's chest. This was the realization of hundreds of wild fantasies and daydreams.

Gideon reverently approached the old trunk. He passed near to Jarvis, who waited patiently for him. Gideon knelt down in front of the trunk. The latches on the leather straps in front hung loosely. With Todd behind him, he reached out and carefully lifted the lid. The excitement and anticipation of the moment was almost too much to bear. He raised his flashlight and peered inside. His heart sank when, instead of gold, he found stacks of old leather bound books. The heart-shaped looping sankofa symbol was carved into the underside of the walnut lid. Disappointment quickly transformed into intense curiosity. Three of the stacks of books were covered with cobwebs and dust. On top of the stack to the far right, however, was a book void of dust and cobwebs. Gideon reached out and picked it up. He stood up and opened the cover. Todd moved in closer and hovered over his shoulder. On the first page were three handwritten words.

Robert Sterling Gervaise

A long white envelope stuck out near the back of the journal. With his fingers Gideon took hold of the envelope and pried the book open to the pages it was tucked between. The page on the right was blank and in the top right corner of the left page was yesterday's date. Gideon looked back at Todd and then over to Jarvis; who stood silently by as usual. He held the flashlight close to the page and began to read.

After much wandering and many wasted years I believe at long last I have found my protégé. If all goes as planned the next entry in this log will be his. I have given my life to this cause and feel a great sense of relief that it will all soon be over.

Although I have failed to pass on my family's name, I have done all within my power to pass on my family's secret. It is right and good that it should be this way; a secret kept too long becomes a poison and this poison has done my family in. I do not bemoan that fact but record it for the benefit of future generations that will engage in protecting our secret.

It has been my great privilege to carry this burden. I only wish I could have been a more faithful steward.

Professor R. Sterling Gervaise

Gideon felt Todd's breathe on his right ear. He leaned forward to give himself some space. He looked to his left and saw only darkness. Jarvis had once again disappeared without warning. Todd reached into the journal and took the envelope that lay between the open pages. He pulled out the papers inside and unfolded them. Gideon shone the light on them as he scanned the typewritten page. It was the last will and testament of Professor Gervaise. It stated that he left his fortune and all his earthly possessions to Gideon Goodwin. Gideon and Todd exchanged astonished looks.

"Less than a twenty souls 'ave seen dis room," said a deep voice from behind them.

They spun around and Gideon shined the light to where the voice came from. Mucaro leaned against the wall by the narrow entrance. He held up his hand to shield his eyes from the glare. When Gideon lowered it, Mucaro stood up straight and walked casually toward them.

"'e wasn't right, up 'ere," Mucaro continued, and pointed to his head.

"The professor?" Gideon asked.

"Yeah man."

"No kidding," Todd said sarcastically.

"Dis place was 'is life but not da life 'e chose, and it took everyt'ing from 'im," Mucaro went on. "'e 'ad a child, a likkle girl. A she was supposed to tek over when 'im gone but when she was very young, she took sick an' died. 'e carried a secret 'e couldn't share an' 'is wife left 'im in 'is grief. Vexed an' alone, 'e blamed dis place. 'e stayed away for y'ears. Mi fadda took care a t'ings alone, until one day 'e returned. When mi fadda died 'im brought mi 'ere an' showed mi dis. Wi 'ave been trusted wit a great t'ing."

Mucaro gestured to the dusty trunk behind them. Gideon and Todd turned around to look at the stacks of books inside. Gideon thought about what incredible stories they must contain. He remembered how often Professor Gervaise referred to documented history as a treasure. Now he stood in front of a treasure chest that literally contained documented history.

"Fi t'ree 'undred y'ears da guardians 'ave recorded our 'istory," Mucaro continued. "Dis is a legacy passed down from parent to child, until today. 'e chose yu fi dis place an' d'ese people."

"I didn't ask for this," Gideon said.

"A man licked down 'is neighbor an' orphaned 'im pickney dem," Mucaro said. "Uno 'ad nothing fi do wit it, but when yu come 'cross dem, will yu leave dem fi starve or will yu tek dem in an' care fi dem? Sometimes yu 'ave no choice."

Mucaro walked past them and placed Jarvis's wet and battered journal in the trunk on top of the stack. Gideon thought of the Arawak people back in the village, a civilization thought to be extinct. But through the extraordinary efforts of a few, it had not only been preserved but remained untarnished by the modern world. He thought about Professor Gervaise and his link in a chain that stretched back generations. This was not simply a chain forged by blood but a chain welded through complete consecration and dedication to a single cause. He thought of what a burden that must have been on him. He felt inadequate and unworthy to even touch this chain, let alone join with it. Mucaro turned and started to exit the room.

"What if I can't do it?" Gideon asked.

Mucaro paused near the exit and turned back around.

"At first I believed yu couldn't."

"And now?"

"Darkness c'yan't drive out darkness," Mucaro repeated.

"Only light can do that," Gideon finished the quote.

Mucaro nodded to him. "Sankofa is da guardian of light inna world full a darkness."

He turned his shoulders, slid into the narrow passage and disappeared out of sight. Gideon looked down at the journal in his hand. He thought about his old friend who stood, as always, faithfully by his side. Todd had not said a word and he wondered what he was thinking. As Gideon stood in the subdued atmosphere of this room of records the consequences of his activities bore down on him. Old aches and pains returned in full force. Fatigue and soreness nearly brought him to his knees. Professor Gervaise's journal, all at once, felt heavy and burdensome. He walked over to the trunk and ceremoniously returned the journal to where he found it. He gazed down on the stacks of books, his scholarly desires were to dive head first into them and bathe in their knowledge. He knew, however, that would have to wait. Right now he needed to check on his friends outside. He needed to think. He needed to somehow find a way to rest. He reached up and took hold of the leather strap in the center. With one last look at the looping heart shaped symbol inscribed beneath the lid, he pulled down on the strap and let it fall closed.

Back to Light

It's been four months to the day since we walked into the cockpits. To say our adventure there changed our lives is an understatement.

I honored my promise to Tara and sponsored both her and Corey. They are currently living in the States and Corey is attending a school tailored to the needs of deaf children. Tara promised Bammy and Mucaro that once Corey completed his education they would return home.

Bigga sold his taxi and enrolled at the University of West Indies. He is majoring in History and Caribbean Studies. He and Todd have become pen pals and write often.

Todd caught the family bug and is working with Joe, right in his own backyard, trying to find Glenn's legendary Apache wind cave in the Superstition Mountains. Thus far, by no small miracle, he has kept the details of our trip to himself. Mucaro made it abundantly clear that were Todd to speak of it to anyone, both he and death would visit him quickly.

I think about Professor Gervaise every day. I think of Ben Jarvis and his legacy, what they lived for and what they died for. Unintentionally perhaps, they taught me of the great inheritance *and onus passed down to each new life. We distinguish ourselves through choices but those choices don't define who we are. A series of decisions and actions can chronicle our time here but they won't change our identity. To know who we are we must look back, we must remember where we came from. No matter where on earth we are born or to who, we are all children of the same Father. We are all children of light. The earth is full of darkness and we have a choice; give in to that darkness or make the world a little brighter. I have made my choice and I choose light.*

Gideon closed his journal and laid his pen down next to it on the bright red wooden desk. On top of the desk, near the journal, was a wooden carving of a black rhinoceros Bammy had made for him; which he named Keitloa. Above the wooden rhino, on a bright yellow wall, hung a framed picture of Gideon, Todd, and Glenn on graduation. Glenn's round face and gap tooth smile gleamed out at him. He stood up from the desk and ritually touched the picture frame as he walked by. He strode across the painted cement floor in khaki cargo shorts and black leather Dr. Marten sandals. Gideon approached a dark brown door. Next to the door was a plaque that read: *A people without a knowledge of their past history, origin, and culture is like a tree without roots. Marcus Mosiah Garvey.* There was a grand tree carved at the center of the plaque above the inscription. Gideon was first introduced to this quote when Professor Gervaise had shown him that very plaque which hung in his office. He pulled open the front door and stepped out onto the veranda.

"Morn'n, Mr. Goodwin," a short portly woman greeted him.

"Good morning, Marlene," he replied warmly.

She happily worked in the front yard and hung his laundry on a clothes line. The sun shone brightly, with not a single cloud in the deep blue sky. Marlene, who could not have been more the five feet tall, stretched up to clip a clothespin on the red wool cloth with orange trim that flapped on the wind like a grand old flag. She wore a light blue dress that went down to her chubby knees. She hummed Bob Marley's 'Three Little Birds.' Gideon had never seen her be anything but cheery. When she smiled, her bright white teeth lit up and consumed her dark round face. She continued to pull clothing from the wash basin and, one by one, hung them on the line.

He left the door to the house open behind him. On a clear day, with the wood slats on the windows already open, he felt no compulsion to keep it closed. The spacious veranda spanned the entire front of the modest cinder block house. The house was perched near the edge of a mountaintop, surrounded by acres of green grass to the east. Gideon stepped to the edge of the porch and took in the majestic view. In front of him, to his right, an enormous valley sprawled out, filled with lush green vegetation that stretched all the way to the ocean. From the wicker lounge chairs on the veranda he had taken in many spectacular sunsets that rivaled anything he had seen back home. The large estate on the mountaintop had no walls and no borders. It was the only home for sixteen kilometers, with one dirt road in the area that led right to his front door.

A crisp cool breeze swept up from the valley, across the grass and through the trees. It whisked up to meet him, as if the island sent its own personal greeting. His hair, which he had let grow first the first time in years, blew in the breeze. He had also grown a beard and was grateful to be just out of the itchy stages. He reached up and took hold of the eaves of the veranda over the top of the steps. The sunlight shone on the tattoo of a backwards facing bird on his right forearm. He closed his eyes and leaned forward to soak in the beautiful contrast of the warm sun and cool breeze.

He smiled broadly and looked out over the distant landscape. He thought of all those who had shared this same view over the centuries.

"*Se wo were fi na wosankofa a yenkyi*," he said to himself.

"What's dat, Mr. Goodwin," Marlene asked.

"Nothing Marlene," he replied. "I was just saying was a glorious day it is."

"Yeah man," she said. "Everyt'ing gonna be a'right."

In the distance he saw a plume of dust rise up from the dirt road and blow away in the wind. The roar of a four-stroke engine grew louder as the lone motorcycle carried its rider nearer. Mucaro eased to a stop just outside the front gate. Gideon descended the steps and walked out to greet his friend.

"Wha'pun mi friend."

"Mi deh yah," replied the dread-laden Mucaro.

"Wha g'wan?"

"*Guarico guake'te.*" He tossed a helmet to Gideon.

"Where's your helmet?" Gideon asked.

With a wry smile Mucaro turned the throttle and revved the engine. Gideon put on the black helmet, embossed with a golden backward facing bird, and hopped on the back of the bike.

"*Han-ha'n catu',*" Gideon grinned. "*Taino-ti'.*"

Mucaro let out the clutch and rocketed down the road toward the lush green valley. As they rode away, Gideon could not help but turn and look back to where he came from.

Acknowledgments

First, to my wife, who is the origin of everything good in my life. I am blessed every day I wake up by your side. Thank you for being my sounding board and my editor. You spare the world from the typographical horror show my writing would produce without you.

Thank you to Emma Parker, the dream maker, for picking me off the slush pile and enduring a barrage of questions from a nervous and overexcited first-time author. Additionally, I'd like to thank Emma and Justin Greer for their work in editing this book. Justin put up with two late-edit plot additions and a rewritten ending, as well as, literally, forty-one minor tweaks the week before it went to the printer. And yes, I counted them.

The Land of Look Behind is in many ways my love letter to Jamaica, land I love. This magical, beautiful island, the amazing Jamaican people, and their rich history inspired this story. To that end, thank you to Carey Robinson and Mavis C. Campbell for *The Iron Thorn* and *The Maroons of Jamaica*, respectively; those books were integral to setting the stage for the historical portion of this tale. Also, I need to thank Saki Mafundikwa for introducing me to Sankofa and changing the course of this story.

You could fill another book with the names of people who inspired the characters in this story and of those who have supported me along my journey. Although I won't attempt to name you all here, your names are forever listed in my heart. I would, however, like to especially mention my children, whose love of reading and enthusiasm for my outlandish storytelling has been a constant motivation to me. I hope I've made you proud.

And finally to you, the reader. Not only did you read my story, but you read the acknowledgments all the way to the end; that's commitment. Well done, you.

About the Author

Born and raised in Arizona, Aaron is proud to call the desert home. He came of age in the suburbs of Sacramento, California, and as a missionary for The Church of Jesus Christ of Latter-day Saints in Jamaica, where he fell in love with the people and their culture, but he was always drawn back to the valley of the sun.

He married his childhood crush, and the girl of his dreams, in 2001. Together they are raising four beautiful and rambunctious children. He worked as a freelance sports reporter for *The Arizona Republic* for nearly ten years, combining his love of writing and sports. When not working, writing, or serving at church, Aaron volunteers as a soccer and baseball coach for his children and enjoys chasing a small white ball around a golf course.

His storytelling draws heavily from his love of history, adventure, his faith, and his own life experiences.